Praise for Anna Schmidt

"Schmidt pens a won... —RT Book... ...w Wife

"Schmidt knows what readers expect in a love story and delivers on all levels. It's refreshing to see characters with their flaws showing, which makes them appear very real."
—*RT Book Reviews* on *Gift from the Sea*

Praise for Linda Ford and her novels

"A tender, sweet love story with characters who only want the best for others and themselves."
—*RT Book Reviews* on *Dakota Cowboy*

"Ford's sweet, charming love story has well-written characters that demonstrate strong faith, even though they stumble along the way."
—*RT Book Reviews* on *The Cowboy's Baby*

Praise for Lyn Cote and her novels

"*Her Healing Ways* is a wonderful love story between two people with different outlooks on life, who together bring out the best in each other. Cote knows what will keep readers interested in the story and uses this knowledge throughout her story. Don't miss this wonderful book."
—*RT Book Reviews* on *Her Healing Ways*

"*Suddenly a Frontier Father* has a little bit of everything: mystery, drama, romance and humor. The two young girls are truly the stars of this story, as they are totally charming and endearing."
—*RT Book Reviews* on *Suddenly a Frontier Father*

Anna Schmidt is an award-winning author of more than twenty-five works of historical and contemporary fiction. She is a three-time finalist for the coveted RITA® Award from Romance Writers of America, as well as a four-time finalist for an RT Reviewers' Choice Award. Critics have called Anna "a natural writer, spinning tales reminiscent of old favorites like *Miracle on 34th Street.*" Her characters have been called "realistic" and "endearing," and one reviewer raved, "I love Anna Schmidt's style of writing!"

Linda Ford lives on a ranch in Alberta, Canada, near enough to the Rocky Mountains that she can enjoy them on a daily basis. She and her husband raised fourteen children—four homemade, ten adopted. She currently shares her home and life with her husband, a grown son, a live-in paraplegic client and a continual (and welcome) stream of kids, kids-in-law, grandkids and assorted friends and relatives.

A *USA TODAY* bestselling author of over forty novels, **Lyn Cote** lives in the north woods of Wisconsin with her husband in a lakeside cottage. She knits, loves cats (and dogs), likes to cook (and eat), never misses *Wheel of Fortune* and enjoys hearing from her readers. Email her at l.cote@juno.com. And drop by her website, www.lyncote.com, to learn more about her books that feature "Strong Women, Brave Stories."

Christmas Under Western Skies

Anna Schmidt
Linda Ford

&

Her Healing Ways

Lyn Cote

H HARLEQUIN® LOVE INSPIRED® HISTORICAL

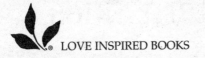

LOVE INSPIRED BOOKS

Recycling programs for this product may not exist in your area.

ISBN-13: 978-1-335-00543-4

Christmas Under Western Skies and Her Healing Ways

Copyright © 2018 by Harlequin Books S.A.

The publisher acknowledges the copyright holders of the individual works as follows:

A Prairie Family Christmas
Copyright © 2010 by Jo Horne Schmidt

A Cowboy's Christmas
Copyright © 2010 by Linda Ford

Her Healing Ways
Copyright © 2010 by Lyn Cote

www.Harlequin.com

Printed in U.S.A.

CONTENTS

CHRISTMAS
UNDER WESTERN SKIES

* * *

A PRAIRIE FAMILY CHRISTMAS
Anna Schmidt

&

A COWBOY'S CHRISTMAS
Linda Ford

A PRAIRIE FAMILY CHRISTMAS

Anna Schmidt

To dear friends who have known the loss of
a first love and made the journey from grief
to acceptance with grace and great dignity.

Only take heed to thyself, and keep thy soul
diligently, lest thou forget the things which
thine eyes have seen, and lest they depart from thy
heart all the days of thy life...
—*Deuteronomy* 4:9

Chapter One

Homestead, Dakota Territories
Late October, 1865

Julianne Cooper coaxed her ox, Dusty, over the rutted and snow-covered path that connected her farm to that of Glory and Sam Foster. The Fosters were freed slaves who had—like Julianne and her late husband, Luke—taken advantage of the Homestead Act of 1862 and headed west to claim their one hundred and sixty acres. The dozen families that had settled in the area had already established a thriving community that they had named "Homestead."

"You should head back, Sam," Julianne called to her friend walking alongside the wagon. "It'll be dark soon and Glory will worry."

Her son, Luke, Jr., had run ahead searching for dried, frozen buffalo chips to stoke the fire when they got home. His twin, Laura, sat huddled under a buffalo robe next to Julianne.

"Mama!"

Luke's cry of alarm had Sam running as Julianne halted the wagon and slid from the seat, sinking in slush that covered her shoes when she landed. "Stay here," she ordered her daughter. "Luke! Are you hurt?"

The boy did not reply, just pointed.

Near the grove of bur oak trees that her late husband had designated as the perfect setting for their house stood a riderless horse, saddled and loaded with gear.

"Can we keep him?" Luke asked.

"Go back to the wagon and stay with your sister," Julianne ordered.

Her mind raced with possibilities—none of them good. Over time, most of the Indians in the area had been moved to reservations by the government. The few who remained had come to accept the reality of settlers from the east; but still, every now and again there were stories of renegades. Or it could be a trap. Some poacher come to claim her land for himself. Or...

"Over here," Sam called and knelt next to a lifeless form half covered over with drifted snow.

Julianne stumbled through patches of frozen high grass stalks. "Is he..."

"Not yet," Sam replied as he hoisted the man over one shoulder as if he were no more than a sack of flour. "But we'd best get him inside and warmed up or he surely will be."

Julianne considered their choices. They could turn the wagon and head back to the Fosters. But Glory was sick in bed. And Julianne's place was closer. Sam eased the man into the back of the wagon and then went back for the horse.

"I'll go with you," he said, mounting the horse.

Julianne nodded and climbed back onto the wagon, her skirt wet and heavy now.

"Is that man dead?" Luke asked, squirming around to study the form in the back.

"Not yet," Julianne replied through gritted teeth.

* * *

Captain Nathan Cook faded in and out of consciousness. One minute he was aware of sliding to the frozen ground from Salt's back, and the next he felt the bone-jarring motion of a wagon making its way slowly over uneven ground. One minute he opened his eyes to see an elderly black man riding Salt, and the next he was sure he heard a woman quietly giving orders as he was moved from the wagon and into a dark, close room that smelled of smoke and damp earth. One minute he was so cold that he was beyond shivering, to stir the embers of inner warmth his body might still provide, and the next he was buried under a soft pelt of dank fur. One minute he was tempted to give himself over to the blessedness of everlasting sleep, and the next he was following orders barked at him like his command officer once had, only these came with a feminine drawl.

"Mister? Open your eyes. Mister? Look at me. Who are you? Where were you heading?"

There was no tolerance for disobedience in that command, no matter how sweet the voice, so Nathan did as she ordered and forced his eyes open. He found himself staring straight into the eyes of what was surely one of God's most beautiful angels.

"California," he murmured, choosing to answer the question that was simplest. Then he closed his eyes again and gave himself over to his fate.

For two days the man lay close to death. But in spite of Sam's thinly veiled hints that Julianne should think about where and how they might bury him and get word back to his people of his passing, Julianne refused to even consider the idea that this man would die in her house.

It never occurred to her that what she was really fighting were the memories of her husband's death, and yet the similarities were astounding. Like this man, Luke had gone out in a storm. Like this man, he had become disoriented. Like this man, by the time they found him he was wracked with fever and at the same time half-frozen.

"This isn't Big Luke," Glory warned her the next day, when she arrived with the ingredients to mix up a generous helping of her special plaster for drawing out fever.

"I know that," Julianne whispered, mindful of her children not ten feet away. Hopefully, Sam had distracted them enough with his game of shadow figures that they had momentarily forgotten about the man lying where they had last seen their father. Even at noon, the house was dark enough for the game.

"It's not the same at all, but for them…" She jerked her head in the direction of the children as she helped Glory lift the man's upper body so they could wrap the strips of torn cotton around the plaster Glory had spread over his bare chest.

He was muscular but too thin, as if it had been some time since he'd had a decent meal. Glory helped her ease the man back onto the cornhusk mattress, then stood with hands on hips and glanced toward the wooden table that dominated the center of the small room. "You make anything of those papers he was carrying?"

"His name is Nathan Cook. He was a captain in the Confederate Army. There's a letter of honorable discharge from General Lee and a paper that shows ownership of his horse. There's a picture of him in uniform and another of a young woman—perhaps it's his wife or sister."

Glory frowned. "A Southern boy? Way out here?"

Glory's expression shifted from concern to wariness. "That can't be good." She stared at the items Julianne had spread out over the table to dry and fingered a small leather-covered Bible. "This was part of his belongings?"

Julianne nodded. "And that journal as well."

Glory picked up the second volume and studied it. "Did you read it?"

"No."

"Read it," Glory instructed. "Folks will lie to your face, but when they write down their thinking, that's something you can take for truth. Might as well know who and what you're dealing with while he's weak as a newborn kitten." She let the diary drop back onto the table and turned her attention to the kettle simmering over the fire. "We'd best start getting some of this broth down him if you're determined to bring him back from the brink."

After ladling up half a bowl of the soup from the simmering stew, Glory perched on the side of the bed next to the man. "His breathing seems to have eased some," she noted. "Sam Foster, stop that foolishness and come help me get this man sitting up so I can feed him."

Julianne gave the children their stew while Glory and Sam attempted to feed the man. He coughed and muttered incoherently, but did not fully regain consciousness and after three attempts, where most of the broth landed on the buffalo robe, Glory gave up. "I'm sending Sam back to our place to get my things," she announced. "Don't know what I was thinking, leaving you here alone with those children and this stranger."

"We're fine," Julianne protested. "As you said, the man is as weak as a kitten. I'll signal if anything changes," she promised, as Glory launched into a fit of coughing that had Sam looking worried and scared. "Go take care of yourself for once."

"Sam will drive me home and be back before dark. Have young Luke there make a fire near the shed. Sam can bed down out there. And you need to allow him to take his shift watching the patient, while you get some rest." She put on her coat and handed Sam his hat.

Julianne saw her friend's plan for the compromise it was and, in the interest of expediency agreed. She stood in the doorway and waved until the wagon had disappeared into the gray afternoon.

Over the next week, she and Sam took turns sitting with their patient through the night, and Glory kept watch during the day. He'd been in and out of consciousness for over a week, and Julianne was beginning to worry that this might be a repeat of Luke's last days.

"Mama!"

Julianne wheeled around to find the man struggling to throw off the covers and sit up. Both of her children stood close enough for him to grab them if he chose to do so.

"Get back," she ordered as she reached for the hunting rifle Luke had mounted over the door on a rack of moose antlers.

Both children, as well as the man, looked back at her. The children's eyes were wide with surprise at the sight of their mother holding the gun. The man's eyes were red-rimmed and half-closed with fever.

"Stinks," he muttered tearing at the bandages on his chest.

"Stop that right now," Julianne ordered, setting the rifle aside, but within reach, as she positioned herself between the man and her children. "Just stop that and lie back down."

He squinted at her, his thick black hair falling over his eyes, further hampering his vision. "Ah, my angel," he said. And to Julianne's shock, the man laughed.

The sound of it was so unusual in this place where laughter had died with Luke that, for a moment Julianne considered taking the children into the yard and firing the rifle for help. She felt the eyes of her children on her, questioning their next move.

She pointed to their bowls of stew—cold now, no doubt, then wrapped her hands around an iron skillet and eased closer to Nathan Cook. "I'm no angel, mister," she warned. "Try anything and I'll use this."

She brandished the skillet in his direction.

His answer was a soft snore.

Seeing that he'd succeeded in loosening the bandages, and yet reluctant to touch him, Julianne pulled up the buffalo robe and dropped it over him. When Sam returned, she would see to the plaster while he stood guard. In the meantime…

"Mama, what's con-fed-er-ate?" Laura asked, fingering the letter of discharge as she picked at the last of her stew.

Luke had insisted there be no talk of the war, once they'd left all that behind them. But now the war had possibly come to their door, in the form of Captain Nathan Cook.

"There was a war," she explained. "One side was called the Confederate Army and the other was—well, the Federal Army, I guess you could say."

Luke Jr.'s ears perked up. "Did Papa fight?"

"No."

"Why not?" The boy was clearly disappointed.

"It's complicated, Luke, but we decided to move out here."

"Klaus Hammerschmit said that's why they came over here from Germany. There was a war and his father decided to move out here."

"I don't like it when people fight," Laura murmured.

"No, neither do I," Julianne agreed, but she couldn't help glancing back at the man snoring away on her bed and wonder if, before this was all over, she might not have to fight. "Now finish up, and then get to your chores before it gets dark."

While the children scraped out the last of their stew and washed out their bowls, replacing them on the cupboard shelf, ready for their supper, Julianne restacked the papers that had sat on the corner of the table since they'd dried out. Sam had collected them from Nathan Cook's saddlebags and pockets and spread them by the fire to dry that first day they'd found him. She slid the papers back inside the cover of the Bible and placed it inside the saddlebag propped at the foot of the bed. She picked up the diary and paused.

Glory had urged her to read it, but what right did she have? Glory had suggested that the journal might reveal information that could help Julianne decide her course of action, should the man recover.

She fingered the cracked leather cover, then the leather thongs that bound the journal pages. *Just the last few entries*, she decided. Surely that would tell her why he'd come this way and where he was headed. The pages crackled as she pressed the small book open on her lap. She turned to the last entry.

Chapter Two

This land is so different from home. No trees, few streams, and the wind is as relentless as the unending, barren landscape. And then this evening, just as the sun was setting, I stumbled across what back home might have been an orchard of apple or pear trees. It was such a beautiful sight after so many long days of nothing but fields of dead grasses and withered crops, that tears sprang to my eyes. I climbed down from Salt and walked among the low branches and saw the shape of a few hardy leafs undeterred by either the wind or the cold. Oak leaves. I had to smile, then laugh aloud, as I thought of the mighty oak trees that dominate the hills back home.

Julianne glanced at the sleeping man, his breath coming a little easier these last few days. He had been here—right outside. Hers was the only farm in this area that fit the setting he'd described. While she and the children had stayed the night with Sam and Glory, he had passed this way. What if she'd been here? Alone with the children? And yet, he had not broken in. The storm had come on suddenly at dawn, as such things did here on the plains—and passed just as quickly.

As if he felt her watching him, he opened his eyes. "Ma'am?" His voice was raspy.

Julianne started and snapped the journal shut, placing it in her apron pocket.

"Right here," she replied, edging cautiously closer to the bed.

He was lying on his side, and for the first time since Sam had carried him inside his eyes were clear. Only the occasional coughing fit told the story of how very ill he still was.

"Don't want to impose," he managed between coughing jags. "Could I have a little water?"

"Of course," Julianne hurried to the bucket and dipped water into a tin cup. When she turned, he had pushed himself to a position of half-sitting, his weight resting on one forearm.

"Appreciate that," he said when she handed him the cup. His drawl was unmistakable.

"You're Virginian?" she guessed.

He nodded. "How did you know?"

"I grew up there—in the western part of the state."

"Hill country." He grinned and sipped the water. In spite of several day's growth of a thick, black beard, his smile was disarming and at the same time captivating.

"And you?" she asked, forcing her attention anywhere but on those white, even teeth and eyes that were now wide open, and the most startling shade of green—like spring grasses come to life on the plains.

"Just outside Richmond," he managed before the coughing started again. The water sloshed from the cup onto the bedding. "Sorry," he mumbled as he tried ineffectively to clean up the spill.

"Never mind." She took the cup from him. "Are you hungry?"

"Famished," he admitted, "but I don't mean to trouble you—I mean, any more then I already have."

She ignored that and stirred the stew, then ladled up half a bowl and handed it to him.

"What day is it?"

"Monday."

She saw him mentally calculating the lost time. "I've been here a week already?"

"As of yesterday, yes." She handed him the soup and could not help noticing the way he seemed to savor every bite. She would have expected him to gobble it down. After all, it had been days since he'd eaten anything of substance.

"Where are you heading?" she asked.

"California, God willing."

"Well, God seems to have led you straight into the eye of the worst early winter storm we've seen for this time of year." Julianne had little patience with people who placed their lives in God's hands. After all, that's what she'd done with Luke, and he'd died.

Nathan Cook paused with the spoon poised over the bowl, his eyes searching hers. "God has His reasons for whatever comes our way, ma'am."

It was her turn to shrug. Once a woman of deep, abiding faith, the events of her life over the last few years had convinced Julianne that she could rely on neither man nor God. She had only herself. "We found your papers, Captain Cook. They were quite sodden but we managed to salvage them along with your Bible."

"We?"

"My neighbor and I found you lying in the snow. We brought you here and stabled your horse with the other livestock." She busied herself peeling potatoes to add to the stew.

"May I know your name?"

"I am Mrs. Cooper." Best withhold the fact that she was widowed for as long as possible, Julianne decided.

"And Mr. Cooper?"

"Is not here," she said, satisfied that she had not told an outright lie. "If you'll tell me who to contact, I can see that your family receives word that you are safe."

Julianne was riveted by the expression of abject sadness that briefly shuttered his eyes. "No need," he replied, and turned his face away, whether because of a fresh coughing jag or because he could not bear for her to witness his pain, she could not say.

Just then the door banged in on its hinges, admitting nine-year-old twins engaged in one of their never-ending debates. "I'm telling you that he was on the losing side," Laura insisted. "The papers said that…"

"Children," Julianne interrupted, and the twins stopped in midsentence as they stared past their mother to the stranger smiling at them. "Captain Cook is feeling somewhat better, but still recovering. Please close the door and lower your voices."

Laura did as she was asked while Luke moved closer to Nathan. "Did you fight for the army that won or the one that lost?"

"Luke Cooper, Junior." Julianne knew she did not need to raise her voice. Using the boy's full name never failed to remind him of his manners.

"Sorry," he muttered, and took a sudden interest in looking at the tips of his wet boots.

"Everybody loses in war, son," Nathan said.

It was so close to the answer that Big Luke would have given the boy, that Julianne felt her breath catch, and she was relieved to hear the creak of the wagon wheels on the frozen ground announcing Sam's return.

"Go help Mr. Foster unhitch Dusty," she told her son, as she gently guided him toward the door where she could hear another wagon arriving. "Laura, please finish peeling these potatoes while I see who's come calling."

Nathan watched the woman hurry across the room and peek through one of several small holes in the heavily oiled paper that covered the house's only two windows.

"Oh, no," she muttered to herself as she straightened, they pressed her palms over the front of her apron before heading to the door.

Under the spotless bibbed apron made of a calico material, she wore a wool dress of dark gray. It suited her in its simplicity, but seemed exceptionally austere for one so young and vibrant. With her golden hair and pale blue eyes, and cheekbones freckled and kissed by the sun, she was like a ray of sunshine in the otherwise gloomy surroundings.

He saw her glance back at him once she'd recognized her visitors. "Everything will be fine," she assured him in a voice intended to placate and soothe. It was almost as if she expected him to make a run for it.

Within moments, the room was filled with cold air, as well as three women who placed prepared dishes of food on the table. They then surrendered their outer garments to the boy who hung them on pegs. An older black man hung up his hat and coat and stood near the door, as if waiting for the women to settle somewhere.

One of the three—a tall, heavyset woman with a voice that could shatter glass—stood by the door and focused her attention on him as she spoke to the Cooper woman. "I don't know what you could possibly have been thinking, my dear." She clucked her tongue against uneven teeth, and the other two women sidled a little closer to her until they formed what Nathan could only view as a solid line of defense against him.

"You take in a complete stranger, and you all alone here with these dear children?" the woman continued.

"How did you hear of—"

"You were not at services yesterday, and so, naturally, I told Jacob something must be wrong. I thought perhaps the children were ill, or you, yourself. Mind you, the way you insist on living out here alone like this—"

"Sorry," the man by the door said to Julianne. "She came straight to us, and, well…" He shrugged and Julianne nodded.

The older woman ignored this, turning her full attention back to Nathan. "Why have you come here, young man?" she demanded, pointing one stubby finger at him.

"I…" Nathan was not at all sure how to best answer that.

"The man was passed out in the snow," the black man drawled, moving fully into the room now and tapping the bowl of his pipe on the hearth. "There was a choice, that's certain. Leave him where he dropped or take him in."

Nathan was speechless that a black man—an ex-slave by his accent—would speak to a white person with such sarcasm and confidence.

"Just hush, Sam Foster. I am addressing this man here. Well?"

Nathan was thinking a coughing fit might save him, when the Cooper woman stepped forward.

"Captain Cook became disoriented during the storm, Emma," she explained. "He, like so many who have passed our way, is on his way west, to California. Ill as he was, there was little choice but to take him in until he could be moved."

The woman called Emma peered more closely at Nathan. "He certainly won't be going to California until spring—not with an early winter already upon us," she announced. "What's your trade, mister?"

Nathan was speechless at the woman's sudden shift in questioning. "I…"

"The captain served as a chaplain during the war."

All eyes turned to Laura, who was adding onion to the pile of apples and chopped potatoes, as if she hadn't spoken.

"Is that right?" Emma demanded of Julianne.

"According to his papers," she replied.

"Mother, a minister," one of the other two women said, as if this were some sort of good news.

"Hush. And from your accent, may I assume that you are Southern?"

"Virginia, born and bred. Same as Mrs. Cooper here." He had no idea why he'd added that, but it seemed an important point to make.

"Well, I suppose it's true. You had no choice but to do your Christian duty," Mrs. Putnam said, backing away. "Sam, I am assuming that you and Glory will see that Mrs. Cooper—"

"I'm staying in the lean-to for the duration," Sam assured her. "You ladies can rest easy that she and the children won't be alone," he added.

"Very well. But make no mistake, young man," she added, turning her attention back to Nathan, "someone *will* be watching you." She reached for her cloak as the other two women prepared to leave.

"It'll be all right," Sam assured the ladies as he escorted them from the cabin.

Nathan processed this newest bit of information as the women huddled on the stoop, communicating with Sam Foster in urgent and worried whispers. *Where was the husband?* He glanced at the boy and girl—twins by the looks of them. The girl kept casting him curious glances, while the boy edged his way closer to her as if to protect her should Nathan try anything.

Outside, a horse snorted and he heard a wagon pull away, then the black man came back inside with Mrs. Cooper. He folded his arms and studied Nathan while she took the freshly peeled vegetables and added them to a pot over the fire. "Children, it's time for you to work on your spelling," she said, as she put away the bread and cake the women had brought.

"Glad to see you're feeling some better, mister, but just keep in mind that I'm right here," the man the Putnam woman had called Sam Foster warned, as he settled himself in the lone chair close to the door.

"Understood," Nathan said and collapsed back onto the bed, his head spinning. Nothing about these people was making any sense. Neither Mrs. Cooper, whose protector was not her husband but this elderly man, nor the woman from town who had interrogated him and then left. Mrs. Cooper looked as fragile as a china doll, and yet left the definite impression that she could take care of herself. The one thing that he'd heard since regaining consciousness that made any sense at all was the Putnam woman's proclamation that he was going nowhere until spring. He stared up at the makeshift canopy, constructed no doubt to protect the Coopers from bugs and such that might fall from the ceiling of the sod house as he considered his options.

"What is this place?" he asked.

"They named the town Homestead," the girl replied, ignoring her mother's look of warning.

"We're a long way from California," Sam Foster commented, as if making an observation about the weather. "Why are you going there?"

"My brother's there," Nathan replied, not yet ready to give them the whole story.

"Well, there's no hope that you're going to find your way across those mountains before spring—late spring at that." The man lit his pipe and drew on it. "I reckon you could stay with me and Mrs. Foster until you figure out your next move. That would probably be best all around."

"I can work, Mr. Foster," he said, seizing this opportunity God had surely placed before him.

"What'd you say was your trade?"

"I was a chaplain during the war. Before the war my family owned a…" He hesitated to call his family's land by its true name.

"Plantation?" Foster asked.

Nathan nodded.

"Things are different out here," the woman murmured. She glanced at him. "In many ways—not just farming."

"I can see that," he told her, cutting his eyes from her to Foster and back again. "After all I saw these last years, it'd be a nice change."

"You might be thinking about helping out some around here," Sam said. "Those windows could do with some fresh oiled paper if they're expected to keep out the wind and cold this winter."

"I'd be pleased to serve in any way I can," Nathan

said. "I'm in your debt, Mrs. Cooper—and yours, Mr. Foster. After all, the two of you saved my life."

"Sam," the older man said. "Just Sam, and my wife's Glory. We'll get you on your feet and then move you over to our place in the next day or so. Let's see how you hold up over the next little bit. No sense in rushing this thing and you having a setback." He sucked on his pipe. "Now, who's gonna help me unhitch that wagon out there?" Both children scrambled to put on their coats and follow him outside.

The silence was suddenly as thick as the smoke-filled air in the close room. The woman picked up some mending.

"May I know your given name?" he asked.

She seemed to consider his request for a long time. "Julianne," she said.

"And your husband's?"

"Luke," she replied, her fingers suddenly still on the fabric. Then she looked up at him, her gaze steady. "My husband died a year ago, Captain Cook."

"I'm so sorry for your loss, ma'am," Nathan said—and he was, but he also couldn't help feeling a certain comfort at the realization that in revealing this information, she had apparently decided to trust him.

Chapter Three

Even after Nathan had been with the Fosters for almost three weeks, it seemed that Julianne Cooper's entire routine had been turned upside down. And she could place the blame for that squarely at the doorstep of one Nathan Cook. The man had a way of being the focus of attention whether he was present or not. Whenever Glory or Sam stopped by, their conversation was about him, and the twins were always curious to know how he was doing. And a parade of townspeople had made it their business to check in on Nathan at the Fosters, and on Julianne, as if they'd suddenly been reminded that she was managing alone now.

On the day that Glory pronounced Nathan well enough to be moved to their farm, Emma Putnam arrived at Julianne's house and, as usual, she was accompanied by her sister, Lucinda, and her daughter, Melanie.

"Good," she announced in her booming voice. "It's high time you got the man out of here, Julianne. It's unseemly for a woman alone—"

"He was too ill," Glory started to protest, but saw the futility of arguing, and pressed her lips together.

"And, Captain Cook," Emma said, turning her attention to him, "you may as well accept that out here on the plains, we don't hold with any social hierarchy. The Fosters are every bit as welcome here and a part of this community as anyone else. I know you're from the South, but—"

"Yes, ma'am," Nathan replied. He leaned heavily on Sam as the older man helped him from the bed and into the wagon. Julianne had followed with the buffalo robe to cover him.

"Oh, no ma'am," he'd protested. "You'll be needing that—you and the children."

"I have another, and Mr. Foster can bring this one back on his next visit," she assured him.

He covered her hand with his, then and peered at her from beneath a fringe of thick, black lashes. "I thank God for bringing me to your home, Miz Cooper."

Julianne had nodded curtly, and slid her hand from between the two of his. She wasn't sure what made her more uncomfortable, the fact that he'd given God the credit for his rescue, or the fact that she could still feel the warmth of his touch radiating through her fingers.

"Come inside this instant, Julianne," Emma called from the doorway, "before you catch your death.

"Captain Cook is quite handsome," Lucinda gushed, once Julianne had returned to the cabin and closed the door.

"Handsome is as handsome does," Emma huffed. "He's a Southerner, and that's cause for concern. We'll see how he handles himself, now that he's regaining his strength, Lucy—before we make any further assessment of the man's positive attributes."

But whatever reservations Emma Putnam, or anyone else in the community of farmers and townspeople, might have had were erased entirely the first Sunday that Glory pronounced Nathan recovered enough to accompany her and Sam to church. It was the third Sunday of the month, and the circuit preacher was scheduled to hold services in the newly built schoolhouse. The children's desks had all been pushed against the walls and replaced with rows of long wooden benches.

The schoolyard was crowded with wagons and carriages, as farmers and townspeople gathered for the service that was as much an opportunity to socialize as it was to worship. But as the clock over the teacher's desk ticked off the minutes and then an hour, it was apparent that the preacher would not be coming.

"Well," Jacob Putnam said as he stood up and moved to the lectern that served as a pulpit. "Seems we'll have no service today, folks. Shall we—"

"Begging your pardon, sir," Sam Foster said, "but we've a chaplain right here. Perhaps he'd be willing to do a reading and give us a few words before we go?"

All eyes turned to Nathan. He was still gaunt and pale, even after weeks of Glory's cooking, but he stood up, his Bible in his hand. "I could say a few words," he said, looking over the congregation, "if that's agreeable with all?"

There was a general murmur of assent and relief as Nathan made his way to the front of the room. In addition to the usual group that regularly attended services, this was the Sunday before the community's annual harvest homecoming, and the beginning of weeks of preparations for Christmas. The room was so packed with men, women and children that it made the fire in the school's potbelly stove almost unnecessary.

Julianne could not help but notice that Nathan was an impressive figure of a man. He was taller than most of the men in the room, and yet his size was not at all intimidating. In fact, he seemed to exude a kind of confidence and leadership that would naturally draw people to him.

He read a passage from the small Bible that Julianne recognized as the one she'd carefully dried along with his other papers—and his journal. She wished now that she had taken Glory's advice and read more of the journal, and couldn't help wondering what entry he'd made in his journal since leaving her cabin. It shocked her to realize that what she was really wondering was whether or not he might have mentioned her.

After a hymn, Nathan cleared his throat and looked out over the gathering. It was as if everyone had stopped breathing as they waited for the message this Southerner would bring them.

"I had the privilege of meeting young Master Luke Cooper a few weeks ago," he began, and all eyes shifted to where Julianne sat between her two children.

"The boy asked me if I'd been on the winning side of the war. Now, all of you good people know the outcome of that conflict by now, but I would say to you the same thing I told Master Cooper. There are no victories in war—only losses. The loss of sons and husbands and brothers and fathers—on both sides. The loss of family ties, as one member chooses one side and another chooses the other. The loss of homes and farms and businesses. The loss of unity among states in a nation founded on unity of purpose. The loss of community. And far above everything, often there has been the loss of faith."

Julianne's head shot up. Was it possible that, in their brief conversation, this man had realized that she had lost her faith when Luke died? That in standing by helplessly as the man who had been her strength and protector faded away day by day, in pain and suffering, with his children watching, Julianne had questioned a god who could allow such a thing. And when Luke finally died, she had not prayed with the others, for she had spent all of her prayers and all of her tears, and it had come to nothing. God had not heard her cries for help.

But Nathan was not looking at her as she had expected. He was looking over the crowded room, his eyes skittering from one upturned face to another. "I am here to testify that faith can survive even the most horrific atrocities that man may inflict upon his fellow man. I am here to say that such faith can not only survive, it can sustain. Indeed, faith in God is man's only weapon against despair."

Across the aisle from Julianne, Glory Foster's eyes brimmed with tears, but she was smiling and nodding and murmuring, "Amen," to each pronouncement out of Nathan's mouth as she clutched Sam's gnarled hand.

"A family is a precious thing," he said, his voice softening. "Every man I ministered to on the battlefield thought first and last of family."

Unconsciously, Julianne placed one hand on Luke's knee and the other on Laura's forearm. *Family. Her family. All she had, now that Luke was gone and her relatives back east had abandoned her because she had defied them to love a Yankee.* She felt her throat close as she thought about the promise she'd made to herself the night that Luke died. His dream—his life—would not have been in vain. She would work the land, maintain the homestead, and protect the legacy that he had wanted for her and their children.

"A community is like family. And although I have only been here a short time, from what I have seen,"

Nathan continued, "this is a community that has come together to sink its roots deep into the tangled soil of the tall grasses. And now, as you enter this season of harvest and holy days, you have opened your homes and hearts to me—a stranger in your midst and I thank God and each of you for that blessing. Let us pray."

In unison, every head bowed—even Julianne's.

After services, the schoolyard came alive with chatter, as everyone angled for a position to have a word with Nathan. Julianne watched from a distance, waiting for Glory and Sam to have their turn, before she and the children drove to the Foster farm for the noon meal, as they had every Sunday since Luke's death.

She heard Jacob Putnam ask Nathan if he might consider a permanent position as minister of the church the community planned to build in the spring. She moved closer, unsure why his answer seemed so important.

"That's very flattering, sir," Nathan replied. "But California is my destination. My brother is there and he's alone. Like I said before—a man needs to know he has family."

"Contact your brother. Perhaps he might consider—"

"I don't know where he is, sir," Julianne heard Nathan admit then he smiled down at the older man. "But I'd be more than pleased to offer services while I'm here, if that helps."

"It does," Jacob agreed. "And don't think you've heard the last of this. For some in this town, gathering for worship is about as close to family as they're likely to get."

Julianne was sorting through the confusion of her feelings. Shouldn't she feel relief that he planned to move on come spring? Instead, her relief seemed to grow from the news that he would stay for the winter. Why should anything Nathan Cook did concern her in the least?

"Is the captain coming for Sunday dinner?" She heard Luke, Jr. ask as Sam led Glory across the snow-patched schoolyard to their wagon.

"Not today," Glory replied. "Seems Emma Putnam has invited the church elders and the captain to her house."

Julianne had little doubt that her friend was more than a little put out with this affront. "Maybe that's a good thing," she suggested. "It certainly seems as if Emma has had a change of heart when it comes to Nathan—Captain Cook."

Glory glanced over to where Emma was talking excitedly—and loudly—to Nathan, and frowned. "Will you listen to that? All of a sudden she's acting like she wanted to ask him to take the pulpit today all along—like it was her idea, not my Sam's."

"Now Glory," Sam placated.

"She's got her eye on him for other reasons, too. You mark my words, she'll have that scrawny daughter of hers sitting right beside him at the dinner table, but that simpering schoolmarm is no match for that young man. No, sir. He needs a woman who'll stand up to him, walk alongside him—not behind."

Julianne could not help but notice that Glory was looking straight at her as she made these pronouncements.

Throughout the noon meal, all conversation continued to focus on Nathan. Julianne was never so glad to be on her way home. But even, there Nathan Cook's presence filled the tiny cabin.

"Mama?"

Julianne looked up from her needlework to see Laura holding the familiar journal.

"I think this belongs to the captain," Laura said.

"Yes, you're right. It must have slipped out of his saddlebag when he left us. I'll see that he gets it," Julianne promised, taking the book from her daughter.

So there was the answer to her silly, girlish ruminations about whether or not he might have made mention of her in his writings. How could he, when the journal had been here the entire time?

She fanned the pages with her thumb, catching a word here and there. "Jake" was a word she saw more than once as were the words "faith" and "blessed".

The jingle of a harness outside the cabin door made Julianne lay the journal aside as the twins abandoned their game of tiddledywinks and rushed to see who might have come to call. For weeks after Luke died, neighbors had dropped by unannounced several times a day. In some cases, they had been simply curious, clearly half-expecting to find Julianne in the process of packing up for the trip back east. Others had been more direct in their purpose. Emma Putnam came with advice—in her view, Julianne was simply being stubborn and doing her "precious little ones" no favor by refusing to leave.

"It's the captain," Luke, Jr., announced, then threw open the door, bringing in a rush of cold air and a dusting of snow. Nathan ducked to clear the low doorway, removing his hat as he did so. He ruffled Luke's hair and smiled at Laura before turning his attention to Julianne.

"Hello," he said softly, his eyes meeting hers with so steady a gaze that she looked away.

"Well, this is a pleasant surprise," she said, sounding more like Emma Putnam than herself. She picked up the journal. "I expect you've come for this," she continued in a more normal tone. "Laura found it under the bed. It must have fallen out of your saddlebag."

Nathan took it from her and chuckled. "Just goes to show how busy I've been. I didn't even miss it. Writing in it was just a way I used to keep myself company on the trail. But since I moved in with the Fosters, and— what did you think of the service this morning?"

Julianne was taken aback at the sudden change of subject, but Luke rushed in to fill the void. "I was kind of hoping for more stories about the fighting," he said.

"Luke, I believe that you and your sister have chores to attend?"

"Yes, ma'am," the twins replied in unison, as they collected their outer garments and headed for the door.

"Want me to stable your horse?" Luke asked.

"He'll be fine, but thank you anyway."

Luke looked disappointed.

"Come to think of it," Nathan called after him, "Ol' Salt would probably appreciate some water if you could crack the ice on that bucket I saw out there."

"Yes, sir," Luke replied, and ran from the house leaving his sister to make sure the door was closed.

"I apologize," Julianne said when they were gone. "Luke gets his directness from his father."

"And Laura her Southern reticence to pry from you?" Nathan guessed this aloud, as he shifted from one foot to the other. Julianne realized he was still standing just inside the door, still wearing his coat, still holding his hat.

She leapt to her feet and held out her hand for his hat and outer coat. "Well, clearly neither child is learning manners from me today. I'm sorry, Captain, please come and warm yourself by the fire. Even after over three years out here, it's hard to adjust to such bitter cold."

"I was thinking on the way over here how, when I was a kid back in Virginia, at this time of year we were still able to be out in our shirtsleeves." Nathan folded his tall frame onto one of the wooden stools that Luke had fashioned for the table. Luke had been a much smaller man—shorter by a good six inches, and stockier. It was unsettling, seeing Nathan sitting where her husband had once sat.

"Would you like some tea?"

"That would be fine. I'd also really like to know what you thought about today's service."

"Why?"

Nathan smiled. "I thought you said your late husband was the direct one."

"Sorry, but I simply don't know why my opinion should matter one way or another."

"The Fosters have a great respect for you, and that tells me that your opinion has meaning."

Julianne felt the heat rise to her cheeks. "Glory and Sam have been like family to me. I'm afraid they may be prejudiced." She set a mug of tea and a spoon in front of him, and another at her place, then slid the sugar bowl across the table. "Do you take milk?"

"No, thank you." He took a long swallow of the hot liquid, then set the mug down and looked at her. "So?"

"I thought it was fine," she replied.

"Not too much? All that business about us all being pioneers and such?"

"Are you fishing for compliments, Captain Cook?"

Julianne laughed, and the sound of it was foreign to her. How long since she had sat at this table and laughed?

Nathan grinned. "Guess I am."

They each drank their tea and Julianne set down her mug and picked up her needlework.

"I'm real sorry for the loss of your husband," Nathan said after a moment. "It must be especially hard this time of year, with Christmas coming and all."

Julianne was so startled that she jabbed herself with the needle and cried out. Nathan reached across the narrow table and examined her finger. "Are you hurt?" He brushed away the single drop of blood with his thumb.

It was the second time the man had taken her hand—the second time she'd been unnerved by the action; and yet, in both cases his attention had been completely innocent and appropriate.

"I'm fine," she assured him. "I often forget to put on my thimble, and I pay the price. Glory says it's because my mind is always on things other than my handiwork," she explained, words coming in a rush, like a creek thawing in spring. "And she may have a point. Certainly, if you look at my work next to Glory's, you'd know at once who paid the attention necessary to get the stitching perfect."

"What other things?"

"What?"

"What are you thinking about when you're stitching?"

The farm. The crops that might never get planted or worse, get washed out if we have a wet spring. The prairie fires that could take everything if we have a dry summer. Having what I need to feed and clothe my children. Making sure that we don't lose this place after all the work that Luke put into it....

Nathan leaned closer and Julianne realized that she had failed to respond to his question. She forced a smile and got up to refill his mug. "Silliness," she said.

"Somehow I doubt that."

"You hardly know me."

"What I know is that it takes a woman of substance to maintain a spread like this, hang on to the only real home her children have ever known. That, and still have the strength to play the Good Samaritan to a stranger stupid enough to try and find his way across the plains with winter coming on."

"How are you feeling?" she asked, relieved at the opening to change the subject.

"Better each day. It's self-defense."

"I don't get your meaning."

Nathan laughed. "Mrs. Foster seems determined to 'fatten me up', as she puts it. She claims I'm skinnier than President Lincoln was, and has this notion that putting food in front of me every couple of hours is the only medicine that can possibly build my strength."

Julianne could not help smiling. "She did the same thing with me after—" She stopped and covered her mouth with her hand. "Would you like more tea?"

"After your husband died?" Nathan guessed.

Julianne nodded and refilled his cup.

"It will ease—the grief and pain," he assured her.

"I'm sure that on the battlefield you experienced death many times over, Captain. Some of those men were probably friends of yours. And yet—"

"It's not the same," he said, and ran his forefinger around the rim of his cup. "You're right, of course. Still, there are all sorts of losses we must endure over the course of a lifetime. I choose to have faith that each has some purpose."

Her eyes flared with anger. "I fail to see the purpose in leaving those two children fatherless and—"

"I understand how you might feel that way," he said.

She wanted to tell him that he couldn't possibly understand unless he had children who depended on him. But she decided to let the matter drop. After all, he was a guest. "I overheard Jacob Putnam ask you to stay on and consider taking the pulpit permanently."

"Thinking back on it, I suspect it was a compliment, nothing more. I mean, who would hire someone to minister after just one sermon?"

"Jacob takes his role as mayor quite seriously. He's determined to establish Homestead as a viable community as quickly as possible. There's a rumor that the railroad company is looking at a route that could come very close to Homestead."

"Well, I wish him well, and I'm happy to fill in for as long as I'm here, but I have to get to California."

"Your brother?"

Nathan nodded and set his cup on its saucer. "Jake was only sixteen when the war started, but my father thought he was old enough to serve. He couldn't understand why Jake wasn't as eager to volunteer as every other youth in our area."

"But surely your mother—"

"She sides with my father no matter the topic. I was already gone, but apparently the argument escalated to the point where one night Jake just took off. He left a note saying he was headed to California because it was as far away from the war as he could get."

"And you didn't know?"

"I found out when I went home last spring after General Lee surrendered. Mother said they didn't want to tell me, for fear it would upset me and I might get careless. They had lost one son, and they couldn't face losing me as well."

"But Jake wasn't lost."

"He was to them. He had dishonored the family, the South. My father never forgave him—not even on his deathbed. He refused to allow Jake's name to be spoken in that house after the day he left."

"And no one has heard from him?"

"No. As I've traveled west I've placed ads in the California papers, always leaving a general address for a reply, if anyone has seen or heard of him—or if Jake—"

"You don't even know if he's alive?"

Nathan shook his head. "Not for sure. But I have faith that God would not send me off on some wild-goose chase. I believe this is the journey I am meant to be on." He looked up and smiled. "Enough of my misery. What about your family? And your late husband's? Are the twins' grandparents in this area as well?"

"No, my parents are still in Virginia, and Luke's are in Boston." She got up and wrapped her apron around the handle of the kettle. "More?"

The door slammed open and Luke, Jr., burst inside, breathless with the cold and excitement. "The land agent's coming," he announced as Laura crowded in the doorway next to him.

Julianne's hand went to her throat and her eyes widened with alarm as she glanced quickly around the cabin. as if checking to be sure it could stand inspection.

"Is there a problem?" Nathan asked, getting to his feet and moving toward the door.

"No. Maybe." Julianne brushed back a wayward strand of hair. "It's just odd he would come on a Sunday."

Chapter Four

Roger Donner was a large man with a barrel-shaped chest that belied his mild, almost shy manner.

"Afternoon, ma'am," he said, then stopped short when he saw Nathan. "Captain," he added. "Fine sermon this morning."

Nathan extended his hand. "Thank you. I don't believe we had the pleasure of speaking after services."

"Roger Donner, government land agent for the territory." His eyes slid from Nathan to Julianne. "Mrs. Cooper, I wonder if we might have a word…in private?"

Nathan saw Julianne's eyes dart anxiously over the spotless room. "I…this is…" she began.

"It's the Lord's Day, sir," Nathan said quietly. "Surely, any business you have to discuss with Mrs. Cooper can wait until tomorrow?"

"Sadly, no," Donner replied. "I leave first thing tomorrow for St. Louis, to file this year's report with the commissioner for the region." He directed his explanation to Julianne.

Nathan saw Julianne's fingers tighten on her needlework. She jabbed the needle through the cloth and shuddered, and he knew she had once again pricked her finger. "I see," she said softly. "This is about this season's crops, is it?"

"Yes, ma'am. I was in hopes that together we might come up with some way of explaining—"

"My husband died," she said.

"Yes, ma'am. Big Luke was a good man and will be sorely missed." Donner bowed his head even further. "Still, the rules of the Homestead Act are clear. Those living on the land—hoping to claim the land—are responsible."

"Surely there is room for compromise," Nathan said, moving around the table to stand behind Julianne, but resisting the urge to place a comforting hand on her thin shoulder.

Donner shook his head. "No, sir. There's plenty of folks waiting for land—and land with fields already plowed and a house—"

"There's got to be a way 'round it," Nathan said.

"The rules are quite clear, Captain Cook," Julianne said. "If the land lies fallow for a period of six months or more during growing season then it is considered to have been abandoned."

"You could buy it outright," Donner suggested.

"I don't have the two hundred dollars, Mr. Donner."

"I was thinking maybe Mr. Cooper's family back east…"

Julianne stiffened. "That's not possible."

Donner nodded and turned to the door. "Just an idea. I'll do my best, Mrs. Cooper. I wanted to let you know that in person."

"I appreciate that," she said. "How long will you be away?"

"I'll be back in time for Harvest Home," he said

brightening a little for the first time since entering the small cabin.

Julianne smiled and pressed his forearm. "Good. We count on you for the music at the festival, you know."

Nathan saw relief flood the man's haggard features, once he realized that he and Julianne seemed to have reverted to their normal friendship. "Yes, ma'am," he said as he left.

"Thank you for riding all the way out here, Mr. Donner. Safe travels," she called, as the man mounted his horse.

"Wait up," Nathan called, taking his hat and coat from the hook where Julianne had hung them. "Mind if I ride along?" He wanted to know more. For starters, why had Donner suggested the dead husband's family and why had Julianne refused so abruptly?

"Not a bit," Donner replied. "Glad of the company."

"I'll stop by later in the week, if that's all right," he said to Julianne, who stood in the yard, her arms wrapped around herself.

"The children and I look forward to it," she replied. "Good afternoon, gentlemen," she called, as the two men rode off together.

Realizing that the way she had been clutching her shoulders had less to do with the weather and more to do with this new bit of worry Donner's visit had brought, Nathan was tempted to turn back to make sure she was all right. But something told him that Julianne Cooper was a woman of pride as well as uncommon strength. She was not likely to appreciate having some stranger see through that pride to the panic and fear he'd seen fill her eyes when Donner had given her his news.

Still, as he and the land agent rode past the fallow fields, snow-covered now, he wondered how any woman alone with two children to raise could possibly live up to the regulations for making the land her own. Acre after acre, the scene was the same—fields clotted with the remains of the last harvest Luke Cooper had gleaned. Roger Donner pointed it all out to him as evidence that he had little choice but to make his report.

"I could lie," he said, "but there's this man who has made a business of buying folks out or reclaiming abandoned land. Miz Cooper's place is one he's had his eye on. It's prime, the way it sits near the river, with its natural supply of water and the way Luke built that soddy so it was protected from the worst of the winter storms."

"She wouldn't want you to lie," Nathan assured the man, and then wondered how he knew that to be true. "God will show her the way," he added. As the two men rode over the uneven and slippery fields, Nathan could only hope that faith was going to be enough.

Later that evening, Glory Foster told him that after Luke Cooper died, something inside Julianne had hardened. "She sees that those children attend church and all, but I've seen it in her eyes that she's lost faith. And who can blame her—all she's had to endure."

She'd gone on to talk about Julianne's family, who had broken with her when she married Luke—a New Englander—a Yankee. "Then there was his people," Glory continued pursing her lips, as if tasting something bitter. "All kinds of money that family has, but he wanted no part of it if they wouldn't accept Julianne as their equal, even though they had education and all. Big Luke was no more than two months in the ground when she gets this letter from some city lawyer telling her not to try and lay claim to any of the Cooper fortune—as if she would, the way they turned against their own son."

That explained her curt answer when Donner had suggested asking the Coopers for the two hundred dollars she needed to buy the land. With each revelation, Nathan's esteem for the young widow deepened into something that he recognized as more than just empathy for her troubles and admiration for her strength. Was it possible that all along God had been guiding his way, bringing him to this place, that sod house—to her? Julianne Cooper needed help. The problem was that everything about her shouted, *No, I don't.*

Julianne was far more shaken by Roger Donner's visit than she had let on. Standing outside the sod house, she had never felt less suited for the task that she had set for herself.

In the spring after her husband's death, she had hitched their ox, Dusty, to the plow, and set out to prepare the fields that surrounded their cabin for planting. But she had made it barely half a row before blisters had formed on her palms and her skirts and boots were coated with mud. She'd looked up then and seen a man astride a large white steed, watching her from the top of the rise.

Two days later the man had come calling and suggested that going it alone was not the answer. If she would allow him to assume ownership of her land...

She'd lost her temper and ordered him off her property. But the man had not given up. He had only changed tactics. Instead of trying to buy her out, he had tried courting her. He would stop by on the pretense of bringing Laura a book he'd seen when the peddler came through town. He offered Luke, Jr., his pocketknife. Julianne had quietly refused every gift, and eventually he stopped coming. But he was out there. She'd heard of a man of his description traveling the region, reclaiming abandoned homesteads and buying out those who found the winters too severe and the summers too hot.

Later that week, as she peeled apples for apple butter and counted the days until Roger would return with news of her fate, she felt the familiar weight of responsibility settle round her shoulders. The rules of the contract were simple—either manage the land or lose it. Even though her neighbors had offered to put in crops for her, she'd been too proud to accept charity. Besides, Roger had made it clear that eventually she would have to find a way to work the land herself.

"Mama, you're cutting too close to the core," Laura reprimanded, as she picked an apple seed out of the bowl and laid it on the table.

Julianne stared at the tiny black seed, her paring knife suspended in midair, the seed reminding her of the thousands of seeds it would take to plant her fields come spring.

The shroud of hopelessness that covered her made her knees shake, and she sank down onto a kitchen stool.

"Mama?"

Laura was peering at her. "Are you sick? Should Luke go for Miz Foster?"

"I'm fine," she assured both children. "We're fine," she added through teeth gritted in determination that she would not fail them.

Ever since President Lincoln had called for a national day of thanksgiving, towns and villages across the land had held prayer services and festivals in observance. The date varied from one community to the next, but the celebration found its framework around faith and food and friendship. Homestead's festival was scheduled for the last weekend in November.

The day of the festival, Julianne braided Laura's hair and ironed a shirt for Luke. She took more time than usual with her own hair and clothing. Ordinarily, she would have chosen the black dress she had worn for Luke's funeral and to every public gathering since. But the anniversary of Luke's death had passed quietly that week, with only Glory taking note. "Time to move on," she'd advised. "Luke would have wanted that for you."

And so she chose her best dress, a woollen homespun the color of pine trees back in Virginia. She braided her hair and then wrapped the long braids around her head in a coronet, fastening them in place with the pair of silver combs Luke had given her as a wedding present.

"You look pretty, Ma," Laura said.

"Yeah—different, but real pretty," Luke added.

"Thank you. Now get your coats and mittens on. Mr. and Mrs. Foster will be here soon and we don't want to be late."

The Putnam barn had been transformed for the festival. Bales of fresh hay did double duty as decoration and seating. Piles of pumpkins, squash and gourds filled freshly swept stalls—the animals having been moved to neighboring farms for the occasion. Dozens of lanterns swung from rafters and cast a warm glow over the festivities below.

In one corner, the children were gathered around their teacher in her new role as organizer of games and contests for the evening. A barrel filled with melted snow and apples waited for the children to try and snag an apple without using their hands. Across the way,

Roger Donner and a trio of farmhands were warming up their fiddles in preparation for a sing-along and dancing. Roger had avoided Julianne since she and the children had arrived, and that more than anything told her that he had likely failed to successfully plead her case with the commission.

"Come along, Julianne," Emma bellowed. "The contest is about to begin." She took Julianne by the arm and steered her to the end of a long bench that had been placed in the center of the barn.

Julianne unwrapped her paring knife from the napkin she used to protect its sharp blade, and sat on the edge of the bench. Lucinda Putnam moved up and down the rows, handing each woman an apple.

"Now, ladies, you have one minute to produce the longest unbroken strand of apple peel," Jacob Putnam instructed, taking out his pocket watch and flicking open the cover. "Ready, set, go."

In seconds, several of the younger and less experienced women were eliminated as the peels of their apples broke. Soon it was down to Julianne and two others. She considered allowing the streamer of peel to break of its own weight, giving one of the others a better chance at the victory, but then she caught Nathan watching her closely.

He smiled and nodded, and she found herself wanting to please him. She narrowed her cut a sixteenth of an inch, to give herself the best chance at having the longest strand.

"Time," the banker called, as Lucinda carefully gathered the peels created by the three finalists and took them off for measurement. "And while we await the outcome," Putnam shouted, "we shall ask the single ladies to take their places and peel one more apple."

There were giggles and excited whispers, as girls and single women took their places on the benches. Julianne started to get up, but Glory placed a firm hand on her shoulder and handed her an apple.

"Let's just see if there's a new man in your future, missy," she said.

"Don't be ridiculous."

"Peel," Glory ordered as, one by one, the others peeled their apple and tossed the skin over their shoulder. Then everyone gathered to see what initial the peel might have formed, for legend had it that the peel would form the letter of a girl's intended.

"Well, look at that. Is that the letter C, or could it be the letter N?" Emma boomed as everyone gathered around.

"I think it's more of a J," someone suggested. "Is it supposed to be the first or last name?"

"First," someone replied.

"Well, now that I study it, that's an N as clear as writing it on the chalkboard," Emma insisted.

"The letters C and N don't look nothing alike," someone shouted, and others murmured their agreement as Emma defended her position.

"Drop yours while they're busy chewing on that," Glory instructed.

"Glory," Julianne protested.

"Just humor an old woman and drop the peel."

Julianne refused to toss the peel over her shoulder as tradition dictated. Instead, she dropped it on the floor in front of Glory, and there was not a doubt in the world that the letter the red apple skin most resembled was an N.

"Told you so," Glory said, scooping up the peel before anyone else could see it and walking off toward where the children were bobbing for apples.

Julianne continued to stare at the dirt floor where the peel had lain. She did not believe in such silliness, but on the other hand, the moisture from the peel had left its imprint, and she could not deny that it formed the first letter of Nathan's name.

It had been a year, and in all that time the idea that she might find love again had been the furthermost thing from her mind. And yet…

"And the winner and new champion of the apple-peeling contest with a ribbon of twenty-three inches is," Putnam shouted, "Mrs. Julianne Cooper."

A cheer went up as Julianne stepped forward to receive her prize, an apron embroidered with apples on the pocket.

"Thank you," she said.

"Louder," someone called.

"Thank you," she shouted, and everyone laughed. "But let us all remember that the champion will always be Mrs. Foster, until her record can be broken."

"And now, ladies and gentlemen, boys and girls, it's time for the judging of the baked goods," Jacob announced. "Captain, will you do the honors?"

The crowd followed Nathan over to where the cakes, pies and sweetbreads were displayed.

She watched as he tasted one sweet after another and announced that choosing the best was an impossible task. In the end, he declared a tie between Emma's pumpkin pie and Glory's apple cake.

"That was very nice of you," she told him later, as they sipped glasses of apple juice and watched the children engaged in a lively game of blindman's buff. "Everyone knows that Emma Putnam has many skills, but baking isn't one of them."

He shrugged. "Some people need that recognition, and it costs nothing to give it to them now and again."

"So you admit it," she pressed.

He grinned. "Between you and me? Yes."

"Why, Reverend Captain Cook, I am shocked." His laughter carried above the squeals of the children, warming the air around them.

"It's getting so close in here, and the night is clear. Would you walk with me, Julianne?"

Outside, several men had gathered around a fire to talk in peace and smoke their pipes as couples strolled hand in hand under the star-filled sky.

"I see Roger Donner is back," he said.

"Yes."

"And?"

"We haven't spoken, but I know that's the answer. If he'd been successful in getting me more time he would have told me right away. He wants me to have this evening to enjoy. He's a good man."

"What will you do?"

"I don't know," she admitted.

He pulled her hand through the crook of his elbow. "We'll figure something out," he said. "Meanwhile, Roger has a good idea. Let's just enjoy this evening."

They walked along in silence until they came to a rail fence, the silence stretching uncomfortably between them. "I hate seeing you so sad," he said finally.

"Not sad so much as…" She searched for the right word. "That is, I was very sad for a long time after Luke became so ill and died."

"Only sad?"

"And angry," she admitted.

"At God?"

"I'm afraid I don't have your strength when it comes to faith," she said. "Yes, I was angry at God—and at Luke."

"For dying?"

"For leaving me and the children, I suppose. Oh, I know that he didn't choose that path—no one does. But life can be so very hard sometimes. Don't you ever feel that?"

He stared out at the horizon for a long moment, and she wondered if he was thinking about his lost brother.

"I'm sorry," she said, touching his shoulder to draw his attention away from the past. "Glory says I spend too much time dwelling on things I can't change." She was struggling to lighten the mood, to bring them back to the place where he was laughing and his laughter made her feel light as air.

"Glory is a wise woman," he said, cupping her cheek with his palm.

In that moment it was as if the world had stopped turning and they were alone in the dark with only the endless horizon and a sky filled with stars surrounding them.

"Julianne," he whispered as he lowered his mouth to hers. And any idea that she had that he might have been mourning his missing brother flew away on the wings of his kiss.

His lips were soft and met hers gently, tentatively, and even when she returned his kiss, he did nothing to take advantage. Instead, he pulled away and rested his forehead on hers. "You could always come to California," he whispered. "You and the children."

Panic laced with confusion threatened to overwhelm her. Her knees shook and she grasped the fence railing for support as she stepped away from him. "How can you think that problems can be so easily solved?" she managed to say.

"I don't. I just…" He reached out to touch her and she backed away.

"I can't leave here," she told him.

"Why not? Think of it, Julianne. A fresh start. California is filled with possibilities."

"You don't know that. You've been taken in by what you've read and heard and you have a purpose in going there. Your brother…"

Now he was the one who took a step back. "And what is your purpose in staying here?"

"I promised," she said, choking a little on the words as she realized that already she had broken that promise, because she had most likely lost the land. She was suddenly aware of music coming from the barn, lively and incongruous to the tension between them. "I have to go," she said. "I need to speak to Roger—to know for certain…."

She did not finish her statement, and as she ran back toward the light of the barn, she realized that she felt only disappointment that Nathan did not try to stop her.

Chapter Five

Roger tried to persuade her that there was still hope in that the commissioner had postponed making any decision until after Christmas, but Julianne saw in the land agent's eyes that he did not believe the decision would be in her favor.

She didn't take the children to church on Sunday. Luke had the sniffles, and while she knew it wasn't serious, that was her excuse. On Monday she found herself listening for the creak of Sam's old wagon, knowing if it came it would most likely be Nathan driving the team.

But Nathan did not come. Glory stopped by to check on the children but remained uncustomarily silent regarding Nathan. A week passed, and an unexpected snowstorm gave Julianne the only excuse she needed to miss church for the second week in a row.

Late on Monday night, after the children had been in bed for an hour already, Julianne heard the pound of hoofbeats coming down her lane. She wiped her hands on her apron and waited for the rider to pass, but the only sound she heard was the relentless wind that whistled around the house seeking any possible entry, and the low murmur of a man's voice instructing his horse.

Then boots, heavy on the stoop outside her door, followed by a light tap.

She glanced at the rifle over the door, then at the lamp she'd left burning while she finished putting up the last of the apple butter that she hoped to trade at the mercantile for toys for the twins' Christmas.

"Julianne?"

The voice was muffled and indistinguishable. Not Sam Foster. But who else might call at this late hour?

"Who's there," she said, standing very close to the door so that there was no need to raise her voice and risk waking the children.

"It's me—Nathan. Look, I know it's late but…" When she failed to answer or open the door, he knocked again louder. "Julianne, please. I need to talk to you."

She grabbed her wool shawl and wrapped it around her head and shoulders, then slipped outside. "The children are sleeping, Captain Cook," she said. "Has something happened to Sam or Glory?"

"Not at all," he assured her. "They're both fine."

"Then why—"

"Walk with me a minute," he urged, taking her elbow.

It was absolutely foolhardy to do as he asked. And yet, even as she took in the restless stirring of the animals in the lean-to and saw that it was a clear night with a sky filled with stars, she did not pull away.

"Captain, really," she protested, but she followed his lead until they were standing in the midst of the apple trees that she and Luke had planted shortly after the house had been completed.

Nathan bent and scraped away snow until he unearthed a fallen apple. "This," he said holding the rotted fruit up as if it were gold, "could be your answer."

"It's an apple," she said slowly, as she might have years earlier when she was teaching the twins to identify objects.

"And how was this year's crop?" he asked, putting an unusual emphasis on the last word.

"It was really the first," she explained. "Luke and I planted the saplings three years ago when we first arrived here. It takes some time for—"

"I know. So how was the crop?"

Again that unusual focus on "crop".

"Captain—"

"Nathan," he corrected.

"Nathan, it is late. It is freezing. And my children are sleeping. What do you want?"

"You harvested these apples—what you could, right?"

She nodded impatiently.

"You probably dried some, put up some butter, perhaps made a pie?"

"Three," she corrected. "In fact, as long as you're here you can carry one back with you for the Fosters." She turned and started back around the house.

But once again he stopped her, his hand taking her forearm and turning her so that she was facing the apple trees and he was standing behind her with his hands resting lightly on her shoulders. "Think of it, Julianne," he said. "Imagine not just these few saplings, but apple trees as far as you can see."

She had lost most of the feeling in her hands and feet, and yet there was a warmth emanating from him that held her where she stood.

"Think of spring and white and pink blossoms everywhere you look, like clouds come down to earth," he said, his voice soft, dreamy. "Think of the blossoms falling like snow, and then the apples coming, green at first, and then brilliant yellow and red, like maple trees back home in Virginia come autumn."

The picture he painted was mesmerizing. She forgot about the cold, forgot about the late hour. "An orchard," she murmured.

"A crop," he corrected. "A legitimate use of the land and one you have already begun. You didn't abandon the land, Julianne. Right here there was a crop."

She turned to face him. "Do you honestly think the commissioner would accept that?"

"I spoke with Roger after I remembered seeing these apple trees the day before the storm came up so sudden, and I got disoriented. I mentioned the idea to Roger and he sent off a letter to the commissioner that very day."

"But Roger said that the best he could do was get a decision postponed until after the first of the year."

"And it may be weeks before you have an official answer. But Roger agrees with me as does Judge Romney." He pulled a paper from his jacket pocket. "This is a copy of the law, and it says right here that you've met the requirements—you raised a crop. You raised and harvested apples."

"It's a few fruit trees," she protested, afraid to let herself surrender to the hope he offered.

"There's nothing in the regulations to specify the size of the crop, Julianne. Roger agrees. It's the intent to farm the land that counts, and these trees show intent."

She felt the way a bird that had just experienced flight for the first time must feel. Weightless. Free. Without thinking, she flung her arms around Nathan's neck. "Oh, Nathan, thank you. It's brilliant. It's…"

She felt his arms tighten around her, his breath against her cheek as he bent his face to hers. Reality hit like a sudden drop in temperature. She reminded herself of the hour, the isolation, the compromising circumstances of being in each other's arms.

"It's freezing out here," she said abruptly, releasing him and stepping back as she clutched the shawl more tightly around her. "Come warm yourself by the stove for a bit before you head back."

She stumbled over the uneven and frozen ground until she reached the front door. Inside, she went first to check on the children, lifting the curtain that surrounded their cots to assure herself that they were both still asleep. She was aware that he had followed her inside and closed the front door.

Without meeting his gaze, she hurried over to the stove and lifted the kettle. "I'll just…"

His hand on her shoulder made her go still.

"Sit down and warm yourself," he said, relieving her of the kettle. "I'll do that."

Gratefully, she did as he instructed, pulling the stool nearer to the fire and holding out her hands to the embers.

He handed her a cup of tea and she wrapped her palms around the warm crockery. Nathan knelt next to her and before she could protest, he had pulled off her shoes and set them on the hearth to dry. Then he wrapped his thick knitted scarf around her feet.

"Better?" he asked looking up at her.

She nodded, unable to find her voice. Unable to decipher the feelings racing through her brain as she looked at him.

"Now then," he said, taking the bench across from her, "you still have to come up with a plan for planting more trees, building the crop. There's still work to be done."

She tried to focus on what he was saying, but could

get no further than remembering the feel of his gentle touch as he swathed her feet in the soft wool of his scarf. He picked up an apple seed that had stuck to the table. "You'll need seeds and—"

"But until we know for certain…" she said, reminded of how Luke had rallied for a few days and then slipped away. She had to stop daydreaming and focus on the hard realities of what lay ahead for her and the children.

"You know. You have it right there in writing," he said, nodding toward the copy of the law he'd given her.

She bent and unwrapped her feet, then folded the scarf in thirds and handed it to him. "Then we'll be fine. Thank you so much, Nathan. You didn't have to—"

"I could help you work out the plan for the planting, order the seeds."

In the days since he'd kissed her she had a lot of time to think, and the one thing she knew was that it would be foolhardy to get any more involved with this man than she already was. Every act of kindness bound her more closely to him and would make his leaving all the more painful. She stood up. "As I said, I am so very grateful for all that you—and Roger—have done for us. We'll be fine now—the children and I."

He stood as well. Slowly, he wrapped the scarf around his neck. "There's an old adage," he said quietly, "that God helps those—"

"What would you have me do?" Her voice was tight and rising. With a glance toward the curtain sheltering her sleeping children, she lowered it to a whisper. "I cannot plant trees when the ground is frozen."

Nathan started to say something, but instead turned and walked the three steps it took to reach the door. His silence made Julianne feel guiltier than if he had argued with her. After all he had come up with this idea—this plan that might make keeping her promise to Luke possible.

"Thank you for coming—for trying to help—for…" Her voice broke then, so that the last word came out on a sob. "…caring."

Nathan turned and pulled her hard against him, holding her as she cried.

"You aren't alone," he whispered. "There are so many people who want to see you succeed. Don't shut them out, Julianne."

She forced a laugh and pulled away, determined to show him that she was fine. "How is it that with everything you've been through, you are so sure things will work out for the best?"

He smiled and pushed a wayward curl behind her ear. "I'll answer that when you tell me how it is that you are so very sure that they won't." He pulled his hat on, anchoring it firmly over his brow. "Goodnight, Julianne."

Chapter Six

In spite of the way she'd tried to refuse his help that night, Nathan made a habit of stopping by every day the following week. In answer to her look of exasperation, he would turn his attention to the children. He would help with the chores and sometimes agree to stay for supper when one or both of the children suggested he should.

While Laura helped Julianne with the housework, Nathan and Luke tended to the evening chores. Through the hole-pocked paper that covered the windows, Julianne could hear the low murmur of Nathan's conversation with her son, although she could not make out the topic. Lately, many of the sentences out of young Luke's mouth seemed to begin with, "The captain says…"

Luke's sudden shriek brought her to the door at a run. Outside, she saw Nathan standing near the lean-to, and he was grinning at Luke who was trying in vain to brush fresh snow off his hair and neck. "Well?" Nathan challenged with a grin.

Luke scooped up a lump of snow and slowly formed it into a ball as he advanced on the preacher.

"Luke, no!" Julianne protested, just as the snowball found its mark smack in the middle of Nathan's chest.

"Good one," Nathan said, even as he grabbed another handful of snow and flung it back at Luke.

The battle was on in earnest now, and before Julianne knew what was happening, Laura squeezed past her, having donned her coat and mittens, and joined her brother in the fray.

"Ganging up on me, are you?" Nathan called, as he ducked a lob from Laura. "Mrs. Cooper, I need reinforcements," he called.

As if she'd traveled back in time to when she was younger, still living in the hill country of Virginia and unencumbered by responsibility, Julianne scooped some snow from the porch and flung it at her children.

"Ma!" Luke protested, but he was laughing and so was Laura, and the sound shattered the last dregs of somberness that had surrounded their home for far too long. Luke was gone, but she had her children. And when Julianne heard her own laughter in chorus with theirs, it was like music in the cold December air, and she felt that somewhere in the heavens above, Luke was laughing with them.

By the time supper was ready, any trace of uneasiness or shyness that might have dampened the meal had been banished by the snowball fight. As they bowed their heads for Laura to offer grace, Julianne could not help but notice that, for the first time in nearly a year, gathering for a meal together felt truly special. And she owed that—like so many changes that had taken place over the last several weeks—to Nathan Cook.

"Thank you, God, for this food we are about to receive," Laura prayed. Assuming his sister's prayer would begin and end as their grace always did, Luke's hand shot out to retrieve the first of the biscuits. But Laura scowled at him from under lowered lashes and continued. "And thank you for sending Captain Cook to us. And thank you for making Mama so happy today. Amen."

"Amen," Nathan added, looking across the table at Julianne.

"Luke, please pass our guest the biscuits first before you serve yourself," she instructed, glad for the excuse of teaching a lesson in manners to avoid meeting Nathan's questioning gaze. The man had to be wondering why her happiness was so unusual as to be a part of the blessing of the food.

"Captain Cook," Luke said, his voice breaking slightly with nervousness. "I know you said nobody wins at war, but can I ask you something else?"

"Yes."

"Did you carry a gun?"

"Yes."

"Then you know how to use a rifle like my Pa's?" Luke glanced at the rifle mounted over the door.

Julianne knew exactly where this was going. Luke's father had promised to teach the boy to fire the rifle and to take him hunting this fall. He'd filled the boy's head with tales of how they would shoot a wild turkey and bring it home for a feast at Christmas. "Luke, this is hardly—"

"I can do that," Nathan replied at the same moment. He looked to Julianne for guidance before continuing. "Tell you what, Mr. Foster and I were talking about doing some hunting. Glory has her heart set on a wild turkey for Christmas dinner. With the snow on the ground, tracking comes easier."

"Yes, sir," Luke said, his eyes sparkling with hope.

"If your mother agrees, Mr. Foster and I could let you come along, help with the tracking."

"Could I, Mom?"

On the one hand, Julianne felt cornered. On the other, she was well aware that this day had to come. And Nathan was offering her son a safe entry into the man's world of hunting.

Taking her hesitation as a good sign, Luke pressed his case. "I'll do all my chores without you having to ask, and I'll practice my multiplication tables and—"

"I suppose, if Mr. Foster is willing. But you'll do no shooting," she said.

Luke started to protest, but Nathan gave the boy a signal that had him agreeing to her terms. "Then I can go?"

"Yes, but on one condition."

His smile wavered.

"I want to hear you recite your multiplication tables all the way to twelve times twelve without looking to your sister for hints," she said. "The day you can do that is the day you can tell Captain Cook here that you are ready to go hunting."

Luke's face fell. Math was not his strong suit.

"I'll help," Laura said softly. "Come on, Luke, it'll be fun. Like playing school."

Luke groaned and Julianne could not hide her grin. Laura's favorite game was "school". She would line up her two dolls and teach them the lessons she'd learned that week. She would also beg Luke to play along, but he usually refused. A chance to make both of her children so happy was not something Julianne was going to pass up.

"I think that's a fine idea, Luke," she said.

"Yes, ma'am," Luke said, admitting defeat. "But once I can say the tables, I don't have to play any more?"

"Seems to me that playing school with your sister every now and again might not be such a bad thing," Nathan said. "Seems to me there might even come a time when you'd play the part of the teacher—maybe teach her about tracking," he suggested.

"Yes," Luke exclaimed, his high spirits restored.

"I should be heading back," Nathan said, as he pushed his plate away and wiped his mouth on his napkin. "I was thinking that tomorrow we might get you a tree to decorate for Christmas."

"Oh, that would be wonderful," Laura squealed. "Last year—" She glanced at Julianne and went silent.

"Last year," Julianne explained, "we didn't really celebrate Christmas. The children's father had recently died, and—"

"Then all the more reason to celebrate twice as much this year," Nathan said, addressing himself to the children. "I expect the two of you have already started on your gifts, right?"

Both children looked blank.

Nathan sighed. "I can see I'm going to have to take charge here—show you folks what an old-fashioned Virginia Christmas looks like."

Julianne was overwhelmed by the sudden need to keep her hands and thoughts busy with something other than the way Nathan looked, sitting opposite her and laughing with her children.

Like he belongs, she thought.

Early the following morning Nathan returned.

"Captain's back," Luke announced excitedly as he ran to the door.

"Good morning," Nathan called out when Julianne and the children came out onto the narrow porch. "Ready to go fetch that tree?"

As usual, the man was in fine spirits. There was something so appealing about that, and she found herself wishing she could find that kind of peace and contentment with life. She realized that she envied him this.

"Good morning," she replied as Luke bolted from her and peered curiously into the back of the wagon.

"What's that?" the boy asked.

"What's that, *sir*," Julianne corrected automatically, her own curiosity piqued.

"Sir," Luke added.

Nathan lifted two flat packages, each wrapped in brown paper and string. "Glass panes for the windows," he explained. "Careful now," he instructed, as he handed Luke one of the packages.

"I can take the second one, sir," Laura volunteered.

"And I thank you for that. Leaves me free to gather these tools," Nathan told the girl.

The twins carried the packages onto the porch as if they were precious gold, and set them carefully on the table that in warmer weather held the pitcher and bowl for washing up.

"I don't understand," Julianne said. "I didn't place an order for glass panes with Mr. Putnam, and this is a sod house, captain."

"I placed the order," Nathan said with a grin. "See, I was thinking that if you had glass in the window openings, then you could start some apple seeds inside— plant them in tin cans there on the window ledge. The sun through the glass would be warmer—like spring, and by spring you'd have a seedling instead of just a seed."

"I really…" She could barely find the words to form the protest.

"Have a little faith, Julianne," he said softly.

Julianne wrestled with her irritation that he would assume she had money for such things. "I cannot…"

Nathan moved a step closer and lowered his voice, his eyes on the children busily unwrapping the precious glass. "You cannot what, Julianne? Afford? Accept?"

"Both."

"It's a gift. My thanks for the care you gave me. I might have died had you not taken me in. Seems to me that a couple of panes of glass is hardly repayment enough for saving a man's life." He gave her a moment to consider his argument. "Please accept this, Julianne."

"Your thanks were enough," she murmured, but her eyes were on the glass pane that Laura was holding up to the light. Glass in the window wells instead of the oiled paper would do far more than help her raise apple seedlings. It would block out the wind and cold. It would allow more light into the cabin—into the lives of her children. "Very well," she said. "I accept, and now it is I who am in your debt."

Nathan laughed. "If you look at it that way, we could play this round-robin of thank-you gifts for years to come, Julianne."

His good humor was contagious, and Julianne smiled up at him. "Would that be so terrible?" It was the kind of flirtatious comment she might have made to Luke in their courting days. She felt the heat rise in her cheeks.

His smile faded and his eyes softened. "Not bad at all," he murmured, then cleared his throat and turned his attention to the children. "What do you say, children? If we work together we can have these panes in place and sealed by noon, and *then* go cut that Christmas tree."

She watched him instructing the children with patience and confidence in their ability to do as he asked. From time to time he would glance her way, as if they shared some bond built around their love of children. And she realized that for the first time since Luke's death, the idea that she might one day marry again was not as far-fetched as she had once thought.

But it could not be Nathan, she thought sadly. She would not keep him from following his dream of reuniting with his only brother and making a fresh start in California. But she would never forget the man who had opened the window to the possibility that she would not fail.

True to his word, the windows were fully installed by noon, and light seemed to pour into the cabin.

"Mama, look," Laura said, "I can see well enough to do my schoolwork here by the window."

"We'll have to make curtains," Julianne replied. "I think I have just the fabric." She rummaged through her sewing basket and pulled out two pieces of calico. "What do you think?"

"I think," Nathan announced, "that if we don't get going we'll not find a tree for Christmas before dark."

She spun around, unaware that Nathan had come inside.

"Oh, you and the children go on," she said.

He frowned. "Choosing and cutting the tree is a family thing, Julianne. Come with us." He took her cloak from the hook and held it out to her.

A family thing, she thought, and wished it might be so.

Chapter Seven

Nathan watched Julianne herd the twins into the back of the wagon bed mounted on runners. She was such a small woman—not more than five feet in height—and yet she carried herself with such strength and determination. He'd have to take care in the way he offered his advice—about the orchard or anything else—for she was also a proud woman. He suspected that underneath that brave front lay the kind of fear that he'd seen more than once on the battlefield. What if an officer could not spare his men from the ravages of the battle they were about to fight? What if that officer made a mistake and chose a path that would lead not to victory but to utter defeat?

"Ready?" he called over his shoulder to the children.

"Ready," they chorused, and then laughed with sheer delight as Nathan snapped the reins and the team took off at a trot across the snowy fields.

Back in Virginia, the challenge of a hunt for the tree was choosing the best one. Here, the problem was finding a tree—any tree. He suspected that Julianne was well aware of his dilemma when he saw her cover her mouth with one gloved hand and pretend an intense interest in the monotonous scenery that surrounded them.

"Not exactly Christmas-tree country," he muttered, and heard her gulp back a giggle. "You might have warned me."

"The first Christmas Luke and I spent here, we searched for hours."

"And found?"

She laughed. "A little scrubby evergreen that we decorated with a single paper star and a strand of ribbon. It was so tiny, that's all it would hold."

The twins were beginning to bicker over shares of the buffalo robe in the back of the wagon. "Are we there yet?" Luke demanded with an exasperated huff. "I'm freezing."

"You're cold," Julianne corrected, "not freezing. And no, we have not seen a tree yet."

"We're not giving up, are we?" Laura asked, and Julianne realized how important this Christmas was going to be for her children. It marked a return to normal, an end to mourning.

"Tell you what," Nathan announced, "let's make a game of the hunt. First one to spot a proper tree wins the prize."

"What's the prize?" the twins chorused.

"Well now, let's see. If Laura wins, then she gets a yard of ribbon from the mercantile. If Luke wins, he gets a nickel's worth of penny candy."

"What about Mama?" Laura asked.

Nathan glanced at Julianne's cheeks, as rosy as a ripe apple. "Apple seeds," he said softly, "for her orchard."

Their eyes met, and for an instant he held her gaze before focusing on her lips.

"Not fair," Luke declared.

"Fair if I'm making the rules," Nathan countered. "When you come up with a game—and the prizes—then you get to set the rules."

He sounded like a father—not *his* father certainly, but the father he and Jake had always wished they might know. How Jake would laugh if he could hear Nathan now.

"Trees," the twins screamed in unison, pointing to a cluster of juniper trees in the distance.

"I win," Luke crowed.

"I saw them, too," Laura protested.

"It's a tie," Julianne said, quieting both children as Nathan snapped the reins and the team of horses trotted across the barren landscape toward the trees.

"Not exactly a forest," Nathan said with a grin.

"It seems a shame to cut even one," Julianne said. "Trees are so very scarce out here."

"Aw, Ma, it's Christmas," Luke groaned, kicking at a branch that had broken off one of the trees.

Nathan bent and picked up the branch, oddly shaped but still green with needles. Then Julianne pulled another small branch from the snow.

"If we tied them together," she said, "they'd almost have the right shape."

Nathan handed her his branch and watched as she arranged the two so that one's greenery covered the other's bare spots.

"Here's another," Laura called, running to collect a smaller branch. "If we find enough we could build our own tree."

The search was on.

"No fair breaking branches off, Luke," Laura instructed.

"Now who's making up the rules," Luke muttered, but released the branch he'd been trying to break off one of the live trees.

* * *

The four of them had soon collected enough greenery to make an impressive tree and then some. "This is fun," Luke shouted as he added another branch to the pile in the back of the wagon.

"No doubt about it," Nathan said, "you two found us a treasure when you spotted this grove."

"We've enough to make a tree for our cabin and one for the Fosters as well." Julianne was beaming. "It will be a wonderful surprise."

"Come on," Luke urged. "Let's get home so we can build the trees."

Everyone piled into the sled and the horses started for home. The scent of juniper berries surrounded them and Nathan could not remember the last time he had felt such anticipation for Christmas to come.

"You know, when Jake and I were just boys," he said, "we used to go into the woods looking for mistletoe. It grew in the tallest trees, and Pa would shoot it down."

"My father did that as well," Julianne remembered. "I always begged him to let me go along, but he said it was a man's job." She got a faraway look in her eyes and frowned. "He was very rigid about such things."

"Sounds like my father," Nathan admitted. "Jake and I always said that if we were ever lucky enough to marry and have kids of our own, things would be different."

"You'd make a wonderful father, Nathan."

It was a simple compliment, and yet the words warmed him as if he'd just downed a steaming cup of hot chocolate.

"Wonder if Jake's a father yet," he mused, embarrassed at the effect her words had had on him.

"You've had no word at all?"

Nathan shook his head. "I keep hoping, and now that I'm to be in Homestead over the winter, I've sent out ads and letters to every community I can think of between here and California. It occurred to me that maybe he stopped along the way and stayed."

"He could be closer than you imagine." Julianne placed her gloved hand on his forearm. "You mustn't give up hope."

But she *had*, Nathan thought. According to Glory, after her husband's death she had locked her heart away.

The jingle of the harness brought Nathan back to the present. The cabin was in sight, the afternoon sun glinting off the newly installed window panes, as a stream of smoke wafted from the chimney and seemed to signal "home" as it dissipated against the overcast sky.

In spite of her resolve not to become more involved with the man, Julianne could think of nothing but Nathan. As she did her morning chores a few days after the Christmas tree outing, she found herself remembering the snowball battle—how the children had shrieked with delight when Nathan had come up behind her and sprinkled snow over her head when she wasn't looking. And how his eyes had sparkled as he gently brushed a melting flake away from her cheek.

She leaned on the pitchfork she'd been using to spread fresh hay for Dusty, and gave her thoughts over to the tenderness of that moment. She even allowed her mind to wander into the dangerous territory of remembering how it had felt to be kissed by Nathan.

"Enough," she muttered and went back to work, slinging the hay with such energy that Dusty turned his head and gave her a quizzical look.

"Well, it's ridiculous," she told the ox. "The very idea that he and I…"

Dusty heaved a disgusted grunt and turned back to his water pail.

"Nevertheless, it's true," she argued. "I know so little about the man. Just because he served as a chaplain in the army and just because his sermons stir hearts and minds all around this community, and…"

Dusty shifted impatiently.

"I know exactly what this is," she continued. "It's this early onset of winter and facing weeks and months of isolation and loneliness. This has nothing to do with Nathan Cook, other than that he is a distraction."

Dusty pawed at the fresh hay, ignoring her.

She set the pitchfork aside and trudged back to the house to check on the twins—both of them sick with a stomachache. After a long night of throwing up and moaning in pain, they had both finally fallen into a peaceful sleep. Julianne brushed Luke's hair off his forehead, testing for fever with the back of her hand pressed gently against his cheek. Then she did the same with Laura. Both of them seemed much improved, and she breathed a sigh of relief.

Wanting to let the children sleep, she went back outside. The day was crisp with a bright blue sky and, for once, no wind to chill her to the bone. She walked over to the grove of bur oak trees, gathering sticks and branches that had snapped off. When she heard a harness jingle, she looked up and saw Nathan and Glory coming over the ridge.

Her heart danced with joy at the sight of them—at the sight of *him*. She waved and saw Glory instruct Nathan to leave the trail and head across to the oak trees.

"Sam was at the schoolhouse stoking the fire, and heard the children hadn't come in today," Glory called as soon as she judged herself to be within Julianne's earshot. "Are they sick?"

Julianne nodded. "Stomach," she explained.

Glory nodded. "Thought that might be it. There's something going around. I brought the makings for my chicory tea. It will help ease the tenderness and help them keep down some food."

Nathan halted the team of horses and jumped down. "Here, let me take those," he said relieving Julianne of the bundle of sticks and branches. In spite of the fact that they were both wearing gloves, her breath caught at the sudden nearness of him. He loaded the kindling into the back of the wagon then held out his hand to her, offering her help in climbing onto the seat.

Riding between Glory and Nathan on a seat designed for two people, Julianne had trouble concentrating on the older woman's chatter.

"...thought Nathan might take a ride over your land and help you decide."

"Decide?"

"Where to put the orchard," Glory said, and she pulled off her mitten and placed the back of her hand on Julianne's cheek. "You're not coming down with this thing, are you?"

"No, I'm fine."

They had reached the yard and the cabin door was open a crack. She could see Luke watching them.

"Luke Cooper," Julianne called, "you shut that door and get back in bed now."

"I'll take care of the children," Glory said as Nathan returned from storing the kindling. "You two head on out while you've got a bit of decent weather."

Julianne was well aware that once Glory settled on a plan, there was no changing her mind, so she scooted herself to the far edge of the wagon seat and waited for Nathan to take the reins.

But the silence that stretched between them as he

guided the team and wagon overland was more unsettling than conversation could ever be. Julianne searched for some normal opener and could not believe that the first thing out of her mouth was, "Why did you never marry, Nathan?"

His fingers tightened on the reins and he was looking at the horizon rather than at her.

"I don't mean to pry," she said. "It's just that there was a photo of a young woman among your things."

"Rebecca." He offered no further explanation.

Now that she had brought the subject up, Julianne could not seem to let it go. "Your sister?"

"No." His normally gentle voice was tense, almost angry.

"Then who?"

He heaved a sigh of exasperation. "Rebecca and I were to be married after the war. She promised to wait for me, but I suppose that she had not imagined it would take four years. She did not wait. She married another."

"I'm sorry," Julianne murmured.

"My best friend," he added, as though she had asked.

"I'm sorry," she repeated, and wished with all her heart she had never brought the matter to light. Clearly, he was still in love with the woman. "So your brother is not the only reason you're bound for California?"

"I came west for two reasons. After the years I spent on the battlefield I wanted to find a place where—a place to start fresh."

"And you wish to be reunited with your brother," Julianne added.

His fingers slackened slightly on the reins and the tension in his shoulders eased. "It's important that Jake know he wasn't disowned by everyone in the family— that he still has a brother."

The wave of disappointment that coursed through her veins took Julianne by surprise. Surely it was beneath her to resent a man she'd never known—would never know—a young man who had left home and family because he thought that was his only choice. But if Nathan was to find his brother, he would have to leave Homestead—and her. Come spring, he would move on.

"There," he said pointing to an area where her land bordered the Fosters. "If you put your orchard there between your trees and those Sam planted, and if the Fosters also plant more trees, then you can both have orchards and double the harvest. You could become partners," he suggested.

"That's a wonderful plan, Nathan," she said. She smiled and smoothed the collar of his coat where the wind had ruffled it. He was such a nice man. How any woman could be foolish enough to turn to another when she had the heart of Nathan Cook was beyond Julianne.

"Nathan," she repeated, treasuring the feel of it against her lips. "Sam knows quite a bit about grafting plants and such. He's promised to teach me," she hurried to add, so that the focus shifted from the two of them to the business of raising apples.

"It won't be the same, growing fruit out here, as it was back east," he warned.

"I know, but until the full five years have passed and the land is truly mine, I have to try something." She could not disguise the shiver that rattled through her at the very idea that she could still fail and lose everything.

Nathan thought the shiver indicated that she was cold, and snapped the reins. The team of horses picked their way slowly and carefully across the rutted fields.

"If things don't work out, Julianne," Nathan said,

not looking at her, "would you take the children and move back east?"

"To Virginia?"

"That's where your family is, right?"

"The children are my family now," she said, and regretted the hard edge to her voice. "My family has made it clear that they believe I made a mistake in marrying Luke. They would take us in, but it would be with pity and self-righteousness. I will not subject my children to that."

"But where would you go?"

Her laugh rang hollow on the cold air. "Believe me, Nathan, that is something I think about all the time. As yet, I have no answer."

"Have you prayed on it?"

She swallowed, suddenly aware that this wasn't just any man. This was a man of God. "No," she admitted.

"Why not?"

She shrugged, and to her relief Nathan did not press the matter, but he also said nothing else until they reached her cabin.

"Come in for a moment and warm yourself," she invited as he helped her down.

"No, thank you. I have some business to attend to in town. See if Glory is ready to go. If not, I can come back for her later." He busied himself checking the harness.

"Thank you, Nathan," she said, "for taking the time and for the idea of working with the Fosters and for…"

"My pleasure," he mumbled. "I hope the children are feeling better. And you should get inside and out of that damp cloak before you come down with something yourself."

She knew when she was being dismissed. She just couldn't understand why—and at her own front door.

Chapter Eight

In spite of the good times they had shared over the last several days, Nathan knew that he was being unfair—to himself and to Julianne and the twins. Every activity that brought them closer was only adding to the cost they would all pay when he left in spring. If only she would agree to come with him…

Still, he had promised her children a good old-fashioned Virginia Christmas, and that was exactly what he intended to deliver. After that he would talk to her, and together they would figure out the best way to distance themselves from one another over the winter until he left.

Once he reached town, he stopped first at the mercantile, where he bought the length of ribbon he'd promised Laura and a nickel's worth of candy for Luke. As Jacob Putnam's sister wrapped his purchases, he spotted a piece of soft wood molding behind the counter.

"How much for that piece of molding?" he asked.

Melanie picked up the wood. "It's left over from when we repaired the counter here. It's just a leftover scrap. Here, take it," she said, and handed it to him. "Another repair at Julianne Cooper's place?"

"Christmas present," he replied, taking his change and pocketing it as he headed for the door. "Mind if I check out back for more scraps of wood?"

"Suit yourself," Melanie replied, then turned her attention to a woman eyeing bolts of fabric behind the counter.

Outside, Nathan found three more cast-off pieces of wood. "These will do nicely," he murmured to himself. So that would take care of Luke. Now for Laura. He frowned. What supplies might a girl need for making a Christmas gift for her mother and brother?

He started past the shop window on his way down the street, and saw Melanie Putnam rolling out yards of fabric for the customer. "Of course, fabric," he said to himself, and reluctantly retraced his steps, knowing that before he could buy the yardage and get back to the Fosters, word would be all over town that Nathan Cook had made some strange purchases that afternoon. But a promise was a promise, and he was not a man to go back on his.

The following afternoon, he arrived at Julianne's homestead about the time he knew that Luke and Laura should be getting home from school. He had tucked the scraps of wood and four assorted squares of fabric into his saddlebag. As he had expected, Luke came barreling out of the cabin the minute he heard Nathan's approach.

"Chore time," he called out and grinned.

"That it is," Nathan agreed, taking note that Julianne did not come to the door as she usually did. "There's some weather approaching," he told the boy. "We'd best get the animals settled in the lean-to as soon as possible. Could be a blizzard, from the looks of that sky."

Luke nodded and went to work. The boy reminded

Nathan of his younger brother. Jake was a good ten years younger than Nathan, and before Nathan went off to war, Jake had shadowed his every move, his every action. There was some of that in Luke, Nathan realized as he watched the boy stable the animals.

"Brought you something," Nathan said, and offered the boy the paper sack of candy.

"I thought you forgot," Luke said, his eyes shining as he accepted the bag. "Did you get some ribbon for my sister?"

"I did. I'll make sure she gets it later." Nathan pulled out his pocketknife while Luke returned to his chores. He started slowly whittling a piece of the soft wood.

"Whatcha making?" Luke asked.

"Just whittling," Nathan replied, concentrating on his work. "You ever try it?"

"No, sir. My pa said he'd teach me one day, but…" He shrugged and returned to the task of pitching fresh hay. "I don't even have a knife."

"I could loan you mine," Nathan said. "If you're careful and all."

Luke leaned on his pitchfork and watched Nathan for a long moment. "Would you teach me?"

"I was hoping you might show an interest," Nathan said, handing the boy his knife and the wood he had started to carve into the shape of a spoon. "How about making a spoon for your mother for Christmas?"

"That would be swell," Luke said, as he carved a large chunk of wood from the side of the piece.

"Easy, son," Nathan said, and guided the boy's fingers to move more precisely. "I brought some extra wood along—and some fabric pieces I thought Laura might find a use for. Maybe make your mother a hand-kerchief."

"We could work on them out here," Luke said. "We could surprise her on Christmas morning."

"I thought that might work. Why don't I go inside and send Laura out to give you a hand? You can let her in on the surprise."

Nathan wanted some time alone with Julianne, and he was sure that the challenge of coming up with hand-made gifts for her would keep the twins occupied. "You might want to think about whittling something for your sister, if you have the time."

"And she could make something for me," Luke said.

"Sounds like a good idea."

"Captain?"

Nathan gave the boy his full attention. "Yes?"

"What if I try to whittle something for Ma and I mess it up."

"You won't," Nathan said, "and besides, she'll love it anyway, because you made it."

The boy beamed. "I'm glad you're here," he said, and started to whittle the wood.

"Me, too," Nathan agreed. But as he passed the pile of branches they had collected to build a Christmas tree on Christmas Eve, he firmly reminded himself that he wouldn't always be here. The twins had lost one father, Was he going to rob them of a father figure as well?

Julianne waited until she heard Nathan stamping the snow from his boots before she went to the door. She avoided looking at him.

Nathan removed his hat and coat and hung them on the peg by the door. He smiled at Laura. "Laura, could you give your brother a hand with stabling the animals before the storm hits? I need to talk to your mother for a few minutes."

Laura glanced at Julianne, then pulled on her coat, mittens and shawl and headed out.

"If there's a storm coming, then you shouldn't have ridden all the way out here," she said, and then turned in surprise when instead of taking offense at her scolding, Nathan laughed.

"You're right. I don't exactly have the best sense of direction when it comes to finding my way through a blizzard, do I?"

Julianne could not help but smile. "You've probably learned the route by now," she said.

Nathan sat across from her and cleared his throat. "I came out today to bring the twins their prizes—the candy and ribbon I promised them."

"You didn't have to do that."

"I also came to see you. I always come to see you," he admitted. "I miss you when I'm not here."

"It's all right. I know you have more things to do than to coddle us—sermons to write and all. Just the other day, when you left you mentioned having to do something," she reminded him.

"I needed to think—work some things out in my mind."

Julianne felt her breath quicken. "And did you?" she asked, picking up her mending.

Nathan chuckled. "I thought I had, but then I was out there with Luke just now and something he said got me thinking another way."

"What was it he said?"

"That he was glad I had come here."

"We all are," Julianne murmured, then looked up and smiled brightly. "I mean, the entire community has benefitted from your being here."

"I'm not thinking about the whole community, Julianne." He stood up and started pacing the small confines of the cabin. "I think you know I have feelings for you, and I think you have some feelings for me as well."

"The children have—"

"I'm not speaking of the children, Julianne. I'm talking about us." He ran his fingers through his thick hair and let out a huff of frustration. "I'm no good at this," he moaned.

Julianne set her mending aside and went to him. She cupped his face in her hands, forcing him to look at her. "You are a good and decent man, Nathan. You have brought laughter back to this house and you have given the children gifts far beyond candy and ribbons. You have helped me find a way to keep this land—this home. I will never forget your kindness and support."

Nathan frowned. "But?"

"But you started on a quest to find your brother. In your heart you made a promise just as I made a promise, to my husband as he lay dying. You set out to find him and reunite with him so that he knew not everyone in his family had abandoned him."

"Come with me," he said, wrapping his arms around her.

"You know that I can't do that. It wouldn't be fair to the children. This is the only home they've ever known. It's the place where their father is buried." She ran her thumbs over his cheeks. "I can't go and you can't stay, so let's give ourselves this time that we have."

She stood on tiptoe and kissed him.

He held her close and whispered. "We can always pray for a miracle," he whispered. "After all, 'tis the season for miracles."

They heard the children outside the front door, stamping their feet and whispering excitedly.

"'Tis also the season for secrets," Nathan said as he loosened his embrace so she could step away before the children burst through the door.

"What have you two been up to?" Julianne asked.

"Chores," Luke mumbled, but then he grinned at his sister and nudged her with his elbow.

Laura giggled.

"I've never known chores to cause you two so much pleasure," Julianne said, winking at Nathan.

"I've got a surprise for you," Luke announced. "I can say my tables all the way to twelve times twelve, which is one hundred and forty-four."

"It's about time," Nathan said, ruffling the boy's hair. "Here it is, just days before Christmas, and Mrs. Foster is still waiting on that turkey."

Julianne sat at the table and Laura and Nathan followed her lead. "Let's hear it," she said.

Luke cleared his throat and began rattling off the numbers. He stumbled only once when he got to six times nine and said fifty-five. Julianne saw Laura signal him to lower the number and he corrected himself and continued. Then he looked at Julianne with a mixture of hope and defeat. "I missed one," he admitted.

"Still, Glory needs that turkey," Nathan reasoned. "Seems to me—"

"You may go," Julianne told Luke, and the boy let out a triumphant shout. "You will mind Captain Cook and Mr. Foster."

"Yes, ma'am," Luke said.

"I wish I could go," Laura said softly.

Julianne wrapped her arm around her daughter's shoulder. "I need you to help me bake a wishing cake," she reminded her.

"What's a 'wishing cake'?" Nathan asked.

Laura grinned. "It's just a cake. But inside we bake a special coin, and whoever gets the piece with coin gets to make a wish."

"What would your wish be?" he asked Laura.

Without a trace of a smile, Laura murmured, "I'd wish that we could stay as happy as we've been today."

"You shouldn't have told," Luke rebuked her. "You're supposed to keep it to yourself."

Laura turned to her mother, her face stricken with worry. "Mama, should I not have told?"

"There's no harm," Julianne assured her. "A wish is the same—spoken aloud or not. It's what you hold in your heart that counts."

"In that case," Luke announced, "my heart just aches for my very own horse. What about you, Captain?"

"Well now, that's a tough one," Nathan said, scratching his head as if deep in thought. "I'd like to find my brother."

"And you will," Julianne said, wondering at her disappointment that his wish had nothing to do with her—with them. And in that moment she realized what she would wish—for him to stay forever. But in spite of the season, Julianne knew from experience that miracles did not happen. Not for her.

Chapter Nine

Two days before Christmas, while the children were in school, Julianne hitched Dusty to the wagon and headed to town with a load of her freshly churned apple butter. She would trade the jars of apple butter to Jacob Putnam for small gifts for the twins. She felt a hint of excitement and realized that she was looking forward to Christmas in a way that she hadn't since she and Luke had left their families behind.

In the years since they'd settled in Homestead, they had had to let go of past holiday traditions and establish new ones. They had shared Christmas Eve with the Fosters, then gone home to trim their tree and lay out gifts for the children to discover on Christmas morning. On Christmas Day they had attended church services in the newly built school. When the circuit preacher could not be there, men from the congregation would read scripture passages and the women would lead everyone in carols. By the time they started for home it would be dusk, but the twins would still be bursting with excitement, for they knew that after supper their father would cut the wishing cake. He would slice it and pass the slices around the table until a metallic clink told everyone that the coin had been found.

But not last year, she thought, as Dusty ambled along. Last year her husband's grave was still fresh and the children were still trying to understand why God would leave them fatherless. Julianne had not had answers for them, and no one had felt much like celebrating.

"Not this year," she vowed. In spite of her worries that the children were building a bond with Nathan that would devastate them when he left in spring, Julianne was determined to make up for the Christmas the twins had missed the year before. "Plenty of time to wean them from being so close to Nathan over the winter," she assured Dusty as the ox made the final approach to Main Street. "Plenty of time," she repeated, but this time she was thinking of *her* need to distance herself from Nathan over the coming months.

"Any mail?" Nathan asked, as he watched Jacob tally his order. He'd promised himself that he wouldn't ask. Jacob would tell him if something came. Everyone in Homestead knew he was hoping for news of his long-lost brother.

"Over there." Jacob jerked his head toward a small stack of letters and packages strewn haphazardly over a desktop near the front door of the mercantile. On top of the desk was a hand-lettered sign that read: EMMA PUTNAM, POSTMISTRESS. "We're always a little shorthanded when Emma is down with one of her headaches. Lucinda helps out after school, but some things just don't get done. Have a look."

Nathan swallowed nervously. He'd been disappointed so many times before. The letters he'd sent and the ads he'd run in newspapers out west had produced nothing. And yet he still hoped.

He was vaguely aware that Jacob had continued to talk, but his focus was on the mail. Postponing what he assumed might be the inevitable, he started with the packages, but there were only three of them, and in no time at all he was down to the letters. He picked up the stack and sorted through them quickly. *Get it over with*, he thought, but still his heart hammered with hope.

A shadow passed the window and he glanced up in time to see Julianne walking across Main Street toward the store. He smiled. Whenever God closed one door, he always opened another, and seeing Julianne Cooper was certainly more than enough to compensate for the absence of a letter.

He heard the jangle of the bell over the shop door, and started to replace the stack of letters on the desk when he noticed the envelope on top.

It was addressed to him.

"Captain, are you all right?" Julianne was at his side, her lovely face turned up as she examined him closely. "Why, you've suddenly gone so pale," she said. "Sit down." She indicated the desk chair. "Are you feeling faint?"

He sat, and then grinned at her fanning the envelope between them. "Seems I've got some news," he said softly, indicating, by a glance toward Jacob, who was cutting yardage for two customers, that he wasn't yet ready to have the entire town privy to that news.

Julianne moved so that she was blocking him from the view of the others. "Very well, Captain," she said in a voice just slightly louder than normal conversation. "And the twins as well," she added, pantomiming that he should open the letter while she covered for him.

"Of course, they are beside themselves with excitement about Christmas."

Nathan scanned the scrawled note on the single sheet of paper inside the envelope, then handed it to Julianne. He watched her lips move as she read the short note.

Nathan,
Not sure how you found me, but find me you have. I cannot wait for you to come out here. There's work here with the railroad, and once that's built there's land we could buy with our wages. Spring can't come too soon for us, my brother. You head west and watch for the railroad crews building toward the east—I'll be there. Jake

"You found him," she said softly, as she carefully folded the paper and handed it to him. "I'm so happy for you both, Nathan. God has blessed you."

It was true, and yet all Nathan felt was confusion. Wasn't this the news he'd hoped for? Been waiting for all these months? Wasn't this the dream he and Jake had always shared—the dream of working together, building a future together? Weren't those the words he had written in his letters home during the war, never realizing that Jake was long gone and had never seen his letters?

"Nathan?"

He looked up at Julianne and felt his eyes well with tears. He had gotten his wish without the need of a slice of wishing cake, and yet all he could think as he looked up at her sweet face was *I don't want to leave her.*

"Anything?" Jacob called out as he rang up the last sale and glanced toward Nathan. "Ah, morning, Julianne. Did you bring those jars of apple butter?"

"I have them in the wagon," Julianne replied. "I'll get them."

"Let me," Nathan said, pushing himself to his feet and folding the letter into the pocket of his vest.

"Any news?" Jacob asked again.

Nathan hesitated, then patted his pocket. "A letter," he replied, not wanting to lie to the man who'd become his friend. "I'd like some time to study on it," he added.

Jacob nodded. "Understood. And while you're at it—now that you've had news—maybe you'll do some studying on that offer we discussed?"

"I will."

Julianne followed Nathan from the store. "What offer?"

"Jacob and the others are asking me to stay on as pastor. They're planning to build a proper church, and they want a regular minister."

"Are you considering it?"

Was that hope he saw in her eyes, or was it just more of his wishful thinking? "I was," he admitted, and fingered the edge of the envelope "when there was no word...."

"But now of course, this changes everything," Julianne said as she busied herself uncovering the jars of apple butter she'd packed into wooden crates in the back of the wagon. "It's not really so bad," she reasoned, not looking at him. "I mean, you can't head west until the weather breaks, and in the meantime the church elders can seek a regular minister—run ads, as you did. Someone will come. It's a good opportunity, as is the opportunity your brother has proposed. Work on the railroad must pay well, and think of the farm the two of you could buy together and—"

Nathan stared at her. Who was this woman, babbling

like a creek running free after a thaw? "Come with me," he blurted the thought that had been uppermost in his mind ever since reading Jake's letter.

She turned and smiled at him. "Of course I'm coming. I'm bartering with Jacob—the apple butter in exchange for some Christmas presents for the twins and Glory and Sam."

Nathan set down the crate he'd picked up and touched her shoulder. "Not to the store, Julianne. Come with me to California."

"How can I?" she whispered hoarsely, and he realized that she was every bit as perplexed by the choice as he was. "I also made a promise, Nathan."

"To Luke."

"To my husband and our children," she corrected. "This is our home, Nathan—the only home the twins have really known. After everything they've had to endure this last year, I couldn't…"

He wanted to take her in his arms and assure her that he understood, that he would never ask her to betray a deathbed promise. But they were standing on Main Street, and in spite of the cold weather, people were out—and watching them with curious glances. So he hefted the crate of apple butter to one shoulder and took hold of her elbow with his free hand. "It's Christmas, Julianne. The season of miracles. How about helping me pick out a gift for the Fosters?"

Back inside the store, Nathan set the crate of apple butter on the counter. "There's one more crate," he told Jacob, and headed back outside.

Julianne watched him go, wondering as always at his certainty that things could possibly work out for them. Well, she had been the cause of Luke's break with his family, and she would not come between Nathan and his brother. Jake had been abandoned by his family once, and his letter—however concise the words—had been filled with his delight at having a connection to family once again.

"How can I be of help, Mrs. Cooper?"

Julianne turned to face Jacob. The older man was always more formal when cast in the role of shopkeeper serving a customer. She pulled a list from her pocket and handed it to him.

"Ah, the ingredients for your wishing cake?"

Julianne nodded. "And I'll need two of those peppermint sticks for the twins," she said, as she focused her attention on the jars of candy that lined the shelf behind the counter. She selected some tobacco for Sam's pipe and a china teapot for Glory, all before Nathan returned with the second crate of apple butter. "Will there be enough to cover all this?" she asked, suddenly aware that she had yet to select an actual gift for the twins—or for Nathan.

"And then some," Jacob assured her as he inventoried the jars and began setting them on a shelf.

Nathan fingered the floral-patterned teapot. "For Glory?"

"Yes. Her favorite teapot was broken when one of the axles on their wagon split on the trip out here. She's never said a word, but every time we come to the store I notice she looks to see if this one is still here."

"What if I gave her the cups and saucers to match?" Nathan asked. "Or maybe not. Maybe that's too—"

"I think she would like that very much."

"I'll need something for Sam."

"He broke the tip on his pocketknife a while back," Jacob said, as he indicated a tray of pocketknives below the glass cover of the counter. "Now, what about those children, Mrs. Cooper? Surely you'll need something beyond the peppermint sticks."

"I was thinking perhaps some paints and brushes for Laura."

Jacob retrieved the items from a shelf near the back of the store. "And young Master Luke?"

Julianne was at a loss. Her son was growing up so fast—both of the children were. She spotted a wooden rocking horse, but Luke was already too big for such a toy, even though his wish had been for a horse of his own.

"How about a hat?" Nathan said, as if reading her mind. "It's not a horse, but it's a start."

"I have just the thing," Jacob said, reaching onto a high shelf for a hatbox printed with a single word: "Stetson". "Young fella by the name of Stetson, from Philadelphia, lived out west of here and came up with an idea for a hat. He went back east and started his own business, but the dandies back there aren't too keen on his design. I picked up half a dozen for next to nothing when Mrs. Putnam and I traveled back east to see family last summer."

He blew the dust off the box cover and pulled it open. "I think this might just be small enough for Luke." He held up a tan felt hat with a high crown and a wide brim. "Waterproof inside and out," he said, "in case Luke finds himself in need of water, with no bucket handy." He made the motion of dipping water from a stream.

"It's dandy," Nathan said, taking the hat from Jacob and perching it on his head.

He looked so ridiculous that Julianne laughed.

"I'm pretty sure I have one in your size as well." Jacob scanned the row of hat boxes.

"Nope. My old one will do me fine," Nathan told him.

"Try it on," Julianne urged. "It will help me imagine what Luke might look like."

Nathan shrugged and accepted the hatbox from Jacob. He pulled out a black version of the wide-brimmed hat and put it on. "I like it," he admitted, adjusting the brim so that the hat fit snugly over his forehead. "Maybe when spring comes." He reluctantly removed the hat and returned it to the box. He turned back to the teacups. "Could you add a couple of those to my tally?"

While Jacob added up the bill, Julianne tried to think of some gift she might choose for Nathan. She looked over the merchant's wares, commenting on this and that and getting absolutely no reaction from the man. She wanted so much to give him something, but she knew that the price of a hat for him, as well as Luke, would be too dear.

"Thanks, Jacob," Nathan said, as he collected his packages, the contents of which were disguised by brown wrapping paper. "Merry Christmas to you and your family."

"And to you," Jacob replied absently, as he gave his attention to wrapping Julianne's purchases.

"Has the captain ever admired anything in particular?" she asked.

Jacob paused in his wrapping and ran one hand over his whiskers. "Not that I can recall. Any time he comes in, it's been to check if there's mail or to get something for the Foster place—or yours. He did seem to like that hat."

"I can't afford two hats, Mr. Putnam."

Jacob considered the hat. "It looked mighty fine on him. Maybe the church elders would agree to give it to him as a token of our appreciation for all he's done since coming here." He winked at Julianne. "You never know. That might just be enough to get him to stay on." He returned to his wrapping. "He'd stay if you asked him," he said after a long moment. "We'd have a full-time preacher and the twins would have a father again."

"Oh, Jacob, that's hardly reason enough to marry. Besides, what would Emma say? She's been trying to match him with Lucinda since he arrived."

"He's not right for my girl."

"Besides," Julianne continued, "he's finally located his brother. It would be selfish of us to want him to stay, when all along his goal has been to be reunited with Jake."

The shopkeeper handed her the parcels and came around the counter to hold the door open for her. "I suppose you're right."

"You know I am. Why, the man has been here only a matter of weeks. We can hardly expect him to change his plans, simply because he's made such an impression on this community. No, we've been given a gift—the gift of having him here for a few months."

"I suppose," Jacob agreed.

But on the drive back to her homestead, Julianne could not help but dwell on Jacob's words. *"He'd stay if you asked him."*

Would he?

"You're being as silly as a lovestruck girl," she admonished herself aloud. "Nathan is attracted to you, but it's different for a man. Men don't fall in love as easily as women do." *As easily as I have*, she thought and she sat upright, tugging on the reins so hard that Dusty stopped in his tracks.

She couldn't be in love with the man, could she?

She'd only known him such a short time, and on the heels of Luke's passing at that. No, surely it was his kindness to the children, the way he had helped Glory and Sam, the ministry he had offered the community as a whole. She admired him, and she couldn't deny that he had eased her grief with his sunny disposition and the way he had a habit of turning up whenever she needed help or was feeling down.

Surely, that was all there was to it. It was part of the passage of mourning, part of the path into widowhood, she assured herself. And yet, when she closed her eyes each night, the last thought she had was of Nathan's kiss, his arms—strong and sure—embracing her, and that smile that seemed to say everything would work out.

Chapter Ten

On the morning of Christmas Eve, Nathan and Sam stopped by to pick up Luke so the three of them could go in search of a wild turkey for Glory to cook for their Christmas dinner. Glory came with them, intent on spending the morning with Laura and Julianne preparing pies, corn bread stuffing and spoon bread to serve at their Christmas dinner.

"And don't forget that wishing cake," Nathan called, as he snapped the reins and Sam's team of horses took off.

"Don't let Luke fire your rifle," Julianne shouted back.

And as the horses and wagon disappeared over the rise, she heard Luke's mournful "Oh, Ma," and she laughed.

"Good to hear you laughing again," Glory said, wrapping her arm around Julianne's shoulders. "Love heals all sorrows, that's certain. Big Luke would be happy for you."

Glory and Sam had taken to calling Julianne's late husband "Big Luke" and her son "Little Luke" on the trail out to the territories. The names had stuck.

"Now, Glory, don't you start. Nathan Cook is just a good friend to all of us. That's all."

"Um-huh," Glory sighed. "And next you'll be telling me that tomorrow isn't Christmas Day," she muttered.

The men returned in record time, their laughter and excited voices preceding them on the cold afternoon air.

"We got one," Luke crowed as he held up their bounty for all to see. "I spotted him and Mr. Foster got off the first shot."

"I can see that it's a beauty," Julianne called, trying hard not to meet Nathan's grin or notice his cheeks red with the cold and excitement for her son.

As always, he filled the small room, not because of his size, but because, with him so near, she couldn't seem to concentrate on anything.

"You planning to bake those biscuits or scorch them," Glory asked with a nudge and a nod toward the pan of dough Julianne had absently set on the hot stovetop. "Where's that mind of yours—as if I couldn't guess?" The older woman chuckled with delight and turned to thrust a wooden spoon filled with cornbread stuffing at Nathan. "Taste this."

"Just like home," he said. "Better."

"Julianne's a good cook."

Blushing furiously and hoping everyone would assume the heat from the fire was the cause, Julianne wiped her hands on her apron and looked around the room. "You know, children, it seems to me this room is missing something."

"The tree," Laura shouted, and Luke echoed her cry. "We have to put it together," they explained in unison to Glory and Sam. "It's going to be the most beautiful tree ever, and we have one for you as well," she confided in a whisper to Glory.

"Put a tree together?" Sam tapped out his old corncob pipe on the hearth. "Where is this tree?"

With the twins leading the way, Nathan and Sam followed them out to the lean-to where they'd stored the two handmade trees. Alone with Glory inside the cabin, Julianne decided to share Nathan's news with her friend.

"Nathan heard from his brother. There was a letter at the mercantile. Jake works for the railroad company, and right now he's living in a camp, waiting for the weather to break so they can continue laying track."

"They're coming west to east then?" Glory continued kneading dough.

"Yes."

"Then knowing his brother is alive and working, Nathan could stay here and wait for Jake to come this way."

"That could be years, Glory. You read the papers. The railroad might not reach us until the next decade. I'd never ask Nathan to wait so long—anything could happen."

"Then go west with him. There's nothing keeping you here—not really."

Julianne wrapped her arms around her friend's thin shoulders. "Only you and Sam and our friends, and this place that I promised—"

Glory wheeled around so that the two women were eye to eye. "Now you listen to me, Julianne, Big Luke would never have wanted you to sacrifice your chance at real happiness for this piece of land. The promise I expect he'd hold you to is the one I heard him ask of you that last night—the one to promise him that you would remarry and make a real home for the twins and yourself.

"He was thinking about here in Homestead, Glory. You know what this place meant to him—and to me," she hastened to add.

"What I know is that living in the past is a pure waste of time and an affront to God Almighty. How many signs do you need, girl?" Glory shook her gently.

Julianne pulled away and turned back to stirring the batter for the wishing cake. "He's asked me about my coming to California with him, but—"

"And you said what?"

"I turned him down. I can't leave and he can't stay, so let's just enjoy this time we have—especially this wonderful Christmas that will be filled with enough memories to sustain us all for years to come."

"Don't know why you'd want to live on memories when you could just as easily have the real thing, but it's Christmas and you're right. Now is not the time to debate the point—we've got all winter for that."

Julianne sighed, knowing her friend would not give up, and nothing she could say would change that. She was relieved to hear the stamping of boots and the giggles of the children outside the front door.

The small, four-foot tree leaned a bit to the left, but it was full and fragrant. Julianne thought she had never seen a more beautiful sight than Nathan standing in the doorway, his arms filled with the branches and snow blowing around his feet, and the twins tugging at his coat as they gave instructions about the trees placement.

"There by the window," Laura said.

"No. Over there," Luke argued, pointing to a spot in the corner. "That way we can see it when we wake up."

"The table," Julianne said quietly. "We're having our main meal tomorrow with Glory and Sam—we can work around it until then."

. "Yeah, the table," Luke agreed. "Plenty of room for
putting presents under those lower branches if we sit
it on the table."

"Table it is," Nathan agreed. "Looks a little bare,
don't you think?"

"Wait," Laura said, and ran to get the strings of wild
berries she'd been working on and the colorful chain
made of scraps of fabric that Glory had insisted she
had no use for.

Everyone gathered around the table and dressed the
tree. Twice Nathan's fingers touched Julianne's as he
handed her part of the berry chain. Twice her fingers
lingered on his a beat longer than was absolutely necessary.

"You did a fine job making these trimmings, Laura,"
Nathan said, and the girl beamed with pride.

"I made something for the tree, too," Luke said shyly.
"It's pretty rough but…" He pulled a roughly whittled
wooden star out from under his bed covers. "I'll do better next year," he assured them.

Julianne felt tears fill her eyes. "You will do no such
thing," she said. "This is our star. It's perfectly wonderful." She hugged both children to her while Nathan
worked the star into the top branches, anchoring it with
a small box he took from his pocket.

Sam blew his nose and Glory sniffed loudly. "Come
on, old man," she ordered. "It's past time we were getting along back. That turkey's not going to cook itself."
She kissed the children on their cheeks and squeezed
Julianne's hand. "We'll see you tomorrow."

Reluctantly, Nathan followed them to the door, then
glanced back at Julianne. "Merry Christmas."

She swallowed around the lump in her throat and rejected the impulse to ask him to stay. "Merry Christ-

mas, Nathan," she managed. "Thanks to you, it's going to be a wonderful Christmas."

After Nathan and the Fosters left, Julianne busied herself getting the children ready for bed. She told them stories until they finally nodded off, then she tiptoed to the wardrobe and pulled down the gifts she'd bought for them and set them under the little tree. While she'd been busy banking the fire for the night, the children had left some gifts on the table as well. One crudely wrapped and misshapen package was addressed "To my sister, from your brother."

Julianne smiled. Next to it were two more gifts, more artistic in their wrapping. Laura had drawn pictures on the plain paper. One gift was for Luke and the other was addressed "To Mama, Love me and Luke." This time she didn't even try to stop the tears, because they were tears of happiness and relief and gratitude for the fact that they had all made it through this long, sorrowful year. Thanks to neighbors who had heard about the plan to turn the farm into an orchard, the deep window ledges were crowded with tin cans filled with dirt and unseen apple seeds that she hoped would blossom into saplings in time for spring planting. Thanks to Glory and Sam, she had managed on her own for a year now. And thanks to Nathan, she had rediscovered her heart.

"Thank you, God," she whispered as she fingered a branch of the tree, setting free its heady perfume. "Thank you for sustaining us through this time of sorrow and for the love of Glory and Sam and for sending Nathan to us."

She paused in her prayer and considered what Captain Nathan Cook had meant to all of them. He had come from five long years of war and despair, and yet his spirit remained positive and strong, so filled with the certainty of better times to come.

"I wish…"

She stopped, horrified at what she'd been about to ask. How many times had she told the twins that prayers were not to be used as substitute for wishes?

She buried her face in her hands. "I love him so," she whispered.

"He would stay if you asked," Jacob had said, and perhaps he would. But was asking him to stay at the expense of reuniting with his brother really love? Wasn't it more a mark of how much she had come to love him that she was willing to let him go? She brushed her tears away with the hem of her apron. "Thy will be done, Lord," she murmured, as she trimmed the wick on the lamp and went to check on the twins.

She had just put on her nightgown and gotten into bed when she noticed the small box nestled at the very top of the tree anchoring Luke's star. It was tied with a green ribbon and there was a small card she had not noticed before. Drawn to the package, she climbed out of bed, wrapping herself in a quilt. She reached up and removed the box, careful not to disturb Luke's star.

"For Julianne…whatever happens, you have won my heart. Nathan"

She untied the thin satin ribbon and opened the box. Inside was a small wooden heart strung on another piece of the green satin ribbon—the perfect length for tying around her neck. She started to put it on but then stopped. She wanted Nathan to tie it around her neck that first time.

"Tomorrow," she whispered, as she placed the small carved heart back in its box. "On Christmas."

Chapter Eleven

Nathan was like a child who couldn't sleep on Christmas Eve. He tossed and turned through the long night. Had she seen his gift? Had she opened it? Would she know it was meant to say so much more than the words he'd finally written on the note?

He slipped out of his bed and dressed in the dark cold of the Fosters' upper loft. As he climbed down the ladder to the main room of the cabin, he could hear Glory and Sam breathing steadily as they slept behind the curtain Glory had devised to give them—and him—privacy. He tiptoed to the door where he pulled on his boots and his coat and hat.

Outside it was still dark, but it had snowed overnight and the white-covered fields gave off a luminescent light. In an hour it would be dawn. By the time he saddled Salt and rode over to her place, Julianne would probably be up and out tending to the morning chores. He checked his pockets for the presents he planned to give the twins, then mounted Salt and rode off across the fields that he had come to know as well as he'd known the way to his father's home back in Virginia.

Home.

It was all that had kept him going those long years of the war. And then he had returned to the place of his youth and found it all gone—the plantation in ruins, his family in disarray and the girl he'd thought would wait for him forever married to his best friend.

But Nathan had gotten through the horror of the war believing one thing—that God had His reasons for everything that happened, and that having faith meant accepting that in time His reasons would become clear. In the meantime, life was short, as he had discovered numerous times on the battlefield, and it was surely a sin not to live out the days given in an attitude of joy and gratitude.

By the time he rode the distance that separated the two homesteads, the sun was starting to rise. It promised to be a splendid day—clear and cold. Nathan saw the curl of smoke before he and Salt topped the ridge and saw the cabin.

As he had imagined, she was out in the yard, scattering feed in a space young Luke had cleared for the chickens. She was wearing the same blue wool dress she'd worn that first Sunday he'd taken the pulpit. She'd covered her head and shoulders with the plaid, woolen shawl that hung with the children's coats next to an empty hook near the door.

That empty hook had held her husband's coat, he was certain, but recently, and without thinking he had taken to hanging his outer jacket there whenever he entered the house.

He heard the squeals of the children as they threw open the front door waving wrapping paper and the gifts she had left for them. Young Luke proudly modeled the wide-brimmed hat. Nathan couldn't see what Laura was holding, but her smile told him she was just as pleased with the art supplies as her brother was with the hat. He tapped Salt's haunches with his heels and the horse trotted down the ridge toward the cabin.

"Merry Christmas," he called, and the twins turned at the sound and began running to meet him. Julianne did not run with them, but she stopped scattering feed and waited for him to admire the children's gifts.

He dropped the reins and let Luke lead Salt to the hitching post, while he pulled Laura up into the saddle with him. She proudly showed him her collections of brushes and paints. "And there's paper as well," she said. "Mama said we would make it into a sketchbook. All real artists have sketchbooks that they carry with them everywhere," she assured him.

They had reached the cabin and he lifted Laura to the ground then dismounted himself. "Good morning," he said, tipping his hat and scanning Julianne's throat for any sign of the heart he'd carved for her.

"You're out early," she replied, and he wanted to believe that the pink on her cheekbones was shyness because she was sorting through her feelings for him and not the cold. "Come in. We're just about to have some breakfast."

"There are more presents," Luke announced leading the way.

Inside, over bowls of hot barley with milk, the twins exchanged their gifts for each other. With Julianne's help Laura had knitted Luke a pair of mittens and Luke had carved her name into a rough board. "It's to be the cover of your sketchbook," he explained. "Mama suggested it."

"It's wonderful," Laura gushed, and hugged her brother.

The boy cleared his throat and reached for the last

package under the tree. "We got this for you, Mama," he said. "Laura wrapped it, but I helped."

"What could it be," Julianne said, carefully untying the ribbons and folding back the paper that Nathan was certain she would keep as a treasured memory of this Christmas. She held up a wooden spoon and a small bag.

"I carved that for you," Luke told her, "and Laura collected the seeds and made the bag. The captain got me the wood and Laura the fabric."

Julianne peeked inside the bag. "There are so many," she gasped slowly pouring them into an empty bowl. "Wherever did you get so many?"

"When we were peeling the apples and making the apple butter I saved them all," Laura explained, "and so did Glory and our teacher and our friends at school. Everyone helped."

"Now you've got seeds enough to plant apple trees from here to forever," Luke assured her. "And the spoon's for stirring the applesauce and butter that you're gonna make and Laura and I are gonna sell to Mr. Putnam at the mercantile. We're going to be rich," he assured her solemnly, "just like Papa dreamed we would be."

"Oh, children," Julianne managed through her tears as she gathered them to her for a hug, "we're already rich beyond Papa's wildest imagination."

As the children buried their faces against her shoulders, she looked up at Nathan. "There's one more present," she said softly. "I found it last night and now that the captain is here I hope he will do the honors."

Nathan took down the small box from the top of the tree, noticing that the ribbon had been retied. "So you peeked," he teased, laughing with joy when Julianne blushed and nodded.

"What is it, Mama?" Laura asked at the same time that Luke admonished her for peeking. "You told us that wasn't allowed."

Julianne held out her hand to receive the box from Nathan, but instead of giving it to her he opened the lid and took out the necklace.

"Oh, Mama, it's so delicate," Laura cooed, moving in for a closer look.

"You carved this?" Luke asked. "I don't think I could ever do anything so tiny."

"It'll take practice," Nathan said, and reached into his pocket. "This might help." He handed Luke a small pocketknife. "Merry Christmas, Luke. Oh, and Miss Laura, I didn't forget you." He reached inside another pocket and handed her a small china doll.

"She's so tiny, but look, Mama," Laura exclaimed, "she has real silk hair and eyes that open and close and—"

"What do you say to the captain, children?"

"Thank you," they chorused, hugging Nathan's waist before running to their beds to examine their new gifts.

Nathan held up the necklace. "May I?" he asked.

"I waited for you," she replied, and immediately understood the double meaning of that statement. As he tied the ribbon around her throat and then rested his hands on her shoulders, she covered his hands with hers crossed over her heart. "I will wait for you," she murmured. "If you want. In spring, go west and find Jake, then come back to us. We'll be here waiting."

He thought his heart would beat right out of his chest, it hammered so hard against the bindings of bone and muscle. "Don't promise what you can't know to be true," he murmured against her hair.

She turned and stared up at him. "Nathan, I don't know why that girl you left behind during the war did not wait. What I do know is that her love was not strong enough. Luke and I defied family and friends to come west—we both knew what we were leaving behind, what we were giving up. I know true love when I have it, and I know that I love you with all my heart. God willing, you return that depth of feeling and will come back to us. In the meantime…"

He kissed her then and she kissed him back, until she became aware of the children's muffled giggles and tried to pull away. "The children," she whispered.

"…are going to have to get used to it," he replied and kissed her again before releasing her. "Now then, Master Luke, how about putting on your jacket and that fine new hat and helping me hitch up the wagon. By the time we go by and pick up Mrs. Foster and get to the schoolhouse, it'll be time for services." He didn't have to add that Sam Foster was already at the little schoolhouse getting a fire started and making sure the benches were in place for an overflow crowd.

"What did you give the captain, Mama?" Laura asked when they were all settled in the wagon and on their way to pick up Glory.

"I…" In her excitement over the necklace he'd carved for her, Julianne had completely forgotten to give Nathan the gift she'd made for him. She'd stayed up late for several nights in a row spinning the fine merino wool she'd bartered from Elton Hanson two years earlier, and then never used because Luke had fallen ill. After his death there had seemed no purpose for such fine wool.

But even in spring, Nathan would need the warmth of

a scarf, and she hoped that such a fine one would remind him of her—would eventually bring him back to her.

"You said you were making him something from all of us," Laura reminded her. "You didn't forget, did you?"

"No. I… Oh, Nathan, I do apologize. Your gift is back at the cabin."

"No matter," he replied cheerfully. "Gives me a good reason to come calling later this evening. Besides—" he winked at Laura "—I'm still hoping to get that wishing coin in my piece of cake today. That would sure enough be a fine present, especially if I get my wish."

"Don't tell," Luke warned.

"He knows that," Laura said. "There's Mrs. Foster," she cried, waving wildly. "I can't wait to show her my doll."

Suddenly it occurred to Julianne how Glory would view the necklace that Nathan had given her. She fingered the small carved heart and considered tucking it beneath the high collar of her dress.

But then she saw Nathan watching her and knew that he had read her thoughts. He had given her far more than a token that morning. The man had offered her his heart, and regardless of what anyone thought, she wasn't about to hide it. She straightened the necklace so that the heart was perfectly centered—and perfectly obvious to everyone. And she couldn't help noticing that a breath of relief preceded the smile Nathan gave her as she scooted closer to him to make room for Glory.

Nathan had worked for nearly two weeks on his sermon for the Christmas service. He wanted to give the people of Homestead a sense of what they meant to him, of how they had taken in this stranger and made a place for him in their community and their hearts. How they had trusted him to lead them in worship and how they had rewarded him by asking him to stay—even though they knew he could not.

If only there were some way…

But he had made a promise and Jake had had enough heartache in his young life without Nathan breaking his word to him. The letter Jake had sent had been filled with dreams for the two of them to start over in a new place together. And wasn't that exactly what Nathan had hinted at in the letters he'd sent home before Jake left?

He hadn't counted on meeting Julianne. He hadn't counted on loving her and her children. He hadn't counted on finding a home in a place he'd barely heard of. After the war and the discovery of his sweetheart's betrayal, Nathan had focused on making life better for Jake, but God had had other plans, and now Nathan had no idea which path to follow, for either way he went seemed destined to lead to heartbreak for someone he loved.

Chapter Twelve

Nathan's sermon was so moving that it brought tears to Julianne's eyes. For the first time since Luke's death, she allowed herself to face squarely the truth of his final days. Luke's toes and fingers had been badly frostbitten by the time they found him that terrible night, and he had cried out in anguish with the pain that followed. Glory and Sam had taken the twins to their place so they wouldn't hear their father's suffering, but even after the initial agony had passed, there had been little hope that Luke would ever again be able to farm the land or walk without considerable help. The idea that he would teach young Luke to hunt and fish was out of the question.

And on Christmas Day, sitting next to Glory on the rough-hewn bench that she and Luke had shared with the Fosters, Julianne finally opened her heart to the truth. In taking Luke, God had shown not vengeance but mercy. For Luke had always been such an active man, so filled with energy, that to live for years dependent on the help of others would have surely been a slow and torturous death.

She saw that in sending Nathan to her door under similar circumstances to how Luke had left her, she had been given a new opportunity—to live, to love and to fulfill the very legacy Luke had been so intent on leaving for his children. Nathan had given her all of that, and she realized now that God's hand had been at the helm of all that had happened since Nathan had arrived.

To wish that he could stay—that they could be together—was simply selfish, and yet...

There had to be a way. *Please, God,* she prayed when Nathan called for a moment of silent prayer, *show us that path.*

She fingered the small carved heart as she prayed, her eyes tightly shut, her lips moving. Only when Glory placed her hand on Julianne's knee did she realize that her tears were flowing freely and that she felt such a release of all the pain and bitterness she had held inside for over a year.

"Amen," Nathan intoned, ending the silent prayer. "And now, as we leave this place for the hearths of home and family that sustain us all, join me in singing 'Silent Night', and may the carol's words echo across these high plains throughout this blessed day."

Slowly, people filed out of the schoolhouse-turned-chapel. They exchanged greetings and farewells with a nod of their heads or the raising of their hands. No words were spoken because everyone was either singing or humming the carol, and as Nathan had suggested, the sounds of their voices mingled with the sound of bells laced onto the harnesses of horses and oxen and drifted over the rises of the fields as they all went their separate ways.

Just outside the schoolhouse, Nathan fell into step with Julianne and the twins, his strong baritone blending with their higher voices as he helped them into the wagon.

* * *

On Christmas Day, the Fosters had established a tradition of opening their home to anyone who did not have extended family with whom to share the day. So it was hardly surprising to see several wagons pulled into the yard by the time Nathan and Julianne arrived. The twins ran off to join the children of a young couple who had recently settled in the area, while Nathan helped Julianne carry in the baskets of cookies and puddings she had made to contribute to the feast.

Inside the cabin, everyone seemed to be talking at once as Sam served up mugs of newly pressed apple cider and Glory made room on the table for what seemed an unending stream of side dishes brought by her guests.

"We'll be eating until the New Year arrives," she exclaimed happily as each new dish was unveiled.

The children settled on the floor near the hearth to play a game of pickup sticks with a pile of wood splinters that Sam had gathered for them. Julianne busied herself helping Glory and tried without much success to avoid stealing looks at Nathan.

"You two need to figure this thing out, and sooner rather than later," Glory muttered when the two women went outside to collect more kindling for the fire. "He must have worked on that necklace most of the night, once he got started on it. Had to begin again at least three times I know of, because the work was so fine he kept breaking it. Wouldn't have done to give you a broken heart, now would it? Although it seems to me you both might be headed toward having your hearts broken if you don't find some way to get together."

"He's given me this token of his devotion, Glory, and God willing, someday we will find a way to be together."

"These are hard times, child, and the one thing life should have taught you so far is that you cannot count on having forever. You and Nathan need to work this business out now." She glanced toward the cabin as Nathan stepped outside. "And I'll leave you to it."

Glory muttered something to Nathan on her way back inside that made him smile. "I think Glory is growing impatient with us," he said, as he removed his coat and wrapped it around Julianne's shoulders.

"She doesn't understand, but I do, Nathan. You made a promise to Jake and you need to honor that promise. Once you've done that—"

"I've been thinking," Nathan interrupted her, running his finger along her cheek. "I made a promise to find Jake and let him know he still had family. Jake and I know where the other one is and there's no possibility we can be together for months to come. I'll be staying here until at least April, and frankly, Julianne, I may be a man of the cloth, but I'm not sure I can be here for that length of time and not be with you."

"You see me and the children practically every day," she protested, but she would not look at him.

He gently lifted her face to his. "You know what I'm saying, what I'm asking, Julianne. Will you marry me?"

"I also have a promise to keep," she reminded him.

"To your late husband."

"To my children. The land Luke and I have homesteaded is their future, their legacy, their connection to their father. I cannot just abandon that and start over in California."

"I understand. So I was thinking that perhaps we could marry, and then, once the weather turns, we could go together to California—a wedding trip."

"But Jake's letter spoke of you working together,

earning the money you need to start your own business in California."

Nathan shrugged. "That's his dream. Mine is right here. I love you and I've come to care deeply for the twins. Will you marry me, Julianne?"

Her heart screamed *Yes!*, but she had to consider the children. Although it was obvious that they liked Nathan and looked forward to his visits, that was a very different matter than having him become part of their family. "I…"

"The children, right?"

She nodded. "They're so young, and they've had so much to deal with this last year."

"If they were in favor, would you say yes?"

It was as if the nodding of her head was completely out of her control.

Nathan grinned. "Then I'll ask the children to marry me as well." Just as he leaned in to kiss her, the laughter and sounds of celebration from the house spilled out into the yard, as the children broke free of the stuffy interior to play outside.

Luke threw the first snowball, missing his target and hitting Nathan squarely in the back instead.

Nathan smiled, kissed Julianne on the nose and bent to scoop up a handful of snow. "Better head for cover," he told Julianne. "There are seven of them, and this could take a while."

Julianne held his coat out to him. "If you insist on playing little-boy games, at least put this on," she ordered.

"See? You're talking like a wife already."

Julianne reached up and shook the canvas that Sam had hung to protect his woodpile from the elements, sending a shower of snow down on top of Nathan.

"Hey," he shouted in protest as she ran for the house.

* * *

The dinner was a feast worthy of kings by any measure. By the time Laura carried the wishing cake to the table and set it in front of Julianne for slicing, there was a chorus of protests.

"I really couldn't eat another bite."

"Perhaps later."

But seeing the disappointment that shadowed the faces of the children, the adults gave in. "Maybe just the smallest slice."

As Julianne sliced the cake, the pieces were passed to her right and around the table, all the way to the guest on her left. More than half the table had been served before she heard the telltale clink of the coin on the plate.

The room went still.

"It appears that the captain will get his Christmas wish," Sam said with a sly grin, as he handed Nathan the plate. "Care to share the wish?"

"Nope. I understand it won't come true if I tell." He winked at Luke and Laura. "Maybe tomorrow," he added, as his gaze met Julianne's. "I mean, if it comes true, then what's the harm in telling?" He glanced at the twins and then back to her.

"No harm at all," Sam replied, nudging Glory as he took a bite of cake.

Nathan saw Julianne and the children home. He wanted to talk to the twins, but had found no opportunity to do so at the Fosters'. Once they reached Julianne's cabin, she told the children to get into their nightclothes and she would make them all some hot milk with vanilla.

She was nervous. "Maybe it would be better to talk to them later," Julianne whispered, as she stirred vanilla into the milk. "They've had such an exciting day already, and well, what if…"

"We won't know if we don't talk to them," Nathan replied. "Would you rather talk to them yourself? I can leave." Of course, he knew he wouldn't get a wink of sleep if she said that would be the best plan.

"No. We should talk to them together."

"Why are you whispering?" Luke asked, then he grinned. "I know. There's another Christmas secret, isn't there?"

"Not a secret exactly," Nathan said, glancing over the boy's head to seek Julianne's help.

"Children, Captain Cook and I have something we want to discuss with you." Julianne set their cups of warm milk on the table.

"It's a bad thing, isn't it?" Laura said, her eyes tearing up. "Like when Papa was—"

"No," Nathan assured her. "It's nothing like that." He pulled her stool closer to his. "Come and drink your milk and we'll tell you."

The children looked warily from one adult to the other, but did as they were told.

Julianne handed Nathan his cup of milk, then turned back to the stove to fill her cup.

"I've been spending a lot of my time here these last weeks and I've come to care about you and your mother a great deal," Nathan said.

"As we have come to care for the captain," Julianne added, taking her seat at the table.

"You're our friend," Luke said with a shrug, "you know, like Mr. and Mrs. Foster are our friends and…"

Laura patted Nathan's hand. "We like you," she assured him.

This was not going to be as easy as Nathan had

hoped. "Well, sometimes when grown-ups get to be friends, they realize that they would like to be even closer—more than just friends or neighbors."

"Oh, you mean like when you kissed Mama? Like mushy stuff?" Luke said, his eyes wide with understanding but at the same time some puzzlement.

Laura clapped her hands together excitedly. "You're getting married? Is that the secret? Was that your wish today when you got the wishing coin?" She looked at her mother expectantly.

"Would you children be all right with that?" Julianne asked.

"Of course," Laura said. "Just think—Christmas and now a wedding? It's wonderful!"

Luke remained quiet and seemed to have taken a great interest suddenly in studying the sparks of the fire.

"Luke?" Nathan said quietly. "What do you think?"

"You'd be our Papa?"

"Only if you chose to call me that someday," Nathan said. "I would be married to your mother and we would all live here together. We would take care of the farm your papa started, and one day the land would officially be your mother's, and after that it would come to you. Just as your father intended."

"I thought you had to go find your brother and live in California," Luke continued, still not looking directly at Nathan.

"I had an early Christmas surprise a week or so ago. I had a letter from my brother. He's working on building the railroad that might one day run right through Homestead."

"If the captain and I were to marry—if we were to become a family—then perhaps in the spring we could all go out to California and meet Mr. Jake."

"He'd be our uncle, right?" Laura said, her eyes ablaze with excitement.

"In a manner of speaking," Nathan said. "Luke?"

The boy looked at his mother. "We'd be a family again?"

She nodded.

"And I could learn to do all the stuff that Papa promised he'd teach me one day?"

Another nod. "And with the captain living here, I expect I wouldn't need quite so much help from the two of you," Julianne added. "Although you would still have chores," she hastened to add.

Nathan reached out and touched each child. "So, what I'm asking the two of you to think about—and you don't have to answer right away—is if it would be all right if your mother and I married and I came here to live."

"Are you still going to preach at the church?" Luke asked.

"If they still want me."

"Luke," Laura said, sidling closer to her brother, "let's say yes. Mama loves the captain and he likes us a whole lot, I think."

"Miz Putnam is always talking about how I'm the man of the family since Papa died," Luke said, looking directly at Nathan for the first time. "Would you be willing to take that on? Because I've got to tell you, there's a lot of worrying and stuff to go with that."

"I'll keep that in mind," Nathan said, trying hard not to smile.

The children sipped their milk and eyed each other over the rims of their cups. Julianne appeared to be holding her breath. Nathan sent up a silent prayer that they were doing the right thing in asking the twins, even if they said no.

Laura made a gesture with her fingers. Luke responded with a nod. "It'll be all right," he said. "I reckon we'll make a good family."

Julianne's breath came out on the wings of her smile. Laura was also beaming. But Nathan solemnly offered Luke his hand. "You won't regret this," he said as he shook Luke's hand and then Laura's.

"We're going to be married," Laura said happily. "I can't wait."

"Neither can I," Nathan admitted, his eyes resting on Julianne's beautiful face. "How about New Year's Day?"

"So soon?"

"No reason to wait that I can think of," Nathan said. "Luke? Any reason to wait?"

"No, sir."

"But," Julianne started to protest. "There's so much to do, and—"

"Miz Foster and the other ladies will help, Mama," Laura told her. "Let's get married right away so we can be a real family again."

"Will you attend me, Laura?" Julianne asked, and the girl started to tear up again, but this time they were tears of joy.

"Come to think of it, I'm going to need somebody standing up for me," Nathan added, as he placed his hand on Luke's shoulder.

"Do I have to wear an itchy suit?"

"I sure hope not," Nathan assured him. "I don't have a suit, so my Sunday shirt and maybe a new pair of trousers is going to have to do."

"I'll wear my hat," Luke decided. "You should get one, too."

"I'll look into it," Nathan said as he raised his cup. "Shall we toast our decision?"

The four cups met over the center of the rough-hewn table, where Nathan hoped they would share meals and conversations and happy decisions like this one for years to come.

Chapter Thirteen

Julianne soon discovered that planning a wedding on the prairie in the middle of winter was a convoluted affair to say the least. In the first place, the citizens of Homestead had come from all manner of communities and cultures back east, and every woman had her own ideas about how the wedding should be handled.

"You'll naturally need to reserve the school for that day, and there's the matter of floral decorations," Emma said, as she ticked off items on her fingers. "My sister Melanie is quite adept at arranging flowers. Will you need a bouquet for Laura as well as yourself, dear?"

Julianne opened her mouth to answer, but Emma wasn't listening.

"Are you quite sure you wouldn't prefer to have someone—well, more mature—attend you? It's a responsibility as well as an honor after all. And what will you wear?"

"In our homeland of Germany," Margot Hammerschmidt interrupted, "it is quite common for the guests to kidnap the bride before the wedding so that the groom must search for her."

"That's barbaric," Lucinda Putnam exclaimed.

Glory rolled her eyes. "And how, may I ask, is that any more uncivilized than grown men racing each other to the bride's house for the reception, just so they can be the first one there and win a kiss from the new bride?"

Emma tapped her pen impatiently on the counter. "We were discussing what our dear Julianne is to wear." She studied the shelves behind her that held bolts of fabric in all the colors of the rainbow.

"I can wear my Sunday green," Julianne said. "At least that's one decision we don't have to fret about."

"Absolutely not," Emma exclaimed. "I will not hear of it." She took down a bolt of fine wool in a pale rose. "White is out of the question, of course, but this…"

Glory ran her palm over the fabric. "It's beautiful." She unwound several yards and let the fabric spill over her tall frame. "Look how it drapes."

Julianne lightly ran her fingers over the fabric. She couldn't help thinking how Nathan's eyes would light up, seeing her in such a beautiful gown. But he would love her no matter what she wore, and the price of fabric, not to mention the time it would take to sew the gown, was just impractical.

"No," she said firmly, and turned her attention to the bolts of lace trimmings. "Perhaps a lace cap."

"That, too," Glory said, testing the rose wool against several of the lace patterns. "Something a little heavier, I should think." She looked at the other women who all nodded in agreement.

"Yes, that cream is perfect," Margot said. "Come over here, Julianne, and let me see it against your skin in the daylight."

Before Julianne could stop them, her friends had gathered around, draping the rose fabric over her shoulders and letting it flow to the planked floor of the mercantile, and then unfurling several feet of the lace to cover her golden hair.

"Perfection," Lucinda murmured. "The captain will be quite overcome when he sees you."

All of the women giggled like young girls, and Julianne could not help smiling. "I suppose I could sell—"

"You will sell nothing," Emma exclaimed, her expression one of horror. "This is our wedding gift to you, dear. Am I not right in saying that, ladies?"

The others nodded. "I think six yards will do," Glory announced, laying the bolt of wool on the counter and measuring out the yardage.

"And perhaps two of the lace?" Margot suggested.

Again, nods all around, and Julianne accepted their incredible generosity, for she understood that it allowed them to play an active role in the wedding—and what woman didn't enjoy that?

"Thank you all so much," she said, hugging each of her friends in turn. "You have made me so happy."

"Well, that was the point," Emma huffed. "Now, we have a good deal of work to complete, ladies. Shall we divide the tasks?"

In short order, Emma had handed out the assignments. Glory would make the gown with Lucinda's help. Melanie was to take charge of flowers and Margot the making of the headpiece.

"And you, Mother?" Lucinda asked.

Emma sighed. "I shall do what I always do, child. I shall make sure it all gets done."

All of the women burst into laughter, and after a moment of trying to hold her composure, Emma joined them. These dear women had become more than just her friends, Julianne realized—they were more like family.

* * *

The days seemed endless to Nathan, in spite of the fact that Julianne hinted that there simply were not enough hours to do everything that needed to be done for the wedding. What did he care of flowers and food and music and such? All he wanted was to stand before the makeshift altar and pledge himself to Julianne— and the twins—for the rest of his days.

"Who will say the words?" Franz Hammerschmidt asked one morning, as the men gathered around the stove in the mercantile, their feet stretched out toward the stove. This was a winter morning ritual, as they smoked their pipes and cigars and considered the problems of the day. "You can hardly marry Julianne and stand in the pulpit at the same time," the German farmer reasoned.

"I could do it," the circuit judge, Matthew Farnsworth, said. "If you can't get the circuit preacher here in time, I have to power to perform weddings."

"We figured, if he couldn't make it on New Year's we'd just delay the wedding a week or so, but Mrs. Cooper and I would be honored to have you marry us, sir," Nathan said. "After all, she was so grateful for your counsel regarding the orchard and how it would qualify as a crop."

Jacob poured himself a tin cup of coffee from the pot on top of the stove. "We're all going to have to stop calling your bride by her former name," he reminded Nathan, and all the men chuckled.

Julianne Cook, Nathan thought and smiled.

"What about the twins?" Another man asked. "You planning to adopt them and give them your name as well?"

"That'll be up to them," Nathan said, and he did not

miss the way the other men glanced at each other in surprise. In their world, the man was the head of the household, the one who made the decisions that mattered. But Nathan had considered the way Julianne had been pretty much on her own for the last year. Would it be fair to suddenly walk into her cabin—her life—and expect to simply take over?

"The twins will have time enough to get used to having me around full-time," he told the others. "No need to rush anything."

Several of the others nodded as if Nathan had presented a concept they had never contemplated, but one that seemed to have some merit.

"Any of those seeds the ladies planted for Julianne showing signs of life?" Jacob asked, after the group had sat in comfortable silence for a long moment.

"Not so far," Nathan admitted.

Franz frowned. "It's been what—three weeks?"

"Something like that. They'll come along," he said. "It's a long winter." But he couldn't help wondering what he would do if the seeds did not germinate. The fields would have to be planted, and he knew very little about such things. Before the war he had studied to become a minister.

"You could move into town once we get the church built," Jacob said, as if reading his mind. "I don't see why we shouldn't build a little house behind the church—a parsonage."

"No. We'll live on that land," Nathan told them firmly. "And we'll make it work."

Sam Foster nodded approvingly. "And you can count on us to be there to give you a hand," he said.

Jacob cleared his throat and took down a large hatbox from a shelf near the circle of friends. "Nathan, we thought maybe you could use this—consider it a wedding present, if you like. The main reason is that we wanted to find some way to let you know that we're real pleased you're going to stay and fill the pulpit for us permanently."

Nathan opened the box and took out the black Stetson. "It's a perfect fit," he said, as he tried it on, "just like me, with all of the good people of Homestead. I thank you, gentlemen, for everything."

Later that evening, while Julianne told the children a story and tucked them in, Nathan couldn't help surveying the cluster of tin cans that cluttered the two deep window wells. Each can was filled with dirt. Each can was carefully labeled with the date of planting. Not one showed the slightest sign of life.

He was so deep in thought about the responsibility he would be taking on in just two days that he was startled when Julianne came up behind him, wrapped her arms around his waist and laid her cheek against his back.

"You're very quiet tonight," she said, her voice muffled against his shirt.

He turned so that he could hold her. "Just thinking about the day after tomorrow," he said, forcing a lightness into his voice that his anxiety for their future could not entirely disguise.

Julianne look up at him. "Nathan, we don't have to do this, you know. If you're having second thoughts about the promise you made to Jake—about..."

He kissed her. "Shhh," he whispered against her hair. "I fulfilled that promise. I found Jake and we are in touch. In the spring you and I will go west and make sure that he is well settled and at peace."

"And if not?"

"Then we will bring him back here with us. He is my brother, Julianne, but you are going to be my wife, and the twins will be our children. I will not abandon my family as my father did his."

"He didn't really—"

"Yes, he did. He left Jake no choice but to leave. He was always so insistent on being right."

"Still, from everything you've told me, he was a good provider—a God-fearing man."

"And that is where he and I differed. The god he followed was an angry and vengeful god."

"And what do you believe, Nathan?"

"I believe that, when all else seems lost, our faith can see us through anything—war, the loss of loved ones. Anything. God is love, Julianne. I believe that with all my heart."

He did not ask the question uppermost in his mind. *What do* you *believe?* He knew that she and her first husband had been devout churchgoers and that after Luke's death she had made sure the twins attended church regularly. But what did she believe?

As if she had read his mind, she cupped his face in her palms. "There was a long period after Luke died when I turned my back on my faith, Nathan. I locked my heart away and refused to allow myself to be comforted by the words of the scriptures or the teachings of the minister who conducted services."

"And now?"

"That first Sunday, when you spoke about the losses of war, I felt something. It was as if there had been the slightest loosening of bonds that had held me so tight for all the months since Luke's death."

"What was it you felt that day?"

"When you spoke about the war and the things you

had seen, I felt as if finally someone understood. I felt for the first time in months that I was not alone."

"But you were never alone. You had Glory and Sam and—"

"Spiritually speaking, I was alone because I had made that choice. Remember that day you came here to ask what I had thought of your service? I did not tell you that I had for the first time in all those long and terrible months thought about others who had suffered, instead of dwelling only on my own suffering and that of my children."

Nathan hugged her to him. "You are going to be a wonderful preacher's wife," he said.

She laughed and tweaked his nose. "Let's see how I do as *your* wife before I have to live up to such a lofty title as 'preacher's wife'."

"I love you, Julianne. I promise you—"

She placed her forefinger against his lips. "Shhh," she whispered. "No need for promises. Love is enough."

And, in that moment, Nathan had never been more sure that God had led him to this place, this woman, and the sacred promise of the life they would share.

For January, the weather was unusually mild—above zero, according to Sam, who had arrived early to take Julianne and the twins to town. There, Julianne was to change into her wedding finery at the Putnam home, and then Jacob and Emma would drive her and the twins to the school, once Sam had assured them that Nathan was waiting inside with Judge Farnsworth.

"It does not do for the groom to see the bride on their wedding day," Emma had lectured both Julianne and Nathan at the dinner Glory gave for them the evening before.

"Why not?" Luke asked. "They see each other all the time."

"It's simply tradition," Emma told him.

"And traditions don't always make a lot of sense," Sam added, "but you learn not to question them."

Luke shook his head and rolled his eyes. "Grown-ups," he muttered.

"Of which you will be one someday, young man," Emma said, effectively silencing the boy, who had clearly never considered this.

Now, as Julianne put on the beautiful, rose-colored gown Glory had stitched for her, and turned so that Emma could place the lace headpiece over her curls, she found herself thinking years into the future. She saw Nathan walking Laura down the aisle of the new church the town planned to build. She imagined other children—those she and Nathan would have together, attending their older sister. She saw Luke, serious and proud like his father had been, with a home and family of his own.

"I'll get your flowers," Emma said with a sigh that said, if she didn't do everything herself it would not get done. Alone with Glory, Julianne stared at her reflection in the mirror.

"I never imagined," she whispered.

"That you would marry again?"

"That I could be so happy," Julianne corrected, her eyes welling with tears of joy as she hugged her friend.

"Now stop that," Glory fussed, wiping away tears from Julianne's cheeks with her thumbs. "You have surely been blessed to come to this day, and it's a blessing we all share in seeing you and those dear ones embarking on this new life together."

"The sleigh is here," Luke bellowed from the foot of the stairs.

"Off you go," Glory said, giving Julianne one last quick hug.

The school had been transformed with ribbons and candles. Laura was holding a nosegay made of dried herbs, and in the vestibule of the school Emma handed Julianne a similar bouquet, enhanced by sprigs of evergreen.

"Ready?"

Julianne nodded and Emma opened the doors a crack and signaled the organist. As soon as they heard the whoosh of the pump organ's bellows, Emma opened the door fully and signaled Laura to start down the short aisle.

Luke moved to Julianne's side and offered her his arm as Emma had taught him to do. "Ready?" he asked and grinned up at her.

Julianne was through the door and partway down the aisle before she looked up and her eyes met Nathan's. In his gaze she saw so much—the days and months and, God willing, years they would share. The children she hoped they would raise together. The community they would embrace and help build. And most of all the blessing God had bestowed upon both of them.

God had not turned His back on her, she realized, as she had thought when Luke died. She was the one who had turned away. God had been there all along, patiently waiting for her to come back to the faith of her childhood.

When she was almost to him, Nathan stepped forward and took her hands in his, and together with Laura and Luke, the four of them walked the rest of the way together.

* * *

The moment the judge pronounced them husband and wife the hall erupted with noisy celebration. The organist pulled out the organ stops assuring the sound would crescendo to its full volume. On both sides of the aisle, women laughed and chattered and men grinned and clapped each other on the backs as if they had just seen a favorite son married. And in the midst of it all, Nathan beamed down at Julianne as if he simply could not believe his good fortune.

"You're supposed to go," Luke coached, tugging on Nathan's trouser leg. "Miz Putnam said—"

"First they have to kiss," Laura corrected her brother, "and then they leave."

The twins looked up at their mother expectantly.

"Miz Putnam has spoken," Nathan said, and held out his arms to her.

When they kissed there was a shout of approval from the men and shushing from the women, but when they turned to make their way back up the aisle, everyone was smiling at them and several women were dabbing at their eyes with lace handkerchiefs.

Emma had insisted that she and Jacob host the wedding reception. "Your home is serviceable, Julianne, but hardly large enough for such occasions. Besides, this way those fools intent on racing to be the first to kiss the bride will have a shorter distance in which to break their necks."

As it turned out, Sam Foster was the first man through the door, other than the bridal couple and their hosts. He seemed inclined to ignore the tradition, but young Luke called him on it.

"You have to kiss Mama—it's tradition," the boy instructed.

Sam leaned in and gave Julianne a dry peck on her forehead. "Be happy, child," he muttered.

"I am," she promised, as she caressed his weathered cheek. "Thank you, Sam, for everything."

"It should be Glory and me thanking you. You and Big Luke made us welcome on the trail out here, and now here you are starting fresh."

At that moment, the entrance to the large house was filled with guests all jostling for a position to extend their best wishes to the bridal couple before moving on into the Putnam dining room for an impressive spread of food.

"How come me and Laura have to stay with Miz Foster tonight?" Luke asked when a quiet had fallen over the room as everyone ate.

"Laura and I," Julianne corrected automatically. "And it's because…" She faltered for the best explanation, looking to Glory for help.

"It's tradition," Glory said. "Now eat your supper or there will be no cake for you, young man."

"But—"

"Come on," Laura said, nudging her brother into the next room. "Let's go sit on the stairs. I'll explain it all to you later."

The rest of the reception went by so fast it was as if Julianne and Nathan were living in a dream. Before they knew it they were being bundled into the Putnam's sleigh. Jacob handed Nathan the reins. "See you tomorrow," he said. He gave the horse a smack on its rump and they were off.

"I like your hat," Julianne said, suddenly shy with her new husband.

"The men gave it to me—a wedding present." He was nervous as well, and that was comforting to his new wife.

She placed her gloved hand on his and he glanced at her and smiled.

By the time they reached their farm, Julianne's head was resting on his shoulder and she had given into the overwhelming exhaustion of an exciting day.

Nathan reined the horse to a stop and kissed her forehead. "You go on in," he said. "I'll unhitch the horse and see to the other animals." He climbed down and came around to lift her to the ground.

They stood for a minute holding each other under the star-filled sky. "I love you, Mrs. Cook."

"Captain, my captain," she whispered and stood on tiptoe to kiss him.

Inside, she stirred the embers of the fire they had left that morning and considered putting on some water for tea, then hearing the whinny of the Putnam's horse, she ran to the window instead. She wanted to see him, to never let him out of her sight. She wanted to remind herself just how blessed she and the children were that this good and gentle man had come into their lives. "Thank you, God," she whispered as she watched him stroke the horse's mane and lead the animal under shelter for the night. "Thank you for all the blessings you have brought to this house."

She had bowed her head and closed her eyes on this last prayer, and when she opened them, she noticed tiny green shoots peeking out of the black earth of several tin cans. She ran to the other window hardly daring to believe her eyes. It was the same there.

She ran to the door and threw it open. "Nathan, we

have apple trees," she cried. "Come see." She grabbed his hand and pulled him to the window.

"Well look at that," he said huskily, and closed his eyes for a long moment. When he opened them he took Julianne in his arms and held her, rocking from side to side.

"Come on," he said grabbing a quilt from the bed and wrapping her in it.

"Nathan, it's nearly midnight and it's freezing," she protested, but she was laughing and she followed him willingly.

Outside, he led her to the small grove of apple trees. "Think of it, Julianne. Trees to the horizon and just there…" He pointed to a low rise that protected a part of the land nearest the river. "We'll build our house and raise our children and cradle our grandchildren and—"

"Stop. You're making us old before our time," Julianne protested, but she was holding him, hugging him to her as they dreamed of the future they would share with God's blessing. She looked up and saw the stars lighting the black of the night and she felt a peace she had not known for over a year.

"Thank you," she whispered to the heavens just before Nathan kissed her. Then he scooped her into his arms and continued kissing her all the way back to the little sod house that in that moment she decided they would always keep to remind them of how truly blessed they had been.

* * * * *

Dear Reader,

It always amazes (and inspires) me when I reach a point in the story that calls for some detail that will be unique to the story. I was very troubled by what gift Nathan might choose to give Julianne for Christmas. Then, without even being aware of my writing dilemma, my husband surprised me on Christmas morning with the most beautiful alabaster heart, and a note that is mine to keep and yours to imagine, that made this heart very, very special for me. The next time I sat down to write the scene where Julianne opens the gift Nathan has left her, I had no problem at all knowing what was inside that box. It was his declaration of love—his heart given to her. Whether you are reading this over the holidays or at some other time of the year, I hope you will find the story of Julianne and Nathan's return to faith and love one that touches you and inspires you to remember that opening your heart to others is a sure path to everlasting joy.

All best wishes to you in this season of faith, joy and love.

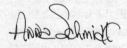

A COWBOY'S CHRISTMAS

Linda Ford

Christmas is a favorite holiday
made all the more special by family gatherings.
This book is dedicated to my family. Without
you, my Christmas celebration would be dull and
uneventful. Thanks to each one of you for making
my life full, busy and joyful. I love you.

For God so loved the world that He gave His
one and only Son, that whoever believes in Him
shall not perish but have eternal life.
—*John* 3:16

Chapter One

1888 Canadian Rockies

A murmur of voices warned eighteen-year-old Winnie Lockwood she'd overslept. Hay tickled her nose and throat. Cold touched her back where the hay had shifted away leaving her exposed.

Exposed! If she was discovered...

She wiggled, but her movement made so much noise she drew in her breath and held it, praying she hadn't been noticed. She cupped her hand to her nose and mouth, forcing back a cough from the dust. The hay had been fragrant and welcoming last night, when she'd sought refuge and warmth. Today she was aware of the musty scent and imagined bugs creeping along her skin. It took every ounce of self-control to keep from squirming.

"I'll fork up feed for the animals," a male voice called.

Was it friendly? Harsh? Dangerous?

One thing Winnie had learned was, you could never be certain what lay beneath the surface of a voice or a face. A kind face readily enough disguised a mean spirit and kind words often enough proved false.

"We need to head for town in good time."

The voice had grown perilously close. She could almost feel the tines of a feed fork pierce her skin, and she bolted upright, gaining her feet in a flurry of hay. She sneezed and swiped her hands over her very untidy coat.

"Who are you? What are you doing in my barn?"

The masculine voice had deepened several degrees and carried a clear warning.

Holding her arms out in a gesture she hoped indicated she meant no harm and had no weapon, she faced the man. Not much older than she, his chin jutted out in a challenging way. Knowing her life depended on a quick evaluation, she took in his dark eyes, the way he'd pulled his Stetson low, how he balanced on the balls of his feet, the pitch fork at ready for defense. A man who would not give an inch, who would tolerate no nonsense. The thought both frightened and appealed.

"I mean no harm. Just looking for a place out of the cold. I'll be on my way now." She glanced toward the door and escape, and made as if to lower her arms, testing his reaction.

"Now hang on. How am I to know you didn't steal something?"

She grinned openly. "Don't hardly see how I'd fit a horse or even a saddle under my coat."

A deep chuckle came from behind the man. "Think she's got a point." An older man, with a grizzled, three-day growth of beard and eyes flashing with amusement, stepped closer. "Seems you should be a little more concerned with why a pretty young woman is sleeping in your barn, than whether or not she might hide a horse beneath her coat."

The younger man grunted. "More likely she's a front

for something else." He shook the fork threateningly. "How many others are there?"

Winnie wiggled her hands. "I'm alone."

"Head for the door and no sudden moves." He waved the fork again and she decided she didn't want to question his sincerity in using it.

"I tell you, I only wanted someplace to get out of the wind." She was on her way to Banff and a job at the sanitorium, but had run out of funds at Long Valley and started walking, hoping to arrive under her own steam or get a ride. Instead, darkness and cold had found her searching for a place to spend the night. She'd planned to slip into the barn for a few hours and be gone again before anyone discovered her.

"Now, Derek—" The older man sounded placating. "Don't be hasty."

"Hasty? Kathy is alone in the house. If your accomplices have—" He indicated she should move.

"My bag."

"Uncle Mac, grab that."

Winnie edged across the expanse to draw the door open and stepped outside, breathing deeply of the fresh air. The day was sunny with a promise of warmth later on. A welcome change from the cold wind of last night that threatened snow and drove her to sleep in the barn of this man. At least there was a Kathy. That gave her hope for a little generosity that would let her get on her way without any more complications.

Sensing the man would not take kindly to her bolting for freedom, and knowing she'd never outrun him, she marched toward the simple ranch house, one-story with a verandah across the side. Welcoming enough under normal circumstances. She kicked the dust from her shoes before she stepped to the wooden floor of the verandah.

"Wait right there." It was the man called Derek. "Your friends have any sort of firearm?"

"I told you—"

"Answer the question." He nudged her with the tines of the fork. They didn't pierce her coat, but she jerked away, not caring to tempt him to push a little harder.

"Now, son, don't be doing anything rash."

"Uncle Mac, I am not prepared to take any chances. Especially when it comes to Kathy's safety." His voice grew gravely, as if Kathy meant more than anything else to him. Seems he was a man who cared deeply. Something quivered in the pit of Winnie's stomach—a familiar, forbidden feeling rolled up in denial. She tried to force anger into that place to quench it but failed miserably. Something in the way this man was prepared to fight assailants, numbers and strength unknown, poured emptiness into her soul. She pushed aside the foolishness. She was headed for Banff and a job. She wanted nothing more.

"I understand that." The older man, Uncle Mac, edged forward. "Why don't I have a look?"

"Be careful. I don't trust her."

Winnie snorted. "Who'd have guessed it?"

Uncle Mac shot her an amused look that fled in an instant when Derek made a discouraging sound. The older man edged forward, slowly opened the door and peeked around. "Don't see nothing."

Winnie bit back a foolish desire to ask if they lived in an unfurnished house.

"Do you see Kathy?

"Nope. Nothing."

"Go in slow and easy. We'll be right behind you.

And I warn you, miss, don't make a sound to alert your friends or I'll be forced to jab this fork in up to its hilt."

Uncle Mac drew his head back and glanced over his shoulder. "You'll do no such thing." Without waiting for Derek's reply he slipped into the house.

Winnie followed. She'd laugh at all this unnecessary drama except she wasn't sure what Derek's reaction would be and he did carry a sharp pitchfork with long tines.

As if to reinforce her doubts, he murmured, "Don't think I'm a softy like Uncle Mac."

"Oh, no, sir. I surely wouldn't make that mistake." She tried her hardest to keep the amusement from her voice but wondered if she'd succeeded. What would it be like to have a man as ready to defend her as Derek was to defend Kathy? Aching swelled in a spot behind her eyes.

She stepped into the room. A big farm kitchen with evidence of lots of living. Messy enough to be welcoming...for the people who belonged here.

"Check her bedroom."

Uncle Mac tiptoed through a doorway.

Winnie grinned, grateful the man behind her couldn't guess how much enjoyment she got from all this.

Uncle Mac returned, a little girl at his side. Winnie put her at about nine or ten.

"She was playing on her bed. As blissful as a lamb." He ruffled the child's already untidy hair.

This must be Kathy.

Winnie studied the girl. Brown hair, beautiful brown eyes, with the innocence of childhood tarnished. Where was the mother? Which of these men was the father?

The child's eyes widened with curiosity when she saw Winnie. "Who's that?" She bent sideways to see

Derek. "How come you got a fork pushed into her back, huh, Derek?"

Guess that meant Uncle Mac was the father.

Derek parked the fork by the door. "So you *are* alone?"

Alone? In more ways than he could imagine. "Just like I said."

"About time we showed some hospitality." Uncle Mac headed for the stove. "Kathy, set the table for four and we'll have breakfast."

Winnie's stomach growled in anticipation. She pretended she didn't notice.

Kathy giggled.

"Kat." Derek warned. "Your manners." His voice was as gentle as summer dew. Winnie blinked as the ache behind her eyeballs grew larger, more intense.

The child scurried to put out four plates, and Uncle Mac broke a stack of eggs into a fry pan.

Winnie followed every movement of his hands. She hoped she'd be allowed a generous portion of those eggs. She'd eaten only once yesterday, and heaven alone knew where she'd get the next meal after she left here. *Lord, you know my need. Provide as You have promised.*

"Sit," Uncle Mac nodded toward a chair. "Tell us your name."

Winnie gave it as she moved the stack of socks and mittens to the floor and sat. Her mouth flooded with saliva like a river suddenly thawed. Her plate had a rim of grease but she didn't wipe it off. She'd have eaten off the table if she had to. Or the floor for that matter.

"I'm Mac Adams. You've met my nephew, Derek. This is my niece, Kathy." His expression softened as he turned to the girl.

Winnie nodded a gracious hello.

Uncle Mac scooped generous piles of eggs to three plates and a tiny portion to Kathy's. He sat at Winnie's right. "Shall we give thanks?"

Grateful for the food and the temporary reprieve, Winnie silently poured out her thanks as Uncle Mac spoke his aloud.

"Amen," he said.

"Amen," Winnie echoed with heartfelt sincerity.

Kathy giggled.

Derek cleared his throat, his warning glance full of affection, and Kathy ducked her head over her breakfast.

Winnie pushed away the longing that threatened to unhitch a wagonload of tears. She only wanted to be on her way to Banff. Winnie forced herself to eat slowly, ladylike.

Uncle Mac picked up the dishes as soon as he was certain she was finished, and added them to the stack on the cupboard by the stove. "Now, young lady, let's hear why you're alone and spending the night in a barn."

She'd known this question was coming, but still hadn't figured out an answer. Her conscience wouldn't allow her to lie. But neither would she tell the whole truth. "Got lost."

"From who and from where?" Derek's question was far more demanding.

"I thought I was on the main road. Obviously I was wrong." She pushed her chair back. "Thank you for the food. Much appreciated. Let me clean up the dishes in exchange, then I'll head back to town."

"No need," Derek protested. "We can manage without help."

Kathy leaned forward, her expression eager. "I don't mind if she helps."

At the same time, Uncle Mac said, "If it's a ride to town you're needing, we'll take you when we go."

They all ground to a halt and tried to sort their conversations out.

Winnie chuckled. "I'll be happy to do the dishes and I'd welcome a ride to town."

Derek looked ready to protest, but Kathy bounced from the table and Uncle Mac slapped his thighs. "It's settled then."

Derek got to his feet so fast Winnie wondered if something had bitten him. "You two stay here while I finish chores and get the wagon ready."

"I'll be along," Uncle Mac said.

"Stay here." He paused halfway across the room and muttered, "No way I'm leaving Kathy alone with her." The door banged shut after him, then swung open again and he grabbed the fork. The slap of the second closing echoed through the room.

And reverberated in Winnie's heart, striking at the feelings she struggled so hard to deny. To have someone who cared that much was a dream beyond her reach.

Winnie pushed to her feet and tackled the stack of dishes, using water hot enough to dissolve the buildup of grease and redden her hands.

Uncle Mac wandered out of the room, leaving her alone with Kathy. She handed the child a drying towel.

Kathy's chin jutted out. Her eyes flashed all sorts of emotions.

She'd try to sidetrack the child. "Shouldn't you be in school?"

Kathy lifted her head. "I get to miss school today because we're going to get my new nanny."

"I see. What happened to your last one?"

"She got married." Tears welled up. "Why couldn't she be happy with us? Now I got to get used to someone else. I hate it. They always have new rules. It makes me sad and mad all at the same time."

Sad and angry explained perfectly the way Winnie felt most of her life. A bitter tenderness touched a place in her heart, that this child should experience the same pain. She closed her eyes and steeled away the gall in her throat, the churn in her chest. As soon as they were under control she concentrated on the girl at her side. *Lord, help me say something to help her before I depart.* "I've felt that way many times. It's pretty confusing."

Tears glittered in Kathy's eyes as she nodded.

Winnie dropped her hand to a thin shoulder, felt the child tense but didn't remove her hand. "It sometimes seems the feelings are eating up your insides, doesn't it?"

Kathy choked back a sob.

"Kathy, it's alright to feel sad. People come and go. Things change. Nothing stays the same except who you are in here." She touched the child's chest. "Nothing can take that away from you. One thing that helps me when I'm feeling bad is to remember God loves me. He holds me in His hands. I am never alone."

"I just want someone with arms to love me."

"I know." Oh, how she knew. But she'd outgrown the need. Now all she wanted was a job, a place to keep warm and no reason to expect more than room and wages. "You have Derek and your Uncle Mac." Uncle Mac seemed kindly and gentle; Derek, an appealing combination of tough and tender. She tried to stifle a longing for devotion like she'd witnessed. She wrenched her thoughts back into order. Not only did she know nothing about Derek, she knew enough not to seek after things unavailable to her.

"I miss my mama." Tears flowed unchecked, leaving a dirty streak on Kathy's face.

Winnie flung about in her thoughts for an answer. Something to help this child deal with her situation. For a heartbeat, she imagined staying for a time and teaching Kathy ways to deal with her sorrow. But she was done working for families. Wanting to belong. Knowing she didn't. Even when she thought she had reason to believe otherwise. "Honey, where's your mama?"

"In heaven. She died in an accident. She and Peter and Susan. Only I didn't. And 'course, Derek, but he wasn't with us."

She guessed that made Derek Kathy's brother. "I'm so sorry. I expect your mama loved you."

"Lots and lots."

"And I expect she liked to see you happy."

Kathy's tears stopped and she smiled. "Mama used to tickle me just to hear me laugh, she said."

"So if your mama could hear you, she'd want most to hear you laugh, I suppose."

Kathy nodded.

"What if she *can* hear you?"

Kathy shook her head. "She's in heaven with Papa. But I don't remember Papa."

"Jesus can hear you."

Kathy waited for her to continue, her eyes wide with consideration.

"I expect He can tell your mama if you laugh or don't." She wasn't sure if people in heaven saw their loved ones on earth or not, but of course Jesus could. She had no qualms about assuring Kathy that.

"I guess so all right." Kathy seemed intrigued by the idea.

"So, even though it's all right to be sad and angry once in a while, don't forget to laugh for your mama."

Kathy brightened. "I won't."

Winnie finished washing the dishes, then poured boiling water on the table and set to scrubbing it.

By the time Derek returned the kitchen was clean, the dishpan hung behind the stove, the towels draped over hooks to dry.

Kathy played with a well-worn stuffed doll.

"Uncle Mac," Derek roared. "Where are you?"

The older man clattered into the room, smoothing his hair.

"You were sleeping? Who was watching Kathy?"

"She was," Kathy jabbed her finger toward Winnie.

Derek's frown deepened, giving his face harsh angles and making his eyes dark and unfriendly. "Kathy, get your coat. We're going to town." The look he favored Winnie with left no doubt. They couldn't wait to get rid of her.

Winnie mentally shrugged as she donned her dusty coat and waited for the others. She was equally anxious to resume her journey. She would not acknowledge the hollowness just behind her breastbone that never quite went away. A longing for home and love—her gaze darted to Derek, who smiled at Kathy, a look on his face as full of affection as any she had imagined. A man who loved openly and freely. Her heart hovering over a deep chasm of emptiness, Winnie jerked away to stare at the door.

The woman—Winnie—was behind him. Uncle Mac shared the back bench. Derek had made sure Kathy sat beside him on the front seat where he could guard her. This little mite of a girl was all he had left of his family. He would never let anything harm her. At twenty-three, he was simultaneously orphaned and thrust into the role of both mother and father to his little sister. A role he did not object to except for the reason for it.

Getting Winnie back to town as soon as possible would ease his mind regarding Kathy's safety. What kind of woman wandered about the country alone and slept in barns? Certainly not the kind he wanted Kathy associating with. He grinned as he recalled Winnie crawling out of the feed, all dusty and dotted with flecks of hay. His heart had missed a beat at how easily he might have jabbed his fork into her. Even in her disarray she was appealing—eyes like strong coffee and every bit as jolting, hair like mink fur.

He flattened his grin. He had no room in his heart or life for pretty gals, no matter how fiery her eyes, how spunky her attitude.

"Fortunate we don't have snow yet," Uncle Mac mused. "Sometimes it's up to the horses' bellies this late in the year."

Derek guessed he meant the latter for Winnie, because it was not news to Derek.

"The mountains are pretty with their snowcap," Winnie said. "Like a glittering necklace."

Kathy giggled. "For a giant."

Derek shifted on the seat and kept silent. Maybe if he didn't add to the conversation, it would end and allow him to settle into businesslike thoughts.

For a few minutes, the soft plod of the horses' hooves on the packed trail was the only sound.

He relaxed and glanced about. The deciduous trees were bare-limbed. The pine and spruce were dark winter green. Yes, they often had snow by now. It was the end of November, after all.

Not a good time to be bringing in a new housekeeper, though he'd discovered there was no such thing as a good time. Why did Miss Agnew have to pick early winter to pack up and leave? Couldn't she put off her wedding until spring? Or at least until after Christmas? Her leaving would make the season even more difficult for Kathy. And she already had enough trouble with missing their mother and sister and brother. He clenched his hand on the reins. His jaw tightened. He should have never let them travel alone. If he'd been with them, he might have prevented the accident, though a train wreck was beyond his control.

Not beyond God's, though, and yet He'd done nothing. Sure made it hard to trust God to take care of them.

Kathy's clear voice sang, "I sing the mighty power of God, that made the mountains rise."

Lonesomeness as endless as train tracks gripped him. It had been their mother's favorite song. She sang it as she washed dishes, as she weeded the garden and as she mended. "Where did you hear that song?"

"Mama used to sing it all the time."

His heart clenched like an angry fist. All Kathy had were memories of their mother. She deserved more. A mother to hug her and kiss her and tuck her into bed at night. He could never replace their mother, and the housekeepers he'd hired only looked on Kathy's care as a job, and moved on as soon as they found a man, which didn't take long out here, where men greatly outnumbered women. "I didn't think you'd remember."

"Yup."

Why was she singing it now? And without tears and sobbing.

Kathy paused. "I think Mama likes to hear me sing. She—" Kathy nodded toward Winnie "—said Mama would like to see me happy."

Derek turned right around to stare at the woman behind him.

She smiled sweetly, her eyes sparking with what he took to be a combination of amusement and challenge. "I'm sure you agree."

His thoughts were a hopeless tangle of memories of his ma. Surprise, pleasure and sadness at hearing Kathy sing their mother's favorite song.

And something nameless, inviting and challenging in Winnie's gaze. He snapped a lid closed on mental wanderings and jerked back to look at Kathy, who regarded him with wide-eyed innocence. "I think Mama would like it very much."

Kathy faced forward and continued to sing.

"I don't know what you said," Uncle Mac murmured, his voice sliding below the sound of Kathy's cheery voice. "But it certainly made a good impression on our Kathy. Thank you."

"I like the song she's singing. Doesn't it give you hope?"

Seemingly unaware of the conversation, Kathy continued. "I sing the goodness of the Lord."

Derek wondered how to rejoice in the goodness of the Lord when it seemed life was so often out of control. But he said nothing. They topped the hill and looked down at Long Valley.

The town had been named for obvious reasons. It lay in a fertile valley between high hills, with the Rockies rising to the west. The Deer River flowed at the foot of the town. It was now iced over though he knew better than to think the ice was solid enough to hold a horse. The weather had been too uncertain.

They rattled down the hill on the road that became the main street. Wood-framed buildings housed businesses of every sort. "Where shall I let you off?" He directed his question to Winnie.

"Wherever you're stopping is fine for me."

He turned toward the rail station.

Kathy fell silent and sat up straight. Her face lost the gentleness and joy she'd revealed while singing, replaced with tightness about her eyes. White circled her lips signaling her tension.

"It's okay, Kit Kat." He squeezed her hands. "I'm getting a married couple. The man is going to work for us, too, so they won't be leaving any time soon."

Young Eric, who helped his father run the station, trotted from the building. "Hey, good to see you, Derek. Saves me a trip to your place with this here telegram." He waved the sheet of yellow paper.

Uncle Mac, who'd been about to jump down and assist their guest to the ground, stopped and waited.

Kathy whimpered.

"No need to get upset," he murmured, but of course she knew a telegram always brought bad news.

No one moved as Eric jogged over to hand Derek the slip of paper. Even Winnie seemed to have forgotten she meant to get off here. Was she aware of the tension in the others? Did it make her limbs as weak as it did his? He dismissed the idea. Of course it didn't. She had no interest in what happened to this family.

He gave the boy a few coins and Eric trotted back to the station. Derek unfolded the page and silently read the words.

Chapter Two

"Who is it from?" Uncle Mac demanded. "What does it say?"

"It's from the Faringtons."

"Weren't they supposed to be here?"

He expected them to arrive to help with Kathy. "They aren't coming until after Christmas. Got a new grand-baby to visit." He crumpled the page and stuffed it into his pocket. Now what was he supposed to do? He didn't like leaving Kathy alone while they worked outside.

"No one wants to take care of me." Kathy's words caught on a sob.

"That's not true. I do."

"You're too busy. 'Sides you're a man." She sucked in a gulp of air and released it in a wail.

Being a man certainly inconvenienced him at times, but he couldn't change that. Kathy's crying intensified.

Eric reappeared in the baggage room doorway, his eyes wide with curiosity. His father stuck his head out the wicket window to see what the racket was.

"Hush, Kathy." Derek tried to pull her to his lap. She shoved him away.

Uncle Mac tried. She pushed him away, too.

"Winnie, what are your plans?" Uncle Mac asked. "You and Kathy got along real well. Perhaps you could stay until these other people arrive."

Derek's nerves jerked. No way would they ask her to stay. Something about her made thinking clearly difficult. He shot Uncle Mac a hard look, but before he could protest, Winnie spoke.

"I'm on my way to Banff."

"What's in Banff?" Uncle Mac seemed set on seeing Winnie as a suitable stand-in for the Faringtons.

"Uncle Mac—"

Again, Winnie spoke before Derek could voice his protests. "The Banff Sanitorium, where people go for the healing waters. Friends of my former employer said it was a lovely place. They are always in need of quality staff."

And she considered herself such? Flecks of hay spattered her coat. Her hair needed a good brushing. And yet, his kitchen had shone after her short visit, and for a few minutes, Kathy had been happier than he'd seen her since the accident. And that was a year and a half ago.

"Can't the sanitorium wait?" Uncle Mac persisted. "We'd pay you as much as you'd make there."

"She don't want to stay with me. No one does." Kathy's cries grew louder.

Winnie leaned forward and touched Kathy's shoulder. "I'd like to take care of you. In fact, I can't think of anything I'd rather do."

Kathy choked off a sob and spun around. "Would you?"

Whoa. All Derek knew about this young woman was she slept in barns at night. That didn't recommend her in his mind, even if she had a reassuring way of calming Kathy. Her presence had the opposite effect on him, leaving him fighting confusion. "Kathy, I don't think—"

She folded into a sobbing heap.

"Derek, it seems you don't have a lot of options."

He flung his uncle an angry look. "We know nothing about her."

"So ask me. I'm right here."

He and his uncle silently challenged each other. Reluctantly, Derek gave in. He edged the wagon away from the station and far enough from the town so they could talk in semi-privacy and no one would stare at them, wondering why Kathy was acting up this time. He shifted around to face Winnie. "Where is your family?"

She shrugged.

"They kick you out?" Had she done something so dreadful they'd disowned her. Though the idea of doing so scraped along his nerves.

"I've been working for some people, but they didn't need me any longer."

"Why?"

"A cousin came west to join them. She took my place."

"Who are these people?"

"I doubt you know them."

At his demanding look, she continued. "The Krauses from Saskatoon. Reginald and Moira."

"You're right. I never heard of them." No way was he going to entrust his little sister to a stranger with no one to say whether or not she was suitable.

Uncle Mac leaned forward. "Seems it would be simple enough to wire these folks."

"Of course." He turned the wagon toward town.

Kathy's sobs subsided. "She's going to stay?"

"Don't get your hopes up. First thing I'm going to

do is send off a telegram. Then we'll wait until we hear back."

At the station, Winnie provided him with the address of the Krauses and he sent the message. "Now we wait for a reply. Kathy, maybe you should go to school."

"No." Her chin quivered. "Don't make me. I have to know if Winnie is staying."

He didn't blame her for not wanting to sit at school worrying about things. "Just for today then."

She twisted the edge of her coat so hard he knew it would end up torn, but he couldn't bring himself to tell her to stop. And the way she worried her lip on her teeth warned him she would have a sore before the day was out.

If only he could provide her with the security she needed and deserved. The Faringtons were meant to help provide that. An older couple eager to stay in one place. At least they wouldn't be rushing off to marry, as all the others had done.

They went to the mercantile. "I'll buy you a penny candy," he told Kathy, hoping to cheer her up.

"Come along." Uncle Mac jumped down and held his hand out to help Winnie. "Buy whatever you need while you're here. No telling when we'll get to town again if winter sets in."

"Thank you." She wandered over to the ladies section.

Derek took Kathy to the counter and they spent fifteen minutes making a selection. She finally selected a red-and-white-striped candy stick. He bought himself a handful of lemon drops and stashed them in his pocket for a time when he craved their sweetness.

Uncle Mac reminded him of supplies they needed, and they waited for their order to be filled. Several times, he glanced at Winnie, but she continued to examine items without making a selection. After a bit, it dawned on him that she likely had no funds. That might provide one explanation as to why she was sleeping in his barn. Lost. No money. No family. Something inside him edged sideways at the thought. He knew the pain of losing family. At least he had Kathy and Uncle Mac. And he intended to do all in his power to protect them.

He wanted to go home, but not until he'd given Mr. Krause a chance to get the telegram and reply. If the man was in his office, a response would take only a few hours. No point in making Eric ride all the way out to the ranch. He turned to Kathy. "What do you say to going over to the hotel for tea?"

Kathy's eyes brightened. "Could we?"

The seldom-indulged-in treat would help pass the time. He signaled to Winnie. Uncle Mac stepped to her side to escort her. Derek clamped down on his teeth as he took Kathy's hand. Let Uncle Mac walk at Winnie's side. Derek didn't care.

Only he *did*. Admitting so scalded his innards.

They spent a tense hour at the hotel, trying to enjoy the tea and selection of baked goodies. Uncle Mac seemed the only one who succeeded. Derek wondered what he was doing, considering asking a young woman to stay, who in a matter of hours had proven such an upset to his thoughts.

Eric strode through the door. "Telegram, Derek."

He read the few words. "Winnifred Lockwood excellent worker. Stop. Honest. Stop. Trustworthy. Stop. Cheerful. Stop. Wouldn't hesitate to recommend her to you. Stop. Reginald Krause."

Derek wondered why they had let such a paragon of virtue leave.

* * *

Winnie wouldn't look at Derek, wouldn't try and guess what the telegram contained. She'd worked hard at the Krauses, but her best efforts had failed to provide her with permanency. She shifted her mind back to the store where she'd admired some fine wool fabric. The burnt-red with tiny yellow flowers would make a lovely dress. Not that she'd ever have such. Her wardrobe consisted of the dress she wore plus one other, both given to her out of the charity of Mrs. Krause's sister. At the sanitorium they provided uniforms. She welcomed the idea. A uniform would give her a bit of anonymity—a young woman doing her job. No need to feel anything toward the patients and visitors except kindness. She would not allow herself to feel more. Doing so in the past caused her nothing but sadness and anger. She had to move on.

Yet she'd agreed to stay with Kathy for a month.

Only because the money would enable her to complete her journey and arrive in Banff looking like more than a vagabond.

"What does it say?" Kathy demanded.

Derek handed the note to Uncle Mac, then turned and pinned Winnie into immobility with his dark eyes. "Seems we would be fortunate to have you work for us."

She swallowed hard, unable to think how she should respond.

"Bear in mind it will be temporary. Only until Christmas, when the Faringtons will arrive."

"I understand, and it suits me fine." This time she would not let herself care about any of them. She'd treat them kindly, of course. She could do no less.

Derek signaled to the others. "She'll be coming home with us. Only until the Faringtons arrive," he warned Kathy.

Disappointment filled Kathy's eyes.

Winnie wished she could assure the child otherwise, but she couldn't. She eyed Derek from under the cover of her eyelashes. Why didn't he marry and provide a permanent arrangement for them all?

She pulled her chin in and faced ahead. Perhaps he had a wife already picked out. After all, he was an attractive man with appealing qualities, such as devotion to his family, readiness to defend and...

She sat up straighter and forced her thoughts into submission. It mattered not one way or another to her. She'd only be here until Christmas.

She ignored the sorrow and anger flooding her soul. There was only one thing she had control over, and that was her spirit; and she had vowed a long time ago that she would not allow a root of bitterness to spring up.

On the way back, Winnie's lungs felt stiff, as if they had forgotten their task was to take air in and out. What had she done? She'd promised herself not to get involved with another family, yet here she was, riding to the ranch with Uncle Mac at her side, Kathy and Derek in front of her. Kathy kept up a steady stream of chatter, but Uncle Mac was the only one who answered. For the life of her, Winnie couldn't manage a sensible thought. Over and over she mentally chanted, *it's only to help Kathy. Nothing more. There's nothing for me here. Nothing at all.* She almost succeeded in not allowing herself to study Derek's back. Ramrod straight. A rock to his family.

Back at the house, Derek let them off. "Show her the housekeeper's quarters. I'll put the horses away."

Uncle Mac led the way to the room off the kitchen behind the stove, Kathy bouncing along at his side. "I hope you'll find it comfortable," Uncle Mac said, as he put her bag on the bed.

Besides the bed that was big enough for a couple, the

room held a dresser and a mirror. The window looked out toward the mountains. "I'm sure I shall."

"We'll give you time to get settled. Come on, Kit Kat."

Kathy paused at the doorway. "I'm glad you're going to stay."

Winnie pushed aside her doubts and smiled at Kathy. "Thank you."

A few minutes later she returned to the kitchen and took over her temporary duties.

Soup simmered on the stove as Derek stepped indoors. Their gazes locked across the room, hers wary, his more than a little annoyed, as if he resented that he had been forced to ask her to stay. She narrowed her eyes. She'd agreed only for Kathy's sake.

But a frisson of tension hovered about her as she served the meal and later cleaned the kitchen. She felt Derek's presence, his watchfulness, even when he wasn't watching her.

To escape the uneasiness she went to her room early.

Three days later she had settled into a routine after a serious talk with herself. This house had everything she wanted and nothing she could have. She had only to accept the fact. Life became easier once she did.

Kathy had returned to school. Derek spent much of his time outside, likely in the barn. Either because of work or to avoid Winnie. Uncle Mac had long naps, then joined Derek. Mornings and evenings were easiest with Kathy present.

Except for one thing. Kathy did not go to sleep easily.

Tonight she cried in Derek's arms as he rocked her, trying to soothe her.

She finally fell asleep, remnants of her sobs shuddering through her. Derek rocked her a few more minutes, then eased from the chair and tiptoed into her bedroom.

Winnie turned from the window where she'd tried to take her thoughts to the silvery moonlight in hopes of ignoring Kathy's distress. She plunked to a chair and let her head fall forward. Her intention had been so simple three days ago—a month of keeping house, seeing Kathy to school and making meals. Nothing more. No emotional connection.

But life never turned out exactly as she planned.

Bedtime was torture for Kathy. She couldn't bear to be alone in the dark. A lamp didn't help. After a few minutes of listening to her sobs, Derek went to her and spent upwards of an hour rocking her, assuring her he was right there and would always be.

Trouble was, all of them knew he couldn't promise forever.

Life was too uncertain.

Winnie had learned that truth at a young age. So had Kathy.

Going to school was equally painful. "How do I know you won't all be gone when I get back?" Tears streamed down Kathy's face.

Winnie had stood aside and let Derek and Uncle Mac deal with Kathy. After all, they were family. They would be here long after Winnie left.

But neither of the men seemed to know how to calm her fears, and the strain on all of them was obvious.

When Kathy started crying tonight, Mac had mumbled something about seeing to the stock and then headed for the barn.

They all knew he was escaping Kathy's distress.

Derek stepped back into the room, deep lines gouged around his mouth, dark misery in his eyes. She'd seen the same distress every bedtime and every morning when Kathy headed down the road to the little school-house on the corner, Derek at her side.

She now knew enough to have a pot of tea ready when Kathy finally went to sleep.

She poured him a cup and edged the sugar bowl closer.

Derek spooned sugar into his tea. At the fourth spoonful, she knew he wasn't aware of what he did and she pushed the bowl away. He stirred his tea. Round and round and round, the spoon tinkling on the china with a cheerless tolling.

"She's been like this since the accident."

Winnie nodded, though he didn't look at her. "She told me her mama and a sister and brother died."

"In a train wreck on their way out here." His voice was harsh. "I was supposed to be with them, but I decided at the last minute to let them travel alone."

She murmured a sound she hoped indicated she heard. If he needed to talk she would listen. She could do that much without getting involved with this family's distress—without letting her emotions crawl up her throat and reach out to Derek.

Then she would go to Banff. A uniform. A job. A room. All she wanted or needed.

"I should have been with them."

Shock jolted through her veins. Did he mean he wished he'd died? "Good thing you weren't. Otherwise, who would take care of Kathy?"

"How can I hope to protect her? Life just happens."

"Life is in God's hands."

He jerked up to face her. "I suppose your life has fit into neat little slots, so it's easy for you to say that."

She laughed. "Yes, that would explain why I was sleeping in your barn."

He looked a little uncertain.

She couldn't resist the urge to further upset his idea of how easy her life was. "I know more about how Kathy is feeling than you could ever believe."

"Huh?"

He doubted her, did he? Well, she would soon enough convince him. "When I was seven, my parents gave me to my aunt and uncle and moved west with no forwarding address."

He looked suitably shocked. Or was he perhaps disbelieving?

"My aunt and uncle were childless and my parents had seven children."

"So you ended up in a better home?"

"One might think so, except my aunt then had two children." After their own children arrived, her aunt and uncle had used Winnie as a servant. She'd moved to an attic room and ran errands from dawn to dusk. She'd done so willingly, eagerly, certain she would earn affection and approval. "My aunt died giving birth to a third who didn't live." Her security had died with her. "My uncle married a young neighborhood woman within a few months, and the new wife wanted nothing to do with a child that belonged to neither of them. At twelve, I was hired out to the Anderson family." She tried to keep her voice light. As if it didn't still hurt.

"How did you come to be working for the Krauses?" No doubt he still thought she was fabricating all the details.

"After four years with the Andersons, they decided they didn't need me anymore." So much for all the talk about how valuable she was. Just like a member of the family. "I was hired by the Krauses then."

"How long were you with them?"

"Two years." She clamped her mouth shut. She would say nothing further. When she went to the Krauses she'd promised herself there would be no more dreams of belonging. She'd do her job well. Give them no reason to dismiss her. But she would be content to be a servant.

Only, Moira and Reginald had invited her to take part in family activities, taken her on family vacations. Given her hope. Fueled her dreams.

She'd been so foolish to think she could belong. All it had taken was a letter from a cousin in Germany saying she wanted to visit, perhaps relocate to the Canadian west, and Winnie had been told her services were no longer needed.

Derek touched the back of her hand. "I'm sorry."

She jerked away, her heart thudding against her ribcage like an overwound clock. "I don't need your pity. I welcome the chance to be able to work in Banff. I hear it's a beautiful place."

He dropped his hand to his lap and looked past her. "I heard that, too."

A thick silence hung between them. She pushed her chair back, intending to excuse herself and go to her room.

"Perhaps you do understand how she feels. I share her sorrow but I don't know how to help her."

Winnie shrugged. "Everyone handles trials in their own way."

Derek's gaze bore into hers, dark, challenging, maybe more. Maybe seeking. "How do you deal with yours?"

A great vacuum sucked at her insides. She tried to

pull her gaze away, couldn't. "That's easy. I trust myself to God's care. He will never leave me nor forsake me. He holds me in the palm of His hands."

His mouth pulled down at the corners. "My mama believed the same thing and look what happened to her." His breath whooshed out. "And despite your trust in God, you spend the night sleeping in a barn. How can you say He is taking care of you?"

She chuckled softly. "Well, I wasn't asleep in the barn of a cruel man, so I suppose He was watching over me." Had God sent her here for a purpose? To help Kathy. What could she do in a month?

Could she risk her heart becoming involved?

The wind sighed about the house as she considered her answer. An alternative sprang to her mind. Something she'd wondered about a few times. "Why don't you get married? Surely, that would give Kathy security."

He jerked to his feet, his fists curled on the table top. "I have no intention of marrying. Ever."

"I can tell you have mixed feelings."

He stared at her then laughed. "Sorry. I was a bit vehement, wasn't I?"

"I barely noticed. But tell me, why are you so set against marriage?"

He settled back to his chair. "I have Kathy to care for. That's my focus."

"Seems to me marriage would make that easier."

His mouth tightened. He shook his head. "I don't need another person to take care of. To worry about. To always know I couldn't protect them as I ought."

"You feel responsible for your mother's death?"

"Wouldn't you, in my shoes?"

She lifted one shoulder. "I have no idea how I'd feel."

"My father died when I was seventeen, after years of illness. His parting words were to take care of the family. I failed completely."

She wanted to comfort him. Give him something to encourage him. Her heart stalled at crossing a boundary she had created to protect herself from growing too close to people.

Quivering with reluctance, she slipped her hand over to rest on the back of his.

He stiffened but didn't pull away.

"You only fail when you don't care."

His eyes darkened enough to match the night outside the window. His gaze searched hers.

She didn't know what he sought, only knew she couldn't provide it. This time she would not let her heart open up to the people of this home. This was a job. Nothing more.

"I care." His voice thickened with emotion.

"I know you do." Despite her best resolve, she ached to experience such caring on her behalf. Determinedly, she pushed aside the yearning, refused to acknowledge it. "So you haven't failed."

He turned his hand and squeezed hers. "Thank you for saying so."

The air between them shimmered with promise. Hope. Unfulfilled dreams. A wish for things to change that could not change, a desire to go back to happier times, happier places. Or better yet, find new happiness. Her heart flooded with sadness as wide as the sky. She scrubbed her lips together and tried to stifle the ache threatening to suck her inside out. Her hand squeezed Derek's without her permission. She tried to pull away. Couldn't make her arm obey. Something deep, gut level, bound her to him.

Chapter Three

Derek blinked, realized he clung to Winnie's hand and pulled away. "Thanks for the tea." And more. Her understanding. The comfort of her touch.

He jerked to his feet. He needed neither. He turned toward the hall, heading for his room. "I'll say good night."

Why had he let himself be drawn into her words? Why had he gripped her hand like Kathy did his on the way to school? He wasn't a frightened child. He needed no one. Wanted no one. Kathy was his responsibility, and he feared he couldn't live up to that adequately. He sat on the edge of his bed and looked at the calendar. December third. The Faringtons would arrive the twenty-seventh. Until then, they had to make do with Winnie's help.

She'd proven herself capable enough at housework. But he didn't need her comfort or words of encouragement.

It sure beat him, how she could believe God was in control when she'd been shoved from pillar to post. He clenched his fists, gritted his teeth. Why did life have to be so harsh? She surely didn't deserve such unkindness.

Any more than Kathy deserved to be orphaned.

He slipped into bed and pulled the covers to his neck, but lay staring at the darkness of his room.

He could only do his best, even if his best had never been enough to protect his family.

He would not let himself care about another person. He'd never marry and take on more responsibility.

Kathy had been hurt by so many people. He must remind her Winnie was only here a month, warn her not to get fond of her.

Next morning, he prepared to walk Kathy to school when Uncle Mac burst into the house. "Derek, the cows are in the feed stack. I need a hand getting them out."

He hesitated. By the time he returned from the school, the cows would have trampled the stacks into bedding.

"I can stay home?" Kathy seemed pleased with the thought.

"Aren't you practicing for the Christmas concert? Seems you need to be there."

She whimpered. "Don't make me go."

"Derek, come on. I can't do this on my own." Uncle Mac waited with his hand on the door. "Winnie, could you take her to school today?"

Kathy wouldn't go to school on her own. But Derek didn't want her learning to depend on Winnie. Wasn't that what he'd decided just last night? Yet Uncle Mac couldn't get the cows out by himself. Derek couldn't be two places at the same time.

Winnie watched him, her eyes knowing and patient, as if she read his uncertainty.

He'd shared too much the previous evening. Given her reason to think she understood him. He composed his face to reveal none of his confusion, and turned to Kathy. "Would you go with Winnie?"

Her face wrinkled, ready for a good wail.

"Just this one time." He hated to turn her over to anyone else.

"I would love to see your schoolroom," Winnie said. "Do you have some work to show me?"

"The teacher hung a picture I drew on the wall."

"Would you show me?"

"I guess."

"Good. That's settled." Uncle Mac opened the door. "Now let's get those cows back where they belong."

Derek hesitated a moment.

"Say goodbye to your brother," Winnie said softly.

He knew her words were meant for him. Telling him to say goodbye to Kathy.

"I'll meet you after school and walk you home," he promised.

Kathy nodded, and he had no choice but to join Uncle Mac.

By the time they chased the cows back and fixed the broken spot in the fence, he was sweating from exertion. He glanced toward the house. "I should have let her stay home until I could take her."

"She'll be fine with Winnie. That young woman has her head on solid. She's good with Kathy. Just what she needs. Just what we all need."

"Hardly."

"Take off the blinders, my boy. She's a good looker—"

"I never said she wasn't." She'd cleaned up real good from his first glimpse of her climbing, bedraggled, from the hay. "That's not the point."

"She's efficient."

"I guess so."

"And steady. Why, I bet she would be loyal to the death."

"All I need is someone else to worry about."

Uncle Mac faced him squarely. "What you need is to stop taking yourself so seriously."

Winnie crossed the yard on her way back from school and went into the house, her step light, as if she had not a worry in the world.

Derek knew better. She had no home, her family was lost to her and what she owned fit into a small bag. She should be weighed down with uncertainty. Was she so simpleminded she didn't realize it?

Uncle Mac must have read his mind. "She's learned to enjoy the present without worrying about the future."

Derek snorted. "Sounds irresponsible to me."

The older man sighed deeply, obviously frustrated with Derek. "Like I said, you take yourself and life too seriously. Sometimes I get the feeling you think you need to tell God how to rule the world."

Derek strode away. If he said what he thought, his uncle would likely have a fit, but it seems God didn't take care of things the way He promised to.

Winnie had tried to stay uninvolved with Kathy's angst as they trudged toward school. But Kathy kept glancing over her shoulder.

"Derek will pick you up after class," she assured the child.

"What if he forgets?"

Winnie laughed softly. "As if he would. He'll never forget you."

"Something might happen to him."

Winnie had stopped and squatted to eye level and

grasped Kathy's shoulders. "Bad things happen. I can't pretend they don't. But you can't change the future by borrowing worry from tomorrow and trying to carry it today. All of us can only live life one day at a time."

Kathy's dark eyes considered Winnie.

Winnie pressed her point. "You miss out on the good things of today by worrying about tomorrow. Hardly seems like a good idea."

Kathy looked back toward the farm. "I can't see the house."

Winnie realized Kathy was a few inches too short to see the peak of the house. "Would you feel better if you could see it?"

"I'd know it was there."

By the time Winnie returned home she had an idea. She dug into a box of rags and pulled out a bit of heavy denim, then headed for the barn.

She found Uncle Mac outside, pounding nails into a raw-looking plank of wood. For some inexplicable reason, she did not make her request to Mac. "Where can I find Derek?"

"Try the pen over there." He pointed down the alleyway. "He was working with one of the young horses. Give out a call so you don't startle them."

"It can wait."

Mac scrubbed at his whiskered chin. "Whatever is on your mind was enough to bring you out here, so you might as well get it done. 'Sides, Derek needs to think about something besides work and responsibility. I'm thinking you might be able to nudge him in that direction."

She wrinkled her nose at him. "That's not exactly what I had in mind."

Mac waved her away. "Don't stop an old man from dreaming dreams."

"Even if I tell you it's impossible? Not what either of us wants?"

"Could be the good Lord brought you here for such a thing as this." He pounded on a nail, making any protest useless. She shrugged and headed in the direction he'd indicated. What difference did an old man's opinion make? Didn't change anything. Any more than her wishes had changed anything in the past. Or Derek's worries could prevent troubles in the future.

Ahead, beyond the wooden rails, Derek's voice came to her, calm, reassuring, just as when he talked to Kathy. Safe, sheltering. Her steps slowed, she dragged her mitten along the rough wood, catching and ripping off slivers, tempting them to stab her, yet knowing pain and blood from an injured finger would not ease the emptiness sucking at her soul. She stood stark still, dropped her hands to her side and drew in air, cool, laden with the scent of animals and snow off the mountains. She let the air settle deep into her lungs, holding it until she'd leeched it of all oxygen. Only then did she let her breath out, and keep within her the strength it had given.

She had no one. She needed no one. Especially not someone who resented another person in his life. She did not need his gentle words. His calm assurance. All she wanted was enough money to continue her journey to Banff.

She'd given her word to stay until the Faringtons arrived.

Her conscience dictated she help Kathy as much as she could. Perhaps that's why God had brought her here.

Not because of Derek, as Mac suggested. *Lord, use me, protect me, help me.*

Strengthened by reality and determination, she called out, "Derek, are you there?" and waited for his response.

Silence filled her ears. Then he answered. "Hang on while I release the horse." A moment later he vaulted the fence. He dragged his gaze over her and glanced beyond her.

"Is something wrong?"

"No. Kathy got to school safely. I met her teacher and saw the room. Admired her drawing. She has a nice touch with crayons and paper. Even the teacher said her drawings were expressive."

He leaned against the fence. "You came here to tell me that?"

It wasn't her purpose in seeking him out, but she was happy enough to relieve the concern he couldn't hide.

"I do have another reason for being here." She explained what she had in mind.

His eyebrows climbed toward his hairline, but before he could voice an opinion she was certain would be contrary, she added, "What does it hurt? And it might help."

He shrugged. "I'll have to get the ladder."

She followed him to a shed where he pulled out a ladder, then she trotted after him to the house and watched as he nailed the flag of denim to a pole and attached the pole to the peak of the house.

"She should be able to see that from the school. It will give her something to watch."

Derek climbed down and stood beside her, staring up at the flapping, faded blue material. "You think it's enough to get her to walk home alone?"

"I can't say. It will take time for her to get over her fears." She refrained from pointing out that he and Mac seem to feed them, rather than give her tools to deal with them. "At the very least, she can look out from the schoolyard and know the house is still here, and by association, assume you and Mac are here as well."

"Seems too easy."

"Sometimes the answers are easier than we anticipate."

He faced her, his eyes full of dark intensity, seeking answers to questions he hadn't voiced—perhaps that he didn't even have words for. "Is that how you see life?" He made the idea sound silly.

"I know life is complicated—"

"Unpredictable? Uncontrollable?"

His driving questions scraped her nerves. She preferred to believe God controlled things. "Personally, I don't want to see the end, the turns in the road. I think if I did, I would live in constant fear."

"You mean like me?" His voice carried a low warning, informing her he didn't care for her evaluation.

She decided to turn the conversation in another direction. "I was thinking of Kathy. Living in fear doesn't change what might come. It only robs you of enjoyment of good things."

"I prefer to call it caution."

She ached to have him understand the difference between the two. Longed to see him know peace. "I learned some hard but valuable lessons. I wouldn't have chosen to be taught by them, but I also don't intend to waste what I've learned."

His look silently demanded an explanation. She couldn't tell if he wanted to understand, or simply to hear her answer so he could refute it. *Lord, You have taught me to trust You even in difficult circumstances. If there is some way I can make him see it's possible, then use me, guide me.*

"I prayed for a home, instead God gave me contentment. I asked for love, instead He gave me peace. I tried to find my family, asked Him to help me. I found no clue of where they had gone, but I found instead, satisfaction in knowing I am loved by God. That is more than enough."

"I don't believe you."

His blunt words hammered at her self-assurance. She clung with deeply embedded fingernails to what she said. "You're accusing me of deceit?"

"I think you've deceived yourself if you believe you are content and happy to be homeless, with no family and alone in the world."

His accusation tore her fingernails away, leaving her heart in shreds. He had excavated a truth she couldn't face. It was too hurtful, too destructive.

"Believe whatever you want." She congratulated herself on keeping her voice gentle, revealing none of the pain pulsing through her. "I know God loves me. What more do I need?" So much more she couldn't face. "Be sure and tell Kathy to watch for the flag and take comfort in the fact that the house is there. You and Mac are here, too." She turned and headed indoors.

"Winnie, I didn't mean to hurt you. I'm sorry."

She gave no indication that she heard him.

Why had he pushed her so hard? What benefit was there in poking at her wounds? In making her acknowledge their pain? He should have quit prodding before he made her bleed.

As he returned to gentling the young gelding he'd bought in the fall, he tried to think how to undo what he'd done. Not that he didn't believe she was hiding her real feelings.

But by the time she clanged the metal triangle to signal dinner, he still didn't know how to explain he hadn't meant to inflict pain.

What *was* his intention? To make her face the truth.

Why? Would he feel better if she worried as much as he did, if she bemoaned the facts of her life?

No. He had come to admire her optimism, perhaps even relish it. But it also accused him. Made him aware of his own shortcomings in trusting God, and that in turn made him defensive.

He followed Mac into the house, stood at the doorway and studied her for some indication of how she felt.

She flashed them both a smile. "Soup's ready. And biscuits hot from the oven."

He let his breath ease past his teeth. So she was willing to overlook his comments, perhaps even pretend he hadn't spoken them? His relief was short-lived. She was a warm person, but only on the surface. Below the gentle smile and kind words was a heart frozen with denial.

How was that better than him worrying?

Mac tossed his hat and gloves onto the narrow bench by the door and shed his coat. "Sure does smell good. A man could get used to being greeted by a warm smile and tasty food. Right, Derek?"

Derek snorted. Uncle Mac was anything but subtle, but protests would only encourage him. "Sure could."

Mac grinned and rubbed his hands together as if he'd succeeded in convincing Derek that Winnie was the answer to all their problems.

Derek knew better.

But he was grateful to enjoy the food and the comfortable atmosphere.

Later that afternoon, he strode down the trail to the schoolhouse to get Kathy. She raced out and joined him in the schoolyard. Her eagerness at seeing him erased the tightness lingering in his thoughts from his unkind words to Winnie. This little sister was his life. All that mattered. He turned her toward the house. "Can you see home?"

She shook her head. "Not until I'm almost there."

"Look again. I think you might be able to."

She giggled. "I'm still not tall enough." But she followed the direction of his finger when he pointed. Her eyes widened. "What is that?"

"It's a flag hanging on the end of the house." He made it sound like it was his idea. "Winnie thought of it. Said you might feel better if you could see where the house is."

Kathy clung to his hand and rocked back and forth on her tiptoes. "I can see it now." The awe in her voice said it all.

How had Winnie known how important this was to his little sister? Why hadn't *he* thought of doing something? A confusion of gratitude and regret twisted his insides.

They headed home. The whole way, Kathy kept her gaze on the flag. Her breath whooshed out when she could finally see the house. "It's right on top."

"Just like I said." He realized not seeing the house had created unnecessary worry for her, and his regret dissipated. Maybe he could find other ways to help Kathy.

He followed her inside.

Winnie waited with milk and cookies. Her welcoming smile faltered a fraction as she saw Derek behind Kathy. "Do you want a snack, too?"

"Sure. Thanks." He didn't normally stop for a midafternoon snack, but she seemed to think the idea was okay.

Winnie put out more cookies, asked if he wanted milk or coffee. He chose the latter. Then she turned to Kathy. "Did you see the flag?"

"Right from the school."

"She likes it," Derek added. "Thanks for the idea."

"I'm glad it helps." He sought her eyes. The air shimmered with tension. Then she blinked, and her barriers were firmly in place.

He didn't know which was stronger—disappointment at her withdrawal, or relief to be allowed to retreat to his own safety.

Winnie wanted to ease bedtime both for Kathy's sake and Derek's. Plus anyone else who might be within the sound of Kathy's cries. Everyone was exhausted from listening to the nightly struggle, when she fought her fears and Derek tried to calm her. Seeing the picture at school Kathy drew had given Winnie an idea.

The first thing she needed was blank paper. She found a stack of folded brown store paper in a closet—along with a trunk full of yarn and yard goods.

She folded and stitched the pages together down the fold line to create a little book. She used Kathy's crayons to color the cover and she put Kathy's name on the front.

Winnie spoke to Derek as the little girl put on her nightgown. "I have a few ideas about how to make bedtime easier. Do you mind if I try them?"

He gave a lopsided grin. "I'm willing to try anything, and if your idea works as well as the flag…" He shrugged.

Kathy came out, her face already tense.

Winnie took over. "Kathy, I was so impressed with your drawing at school. I told Derek how wonderful it was. I think you have a gift." She hoped to do far more than encourage an interest in drawing. "I made you a little art book." She showed the brown paper book to Kathy. "I think you have time to draw something tonight."

"Before bed?"

"What's wrong with that?"

"What will I draw?"

"Whatever you like, but if you need a suggestion, why not think about your day and draw something that shows the best part of the day for you?"

Kathy put her stuffed bear on the table and picked up a crayon. "Does it have to be something good?"

"Do what you want."

She drew a big black circle.

Winnie sat across the table and Derek stood behind Kathy, watching over her shoulder. Winnie felt his tension, wondered if Kathy did, too. "Why a black circle?"

"That's what bedtime feels like."

"Why?"

"'Cause I'm afraid."

"Maybe we can think of something to put inside the black circle to make it happy instead of scary."

Kathy looked intrigued. "What would *you* draw?

Winnie felt Derek's quiet study as she picked up a red crayon and drew a heart inside the black circle. "This heart stands for love, to remind you that Derek and Uncle Mac love you, and so does God." She met Derek's gaze then, managed to ignore her shock of awareness at the surprise and gratitude in his eyes. "What would *you* draw, Derek?"

He shook his head. "I'm not good at this sort of thing."

"You must be able to think of something."

He studied the drawing a moment, then picked up a pink crayon. He made a circle, added eyes and a smiling mouth, selected a brown crayon and drew hair on the head. "This is Kathy. Thinking of her makes me happy."

Kathy giggled. "I don't look like that."

"A heart doesn't look like that either." He touched the red heart Winnie had drawn.

"It's a val'tine heart," Kathy said with utmost sincerity.

"Now it's your turn," Winnie said to the child, hoping she would think of something to help her overcome her fears of the dark.

"Just one thing?"

Winnie laughed. "As many as you want."

Kathy grabbed a crayon and bent her head over the page.

Winnie shot Derek a glance and saw he was as amused by Kathy's enthusiasm as she. Their gazes collided. In her heart, something burst free. Hope. Her lungs caught on an inhalation. Hope had left her too often disappointed. She lowered her eyes, pushed things back where they belonged and concentrated on Kathy.

After a few minutes, Kathy lifted her head and pushed the book forward for the others to see. "It's a flag. This is my teddy bear. This is Derek."

Winnie chuckled at the long-legged stick figure with more hat than head. There was another stick figure—a woman, if Winnie guessed correctly. "Your mother?"

Kathy shook her head. "You."

"Me?"

"You said to draw things that make me happy."

She made Kathy happy? *But I'm not staying.* She swallowed the words, rather than steal any of Kathy's contentment. Instead, she patted Kathy's head. "Thank you." And before anyone, namely Derek, could offer a comment, she hurried on. "I really liked it the other day, when you sang that song. Do you remember?"

"You mean—?" and she started to sing the words. "I sing the mighty power of God...." She sang it clear through.

"I like that."

Kathy smiled. "Me, too." She pushed away from the table and turned to Derek. "I'm ready to go to bed." She took his hand and led him away.

Derek shot a look over his shoulder. Winnie almost laughed at the doubt wreathing his face. He came back ten minutes later. "I can't believe it's that easy."

"It might not be. Her fears won't automatically disappear in one night, but given time..."

As if to prove her correct, Kathy's scream filled the air.

Derek bolted to his feet and came back with Kathy in his arms. He cradled her in the rocking chair. His eyes filled with desperation as he met Winnie's gaze across the room.

Oh Lord, calm her fears.

"Derek?" Kathy managed through her tears. "Sing Mama's song."

Derek nodded and began the song Kathy had finished a short time before. She sighed back a sob and fell asleep in a matter of minutes.

Derek carried her back to bed, then joined Winnie in the kitchen. "Still better than most nights."

"It's a start. Give her a few tools and she'll figure out what works for her."

"I guess I should thank you." He walked to the window and glanced out, then turned and faced her.

She wasn't sure what the look in his eyes meant.

He grabbed his coat and rushed out of the house.

Her heart followed him into the cold. How hard it must be to watch his sister struggle with her fear and loss, and to feel so powerless to do anything.

If she could help even a little, she would gladly do so, then walk away with a clear conscience that she had done what she could, and perhaps what God was calling her to do.

At the idea of walking away, her rib cage tightened until she hunkered over against the pain. She had never found leaving easy, but this time she vowed she would do so without feeling as if her world was crashing down around her feet.

God help her. She would do so.

But even as she prayed for protection against involvement, she knew she had already crossed a line in her emotions. And not just with Kathy. She only hoped she could backtrack when the time came.

Chapter Four

Derek strode to the barn. He needed to think. He leaned against the pen and stared at the horse without any purpose in mind but to sort out his feelings.

"Whatcha' doing here, son? Is Winnie settling Kathy?"

Derek jumped as Mac spoke at his elbow. He'd forgotten his uncle was still in the barn. "Kathy is already sleeping."

"Really? What did you do?"

"Nothing. It was Winnie." He described the drawing book and the song.

Mac let out a long sigh. "That's good."

He understood his uncle's relief at knowing Kathy's distress was short-lived tonight. "Kathy's getting too fond of Winnie. She's going to be hurt when she has to say goodbye." His insides twisted. He should send Winnie away now. Before Kathy got any more attached. Before any of them did.

"I think you're missing the point. Even if she cries when Winnie leaves, Winnie's help will still be with her. Son, from the first day when she helped Kathy realize your mother would enjoy seeing her laugh, to this afternoon when she hung the flag, that young lady understood more of Kathy's problems and how to address them then we have in over a year."

"No doubt you mean that to be comforting."

"It's not?" Uncle Mac's voice was low, not expressing any opinion, though Derek was certain he had one. "This is the first night Kathy has settled down in less than an hour."

Derek banged his palm on the plank. "Why didn't I think of doing something different? I'm supposed to be the one who gives her what she needs."

"Sometimes a person is too close to the problem."

Derek suspected Mac meant more than helping Kathy settle for the night, but he wasn't going that direction.

"Maybe God sent Winnie to us for just this reason— to help us know how to deal with Kathy. My advice? Take the gifts she brings and don't worry about what will happen when she leaves."

"I suppose you're right."

"You know I am." He clamped his hand on Derek's shoulder. "I'm hoping you'll see I'm right for more than Kathy's sake."

Derek stared into the dark recesses of the barn. "Don't be hoping on my account. I will never marry."

"So you say. In fact, if you've said it a hundred times, you've said it a thousand—you don't need the responsibility. 'Course what you mean is you're afraid of getting hurt."

Derek jerked away and headed for the door.

Uncle Mac didn't understand that what Derek feared was failing yet again to protect those under his care. As to being hurt when Winnie left…he kind of guessed he had already stepped into that territory. But Uncle

Mac was right about Winnie helping. He could live with knowing each day made saying goodbye to Winnie harder to contemplate, if having her stay helped Kathy.

He paused in the cold air and looked up at the stars. No snow tonight. The early snow of October and November was long gone. Maybe they'd have a brown Christmas.

Christmas. His stomach churned. He no longer anticipated the season, full now of painful memories of those gone, and a burning sense of helplessness. His father would be disappointed at Derek's failure to take better care of the family.

Uncle Mac joined him. For a moment, neither spoke; and then the older man said, "Come on, son. Let's see if Winnie has any raisin pudding left."

He let himself be led indoors. Would Kathy still be asleep? Blissful silence filled the room.

"Not a peep from her," Winnie said. A bundle of bright objects lay on the table before her.

His gaze riveted to the shiny red ball. He'd been four, his father still healthy, when Pa lifted him to the tree and helped him attach the ball, then stepped back. "Now it's Christmas." Derek would never forget the specialness of that day.

He forced his gaze from the red ball but continued to stare at the pile of Christmas things. They hadn't celebrated much last year, still recovering, as they were, from the deaths of three family members. He hadn't thought to do anything special this year. A gift or two, but that's about all.

"Got any more pudding for two hungry cowboys?" Uncle Mac said.

"Certainly." Winnie put out two generous portions. "Tea?"

"Thanks. We'd appreciate some." Uncle Mac gave Derek a funny look. "Sit down. Take a load off."

Derek's knees seemed to have forgotten how to work, and he had to concentrate on lowering himself to a chair as he fought the memories associated with Christmas. The season was supposed to be happy, but his thoughts were laced through and through with regrets, loss and a deep sense of failure.

Would he ever again enjoy Christmas?

Winnie poured tea and sat across from him. "I found these ornaments and wondered what special traditions you have."

Derek swallowed hard and shifted his gaze upward to look at her. Her face fairly glowed with pleasure. He struggled to focus on her question.

"I remember when I was a boy," Uncle Mac began. "Your father was a little gaffer." He nodded at Derek to make sure Derek understood who he meant. "I was probably twelve or so. There were three girls in between us. We lived on a dirt-poor homestead in Kansas. Not a tree in sight. I remembered big pine trees in Grandma and Grandpa's house. But little Georgie had never seen one. I told my parents we had to have a tree. My pa was gone three days and came back with a tree no more than two feet tall. I don't know where he found it, but he'd dug it up rather than cut it, and after Christmas we planted it outside. Would you believe that thing grew? Every year, we decorated it."

Derek had heard the tale before, but still enjoyed it.

"What a lovely story," Winnie said.

"The folks are gone now, but my sister and her husband live there." Uncle Mac got a faraway look in his eyes. "The tree must be twenty feet tall or more by now. I wonder if they still decorate it."

Derek felt Winnie's gaze on him, felt it burn past his memories to a depth in his heart he wasn't aware of. He pictured himself sharing Christmas with her.

This year only.

He stuffed back a twinge of regret. Realized she waited for him to say something. He plucked the red ball from the pile. "I remember—" He told them his memory.

"It was the last Christmas my father was well." Suddenly he recalled something else. "But Pa always wanted me to hold up the youngest child and have her hang the red ball. Everytime, he would say, 'Now it's Christmas'."

Her eyes filled with warmth and she sighed. "That's so special."

Did he detect a hitch in her voice? Something invisible seemed to pass from his heart to hers. A shared enjoyment of the story, but more, perhaps a shared acknowledgment of the pain of disappointment. His had a different path than hers, but he understood she must have watched family gatherings from the sidelines and dreamed of belonging.

He was equally certain she would deny it. No doubt she'd tell him how eager she was to get to Banff and the job there. They both understood her stay was temporary.

"Kathy was the youngest, wasn't she?"

Her question jolted him back to the conversation and he nodded.

"So you held her up to hang the red ornament on the tree since she was tiny?"

"Every year since she was born." He fell silent as he recalled the exception.

"Didn't have much of a Christmas last year." Uncle Mac sounded woeful.

"I was thinking," Winnie spoke softly, slowly. "Perhaps we can make Christmas special this year. Incorporate some old traditions like this red ball, but add new ones so it's less of remembering the past and more about facing the future, enjoying the present."

Derek wanted to protest. He simply didn't have any enthusiasm about celebrating a day filled with bittersweet memories.

"I wouldn't have any trouble finding a pine tree," Uncle Mac said. "I'll take Kathy with me."

"That's a wonderful idea." Her gaze jerked back to Derek before he could sort out how to deal with this latest interference from a temporary housekeeper. And before he could deny the tangle of regrets over knowing she would leave.

He should have known from the first she would find a way to upset their lives. Only, he didn't regret the things she had done. After all, so far they had been for Kathy's good. Even this latest suggestion was meant for Kathy. He could hardly protest. Even though he knew every time she spoke—earnest, concerned with Kathy, full of cheer and good humor—she gained a larger portion of his heart. He seemed powerless to prevent it.

"Mama used to make popcorn on Christmas Eve, and we always read the Christmas story. The children were allowed to stay up late." He grinned. "I think the adults hoped they would then sleep a little later Christmas morning."

Uncle Mac pushed aside his empty bowl and yawned hugely. "Speaking of staying up late…it's my bedtime. I'm going to leave you young ones to plan Christmas."

Derek waited for his uncle to leave the room, then turned to Winnie, a question burning on his lips. "Do you have memories from when you were a child and lived with your family?"

She jerked back, sat up straighter. Her expression flooded with denial.

Before she could answer, he pulled back his question. "Never mind."

Then she smiled and her eyes glistened. "I remember the year my mama made me a rag doll. I felt so loved."

How could parents give a child away? He would protect Kathy with his very life, and she wasn't even his child. But being her brother and the stand-in for her parents, he guessed it was almost the same.

Winnie recovered her usual focus on others. He was beginning to suspect it was her way of escape. "So Uncle Mac will take Kathy to get a tree, you'll help her hang the red ball and I'll make popcorn. Any other suggestions?"

He knew she meant in regards to Kathy, but he had other intentions. "You seem set on proving you don't want to be part of a family."

She grew so still, he wondered if she even breathed. Her mouth was narrow and straight. Then she sucked in air until he thought her lungs must have a hole in the bottom. She released her breath slowly. "In case you haven't noticed, I am *not* part of a family. I have learned to accept that fact and not let it rob me of enjoying life."

"By making everyone else's family work like clockwork?"

Her eyes narrowed. "If I can help someone, why would you consider that a problem?"

He studied her. Saw the pain behind her eyes she didn't manage to hide. Knew she would deny it if he mentioned it. "I don't... I guess."

They regarded each other like wary combatants.

Then she laughed. "Why are we arguing? I only wanted to talk about Christmas preparations. If you want to turn anything into a tradition, that will be up to you. I'm won't be here next Christmas."

He wondered if he again glimpsed a flash of pain behind her steady gaze.

"My only wish is for Kathy—and you and Mac—to have a special time."

"I'd do anything to make Kathy happy. So—whatever you suggest." He would have no objection to seeing Winnie enjoy the season as well. But how? The one thing she needed despite her denials, he could not, would not offer her.

He would bid her goodbye December twenty-seventh, when the Faringtons arrived.

Winnie looked out the window. Mac and Kathy were out getting a tree. They would all decorate it tonight. The skies were heavy. Perhaps they would get snow. A white Christmas would help make for a perfect holiday, and she was determined to make this the best Christmas ever for Kathy.

Winnie turned from the window and rearranged the decorations, awaiting the time to hang them on the tree.

She picked up the red ornament. Recalling Derek's story of what this ball meant to his family filled her with sweetness that crowded at her careful boundaries. What a special memory of his father.

She pushed the trinket away and strode to the kitchen.

Derek had no right to remind her she wasn't part of a family or to suggest she truly wanted to be. God had seen fit to make her a solitary young woman. She would not let bits of longing and loneliness turn life's joys into dust.

She would not be sucked into the bottomless barrel of wanting what she couldn't have.

Trouble was, her heart did not obey her mind.

She quietly shut out the treacherous thoughts. Come December twenty-seventh she would be on her way to Banff.

Kathy burst through the door. "We got it." Her voice was shrill with excitement.

Behind her stood a tree. Winnie laughed. "Did it walk here on its own?"

"Uncle Mac brought it."

"I don't see him." She did her best to sound puzzled.

Kathy turned and giggled. "He's behind."

"You're sure?"

"I'm here." Mac's voice came from the tree.

Winnie gasped. "A talking tree."

Kathy giggled some more. "Trees don't talk."

The tree pushed into the room and Uncle Mac leaned it against the wall. He dusted needles from his coat. "She went and picked the fattest one in the forest."

"It's the best tree ever." Kathy sighed her pleasure.

Derek stomped his feet on the verandah floor and stepped into the open doorway. "Nice tree, Kit Kat."

"I know. This is going to be such a good Christmas. I can hardly wait." She flung herself at Derek. He caught her and lifted her to his chest.

Winnie's breath caught halfway. She tried to look anywhere but at Derek, but lately her eyes had developed the habit of seeking him whenever he was in the room. Seeing his love for Kathy did funny things to her heart. Made it feel mushy. He was a man who would never shirk his commitment. His strength provided Kathy with more security than he could begin to imagine. He was the sort of man a woman could safely depend on.

She turned away to recapture her wayward thoughts.

A pot of thick soup simmered on the stove. She had brownies baked and hidden in the cupboard—as a treat to go with hot cocoa when they decorated the tree later.

Her self-control firmly in place, she turned to the others.

"Can we decorate now?" Kathy begged.

"Sorry, Kat, Uncle Mac and I have to do chores before dark."

"Aww."

"I'll tell you what. We'll set the tree in place, so as soon as we've eaten we can get right at decorating. How does that sound?"

"I guess I can wait." Kathy managed to pour a great deal of doubt into her words.

"I've got a pail of sand ready." Uncle Mac headed outside.

Derek looked around for a place for the tree. "How about by the window?" He sought Winnie's approval, catching her with her heart too close to the surface.

His eyes narrowed as if he'd read things she could not admit.

She steeled herself to reveal nothing but excitement over Christmas. "What do you think, Kathy?"

"I'd be able to see it when I'm outside, wouldn't I?"

"Sure could." Derek didn't take his eyes off Winnie.

She looked out the window but couldn't stay focused on the distant scene. She allowed herself to glance at the tree. Nice tree. It would look good decorated. Forbidden, her gaze shifted directly to Derek's dark, steady eyes. She couldn't pull away, any more than she could deny she found there something she'd ached for for many, many years.

Slowly he smiled, his teeth a flash of white against his weather-bronzed face.

Her heart split in half and long-denied, always forbidden emotions burst forth. She scrubbed her lips together as her throat tightened with—

No. She only wanted to make this a good Christmas for Kathy. And then she would continue as she'd planned.

No regrets. No pain. No wishing for things that couldn't be hers.

He must have read her determined withdrawal, for his smile soon faded.

She pressed her lips together more tightly and told herself she didn't feel abandoned.

Uncle Mac returned with the pail and the two men struggled to get the tree in place with Kathy's eager help.

Winnie was grateful she had a few moments, unobserved, to get her thoughts and emotions under control.

Satisfied, the men stood back to admire their work.

Kathy clapped her hands. "Now go do chores."

Uncle Mac chuckled. "What's the hurry? I thought I might have a nap first."

Kathy grabbed his hand. "Oh, please, Uncle Mac. Hurry so we can decorate the tree."

Uncle Mac made a great show of yawning and stretching. "It was hard work getting that tree home."

"Uncle Mac." Kathy dragged the words out.

Derek swung her off her feet. "He's teasing you. We're going out right now. You want to help?"

The words were barely out of his mouth before she

dashed for her coat and stood bouncing from foot to foot as she waited.

Uncle Mac chuckled and grabbed his outerwear.

"Think she's having fun yet?" Derek murmured as he passed Winnie.

"Not a bit," she replied.

As soon as the door closed behind them, she collapsed on a chair and buried her face in her hands. *Oh, God, help me. All I want is to give them a good Christmas, help them move forward. Oh, and please, God, let me be able to leave without leaving behind my heart.*

They had never eaten supper in such a hurry, and Winnie promised she would leave the dishes until after the tree was done.

She stood back as Derek handed Kathy decorations and helped her put them in place. The red ball was pushed to one side.

Kathy gave a gold bow to Uncle Mac. "You have to help, too." She handed a wooden toy soldier to Derek.

"You, too." Derek carried a silver metal icicle to Winnie.

She shrank back. Being part of this event would only make it harder to keep herself distanced from them. She shook her head.

But Derek didn't retreat. His eyes filled with dark determination and soft kindness. He wasn't about to take no for an answer, so she took the icicle and slowly circled the tree, pretending to look for the best place.

Uncle Mac and Kathy were too occupied to notice, but she felt Derek's watchfulness, even as he continued to hang ornaments.

She blindly hung the bit of twisted metal. She would not let him guess how difficult this was, how she knew she would not leave without tearing her heart from her chest, leaving it bleeding on the doorstep. But leave she would. She must.

"Do you remember this?" Derek asked as he picked up the red ball.

Kathy nodded, her eyes wide.

Winnie ventured a guess the child had forgotten to breathe.

Kathy took the ball and waited for Derek to lift her so she could hang it high on the tree.

The three of them admired the tree.

Kathy sighed. "Now it's really Christmas."

Winnie hung back and watched. This was what she had wanted to accomplish—help them return to the joy of the season—and if it exacted a price from her, she would not complain.

Kathy turned to Derek. "Do you remember Mama's favorite Christmas song?"

In his rich baritone, Derek sang, "Joy to the world! The Lord is come."

Kathy joined with her thin child's voice. After a few bars, Uncle Mac added a quivery, uncertain sound.

Derek reached out and pulled Winnie to his side. Warm, sheltered, she sang with the others. For just this moment, she would let herself be part of a family. As if she really belonged.

Her voice caught on the words, but she forced herself to continue. Derek's arm tightened across her shoulders and she knew he had heard the strain in her throat.

She slipped away as soon as the song finished. "Anyone for cocoa and brownies?"

The four of them hunkered around the table. It was Saturday, so Kathy was allowed to stay up late.

A sudden memory of childhood flitted across Winnie's mind—just a flash, like a bird startled from an overhead tree branch. She stiffened, tried to capture it, identify it. It hovered, teasingly, then fluttered away. She let out the breath of air she hadn't realized she was holding.

Derek reached across the table and cupped his hand over hers. "Something wrong?"

She shook her head, avoided looking directly at him, lest she see kindness and concern. Such a look would bring the tears. She must never start to cry, for if she did, she would never stop.

"Guess what I'm going to draw in my book tonight?" Kathy asked. It had become a nightly ritual, one that seemed to give them all pleasure as they shared both good and bad from their day.

Kathy opened the pages and drew a big Christmas tree. No surprise there. Nor the prominence of the red ball and four stick people with circle mouths. "To show them singing," she explained.

Then she drew four more stick figures. It seemed two were children—a boy and a girl. The other two adults—a man and a woman hovered above the tree.

"It's Mama, Papa, Peter and Susan having Christmas with us," she said, still concentrating on her drawing.

Winnie felt the waiting stillness of Derek and Uncle Mac matching her own. Would Kathy react to this reminder of her loss?

But Kathy continued to work. Finally, she leaned back, allowing them to see what she'd done. She framed the picture with little drawings of the ornaments and star shapes. "Snowflakes," she explained.

Again, something tickled the edges of Winnie's brain. She grew still, waiting, hoping for the thought to reveal itself.

There was a snowstorm. She remembered that much but no more.

Kathy yawned.

"It's time for one little girl to go to bed," Derek said. "Run and get your nightgown on."

Kathy opened her mouth to protest, then smiled. "I guess I am tired."

Winnie stared at the table before her. The memory had retreated, she realized with a sigh of gratitude.

Derek reached for her hand and she knew he had again been aware of her shift of emotions. Rather than let him touch her, she grabbed the empty cups and stacked them together.

Kathy returned and went to Derek's side. "Are you going to sing Mama's hymn to me?"

It had become another part of the nightly ritual.

"If you'd like."

Kathy hugged and kissed Uncle Mac good-night, then went to Winnie's side to do the same. "Thank you for making Christmas so much fun," she whispered.

Winnie blinked back the moisture in her eyes. Despite her best resolve, she had grown exceedingly fond of this sweet child.

Derek took Kathy to the rocker and held her while he sang. She fell asleep in his arms and he carried her into her room.

Restless, Winnie went to stare out the window. A few fluffy snowflakes drifted toward the ground.

"Maybe we'll get snow for Christmas." Derek stood close. She felt him in every pore. Solid as a rock.

Again, the shadow of a memory flickered. She concentrated on the falling snow, willing the memory to the surface. It was so close. She could almost touch it. She shivered, both afraid of the memory and hungry for it.

He draped an arm across her shoulders. Perhaps he thought her shiver meant she was cold. At his touch, her heart reacted like an overexcited puppy. She should pull away. But she didn't.

"I want to add my thanks to Kathy's. You've made the season one to remember."

She could only nod mute acknowledgment.

She would have to fight hard to forget this season, but forget she must, or turn into a mournful woman.

Chapter Five

The stillness of the night wakened Derek. He slipped from his bed, ignoring the iciness of his room, and padded to the window. Snow. Enough to cover the ground and still falling, promising a perfect Christmas.

Not too long ago he'd dreaded the day. Now, he was almost as eager as Kathy. Thanks to Winnie, he realized he had memories to cherish and carry with him, and an opportunity to create new ones.

Winnie had done so much for him. *Them*, he mentally corrected. Kathy especially.

He recalled the many things she'd done to make their lives more pleasant. He wanted to do something in return. Somehow make the day special for her as well. But what could he do?

He suddenly smiled and returned to bed, but as soon as it was light, he tiptoed out to the barn, selected the appropriate piece of wood. He would honor the Lord's day and wait until Monday to start work on his project.

Kathy waited as he opened the door. "Did you see the snow?"

He shook flakes from his hat to her face. "You mean this wet, sticky stuff?"

She squealed and ducked behind Winnie when he threatened to shake his coat at her.

"It's beautiful out," Winnie said.

Uncle Mac came from his room yawning. "Who can sleep with all this racket?"

Kathy bounced across the room. "Snow. Snow. Snow." She danced to Derek's side. "Let's go play in it."

"Breakfast is ready." Winnie smiled at Kathy's enthusiasm.

"After breakfast. Pleeease." She dragged the word out for ten seconds.

Derek pretended he had to contemplate the question, but the truth was, he couldn't think of any excuse. Playing in the snow with his baby sister sounded just fine. Especially if they could persuade Winnie to join them.

He forced himself to eat slowly, calmly. But something inside him felt as bouncy as Kathy, who teetered precariously and impatiently on the edge of her chair.

The meal over, she dashed for the door and pulled on woolen pants and coat. "Hurry up, Derek."

He shifted his gaze to Winnie. She watched Kathy with affection and maybe just a touch of longing. He couldn't say if the longing took the shape of wanting to belong to a family, or regret at knowing her stay was almost over. But before he got lost in questions he couldn't answer, he spoke. "Winnie, leave the dishes for now and come enjoy the snowfall."

"I'll do them," Uncle Mac offered. "I've enjoyed the scenery often enough. I think it's your turn."

She hesitated a moment, glanced out the window, then smiled. "Sounds like fun."

Kathy raced ahead, dashing from one side of the trail to the other, picking up handfuls of snow, tossing it into the air and letting it fall on her upturned face.

Derek and Winnie laughed.

He took her mittened hand and swung their joined hands.

"There's something about snow."

"You sound as if you aren't sure you like it."

"Oh, it's beautiful. Like a gossamer curtain over the land. But…" She paused. "Something about snow has been tugging at my mind since last night. It's just out of reach. I wish I could recall what it is." Her voice cracked. "Or maybe I don't."

"Sometimes when I push too hard to remember or forget, it makes it impossible to do so."

She laughed. "You mean if I forget about it, I'll remember?"

"Something like that."

"So I need to forget to remember? Or is it remember to forget?"

"Yes."

She jerked his hand. "Oh, you! You're talking in riddles."

He burst out laughing, which brought Kathy to their side.

"What's so funny?"

"Winnie can't remember if she is supposed to remember or forget something."

Kathy shook her head. "That's silly."

"Indeed it is." He tried to make his face appropriately disapproving, but knew he failed.

Winnie's smile caught him in his solar plexus with its gentle sweetness. Despite the sorrows and hardships of her life, she found ways to pour happiness into the lives of others. A true blessing to those she came in contact with.

Kathy grabbed his hand and begged him to play.

They started a game of tag that included Winnie despite her protests. She squealed and raced away when he reached to tag her. He easily overtook her. She stumbled as she tried to escape. He caught her, pulled her close, safe in his arms.

Her breath came in gulps. She rested against his chest until her breathing returned to normal, then she stepped back. "Thank you," she murmured, her gaze lowered.

"My pleasure." His voice had a husky note. He cleared his throat, hoping she would think the cold or snow or exertion caused it. Not a foolish desire to hold her close, keep her safe....

He turned away. He was a miserable failure at keeping his loved ones safe.

Kathy danced by Winnie. "Can't catch me. Can't catch me."

With a speed that surprised both Kathy and Derek, Winnie caught her, trapping her in her arms. Kathy wriggled, trying to escape, while Winnie tickled her and wouldn't let her go.

They both tumbled to the ground in a tangle of arms and legs and giggles.

Derek stared down at the pair, his hands jammed to his hips in mock scolding. "How am I supposed to know whose turn it is?"

They stilled and stared up at him. A second too late, he saw the flash of mischief in Winnie's eyes and the way she squeezed Kathy's hand. Before he could back away, they each grabbed an ankle and yanked. He went down like a tree tackled by an axe. His lungs emptied with a whoosh and he lay staring at the sky.

Kathy plunked to his chest and grinned.

"Two against one. No fair."

"You're bigger."

"Can't say I feel a lot bigger lying on the ground with a half-pint gal on me."

Winnie crept closer, on her hands and knees. "We didn't hurt you, did we?"

He groaned. "I think I busted a rib. Maybe two." He groaned again for good measure.

Winnie knelt beside him, her face wreathed in concern. "Should I get Uncle Mac to assist you to the house?"

He snaked out a hand, grabbed one of her wrists and yanked so that she tumbled to the ground. She grunted and flipped to her back. "You tricked me."

"Guess that makes us even."

Kathy flopped from his chest and rolled to the ground, cuddling close. Winnie lay at his other side, their shoulders barely touching. He stared up into the falling snow, blinking when it landed on his eyelashes. If not for the cold seeping into his limbs, he might be tempted to stay as they were—peaceful and content.

He pushed to his feet, untangling from Kathy's clutches. "I think we'd better go inside and get dried off." He pulled Winnie up and kept her hand in his. He grinned when she made no effort to pull away.

Christmas Eve was on a Sunday, so the church had decided to do the Christmas evening service a week prior to the actual date. Kathy had been bouncing around all afternoon, as if she could make the time go faster by her efforts.

Winnie put the last touches on the cake she would be bringing for the tea after.

Uncle Mac wandered in and out all day, as restless as Kathy.

Derek pretended to read the stack of month-old newspapers, but his mind followed Winnie's movements back and forth. Would she like what he planned to make her? Receive it in the spirit in which he gave it?

And what spirit was that?

Gratitude, he insisted to his mocking mind. Well-wishes for the future. Nothing more. Absolutely nothing more.

He tossed the paper aside.

Winnie gave him a startled look.

"We need new papers," he muttered.

She glanced at the clock over the sofa. He sought the same escape. "Time to get ready."

Kathy dashed to her room. He took his time going to his.

A few minutes later he emerged, a little self-conscious, in his black suit with his new black Stetson. Kathy stepped from her room in a green velvet dress. "Where did you get that?"

"Winnie made it for me." Kathy twirled to show him her dress from every angle. "She did my hair, too."

"Looks good." Brown ringlets tied back by a green bow. "When did she get time to do all that?"

Winnie entered. "It wasn't that difficult."

His eyes widened. Normally Winnie wore a simple frock, which she kept covered by a generous apron. Normally she wore her hair in a simple bun thing, or with braids wrapped about her head and pinned in place, but now... Now she wore a dark red dress with wide sleeves. Now she had her hair parted in the middle and somehow fashioned in rolls behind her ears, making her eyes seem wider. In fact, she was downright attractive. And no doubt every young buck in the territory attending the Christmas service would take note.

A flare of protectiveness seared through his veins. He would be kept busy keeping them away from her tonight.

She backed up, glanced down at her dress. "Is something wrong?"

"No. You look fine. Real fine."

Pink color pooled in her cheeks. "Thank you. So do you."

He turned away as his own face burned. "Where's Uncle Mac?"

"At your service," Mac called from the doorway. "Your ride awaits."

Derek indicated Winnie should go first and reached for Kathy's hand to follow. Winnie stepped outside and gasped, "A sleigh."

"Thought it appropriate for the occasion."

Derek wondered if there was enough snow for the runners but decided it didn't matter. He sat in the middle with Winnie on one side and Kathy on the other. Mac took the reins. Mac had found buffalo robes and Derek covered them with the warm furs.

"This is really like Christmas, isn't it?" Kathy's voice was filled with awe. "I don't see how I'm going to wait one more week."

"Some of us still have things to do," Derek said. He wasn't anxious for the days to fly past. But time did seem to speed up. The trip took far less time than normal.

After Winnie took the cake to the fellowship hall beside the church, they crowded into the sanctuary with most of the community and found a spot big enough for three of them on the end of a pew.

"I'll sit back here." Uncle Mac indicated the pew two rows behind.

They squeezed in, but Derek didn't mind. He liked having both Winnie and Kathy close and safe.

Kathy left after the congregation sang several Christmas hymns. She'd been disappointed she wasn't chosen to be Mary, but Winnie had made her understand Christmas would be pretty dull if there had been only Mary—"No donkeys, no sheep, no shepherds. It would be so empty."

"She's anxious to be a shepherd now," he whispered to Winnie, breathing in the scent of her hair as he leaned close. She smelled as fresh as the snow, as clean as water in the mountain rivers and as sweet as sunshine on a spring meadow.

He pushed his attention back to the front of the church, where one of the older boys began to read the Christmas story as the younger children performed a silent tableau. Well, no doubt it was supposed to be silent, but one little boy dressed as a lamb kept bleating. His shepherdess continually whispered for him to hush. Her whispers grew louder and louder until Derek could hardly keep his amusement silent.

Winnie pressed her hand to her mouth. Her eyes watered with suppressed laughter.

Finally, a red-faced mother marched to the front and jerked the ear of the innocent lamb, who put on the most injured expression Derek could imagine was possible.

Beside him, Winnie shook with silent laughter and squeezed his hand as if she needed to hang on in order to keep from breaking out in loud guffaws. He choked back his own laugh.

And then Mary and Joseph entered and knocked on the paper door. Belatedly, someone off-stage hollered, "Knock, knock."

Derek clamped his fist to his mouth. The fact that someone behind him laughed aloud didn't help his self-control.

"No room. No room." The innkeeper was a red-headed boy with a brown dressing gown bundled at his wrists and drooping on the floor.

The rest of the story proceeded with further amusement, and when it ended, people laughed and clapped.

Winnie pulled her hand from his. She slipped from the pew and headed down the aisle.

He glanced after her. No doubt going to help set up tea. She always sought ways to assist, to make others happy.

Not that he was objecting. Except there was a tiny argument niggling at his thoughts.

Who made *her* happy? Or was she as content as she wanted him to believe? It burned at the back of his throat to think she might not be. He had eight more days to do what he could to give her a taste of happiness—something to carry with her. A memory she could cherish.

The congregation began to move to the fellowship hall. He joined Uncle Mac. Kathy waited for them at the door. Inside the hall, the crush of people made it impossible to locate Winnie. It took several minutes for people to settle themselves at the tables.

Derek glanced about. Winnie wasn't dispensing cake, making tea or pouring water for the children. Perhaps one of the bachelors had latched onto her. He looked around the room again, prepared to take her away from any man who thought to claim her. But he didn't find her in the crowd.

"Have you seen Winnie?" he murmured to Uncle Mac.

"Saw her leave the pew and head outside. Haven't

seen her since." He gave a quick look around the room. "She's not here."

"I'll find her." He told Kathy to stay with their uncle and strode toward the door.

The air outside was a cool relief to the crowded room. Behind him rose the murmur of voices, but two more steps took him into blessed quiet. A muffled sound to his right pulled his attention that direction. Two lads, too old to be in school, too young to be smart, hunkered down over something. Derek turned away. He didn't even want to know what they were doing.

He strode past them, walked around to the front of the church where a lamp shone on the small crèche scene. That's when he saw Winnie kneeling in the snow before the manger, her hands pressed to her face. Her shoulders seemed to move up and down. Was she crying?

With a muffled protest, he hurried to her, knelt at her side and pulled her hands from her face. He touched his finger to her chin and tipped her toward him. Silvery droplets clung to her lashes. He wiped them away with his thumb. The warmth of those salty tears raced along his blood stream and pooled in his heart, crashing like waves of the ocean. "What's wrong?"

She shook her head.

How could he stop her sorrow if he didn't even know what caused it? He pressed her to his shoulder. "I don't want to see you cry."

"I'm done."

"Done or not—"

She shifted toward the manger. "I remember what I wanted to remember about snow. Only maybe I wanted to forget."

He squeezed her closer.

"Snow was falling the day my parents sent me away. I remember looking back and seeing the light in the windows through a veil of snow. I thought I was going to my aunt and uncle's for a special treat. When I got there they told me I had to stay. They said my parents had no room. No room for me." Her voice wavered.

He clamped down on his back teeth until they hurt. How could anyone treat her so callously?

"I thought I would stay with my aunt and uncle, but my new step-aunt said they didn't have room for a child who wasn't theirs. No room." She sobbed once and quieted. "They had no room for baby Jesus either."

She sat up and pulled away from his arms, leaving him helpless. "I won't feel sorry for myself. I'll make my own room." She spoke with determination.

He touched her chin and gently turned her to face him. "You don't have to. There's room with us. Marry me." It made such perfect sense, he wondered why he hadn't realized it from the first.

She blinked, wiped her eyes and stared at him. "What on earth do you mean?"

His smile was one-sided. Was it so hard to contemplate life with him? "Marry me. It's the perfect solution. It would provide Kathy the stability she needs. And it would give you a home."

"What would it give you?"

He cared enough about her to want to keep her safe. The best way he could do that was keep her close. "Figure I'll be happy knowing you and Kathy are taken care of."

She sat up and studied him closely.

He met her gaze steadily. He had nothing to hide. He hadn't offered her love. Only safety and security. Love was going too far. He couldn't do that.

"I recall you saying you didn't want the responsibility of marriage."

"Maybe I've changed my mind."

She continued to study him, her gaze searching his eyes, examining his cheeks, his chin, his mouth and returning to his eyes. "Aren't you afraid of the risks?"

"Didn't you once say we should leave the future in God's hands?"

He hadn't exactly said he was prepared to trust God. Better to take whatever steps he felt were necessary, and marrying Winnie was the only way he could think to keep her safe. His answer seemed to satisfy her for she nodded. "I'll marry you and do my best to make you happy."

He nodded. "Thank you." Considered her sweet, trusting face. "May I kiss you?"

"Of course." She turned to him and he gently claimed her lips. He did not linger, though. Neither of them needed to get the wrong idea about the marriage they had agreed to.

Somehow Winnie made it through the rest of the evening. She must have answered questions correctly, taken part in conversations and held her teacup in an acceptable fashion, because she didn't notice any raised eyebrows or startled looks. Derek stayed close. One thing she could be certain of was his protection.

Neither of them had spoken of love. She didn't expect he would. His only reason for offering marriage was to give Kathy a permanent caregiver.

Her only reason for agreeing was to give herself a permanent home where she would always be welcome.

She wanted no more. Expected no more.

She would never give him cause to regret his offer.

And she would never be so foolish as to expect or demand love. A tiny, almost unheard voice, one she almost managed to ignore, whispered she didn't deserve love.

They had decided not to say anything at church and to wait until morning to tell Uncle Mac and Kathy.

As soon as Kathy had settled for the night, Winnie slipped away to her own room to think. She opened her Bible and searched the scriptures for assurance she was doing the right thing. She turned to the Christmas story in Luke, chapter two. She got as far as "There was no room for them in the inn," and stopped. It was the phrase that had sent her shivering into the cold to kneel before the manger.

She'd cried out her heart to God. Why did no one have room for her? Despite her brave words and determination, she longed for a place where she belonged. She'd begged God to help her. That's when Derek had knelt at her side.

She closed the Bible. She had to believe God had sent Derek, prompted his offer of marriage in answer to her prayer. Comforted, she prepared for bed and fell asleep almost instantly.

"You're going to be my mama? This is the best present ever, and it's not even Christmas yet." Kathy hugged Winnie, then turned to hug Derek. "I knew you wouldn't let her go. So did Uncle Mac. Didn't we, Uncle Mac?"

"I had my hopes for both of you." He hugged Winnie. "He's got a long ways to go yet, but don't give up on him."

"I won't." Though she had no idea what he meant. She thought Derek quite acceptable as he was. If anyone had a long way to go, it was she.

She'd awakened in the night, shivering with apprehension. Would he change his mind and send her away?

Uncle Mac clapped Derek on the back and gave him an awkward hug. "Wise move, my boy. Wise move. Glad to see you listen to an old man's advice occasionally."

Winnie raised her eyebrows.

Derek grinned. "He's been telling me you're the best thing to ever venture into my world."

"She is," Kathy said. "But we despaired of you ever coming to your senses."

At her resigned sigh, they all chuckled.

Later, after dinner, Uncle Mac went to his room for a nap and Kathy shooed them away. "You two go for a walk and make kissy faces, or whatever you're supposed to do. I have something to take care of."

Winnie laughed, even as she knew the heat stealing up her neck would be visible on her face. She wanted to explain their marriage wasn't going to be like that, but Derek grabbed her hand and dragged her outside. "Seems she has important stuff to attend to. We'd better get out of her way and let her do it."

Winnie's heart kicked into a faster pace as Derek took her hand and led her along the snowy path. They paused at the end of the corrals to admire the snow on the mountains.

"Pa dreamed of bringing the family out west. He hoped he'd make it, too. Maybe the air would have cured his lungs."

She squeezed his hand. "Tell me about your father." Mac had said enough for her to know Derek's father had been ill a long time, and more and more of the family responsibility fell on Derek's shoulders.

"He tried hard not to be sick, but by the time I was

seven or eight, he would come home from work and collapse on the bed. I can't imagine how he managed to drag himself to work every day, sometimes shoveling coal for hours. I think his boss must have felt sorry for him and let him drive the delivery wagon. By the time I was twelve he could no longer do it, and I took his place. I hoped if he could rest he would get better. But he didn't. Uncle Mac said his lungs were shot."

"Some things you can't change." The words were empty, meaningless, but she didn't dare offer what she really wanted to—her assurance she would always stand by his side. The best she could do was lean against his shoulder.

"On his deathbed, Pa asked me to do two things. One was to look after the family. I've certainly failed."

"Because of the accident? You can hardly control the universe. Only God can."

"So why doesn't He?" His words tore through her.

"God hasn't forgotten you."

He shrugged. "I couldn't believe it when I got the news. Uncle Mac went with me to take care of the bodies and get Kathy. It's amazing she escaped without a scratch."

"We should always be thankful for God's intervention."

He stared down at her. "You're right. I'm ever so grateful Kathy survived."

Tension eased from her stomach as he smiled. "What was the other thing your father asked of you?"

"To move the family out west. He wanted Uncle Mac and me to continue with their plans. Uncle Mac came ahead and got this place ready. Then I came out to make sure things were suitable. Ma and the kids followed." His voice deepened.

"I think your father would be very proud of you."

"You do?"

"Certainly. You've never shirked from the responsibility his illness and death thrust upon you. You've done your best to fulfill his dream of giving them a new life. He would certainly not hold you responsible for things beyond your control, any more than you would hold Kathy responsible for the accident that killed the others."

"Of course I wouldn't. What a dreadful thing to suggest."

"Exactly my point."

He grew still, as if he didn't dare breathe. She prayed he would see the truth in her words—he couldn't blame himself for things beyond his power to control. "I see what you mean." Suddenly he laughed. "I have not disappointed my father." He hugged her. "Thank you. You've given me so much. I wish I could give you more."

"You give me all I need." Perhaps not all she wanted, but she was only now beginning to understand what it was she wanted.

He rested his chin on her head and looked about. "It's a good land. A good place to raise Kathy."

He hadn't mentioned having children of their own. Of course not. Their marriage was simply a business deal. He did not want more responsibility. Even as she did not want the risk of admitting she loved him.

Chapter Six

Derek turned her to face him and looked so long and hard at her that she lowered her gaze.

"What's wrong? Have you changed your mind?" She wouldn't be surprised if he did.

"No. Of course not." He brushed his knuckles along her jaw. "I'm not the sort to back out of a promise."

She knew that. "I wouldn't want you to feel beholden, just because you said something and later changed your mind."

"The only thing I'm 'holding' right now is you. And I'm thinking it was no mistake you ended up in my barn that night." His fingers lingered at her earlobe, then he cupped the back of her head and leaned close.

She knew he meant to kiss her. Not to seal a marriage agreement. No. This time it was gratitude that she'd landed in his life and proven herself valuable to Kathy's happiness. But she didn't mind. Being valued for any reason made her feel safe. She met his kiss halfway.

His lips were warm. His kiss tentative, gentle. She leaned closer, wrapped her arms about his neck and let her kiss speak her heart.

But then she pulled back, appalled at her own behavior. She'd only meant to inform him she appreciated his kindness. "We should return."

He kept his arm across her shoulders as they walked to the house. Surely, he was only being kind. Protective. He would always be protective out of a sense of duty. He would never guess the simple gesture flooded her heart with impossible longings.

She ached for more than a safe home. She wanted to be loved.

Slowly, she took a deep breath. She would not allow herself to discount the gift Derek had given her—an offer of marriage, a place of permanency—by wishing for more.

They reached the house. He opened the door and they stepped inside. The table was set, china teacups that normally sat far back on the top shelf had been washed and set out. Two of them. Kathy had covered a sheet of brown paper with hundreds of flowers to use as a tablecover.

"Surprise," Kathy called.

Uncle Mac leaned against the door frame, grinning.

"What's the occasion?" Derek asked.

"It's a 'gagement party. Miss Parker at school told us about the 'gagement party she went to for her friend." Kathy's eagerness fled, replaced by uncertainty. "I wanted to do something special for you."

"What a wonderful idea." Winnie hugged Kathy. "We really appreciate it, don't we, Derek?" She shot the startled man a prodding look.

He blinked. "Of course we do."

"Good. Sit down beside each other and Uncle Mac and I will serve you."

Feeling like a cross between royalty and a Barnum and Bailey circus act, Winnie sat, Derek beside her.

Uncle Mac stepped forward as if he'd been coached, and poured tea. Kathy brought a plate of cookies from the cupboard. "I wanted to make some for you, but Uncle Mac said to use the ones Winnie made."

"Probably a good thin—" Derek began. Winnie plowed her elbow into his ribs in time to stop him. "This is fine. Just fine."

They each selected a cookie and took a bite.

Kathy waited, facing them across the table. Winnie sipped her tea, nudged Derek to do the same. She stole a glance at him and wished she hadn't. He looked as awkward as if he'd been dropped into the ladies' home sewing circle. She had to press her lips together to keep from laughing.

Kathy sighed. "I wanted this to be special."

"We'll never forget this, will we, Derek?" Another nudge to his ribs—gentle this time.

"Not as long as we live."

Winnie concentrated on her teacup so Kathy wouldn't guess at how hard she struggled to contain her amusement.

Kathy pulled out a chair and sat across from them, her elbows planted on the table, her chin resting in her palms. "Tell me about getting 'gaged. Miss Parker says it's romantic when the man who loves you asks you to marry him." Kathy sighed dreamily. "Was it romantic?" She pinned Winnie with the question.

"Indeed it was."

Derek sputtered tea and grabbed for his handkerchief to wipe his eyes.

Winnie gave him a narrow-eyed scowl. So maybe he didn't see the romance in sitting in the snow, blurting out an offer to marry, but the way he'd held her, the way he'd tenderly wiped tears from her cheeks, and the gentle kiss, were romantic even if they weren't meant to be.

"Tell me," Kathy begged.

"I think they might want to keep the details private for now," Uncle Mac said.

"Aww."

"I can share one thing." Derek nudged Winnie.

Her heart tightened. Was he going to tell the truth? That their planned marriage wasn't based on romance?

He grinned at her, then turned back to Kathy, leaned on his elbows and got dreamy eyed. "Snow was falling, and each little flake that landed on Winnie's skin looked like a tiny diamond from heaven."

Winnie stared, realized her mouth had dropped open, and closed it. The man had a poetic streak in him. What other talents was he hiding?

Kathy let out an expansive sigh. "That's romantic. Now you have to kiss."

"Kiss?" Winnie tried not to sputter. "Why?"

"Miss Parker said that's how you make the 'gagement 'fficial."

Derek edged his chair closer. "You don't mind, do you?" he murmured in her ear.

He was so close, she saw the ebony lights in his eyes, as well as a healthy dose of teasing. She scrubbed her lips together. A kiss? In public? That would make it official?

Derek took her silence for agreement. He cupped her head with his steady hand and leaned forward. His kiss was firm. Solid. Full of promise.

He eased back and grinned at her.

She swallowed hard. Promise for what? Taking care of her? Giving her a home? She lowered her gaze, lest he see confusion and longing in her eyes.

* * *

Derek hummed as he worked on Winnie's gift.

"Good to hear you so happy." Uncle Mac had slipped up behind him unnoticed. The old man had a knack for doing that of late.

"'Course I'm happy."

"Thanks to Winnie."

"Yup." Knowing she was staying solved a lot of his worries.

Uncle Mac shuffled off and Derek returned to his work and his happy thoughts.

The past three days had been pleasant beyond expectation. There was something about walking into the house, knowing Winnie would glance up and smile a welcome. Knowing he could expect the same face, the same smile in the future. Kathy had settled down, back to the cheerful child he recalled before the accident.

He and Winnie went for walks in the early afternoon and often again after supper. So far, the weather had not grown too cold for them to venture out. They talked about their past and planned their future. He learned about the homes she'd been in and understood she tried to make herself indispensible so they would appreciate her and keep her.

He sat up straight and faced forward. If any one of the homes had valued her, she would not be here. Seems the bad things in her life ended up a benefit for him. He rubbed his neck, trying to ease the sudden tightness, feeling selfish to be grateful for his sake, when it had cost her so deeply.

Something she'd said echoed in his head. "We never know how God is using the events of our lives. We could make ourselves crazy trying to make sense of things like accidents and injuries. Or we can accept that God is in control, and even if we never understand the whys, or see the good in something that's come our way, at least we can rest in His love and leave the questions with Him."

Tension eased from his neck. He might take a while to truly learn that lesson, but he intended to start working on it.

The sound of an approaching wagon pulled his attention from his thoughts. Visitors? He didn't see how news of his engagement could have reached his neighbors. With no school for a few weeks, Kathy hadn't been able to tell anyone, and they hadn't been off the ranch since Sunday.

Best go see who it was. He set aside his work, threw a blanket over it to hide it from curious eyes and went outside.

"Hello, Derek. A few days early but Merry Christmas."

"Hello, Sam, Jean. Merry Christmas to you, too. Come on in and visit."

Sam lived further up the river. He jumped down and helped to the ground the wife he had sent for last spring.

As Jean smoothed her skirts, he saw she was in the family way.

A baby. Marriage often resulted in one. He swallowed hard, realized he was staring, then led the way to the house.

"We have guests," he told Winnie, who was already pulling the kettle forward on the stove.

He couldn't take his eyes off her. Would she like to make a baby with him? He hadn't thought of marriage as anything more than having a permanent housekeeper. A way to keep Winnie close.

His cheeks burned as he thought of becoming a real family.

A baby. But wasn't birth risky?

He jerked his gaze from Winnie and his thoughts from treacherous paths. He intended to avoid such risks.

"Sam and Jean, this is Winnie Lockwood, my fiancée," he said, with an air of possessiveness.

"Fiancée? Well, congratulations." Sam slapped Derek's back and shook Winnie's hand.

Jean shyly offered her hand to Derek. He shook it gently, then she turned to Winnie and hesitated. With a little giggle, she hugged Winnie. "I hope you'll be as happy as I am."

Winnie's gaze met Derek's, her eyes dark and bottomless. He couldn't read her emotions. He only knew it felt like an accusation and drove a harsh fist into his gut.

Then she smiled. "I'm sure we'll be very happy." She extricated herself from Jean's arms. "I'm just making tea. Sit and visit."

Sam held a chair for his wife and eased her gently onto the seat.

Derek didn't move. The gentleness in his friend's care was like watching a mare with a newborn foal—a combination of tenderness and responsibility. Seems the idea of a baby made Sam aware of the load he would carry. Though looking at the man, one would think he relished the idea.

Uncle Mac came in and greeted the pair, then Kathy joined them.

They visited over tea and cookies. Jean wanted to know where Winnie had come from and what brought her to the Adams's ranch.

He waited for her reply, wondering how much of the truth she would tell.

She smiled at him, then turned to Jean. "You might

say God led me here. I actually had other plans." She told about her desire to work in Banff.

He hadn't thought of her initial goal. Was he asking too much of her, to give up her dream to marry him?

In turn, Jean told how she and Sam had met at her father's house a year before their marriage. "My brother had come west. He's got a place down by Pincher Creek. Sam wanted details, as he was thinking of moving west. Mother was out, so I served them tea. You might say I liked what I saw."

Sam took her hand. "No more than I."

Kathy let out a long sigh. "It's so…"

He knew she was going to say "romantic". And given half a chance, she'd be asking for details, likely to repeat every tidbit to Miss Parker, who seemed to need to get her adventures vicariously. He didn't want to embarrass his guests. "Kathy, would you pass the cookies again, please?"

Kathy shot him a surprised look, but she must have read the warning in his face, for she clamped her lips together and passed the plate to Jean, who took one.

"These are delicious."

"Derek's favorites," Winnie said.

"So you make them often." Jean giggled, as if Winnie made the cookies specially for that reason.

Ginger cookies. Soft and moist. They *were* his favorite, and come to think of it, seems there were always some to accompany his tea. Did she make them solely for him?

But as Uncle Mac took four more, Kathy—at his warning nod—took one and the guests each took one more, he knew he wasn't the only one who liked them. She liked to please others. Not just him.

Why didn't that make him feel better?

Sam cleared his throat. "We brought you a present. But before I give it to you, I want you to know it's fine to say no."

What sort of gift would a person say no to? Unless…

Sam went outside and returned with a small crate. From inside came excited yips.

Unless—he finished his thought—it was a pup.

"We rescued a pair of puppies from an old man up the river. He was going to drown them."

Kathy gasped.

"Sorry, Kathy, but as he said, he had no use for three dogs. We picked one to keep, but thought you folks might like the other." He faced Derek squarely. "If you prefer not, we're fine with that. Just thought we'd give you first chance at refusal."

Kathy had bolted to her feet and rocked back and forth in front of Sam. "Can we see him?"

"Derek?" Sam asked.

He'd had a dog once. Remembered how much fun it had been. If this mutt was friendly with Kathy, he might consider the idea. "Let's have a look."

Sam put the crate down and removed the lid. A furry brown-and-black bundle scampered out and turned circles on the floor, as if assuring himself he was free. He saw Kathy and wriggled up to her, whining.

Kathy scooped him into her arms, where he wiggled and tried to lick her.

It was a done deal. No way he could take that bundle of joy away from his little sister, but he needed to ask Winnie her opinion first. He turned to her. She watched Kathy, a smile of such sweetness on her face that Derek forgot his question. She truly cared for Kathy. He'd never doubted it, but seeing how it flooded her expression gave him a wonderful sense of doing the right thing by marrying her.

She jerked toward him and her frank love went into hiding.

He obviously did not warrant the same emotion Kathy did. "Would you mind Kathy having a pup?"

She smiled. "Not at all." She stroked the puppy's head. "He's sweet."

"Can I keep him? Really?" Kathy asked.

"Let me have a look at him." He took the pup and examined his limbs, looked in his mouth and ears, which proved a challenge, as the dog wanted to lick him and almost wriggled from his arms.

Kathy giggled. "He says he's healthy. No need to check."

Satisfied as to the general condition of the animal, he let the pup snuggle into the crook of his arm, where it snuffled once and fell to sleep.

Sam chuckled. "He knows he's safe."

"Home sweet home," Jean said.

Home. Safety. It's what he wanted for himself, for Kathy and for Winnie. It was enough. Wasn't it?

He passed the pup back to Kathy and she sat on the floor to play with him.

The women turned their attention to talk of Christmas plans.

"I wish I could get a turkey," Winnie said. "It would make a special Christmas meal."

"You can. Tell them, Sam." Jean turned to her husband, her face aglow with love.

Sam's gaze lingered on his wife before he turned to Derek. "You remember that German family that took up a homestead over on Bear Coulee?"

He nodded. Of course he did. He wondered how they

would make it. Starting from nothing, with half a dozen kids to provide for.

"They raised turkeys and are selling them. I can tell them to butcher one for you if you like. You just have to pick it up before noon on Christmas Eve day."

At the look of eagerness in Winnie's eyes, he would have agreed to ride to Calgary to pick up the bird. "Tell them we'll take one."

Winnie's smile of appreciation made him feel he had done something special.

He shook his head. All this confusion was only because he had agreed to more responsibility. First marriage to Winnie, and now a puppy.

He was afraid to think about how many things could go wrong.

Chapter Seven

Winnie had the house to herself. Derek and Kathy had taken the pup, christened Beau, for a walk. The pup would provide Kathy with lots of company. Just what the little girl needed. After all, she'd once had a brother and sister to play with.

Winnie appreciated meeting Sam and Jean. Nice to know there were other young couples in the neighborhood, even if their situations were different. Sam was so in love with Jean, Winnie's eyes hurt to watch how he did his best to anticipate and meet her every need.

And Jean had confided her love for Sam. "My heart can only work the way it should when he's around." She'd laughed. "I'm sure you know what I mean."

Winnie bent over the shirt she meant to finish for Uncle Mac for Christmas. She did know what Jean meant. Despite her fears and caution, she'd fallen in love with Derek. Her love required sacrifice from her.

How was she to tell Derek she couldn't marry him?

She prayed for the right words. For the courage.

She heard Derek and Kathy returning and slipped her sewing basket out of sight. She hoped to surprise them all with her gifts.

The pair burst into the room. Beau raced around, checking to make sure he remembered the place.

"I just thought of something," Derek said. "I need to wire the Faringtons to let them know I no longer need them. Do you want to come to town with me?"

"I need to get popcorn." She had to tell him before they reached town.

"Do you want to go, Kathy?"

"Can I stay home with Beau?"

"If Uncle Mac wants to stay."

Uncle Mac came from his room, his hair tousled from his nap. "Did I hear someone say my name?"

Derek explained.

"I'll gladly remain and watch this pair of youngsters."

"It's settled then." Derek went to his room to get his purse and Winnie scurried to hers to tidy her hair. She paused to look in the mirror and forced herself to take a slow, steady breath. *Lord, give me courage.*

Derek chose the sleigh again. A new snowfall made the road suitable for the conveyance.

She climbed in beside him and let him tuck the robes around her knees. Gave a shaky smile when he paused, his face close enough to kiss.

Only he didn't kiss her. Instead, he flicked the reins and they glided down the road. He'd hung bells on the harness. She settled back, allowing herself to enjoy this ride. The last ride she would make as part of his family.

Her nerves twitched as they neared town. She must speak to him before he sent the telegram. Twice she opened her mouth, but the words wouldn't come.

She squeezed her fists open and closed. *Now.* She must do it now. She reached for his hand to ask him to stop.

He misinterpreted her gesture and turned his hand to twine his fingers through hers.

She closed her eyes and prayed for strength to do what she knew she must do. But her heart grew stubborn and insisted she enjoy his touch, his smile and the way he shifted closer so their shoulders and arms pressed together.

She shuddered at all she must give up.

"Are you cold?" He reached around her to tuck the robe tighter.

"Derek, stop."

He jerked back. "I'm sorry. I thought you were cold."

"No. Stop the sleigh."

He pulled on the reins and the horses stood still, steam blasting from their nostrils.

She mustn't take too long or the horses would get chilled. "I don't think you should send that wire."

He twisted to face her. "To the Faringtons?"

She nodded, wishing she had more courage.

"Why not?" His eyes narrowed. "You've changed your mind, haven't you?"

"I must. You deserve to marry someone you can love."

He contemplated her silently.

She lowered her gaze and studied the buttons on the front of his coat. Big. Black. Her sluggish mind could think of nothing more. "I don't want to tie you into a marriage of convenience."

"Isn't that *my* decision? Perhaps it's all I want. I fully intend to send that wire today." He turned and flicked the reins. "I expect you to keep your word. Just as I intend to keep mine."

Her heart lay leaden in her chest. She had succeeded only in making him angry. What was she to do?

They arrived in town. He stopped in front of the store, jumped down and went around to assist her. She put her hand in his, felt him stiffen. "I'm sorry," she murmured.

His hard expression didn't flicker. "Get the popcorn and whatever else you need. I'll be back as soon as I send the wire."

She got what she came for, put it on Derek's bill and then waited for him without even bothering to glance at anything else in the store. There was no pleasure in even looking. In two minutes he returned, helped her in and tucked the robe around her. He would always make sure she was safe, even if he was angry.

Derek avoided the house as much as possible that evening and the next morning. He wished he didn't have to spend time with Kathy and the pup, forcing him to be in the same room as Winnie. To feel her wish to leave. Was Banff so enticing?

He could hardly wait until he could leave to get the turkey and rode out of the yard at a gallop. He slowed as soon as he was out of sight.

How could he persuade her to stay?

By telling her he loved her.

The words blared through his brain.

Love? He had loved his family and lost them, except for Kathy. If anything happened to her, he would break into a million little pieces.

If he loved Winnie, he'd face the same agony.

He couldn't endure it.

He reached his destination, paid the German and headed home with the turkey, refusing to think any further about love. All he had to do was convince her that a marriage of convenience was the best solution for them both.

No risks.

Except to hurt her by not giving her the very thing she needed. Not a permanent home. Not appreciation. Love.

He shook his head. It was the one thing he couldn't give.

He arrived home and handed Winnie the turkey.

"Thank you." She barely let her gaze touch him before she returned inside.

It suited him just fine. He needed time alone. He headed for the barn.

He must finish her gift tonight. He slapped his hat on his thigh. His gift would convince her they could make memories based on something besides love.

He hunkered down on the wooden seat in the corner of the barn and set to work.

Jesus loves you.

Where had that come from?

The words came again. *Jesus loves you.*

Even when things go wrong?

He sat up and stared in the distance, seeing nothing. His heart waited. His thought stalled. A thousand bits and pieces flooded his brain. Jesus becoming flesh and being born a baby. Jesus coming to the world He made and being rejected. Jesus dying on the cross.

Jesus loves you.

Even though it cost Him His life, Jesus loved him.

He wiped away tears he didn't know he cried until they dripped from his chin.

How did God feel when He sent His son to earth, knowing He would endure such horrible things? What a sacrifice it had been for the Father. All to give salvation, hope and an answer to fears. What a shame if people ignored the gift.

What a waste if he refused to let love into his heart.

He breathed deeply. *Lord, forgive my anger at You. Thank You for sparing Kathy. I give You my future to hold in Your hands of love.*

The cracks in his heart mended, and he could look at the truth: he loved Winnie so much it scared him.

Dare he let her into his heart? Risk loving and losing? Feeling he couldn't protect those he loves?

Could he choose to trust God and accept the gifts sent his way. Like Kathy, Uncle Mac and—

Winnie?

He smiled. He might be a fool at times, but he wasn't a big enough one to throw away the chance to love Winnie.

All he had to do was find a way to convince her.

He returned to work on his project. *Please God, I know I don't have the right to ask favors after I've been so stubborn and prideful, but help me tell her how much I love her and let her be willing to make a marriage between us work.*

He finished his original project and added one more thing. Then he went in for supper.

The house was warm and friendly. Kathy and Beau raced over to greet him. Uncle Mac looked up from the table where he was writing something on a piece of paper and nodded.

Winnie waited for him to look at her, and then smiled, tentatively, as if she expected him to still be angry. When her eyes grew wide, he knew he hadn't been able to hide how he felt.

Now for a chance to explain. Perhaps once the others went to bed, but no one wanted to go to bed early.

Winnie popped corn and they gathered around the tree.

Kathy wanted to sing the Christmas songs she remembered their mama singing. Derek's heart softened at the memories. It was sweet to have good things in his past.

Better yet to anticipate good things in the future.

They finished singing and grew silent.

Kathy lay on the floor, her head cradled against Beau.

Derek leaned over to look closely. "She's fallen asleep. I'll take her to bed."

"I'm ready to hit the hay myself." Uncle Mac stretched and yawned.

Derek hesitated. He did not want Winnie to leave before he got back. "Wait for me?"

She nodded. He couldn't make out her expression well enough in the dim light to know if the idea frightened or appealed.

He hoped she would think it the latter by the time he finished.

Kathy barely stirred as he slipped her dress off, eased her nightgown over her head and pulled the covers to her chin.

He paused at her doorway to calm his nerves. Now that he had admitted he loved Winnie, he realized how much he had to lose if she didn't return his feelings.

But he would not let fear deprive him of this opportunity.

He stepped into the main room. Ensconced in the wooden rocker, she turned and gave a tentative smile.

"I'll be right back." He grabbed a lantern and trotted to the barn to grab his gift.

Returning, he burst into the house and forced himself to slow down. Suddenly he didn't know how he was going to present the gift, what words would express his heart.

She waited, watching him.

He had to do something, say something. "I made this for you." He placed the present in her lap.

He felt awkward towering above her, forcing her to tip her head to look at him, so he squatted at her knees. "Unwrap it."

She folded back the towel he'd covered it with.

"A box."

"A memory box." He tipped the lid toward her so she could read the words.

"Winnie's Memories."

"I remember you saying how we should keep the old memories and add new ones, or something like that."

She stroked the wood he had sanded and polished to a fine patina. "It's lovely. Thank you. I have something for you, too."

But he held both arms of the chair and trapped her in place. "There's more. Open the box."

She lifted the lid and pulled out a carved wooden heart.

He swallowed hard as he sought for the right words. "It's my heart." He plucked it from her palm. "I give you my heart." He pressed it back into her hand and curled her fingers around it. "I love you with my whole heart. I want to marry you because I love you and want to share my life with you."

The seconds ticked by. She shifted her gaze back and forth from her hand clutching the heart to his eyes. He couldn't read her thoughts. But if he had to guess, he would venture to say he'd frightened her.

"I hope you'll learn to love me. I'm willing to wait for that day. In fact, I want to marry you, love you and take care of you for the rest of my life, even if you never return my love."

She nodded.

He pulled her to her feet, keeping her within the circle of his arms. "There is no pressure. My love is free. No obligation." He wanted to kiss her, but he wanted her to know he would not take advantage of her in any way. "Now, off to bed, and I'll see you Christmas morning."

"Your present—"

"Give it to me then."

There was only one Christmas present he wanted.

He loved her.

Winnie stared into the darkness.

No one ever loved her before. No one except God.

Others had said they did. She recalled her mother saying it and then giving her away. Her aunt and uncle had never spoken actual words of love, but said how precious she was. "A gift from God." Until their own babies came. The others hadn't pretended to love her. She wouldn't have believed them if they said they did.

She didn't trust the words. Far easier to live pretending love didn't exist.

She clutched the wooden heart to her chest.

I give you my heart.

She shook but not from cold. From nerves.

Could she trust love?

Lord, this is everything I've ever wanted, but I am so afraid it isn't real. Or it might not last. Please send me an answer so I know what to do. What to say.

Derek said he was willing to accept a marriage without her love, but it wasn't that she didn't love him.

She was afraid if she spoke the words aloud the dream would vanish.

How can I be sure it won't?

Her thoughts circled endlessly.

She focused on the season. Christmas.

Glory to God in the highest and on earth peace, good will toward men.

Jesus—God in flesh. A gift. To bring us peace. Peace with God. The peace of God.

The words mocked her. She had no peace.

Trust in God.

She did trust God. She had most of her life.

But you don't trust God to be able to work through others. You want only to let Him into your heart.

She had good reason to distrust people.

But if she wanted the one thing she needed—love and belonging—she had to trust God would keep both her and Derek in the palm of His hand.

Was that too much to trust Him for?

She knew the answer to her question. Peace descended and sleep finally claimed her.

She woke to Kathy calling, "It's Christmas morning! Get up, everyone, so we can open gifts. Hey, where are the gifts?"

The adults had decided not to place them under the tree until morning so as not to tempt Beau to explore.

Winnie dressed hurriedly, as anxious for the day as Kathy, but for an entirely different reason. Scooping up her parcels, she hurried from her room. Uncle Mac and Derek stepped from theirs at the same time, both with arms full as well.

"Merry Christmas," they said in unison.

Winnie laughed. She suspected her eyes overflowed with joy for the day.

"Hurry, hurry," Kathy called.

Laughing, the three of them hurried to the tree and deposited the gifts. Already the smell of the turkey cooking filled the room. She was glad she'd put it in the oven the night before. The aroma made Christmas more real.

Beau caught Kathy's excitement and tore around the room yapping. Derek caught him and held him to calm him.

"Can I open a gift now?"

Everyone agree Kathy should go first. She opened the biggest one, which was from Uncle Mac—a nice bed with a little mattress for Beau.

The next one was from Derek. She folded back the paper to find a real drawing book with thick, smooth pages. "Ohh, I can hardly wait to draw in it."

Then she took the gift Winnie handed her. She unwrapped a rag doll complete with cherry-red cheeks and black braids, her dress of the same material as Kathy's new dress. "I love her! Thank you." She hugged each of the adults.

"I made everyone something." She passed them each a gift. They opened up drawings. She had not drawn stick figures. In fact, her drawings were quite good. Derek's showed him riding his horse. Uncle Mac leaned against a fence before the barn. Winnie stood in front of the house, the mountains rising behind it. She looked like she was welcoming someone home. Kathy had titled it *"Home, Sweet Home."*

"How lovely. I'll find a nice frame and hang it where I can see it every day. In fact, we'll frame all three of them."

The men had gifts for each other—a new lariat for Derek, a new belt for Uncle Mac.

Uncle Mac gave Winnie a nice serving tray.

She gave Uncle Mac his gift from her. He displayed his new shirt proudly.

The last gift was for Derek. He pulled out a shirt. "It's fine. Really fine." She hoped he was pleased.

"Try it on."

He shook the folds out and a small package fell to his lap. He opened it. Her aunt had given her the small hanging that Winnie had carried with her since she left her uncle's house. The edges were dog-eared, and stained where she had pressed her finger to it many times. "I'm sorry it's not new."

He read the words aloud. "'Many waters cannot quench love, neither can the floods drown it.' Song of Solomon, eight, verse seven."

"All my life I have hoped and prayed for that kind of love. I have found it here. Thank you." She meant to include them all, but couldn't tear her gaze from Derek's dark eyes.

Uncle Mac cleared his throat and pushed to his feet. "Kathy, I think Beau needs to go for a walk."

Winnie barely noticed the pair leave the house, with Beau tearing out the door ahead of them.

Derek slowly rose and stood before her. He pulled her to her feet and held her shoulders. "Winnie, do you mean to say you love me?"

"I certainly do. I've known for a while, but feared to trust it."

"No more fears?"

"God has given me what I always wanted. I'd be foolish to throw away such a wonderful gift."

Derek sought her gaze hungrily. She knew he waited to hear the words—the same words that had melted the resistance in her heart. "I love you, Derek Adams. I will gladly share your life, help raise your little sister and build a solid home here in the west."

He still kept her at arm's length. "Winnie, I promise to love and protect you always. You and any children God blesses our union with. You have completed my life and given me real happiness."

He finally pulled her close and she lifted her face to meet his kiss, giving her whole heart into their promise.

* * * * *

Dear Reader,

In an earlier book, *The Path To Her Heart*, I mentioned the tragedy of children taken from families against their will. It got me to thinking of children who suffered even worse—given away by parents because of economic or health restrictions. Thus Winnie was born. Okay, created. I wanted to tell her story but to set it in a positive light. What better way than to give her Christmas?

I love the simple message of Christmas—God's love sent to us in the form of a baby. Yet so often I miss the simplicity of the message as I add commercialism, consumerism and other-isms. Writing this story was a joy because my characters brought me back to the true meaning of the season. Wouldn't it be great if all of us could get down to the basics of love and joy this Christmas? I pray that will be the case in my family and yours.

I like to hear from readers. Contact me through email at linda@lindaford.org or lindaford@airenet.com. Feel free to check on updates and bits about my research at my website www.lindaford.org.

Linda Ford

HER HEALING WAYS

Lyn Cote

To Irene, Gail, Lenora, Patt, Carol, Kate, Val, Lois and Marty! Thanks for being my friends.

There is no difference between
Jews and Gentiles, between slaves and free men,
between men and women; you are
all one in union with Christ.
—*Galatians* 3:28

Also, if two lie down together, they will keep warm.
But how can one keep warm alone? Though one
may be overpowered, two can defend themselves.
A cord of three strands is not quickly broken.
—*Ecclesiastes* 4:11–12

Chapter One

Idaho Territory, September 1868

High on the board seat, Mercy Gabriel sat beside the wagon master on the lead Conestoga. The line of the supply train slowed, pulling into the mining town Idaho Bend. Panicky-looking people ran toward it with bags and valises in hand. What was happening here? Like a cold, wet finger, alarm slid up Mercy's spine.

She reached down and urged her adopted daughter, Indigo, up onto the seat beside her, away from the onrushing people. Though almost sixteen now, Indigo shrank against Mercy, her darker face tight with concern. "Don't worry," Mercy whispered as confidently as she could.

She looked down at a forceful man who had pushed his way to the front. He was without a coat, his shirtsleeves rolled up and his colorfully embroidered vest buttoned askew. From the flamboyant vest, she guessed he must be a gambler. What would he want with them?

With one sweeping glance, he quelled the people shoving each other to get closer to the wagons. A commanding gambler. In her opinion, an unusual combination.

"Are there any medical supplies on this train?" he asked in a calm tone at odds with the mood of the people crowding around. "Two days ago, we telegraphed to Boise, asking for a doctor to come. But no one has. We've got cholera."

The dreaded word drenched the brave, brawny wagoners; they visibly shrank back from the man. It set off the crowd clamoring again.

Mercy's pulse raced. *No, not cholera.* Yet she hesitated only a second before revealing the truth about herself. Until this moment, she'd just been another traveler, not an object of mirth, puzzlement or derision. She braced herself for the inevitable reactions and rose. "I am a qualified physician."

Startled, the frantic crowd stopped pushing. As usual, every head swiveled, every face gawked at her.

"You?" the gambler challenged. "You're a woman."

Mercy swallowed a number of sardonic responses to this silly comment. She said, "I am a recent graduate of the Female Medical College of Pennsylvania. I also worked alongside Clara Barton as a nurse throughout the Civil War."

"You nursed in the war?" The gambler studied her, a quizzical expression on his face.

"Yes." Leaning forward, she held out her gloved hand. "I am Dr. Mercy Gabriel. And this is my assistant, Nurse Indigo."

He hesitated only a moment. Then, reaching up, he grasped her hand for a firm, brief handshake. "Beggars can't be choosers. I'm Lon Mackey. Will you come and help us?"

She wondered fleetingly why a gambler was taking charge here. She would have expected a mayor or—

Renewed commotion from the crowd, almost a mob now, grabbed her attention. People were trying to climb aboard the supply wagons. "Get us out of this town!" one of them shouted.

No, that would be disastrous! "Stop them," Mercy ordered, flinging up a hand. "No one from this town should be allowed to leave. They could infect everyone on the supply train and spread the disease to other towns."

At this, the wagoners rose and shouted, "Keep back! Quarantine! Quarantine!"

This only spurred the people of the mining town to try harder.

The head wagoner put out an arm, keeping Mercy and Indigo from getting down. "Wagoners, use your whips!"

The drivers raised their whips and snapped them expertly toward the mob. Mercy was horrified. Still muttering mutinously, the crowd fell back until safely out of range. Mercy swallowed her fear, her heart jumping.

"We will unload the shipment of supplies," the wagon master barked, "then we're leaving for the next town right away. And we're not taking on any new passengers."

People looked ready to make another charge toward the train, their expressions frantic, desperate.

"Thee must not give in to fear," Mercy declared. "There is hope. I am a qualified physician and my nurse is also trained." A silent Mercy stood very straight, knowing that her petite height of just over five feet didn't add much to her presence.

"You have nothing to fear, Dr. Gabriel," Lon Mackey

announced, pulling a pistol from his vest. "I came to see if anyone could send us assistance. I didn't expect a doctor to be on the supply train. Please come. Lives are at stake."

Mercy moved to descend from the high buckboard. The wagon master let her go, shaking his head. Again he raised his whip as if ready to defend her. Barely able to breathe, Mercy descended, with Indigo in her wake. She addressed Lon Mackey. "I have medical supplies with me. Someone will need to get my trunk from the wagon."

"Get her trunk!" Lon ordered. "We need help. Thirteen people have already died in only three days."

The wagon master roared names, and another two wagoners got down and started to unload Mercy's trunk, one cracking his whip to keep people back. The sullen mob still appeared ready to rush the wagons.

"No new passengers! Now back off or I start shooting!" The wagon master waved his pistol at the people about to surge forward. The sight of the gun caused a collective gasp. The mob fell back.

A wagoner pulled Mercy's bright red trunk, which was on casters, to her and Indigo. He touched the wide brim of his leather hat. "Good luck, ma'am."

Lon Mackey, also brandishing his pistol, led Mercy and Indigo through the crowd.

Indigo hovered closer to Mercy. They both knew what damage a bullet could do to flesh. And how a crowd could turn hostile. Mercy held tight to her slipping composure. *Father, no violence, please.*

Mercy called out a thanks and farewell to the gruff yet kind wagoners who had been their traveling companions for the past ten days on their way to Boise.

Lon Mackey led Mercy into the charcoal-gray twilight. She drew in the cool mountain air, praying for strength. The crowd milled around them, following, grumbling loudly, angrily.

Mercy tried to ignore them. She understood their fear but knew she must not get caught up in it. "Lon Mackey, has the town set up an infirmary?"

"We have concentrated the sick in the saloon. It was where the cholera started and it's the biggest building in town."

Mercy touched Lon's shoulder. "Cholera can snatch away life within a day. I'll do my best, as will my nurse-assistant. But people are going to die even after treatment. Cholera is a swift, mortal disease."

"That's why we got to get out of town, lady," one of the people in the surrounding crowd complained.

She looked at them. "Go to thy homes. If there has been anyone sick in thy house, open all the doors and windows and begin scrubbing everything—clothing, walls, floors, ceilings. Everything! Scrub with water as hot as thee can stand to use and with enough lye soap mixed into it to make thy eyes water. Use a scrub brush, not a cloth. That's thy only defense."

The crowd gawked at her.

"Now! Go!" Mercy waved her hands at them as if shooing away children. Several in the crowd turned and began to leave. The rest stared at her as if unable to move. "If thee acts quickly, thee and thy families may not succumb!"

This finally moved the people. They began running in several directions.

Lon Mackey started walking faster, waving for Indigo and Mercy to follow him. Mercy didn't complain about the brisk pace he set, but she had trouble keeping up. She forced herself on. People were dying.

The sun was sliding below the horizon of tall green mountains. How many evenings like this had she been faced with? People were dying. And she must help them. It was her calling and her privilege.

The gaudy front of the saloon loomed above the street, sticky with mud. Mercy and Indigo followed Lon Mackey inside, where another man was lighting the hanging oil lamps. Mercy gazed around and assessed the situation. Perhaps twenty people lay on blankets spread over the floor and the bar. Most were alone, but some were being ministered to by others, probably relatives.

Many of the patients' faces were bluish, the sign that cholera had already accomplished its pitiless, deadly work. The gorge rose in Mercy's throat. *Father, let my knowledge—as flimsy as it is—save some lives. Help me.*

Mercy took off her bonnet. "Good evening!" she announced in a loud, firm voice, though her stomach quivered like jelly. "I am Dr. Mercy Gabriel. I am a graduate of the Female Medical College of Pennsylvania. I nursed with Clara Barton throughout the war. I am here to see if I can save any of the sick. Now first—"

As she expected—dreaded—hoped to avoid, a sudden cacophony of voices roared in the previously quiet room.

"A woman doctor!"

"No!"

"Is this a joke?"

Mercy had heard this so many times before that it was hard not to shout back. A sudden wave of fatigue rolled over her. She resisted the urge to slump against the wall. As was common on most wagon trains she and Indigo had walked most of the ten days from the nearest railhead. She'd been looking forward to a hotel bed tonight. And now she must face the ridiculous but inevitable objections to her profession. The urge to stamp her foot at them nearly overwhelmed her good sense.

She endeavored to ignore the squawking about how she couldn't be a doctor. Who could trust a female doctor, they asked, and was that the best the gambler could do?

"Quiet." Lon Mackey's solid, male voice cut through the squabbling voices. He did not yell, he merely made himself heard over everyone else. The people fell silent. "What should we do to help you, Dr. Gabriel?"

In this chaotic and fearful room, Lon Mackey had asserted control. He was an impressive man. Mercy wondered what made him so commanding. She decided it wasn't his physical appearance as much as his natural self-assurance.

Mercy cleared her throat and raised her voice. There was no use sugarcoating the truth and doing so could only give false hope. "I am very sorry to say that those who have been sick for over twenty-four hours are without much hope. I need those cases to be moved to the far side of the room so that I can devote my energies to saving those who still have a chance to survive."

Again, the babble broke out.

Lon Mackey silenced all with a glance and the lifting of one hand. "We don't have time to argue. You wanted help, I got a doctor—"

"But a woman—" someone objected.

He kept talking right over the objection. "The mayor's dead and no one else knew what to do. I went and got you a doctor, something I thought impossible." He propped his hands on his hips, looking dangerous to any opposition. "If Dr. Gabriel nursed in the war, she knows more than we do about taking care of sick people. If you don't want her to nurse your folks, then take them home. Anyone who stays will do what they're told by this lady doctor. Do you all understand that?"

Mercy was surprised to see the opposition to her melt away, even though Lon Mackey's pistol was back in his vest. She looked to the man again. She'd been distracted by his gambler's flashy vest. Now she noted that the shirt under it was of the finest quality, though smudged and wrinkled. Lon Mackey had once bought only the best.

He wasn't in his first youth, but he was also by no means near middle-aged. His face was rugged from the sun and perhaps the war—he had that look about him, the look of a soldier. And from just the little of him she'd seen in action, he was most probably an officer. He was used to giving orders and he expected to be obeyed. *And he is a man who cares about others.*

Mercy raised her voice and repeated, "I will set up my medical supplies near the bar. If thee isn't nursing a friend or loved one, I need thee to get buckets of hot water and begin swabbing down the floor area between patients.

"And get the word out that anyone who has any stomach cramps or nausea must come here immediately for treatment. If patients come in at the start of symptoms, I have a better chance of saving their lives. Now please, let's get busy. The cholera won't stop until we force it out."

The people stared at her.

She opened her mouth to urge them, but Lon Mackey barked, "Get moving! Now!"

And everyone began moving.

Lon mobilized the shifting of the patients and the scrubbing. And, according to the female doctor's instructions, a large pot was set up outside the swinging doors of the saloon to boil water for the cleaning.

He shook his head. A female doctor. What next? A tiny female physician who looked as if she should be dressed in ruffles and lace. He'd noted her Quaker speech and the plain gray bonnet and dress. Not your usual woman, by any means. And who was the young, pretty, Negro girl with skin the color of caramel? The doctor had said she was a trained nurse. How had that happened?

"Lon Mackey?"

He heard the Quaker woman calling his name and hurried to her. "What can I do for you, miss?"

"I want thee to ask someone to undertake a particular job. It has to be someone who is able to write, ask intelligent questions and think. I would do it myself, but I am about to begin saline infusions for these patients."

"What do you need done?"

"In order to end this outbreak, I need to know its source."

"Isn't it from the air?" Lon asked.

She smiled, looking pained. "I know the common wisdom is that this disease comes from the air. But I have done a great deal of study on cholera, and I believe that it comes from contaminated water or food. So I need to know the water source of each patient, alive or dead—if they shared some common food, if there was any group gathering where people might have drunk or ingested the same things. You said that the cholera appeared here in this saloon first. Is that correct?"

"Yes." He eyed her. *Contaminated water?* If there had been time, he would have liked to ask her about her research. But with people in agony and dying, there was no time for a long, scientific discussion. He rubbed the back of his neck and then rotated his head, trying to loosen the tight muscles.

"Was the person first taken with cholera living on these premises or just here to socialize?" she asked.

He grinned at her use of the ladylike word *socialize*. Most people would have used *carouse* or *sin* for stepping inside a saloon. This dainty woman continued to surprise him.

"It was the blacksmith. Comes in about twice a week for a beer or two. I think McCall was his name."

She nodded. "Has anyone at his home fallen ill?"

"Yes, his whole family is dead."

Her mouth tightened into a hard line. "That might indicate that his well was the culprit, but since the cholera seems to be more widespread…" She paused. "I need someone to question every patient about their water and food sources over the past week. And about any connection they might have had with the first victim." A loud, agonizing moan interrupted her.

"Will thee find someone," she continued, "to do that and write down the information so that I can go over it? This disease will continue to kill until we find its source and purify it. I assure you that the cholera epidemics that swept New York State in the 1830s were ended by cleaning up contaminated water sources."

He nodded. "I'll do it myself." From his inner vest pocket, he drew a small navy-blue notebook he always carried with him.

"I thank thee. Now I must begin the saline draughts. Indigo will try to make those suffering more comfortable." She turned to the bar behind her and lifted what he recognized as a syringe. He'd seen them in the war. The thought made him turn away in haste. *I will not think of syringes, men bleeding, men silent and cold…*

Several times during the long day, he glanced toward the bar and saw the woman kneeling and administering the saline solution by syringe to patient after patient. The hours passed slowly and painfully. How much good could salt water do? The girl, Indigo, was working her way through the seriously ill, speaking quietly, calming the distraught relatives.

He drew a long breath. He no longer prayed—the war had blasted any faith he'd had—but his spirit longed to be able to pray for divine help. Two more people died and were carried out, plunging them all into deeper gloom. He kept one eye on the mood of the fearful and excitable people in the saloon. A mob could form so easily. And now they had a target for blame. He wondered if the female doctor had thought of that.

Would this woman, armed with only saline injections and cleanliness, be able to save any lives? And if she didn't, what would the reaction be?

Much later that night, candles flickered in the dim, chilly room. When darkness had crept up outside the windows, voices had become subdued. Lon saw that for the first time in hours the Quaker was sitting down near the doors, sipping coffee and eating something. He walked up to her, drawn by the sight of her, the picture of serenity in the center of the cruel storm. Fatigue penetrated every part of his body. A few days ago he had been well-rested, well-fed and smiling. Then disaster had struck. That was how life treated them all. Until it sucked the breath from them and let them return to dust.

As he approached, she looked up and smiled. "Please wash thy hands in the clean water by the door, and I'll get thee a cup of fresh coffee."

Her smile washed away his gloom, making him do

the impossible—he felt his mouth curving upward. She walked outside to where a fire had been burning all day to heat the boiled water for the cleaning and hand-washing. A large kettle of coffee had been kept brewing there, too. If he'd had any strength left, he would have objected. She wasn't here to wait on him. But it was easier to follow her orders and accept her kind offer. He washed his hands in the basin and then sank onto a wooden chair.

The Quaker walked with calm assurance through the swinging saloon doors as if she were a regular visitor of the place, as if they weren't surrounded by sick and dying people. She handed him a steaming cup of hot black coffee and a big ginger cookie. "I brought these cookies with me, so I know they are safe to eat."

It had been a long time since anyone had served him coffee without expecting to be paid. And the cookies reminded him of home, his long-gone home.

He pictured the broad front lawn. And then around the back, he imagined himself walking into the large kitchen where the white-aproned cook, Mary, was busy rolling out dough. But Mary had died while he was away at war, a sad twist. He shrugged his uncharacteristic nostalgia off, looking to the Quaker.

She sat across from him, sipping her coffee and nibbling an identical cookie. He gazed around him, smelling the harsh but clean odor of lye soap, which overpowered the less pleasant odors caused by the disease.

"You're lucky to have a maid who can also nurse the sick," he said. Ever since the unlikely pair had entered the saloon, the riddle of who the young black girl was had danced at the edge of his thoughts.

"Indigo is not my maid. She is my adopted daughter. I met her in the South during the war. She was only about seven at the time, an orphaned slave. Now she is nearly a woman and, as I said, a trained nurse."

He stared at her, blowing over his hot coffee to cool it. He'd never heard of a white person adopting a black child. He knew, of course, that Quakers had been at the forefront of abolitionism, far ahead of popular opinion. What did he think of this unusual adoption?

He shouldn't be surprised. Just like him, Dr. Mercy Gabriel obviously didn't live her life guided by what others might think. A woman who had nursed in the war. He recalled those few brave women who tirelessly nursed fallen soldiers, both blue and gray. As he sipped more bracing hot coffee, he studied this courageous woman's face. The resolve hardened within him. *I won't let any harm come to you, ma'am.*

"Will thee tell me if thee has found any connection between the first victim and the others?" she asked.

Glad for the distraction from his contemplation of her, Lon pulled the notebook out of his pocket and flipped through the pages. "The first victim, McCall, had just butchered and sold a few of his hogs to others in town. But some people who have died were not connected with this hog butchering or sale."

She nodded, still chewing the cookie. She daintily sipped her coffee and then said, "Once a contagion starts, others can be infected by coming into contact with those who have fallen ill."

"Are you certain it isn't due to an ill air blowing through town?" His large round cookie was sweet, spicy and chewy. He rested his head against the back of the chair.

She inhaled deeply. "Over a decade ago, Dr. John Snow in London did a study of the water supplies of victims of cholera in a poor district in London. The doctor was able to connect all the original cases to a pump in one neighborhood."

If Lon hadn't been so tired, he would have shown shock at this calm recitation of scientific information. This woman was interested in epidemics in London? Few men hereabouts would have been. He studied her more closely.

Her petite form had misled him initially, but she was no bit of fluff. Despite death hovering in the room with them, her face was composed. She had taken off her bonnet to reveal pale, flaxen hair skimmed back into a tight bun, though some of the strands had managed to work themselves free. Her eyes—now, they stopped him. So blue—as blue as a perfect summer sky. Clear. Intelligent. Fearless.

He recalled her tireless work over the past hours, her calm orders and take-charge manner. Some men might resent it. He might have resented it once. But not here. Not now. Not in the face of such a wanton loss of lives. This woman might just be able to save people. Maybe even him.

"Do you think you're having any success here?" he asked in a lowered voice.

She looked momentarily worried. "I am doing my best, but my best will not save everyone who is stricken."

The swinging doors crashed open. A man holding a rifle burst into the saloon. "She's dying! I need the doctor!"

Chapter Two

Everyone around Lon and Mercy Gabriel froze.

"Did you hear me?" the man shrieked. "I was told a doctor's here! My wife's dying!"

Dr. Gabriel put down her cup, swallowing the last of her cookie. She rose and faced the man. "I am sorry to hear that. Why hasn't thee brought her here?"

"She won't come! She won't come into a saloon!" The man swung his rifle toward the Quaker. "You gotta come with me! Now! Save her!"

Lon leaped to his feet, pulling out his pistol, ready to shoot.

"Friend, I am heartily sorry for thee, but I cannot leave all these patients—" the woman motioned toward the crowded room "—to go to one. Thee must bring thy wife here."

"What?" The man gawked at her and raised his rifle to his eye to aim.

Lon moved toward the man slowly. He didn't want to shoot if he didn't have to.

"Thee must bring thy wife here. And then I will do whatever I can for her."

Lon marveled at the Quaker's calm voice. It shouldn't

have surprised him that the man with the rifle was also confounded. The man froze, staring forward.

Dr. Gabriel moved away to a patient and began to give the woman another dose of the saline infusion.

"You have to come with me, lady!" the man demanded. "My wife won't come here."

Dr. Gabriel glanced over her shoulder. "Is she still conscious?"

The man lowered his rifle. "No."

"Well, then what is stopping thee from carrying her here? If she is unconscious or delirious, she won't know where she is." The Quaker said this in the same reasonable tone, without a trace of fear. Lon had rarely heard the like.

This woman was either crazy or as cool as they came.

The man swung the gun above Mercy's head and fired, shattering one of the bulbous oil lamps behind the bar.

Lon lunged forward and struck the man's head with the butt of his pistol, wrestling the rifle from him. The man dropped to the floor.

"Does he have a fever?" the Quaker asked as she gazed at the fallen man.

Lon gawked at her. Unbelieving. Astounded.

"Does he have a fever?" she prompted.

After stooping to check, Lon nodded. "Yes, he's fevered. Doctor, *you* are very cool under fire."

She gazed at him, still unruffled. "Unfortunately, this is not the first time a weapon has been aimed at me." She turned away but said over her shoulder, "Set him on the floor on a blanket. Then please find out where this poor man's wife is and see if she's alive. I doubt there is anything I can do for her. But we must try. And, Lon Mackey, will thee please keep asking questions? We must get to the source before more people die."

Lon carried the unconscious man and laid him down, then asked another person where the man's home was. As he turned to leave, he snatched up the rifle and took it with him. He didn't want anybody else waving it around.

Since the war, nothing much surprised him. But Dr. Mercy Gabriel had gotten his attention. *She could have gotten herself killed. And she didn't even so much as blink.*

Mercy went about her round of injections, thinking of Lon and the ease with which he'd subdued the distraught man. She had never gotten used to guns, yet this was the second time today men had been forced to draw guns to protect her.

A young woman with a little girl in her arms rushed through the swinging doors. "My child! My Missy is having cramping. They said that cramping…" The woman's face crumpled and she visibly fought for control. "Please save her. She's only four. Please." The woman held out her daughter to Mercy.

"Just cramps, nothing else?"

"Just cramps. She started holding her stomach and crying about a half hour ago." Tears poured down the woman's face.

"Thee did exactly right in bringing her here so quickly. I will do what I can." Mercy lifted the child from her mother's trembling arms, tenderly laid the little girl on the bar and smiled down at her. "Thee must not be afraid. I know what to do."

Mercy felt the child's forehead. Her temperature was already rising. Mercy fought to keep her focus and not give in to worry and despair. God was in this room, not just the deadly cholera.

The mother hovered nearby, wringing her hands.

Mercy bent to listen to the child's heart with her stethoscope. "Missy, I need thee to sit up and cough for me."

The mother began to weep. Mercy glanced at Indigo, who nodded and drew the woman outside. Then Mercy went about examining the child. Soon she glanced over and saw that Indigo had left the woman near the doors and was continuing her rounds of the patients. Indigo bathed their reddened faces with water and alcohol, trying to fight their fevers.

Mercy listened to the little girl's abdomen and heard the telltale rumbling. No doubt the child had become infected. Mercy closed her eyes for one second, sending a prayer heavenward. *Father, help me save this little life.*

A call for help came from the far side of the room. Mercy looked over and her spirits dropped. One of the patients was showing signs of the mortal end of this dreaded disease. A woman—no doubt the wife of the dying man—rose and shouted for help again.

Mercy watched Indigo weave swiftly between the pallets on the wood floor to reach the woman's side. Mercy looked away. She hated early death, needless death, heartless death. Her usual composure nearly slipped. As the woman's sobbing filled the room, Mercy tightened her control. *I cannot give in to emotion. I must do what I can to save this child. Father, keep me focused.*

Mercy mixed the first dose of the herbal medication her mother had taught her to concoct, which was better than any patented medicine she'd tried. "Now, Missy, thee must drink this in order to get better."

"I want my mama." The little girl's face wrinkled up in fear. "Mama. Mama."

Mercy picked up the child and cradled her in her arms. "Thy mama's right beside the door, see?" Mercy turned so the child could glimpse her mother. "She wants me to make thee better. Now this will taste a little funny, but not that bad. I've taken it many times. Now here, take a sip, Missy. Just a little sip, sweet child."

Missy stared into Mercy's eyes. Then she opened her mouth and began to sip the chalky medicine. She wrinkled her nose at the taste but kept on sipping until the small cup was empty.

"Excellent, Missy. Thee is a very good girl. Now I'm going to lay thee down again, and thy mama will come and sit with thee. I will be giving thee more medicine soon."

"It tasted funny."

"I know but thee drank it all, brave girl."

About half an hour later, Mercy was kneeling beside the man who had burst into the saloon and was still unconscious. She carefully gave him a dose of saline water. It seemed a pitiful medicine to combat such a deadly contagion. But it was the only thing she knew of that actually did something to counteract cholera's disastrous effect on the human body. And no one even knew why. *There's so much that I wish I knew—that I wish someone knew.*

It was nearly dawn when she heard her name and glanced up to see Lon Mackey. "Did thee find this man's wife?"

His face sank into grimmer lines. "She's dead."

The news twisted inside Mercy. She shook her head over the loss of another life. Then she motioned for him to lean closer to her. She whispered, "We must find the source or this disease will kill at least half in this community."

The stark words sank like rocks from her stomach to her toes. She forced herself to go on. "That is the usual death rate for unchecked cholera. Has thee found out *anything* that gives us a hint of the source?"

"I've talked to everyone. The little girl's mother told me something I've heard from several of the others."

"What is that?" Mercy asked, turning to concentrate on slowly infusing saline into the man's vein.

"Wild blackberry juice was served at the church a week ago Sunday. There was a reception for the children's Sunday-school recitation," he murmured.

Mercy looked up into his face. "Wild blackberry juice? Who made it?"

"It was a concoction Mrs. McCall made from crushed berries, their good well water and sugar. Mrs. McCall was the wife of the first victim. And the whole of his family was ailing first and all succumbed."

Mercy sat back on her heels. Closing her eyes, she drew in a slow breath, trying to calm her racing heart. Lon Mackey may have found her the answer. "That tells me what I need to know. Thee must do exactly as I say. Will thee?"

Hours ago Lon wouldn't have done anything a female stranger told him to do. But he would do whatever Mercy Gabriel asked. He just hoped it would work—passions were running high outside the saloon. "What must I do?"

"Go to the McCall house and examine the water source. Examine the house and the grounds with great care. Take a healthy man with thee as a witness."

"What am I looking for?" he asked, leaning closer. The faint fragrance of lavender momentarily distracted him from her words.

"After the 1834 cholera epidemic, New York State passed laws forbidding the discarding of animal carcasses in or near any body of water. Does that help thee?" she asked.

Without a word of doubt, Lon rose and strode outside. He motioned to the bartender, Tom Banks, who was adding wood to the fire under the kettle of water the Quaker required to be kept boiling. "We've got a lead on what might have caused the cholera. Come with me. She told me what to look for and where," Lon said.

The two of them hurried down the empty street. Dawn was breaking and normally people would be stirring, stepping outside. But every shop in town was closed up tight and all the houses were eerily quiet. No children had played outside for days now. Even the stray dogs lying in the alleys looked bewildered.

"Do you think this Quaker woman, this *female* doctor, knows what she's doing?" the bartender asked.

Lon shrugged. "Proof's in the pudding," he said. But if he had to wager, his money would be on Mercy Gabriel.

At the McCalls, the two of them walked around the empty house to the well. He was used to violent death and destruction but the unnatural silence and creeping dread of cholera was getting to him. Everything was so still.

"The Quaker told me to examine the well and any other water source."

"Doesn't she know that contagions come from bad air?" Tom objected.

"She knows more than we do," Lon replied. "Every

time I talk to her, I know more about this scourge than I did before." Of course, that didn't mean she could save everyone. In times like these, however, he'd found that a show of assurance could avert the worst of hysteria. He didn't want anyone else bursting into the saloon and letting loose with a rifle.

The two of them approached the well. It was a primitive affair with the pump sitting on a rough wooden platform.

"I don't know what we'll find that's not right," Tom grumbled. "From what I heard, the McCalls always had sweet water. That's why they always brought the juice."

Lon stared down at the wooden platform. Part of it was warping and lifting up. "Let's find a crowbar or hammer." They went to the barn and found both. Soon they were prying up the boards over the McCalls' well.

Both of them cursed when they saw what was floating in the water.

They cleaned out the well and then pumped water for a good half hour. Then they capped the well cover down as tight as they could. Tom and Lon walked silently back to the saloon. Lon hit the swinging door first and with great force, his anger at the senseless loss of life fueling a furious fire within. The two swinging panels cracked against the wall. Every head turned.

Lon crossed to the Quaker doctor. "We found dead rats floating in the McCalls' well."

The Quaker rose to face him, looking suddenly hopeful. "That would do it. Had the well cover become compromised?"

"It was warped and loose."

She sighed and closed her eyes. "We need to find out if everyone who is ill has been brought here. Anyone who drank the juice or who came in contact with a person falling ill from it should be checked. Then we need to make sure that every house where the illness has presented is scrubbed completely with hot water with a high concentration of lye soap."

"That will end this?" Lon studied her earnest face, hoping against hope that she would say yes.

"If we kill off all the bacteria that carry the disease, the disease will stop infecting people. The bacteria most likely move from surface to surface. I believe that in order to become ill, a person must ingest the contaminated water or come into contact with something an infected person has touched. Does thee need anything more from me to proceed?"

"No, you've made yourself quite clear."

She smiled at him. "Thee is an unusual man, Lon Mackey."

He couldn't help but smile back, thinking that she was unusual herself. He hoped she was right about the cause of the cholera. Only time would tell.

The last victim of the cholera epidemic died seven days after Mercy and Indigo came to town. When people had begun recovering and going home, the few remaining sick had been moved to one of the small churches in town after it had been scrubbed mercilessly clean. And the vacated saloon was dealt with in the same way. The townspeople doing the cleaning complained about the work, but they did it.

Eight days after getting off the wagon train, Mercy stood in the church doorway. She gazed out at the sunny day, her body aching with fatigue. She had slept only a few hours each day for the past week, and her mind and body didn't appreciate that treatment. Only three patients lingered, lying on pallets around the church pulpit.

The new mayor came striding up the path to the church. "The saloon is clean and back in business."

She gazed at him. Even though she was glad there was no longer a need for a large hospital area, did he expect her to say that the saloon being back in business was a good thing?

"I took up a collection from the people you helped." He drew out an envelope and handed it to her. "When do you think you'll be leaving town?"

Mercy made him wait for her answer. She opened the envelope and counted out four dollars and thirty-five cents. *Four dollars and thirty-five cents for saving half the lives in this town of over a thousand.* She wasn't surprised at this paltry amount. After all, she was a female doctor, not a "real" doctor.

Mercy stared into the man's eyes. "I have no plans to leave." She had thought of going on to Boise, but then had decided to stay where she had shown that she knew something about doctoring. Many would discount her efforts to end the epidemic, but others wouldn't—she hoped. "And, friend, if this town doesn't want a recurrence of cholera, thee should have all the people inspect their wells and streams."

The mayor made a harrumphing sound. "We're grateful for the nursing you've done, but we still believe what real doctors believe. The cholera came from a bad wind a few weeks ago."

Mercy didn't bother to take offense. *There are none so blind as those who will not see.* "I am not the only doctor who believes that cholera comes from contaminated water. And thee saw thyself that the McCalls' well was polluted. Would thee drink water with a dead rat in it?"

The mayor made the same harrumphing sound and ignored her question. "Again, ma'am, you have our gratitude." He held out his hand.

Mercy shook it and watched him walk away.

"The thankless wretch."

She turned toward the familiar voice. Lon Mackey lounged against the corner of the small white clapboard church. He looked different than the first time they'd met. His clothing was laundered and freshly pressed, and his colorful vest was buttoned correctly. He was a handsome man. She chuckled at his comment.

"It is so predictable." She drew in a long breath. "I've heard it all before. 'You're just a woman. What could you possibly know?' Over and over."

"Why do you put up with it?"

She chuckled again.

The sound irritated Lon. "I don't know what's funny about this. You should be taken seriously. How much did the town pay you?"

Mercy sighed, handing him the envelope. "Human nature is what's funny. Even when confronted by the truth about the cause of the epidemic, the average male and most females refuse to believe a woman would know more than a man would."

They'd paid her less than five dollars. He voiced his disgust by saying, "But your idea about the cause of cholera is based on what male doctors have discovered, isn't it?"

She nodded, tucking the envelope into the small leather purse in her skirt pocket. "But I could have gotten it wrong. I am, after all, just a poor, inferior, weak female who must always defer to men who *always* know better than women do."

Her words grated against his nerves like sandpaper on sensitive skin. Why? Was he guilty of thinking this, too? He found himself moving toward this woman. He shut his mouth. He didn't want to know more about Dr. Mercy Gabriel. He didn't want to walk toward her, but she drew him. He offered her his hand to cover how disgruntled and confused he felt by his reaction to her.

She smiled and shook it. "I thank thee, Lon Mackey. Thee didn't balk very much at following a woman's directions."

He didn't know what to say to this. Was she teasing him or scolding him? Or being genuine? He merely smiled and turned away. The saloon was open again and he had to win some money to pay for his keep. He would be staying in the saloon almost round the clock for the next few days—he'd seen the men of the town coming back full force. How had he come this far from the life he'd been born to? The answer was the war, of course.

He walked toward the saloon, hearing voices there louder and rowdier than usual. No doubt watching the wagons carrying people to the cemetery made men want to forget the harsh realities of life with lively conversation and laughter. Nearly seventy people had succumbed to cholera. How many would they have lost if Dr. Mercy Gabriel hadn't shown up? Was he the only one who wondered this?

And why wouldn't the Quaker woman leave his mind?

Images of Mercy over the past few hectic days popped into his mind over and over again. Mercy kneeling beside a patient and then rising to go to the next, often with a loud, burdened sigh. Mercy speaking softly to a weeping relative. Mercy staggering to a chair and closing her eyes for a short nap and then rising again. He passed a hand over his forehead as if he could wipe away the past week, banish Mercy Gabriel from his mind. But she wasn't the kind of woman a man could forget easily. *But I must.*

Chapter Three

The morning after the final patient had recovered,
Mercy decided it was time to find both a place to live
and a place to start her medical practice. She wondered
if she should ask Lon Mackey for help.

As she stood looking down the main street of the
town, Indigo said, "Aunt Mercy?"

Mercy looked into Indigo's large brown eyes. Indigo had always called her Aunt Mercy   the title of
"mother" had never seemed right to either of them.
"Yes?"

"Are we going to stand here all day?" Indigo grinned.

Mercy leaned her head to the side. "I'm sorry. I was
lost in thought." She didn't reveal that the thoughts had
been about Lon Mackey. He had vanished several days
ago, returning to the largest saloon on the town's one
muddy street. His abrupt departure from their daily life
left her hollow, blank, somehow weakened.

Indigo nodded as if she had understood both Mercy's
thoughts and gaze.

Mercy drew in a deep breath and hoped it would revive her. This was the place she had been called to. Only
time would reveal if it would become home. "Let's pull

the trunk along. There must be some rooming houses in a town this size." The two of them moved to the drier edge of the muddy track through town.

Mercy's heart stuttered as she contemplated once again facing a town unsympathetic to a female doctor and a black nurse. Lon Mackey's withdrawal from her sphere also blunted her mood. As she strode up the unpaved street, she tried to center herself, calm herself. *God is a very present help in time of trouble. Lon Mackey helped me and accepted me for what I am—there will surely be others, won't there?*

A large greenwood building with big hand-painted letters announcing "General Store" loomed before her. Mercy left the trunk on the street with Indigo and entered. Her heart was now skipping beats.

"Good day!" she greeted a man wearing a white apron standing behind the rough wood-slab counter. "I'm new in town and looking for lodging. Can thee recommend a boardinghouse here?"

The man squinted at her. "You're that female doctor, aren't you?"

Mercy offered her hand. "Yes, I am Dr. Mercy Gabriel. And I'm ready to set up practice here."

He didn't take her hand.

She cleared her throat, which was tightening under his intense scrutiny.

"I'm Jacob Tarver, proprietor. I never met a female doctor before. But I hear you helped out nursing the cholera patients."

"I doctored the patients as a qualified physician," Mercy replied, masking her irritation. Then she had to suffer through the usual catechism of how she'd become a doctor, along with the usual response that no one would go to a female doctor except maybe for midwifing. She could have spoken both parts and he could have remained silent. People were so predictable in their prejudices.

Finally, she was able to go back to her question about lodging. "Where does thee suggest we find lodging, Jacob Tarver?"

He gave her an unhappy look. "That girl out there with you?"

Mercy had also been ready for this. Again, she kept her bubbling irritation hidden. If one chose to walk a path much different than the average, then one must put up with this sort of aggravation—even when one's spirit rebelled against it. "Yes, Indigo is my adopted daughter and my trained nursing assistant."

The proprietor looked at her as if she'd lost her mind but replied, "I don't know if she'll take you in, but go on down the street to Ma Bailey's. She might have space for you in her place."

Mercy nodded and thanked him. Outside, she motioned to Indigo and off they went to Ma Bailey's. Mercy's feet felt like blocks of wood. A peculiar kind of gloom was beginning to take hold of her. She saw the boardinghouse sign not too far down the street, but the walk seemed long. Once again, Mercy knocked on the door, leaving Indigo waiting with the red trunk.

A buxom woman in a faded brown dress and a soiled apron opened the door. "I'm Ma Bailey. What can I do for you?"

Feeling vulnerable, Mercy prayed God would soften this woman's heart. "We're looking for a place to board."

The interrogation began and ended as usual with Ma Bailey saying, "I don't take in people who ain't white, and I don't think doctorin' is a job for womenfolk."

Mercy's patience slipped, a spark igniting. "Then

why is it the mother who always tends to sick children and not the father?"

"Well, that's different," Ma Bailey retorted. "A woman's supposed to take care of her own."

"Well, I'm different. I want to take care of more than my daughter. If God gave me the gift of healing, who are thee to tell me that I don't have it?"

"Your daughter?" The woman frowned.

Mercy glanced over her shoulder. "I adopted Indigo when she was—"

"Don't hold with that, neither."

"I'm sorry I imposed on thy time," Mercy said and walked away. She tried to draw up her reserves, to harden herself against the expected unwelcome here. No doubt many would sit in judgment upon her today. But she had to find someone who would take them in. Lon Mackey came into her thoughts again. Could she ask the man for more help? Who else could put in a good word for them?

Heavenly Father, plead my case. For the very first time, she wondered if heaven wasn't listening to her here.

Midafternoon Lon took a break from the poker table. He stepped outside and inhaled the cool, damp air of autumn. He found himself scanning the street and realized he was looking for *her*. He literally shook himself. The Quaker was no longer his business.

Then he glimpsed Indigo across the mud track, sitting on the red trunk. As he watched, the female doctor came out of a rough building and spoke to Indigo. Then the two of them went to the next establishment. Dr. Gabriel knocked and went inside. Within minutes, she came back outside and she and the girl headed farther down the street to the next building. What was she doing? Introducing herself? Or trying to get a place to stay? That sobered Lon. No one was going to rent a room to a woman of color. Lon tried to stop worrying and caring about what happened to this unusual pair. *This can't be the first time the good doctor has faced this. And it's not my job to smooth the way for them. In fact, it would be best if they moved on to a larger city.*

He turned back inside, irritated with himself for having this inner debate. The saloon was now empty, sleepy. Since his nighttime schedule didn't fit with regular boardinghouses, he'd rented a pallet in the back of the saloon. He went there now to check on his battered leather valise. He'd locked it and then chained it to the railing that went upstairs, where the saloon girls lived. He didn't have much in the valise but his clothing and a few mementoes. Still, it was his. He didn't want to lose it.

Mentally, he went through the few items from his past that he'd packed: miniature portraits of his late parents, his last letter from them as he fought in Virginia and the engagement ring Janette had returned to him. This last article wasn't a treasured token but a reminder of how rare true love was in this world. He wondered if Mercy Gabriel had ever taken a chance on falling in love.

That thought ended his musing. Back to reality. He'd have to play some very good poker tonight and build up his funds again. He lay down on his pallet for a brief nap. The night was probably going to be a long, loud one.

Mercy faced cold defeat. She had been turned away at every boardinghouse door and had been told at the hotels that they had no vacancies. She sensed the reason was because of Indigo's skin color, a painful, razor-sharp thought. A cold rain now drizzled, chilling her bone-deep. She and Indigo moved under the scant cover of a knot of oak and elm trees.

"Well, Aunt Mercy, this wouldn't be the first time we've slept under the stars," Indigo commented, putting the unpleasant truth into words.

Mercy drew in a long breath. She didn't want to reply that those days had been when they were both younger and the war was raging. Mercy had found little Indigo shivering beside the road, begging. Mercy had turned thirty-one this January. The prospect of sleeping out at twenty-one had felt much different than sleeping without cover nearly a decade later. Both she and Indigo sat down on the top of their trunk. *Father, we need help. Soon. Now.* Then defeat swallowed her whole.

The acrid smoke from cigars floated above the poker table. Lon held his cards close to his chest just in case someone was peeking over his shoulder for an accomplice, cheating at the table. So far he hadn't been able to play for more than chicken stakes. Piano music and bursts of laughter added to the noisy atmosphere. He was holding a flush—not the best hand, but not the worst, either. Could he bluff the others into folding?

"You got to know that strange female?" the man across from him asked as he tossed two more coins into the ante pile. The man was dressed a bit better than the other miners and lumberjacks in the saloon. He had bright red hair and the freckled complexion to match. Lon thought he'd said his name was Hobson.

Lon made an unencouraging sound, hoping to

change the topic of conversation. He met the man's bid and raised it. The coin clinked as it hit the others.

"You know anything about her?" Hobson asked.

Lon nodded, watching the next player, a tall, lean man called Slattery, with a shock of gray at one temple. He put down two cards and was dealt two more.

"You know anything about her? I mean, can she really doctor?" redheaded Hobson asked again.

"She's a doc all right," Lon conceded. "I saw her certificate myself. She showed it to me the second night she was in town. It's in her black bag."

"We need a doc here," Hobson said as the last of the four players made his final bet of the game.

"Don't need no woman doctor," Slattery replied. "She's unnatural. A woman like that."

Lon started a slow burn. Images of Mercy Gabriel caring for the cholera victims spun through his mind. "She's a Quaker. They think different, talk different."

The other player, a small man with a mustache, grunted. "Forget the woman doctor. Play cards."

"She's honest and goodhearted." Lon heard these words flow from his mouth, unable to stop them.

"I don't hold with Quakers' odd ways," Slattery said.

Hobson glared at Slattery as he laid down his cards. "My grandparents were Quakers. You could look your whole life and not find finer people. So what if they say 'thee' and 'thy'? It's a free country."

As Lon laid down his own hand, he sighed. His flush beat every other hand on the table. A tight place within him eased—winning was good. He scooped up the money in the ante pile.

"Well, nobody would take them in," Slattery said, looking irritated at losing but satisfied to be able to say something slighting about Dr. Gabriel. "She has a black girl with her. Tells everyone she adopted her. If nobody takes them in, they'll have to go elsewhere. And good riddance, I say." Slattery shoved away from the table and headed toward the bar.

Hobson looked after him and turned to Lon. "We need a doctor in this place. Logging and mining can be dangerous. Anybody see where those two women went?"

"When I came in, they were wrapped in blankets, sitting on the trunk under that clump of oaks at the end of the street," Lon said.

Hobson stood up and headed toward the door.

The quiet man with the mustache looked to Lon. "Let's find a couple more—"

Two other men came and slid into the seats left vacant by Hobson and Slattery. Out of the corner of his eye, Lon glimpsed Hobson leaving.

Lon hoped Digger was going to help out the two stubborn women. He didn't like to see anyone homeless, but they had chosen a path that put them at odds with popular sentiment. In any event, how could he provide them with a place to stay? Would they want to bunk in the back of the saloon, as he did? Of course not. With regret, he turned his mind to his new competitors.

Mercy shivered as the night began to fold them into its cool, damp arms. She and Indigo had wrapped themselves in their blankets and perched on top of the trunk, which was wedged between two trees so it wouldn't move. Oil lamps and candles shone in the dwellings so they weren't sitting in complete darkness. Mercy kept her eyes on those lights, kept praying that someone would offer them a place, someone would come out—

A man was striding down the street in their direction. Was he headed past them for home? She heard him coming, splashing in the shallow puddles. A lantern at his hip glimmered.

"He's heading straight toward us," Indigo whispered.

Mercy caught the fear in Indigo's voice, and it trembled through her. Was violence to be added to insult here? She leaned against Indigo, her voice quavering. "Don't be afraid. No one is going to harm us."

"You that woman doctor?" the man asked in a brisk tone, his copper hair catching the lantern light.

"Yes, I am." Mercy didn't know whether she should stand, or even if she could.

"You two can't sleep out here all night. Follow me." The man turned and began striding away.

His unforeseen invitation sent her thoughts sprawling. "Please, friend, where is thee going?"

He turned back and halted. "I'm Digger Hobson, the manager of one of the mining outfits hereabouts. I'm going to take you to the mining office for the night."

She didn't want to turn the man down, but how would they sleep there? Her nerve was tender, but she managed to ask, "Mining office?"

"Yeah, I bunked there till I got a place of my own. Now come on. Let's not waste time." The man strode away from them.

With a tiny yelp, Indigo jumped off the trunk, swirled her blanket higher so it wouldn't drag in the mud, and began hauling the trunk behind her.

Coming out of her shock, Mercy followed Indigo's example and grabbed the valises, hurrying on stiff legs through the mud. The two of them caught up with Hobson where he had stopped. The building had a hand-painted sign that read "Acme Mining Office."

"Come on in. It's not much, but it's better than sleep-

ing out under the trees all night. I can't understand why
no one would take you in."

Mercy could only agree with him. But she was so
unnerved she didn't trust herself yet to speak.

"Some people don't like me because of my color,"
Indigo said, surprising Mercy. Mercy hadn't mentioned
the rude comments people had made about Indigo. But
since none of them had kept their voices down, Indigo
had probably overheard them. The area around Mercy's
heart clenched.

"I fought in the war to set you free," Digger said.
"Some folks think you all ought to go back to Africa.
But I don't think I'd like to go there myself."

"Not me, either, sir. I'm an American," Indigo stated.

"Thee is very kind, Digger Hobson." Mercy found
her voice. She wondered why this welcome hospitality
still left her emotionless inside. Perhaps rejection was
more powerful than kindness. But that shouldn't be.

"We need a doctor here. I wouldn't have asked for
a female doctor, but if you really got a certificate and
everything, then we'll make do with you. Mining can
be a rough trade."

Mercy tried to sort through these words but the unusual numbness she hoped was due to the chill and fatigue caused her only to nod. Certificate? Who knew
she had a certificate?

Her dazed mind brought up a scene from the saloon
infirmary. Lon had been looking over her shoulder as
she had dug into the bottom of her black bag. She'd taken
out her framed certificate so she could search better.

So Lon had been talking about her? What had he
said?

"Dr. Gabriel is tired," Indigo said. "Where are the
beds?"

Mercy realized that she had just been standing there, not paying attention to this kind man.

"There are two cots in the back room. I'm going farther up the mountain now, to get to bed. Have a busy day tomorrow." As he spoke, he led them through an office area into a back room where there was a potbellied stove and two bare cots.

"Do you have bedding with you?" he asked.

"Yes, yes, thank you," Indigo stammered.

As Hobson turned to leave, he lit a tall candle on the stove. "Good night, ladies." He handed Mercy the key. "Lock up behind me. Two women alone can't be too careful."

When Mercy did not move, Indigo took the key and followed him back through the office. Mercy waited, frozen in place, watching the flickering, mesmerizing candle flame. She had heard of people falling asleep standing up. Was that happening to her?

Indigo entered, helped Mercy off with her blanket and steered her into a wooden chair beside the stove. "You sit here, Aunt Mercy. You look really tired."

Mercy sat, the numbness still clutching her. This was more than the usual fatigue, Mercy sensed. Indigo began humming "Be Thou My Vision" as she opened the trunk, got out their wrinkled sheets and pillows, and made up the two cots. "God has provided for us again."

Mercy wanted to agree. But her tongue lay at the bottom of her mouth, limp and wayward. Then Indigo was there in front of her, kneeling to unbutton her shoes. "You're just very tired, that's all. I think you need a few days of rest and good food. And you'll be right as a good spring rain."

Indigo led Mercy over to the cot nearest the stove. "I think I'll make up a small fire and brew a cup of tea for both of us. Then we'll go to bed and let the fire die down on its own. It's not that cold, not as cold as it can be in Pennsylvania in late September."

Indigo kept up small talk as she cared for them both. Mercy let herself sit and listen. She could do nothing more. She was tired, not just from the cholera epidemic or walking behind the wagons to get here. She was tired to the marrow of her bones from the unkind way people treated each other.

The mayor's insults the other day, diminishing her role in stopping the epidemic which could have killed him. The unfriendly and judgmental way people had looked at them today as they walked down Main Street. And Lon Mackey, who she'd begun to consider an ally, disappearing from her life when she most needed help. These had leeched the life from her.

In this whole town, they had encountered one kind man out of how many? The others, when they had ample room to take them in, would have let her and Indigo sleep outside. Well, she shouldn't be surprised. There had been no room at the inn for Mary and Joseph. And baby Jesus had been born among the cattle. Lon Mackey's face came to mind clearly. She had been hoping he would come to their aid, clearly. Foolish beyond measure. She sighed and closed her eyes. Whatever connection she had felt with him had been an illusion. Something inside her flickered and then went out, extinguished.

Despite his best efforts, Lon woke while it was still morning. Dr. Gabriel's face flashed before his eyes. He rolled over. Around four o'clock in the morning, when the saloon had finally shut its doors, he'd been unable to keep himself from going out with a lantern and checking to see if the two women were still sitting under the tree. This concern for their welfare could only spring from the life-threatening circumstances under which they'd met and nothing else, he insisted silently.

When he'd found, in the early morning light, that they were no longer under the tree, he'd been able to go to his bed and sleep. He would let the God they believed in take care of them from now on.

Though it was much earlier than he ever cared to be awake, he found he could not go back to sleep. He sat up, disgusted with himself. After shaving and donning his last fresh collar, he strode out into the thin sunshine to find breakfast. The town was bustling. He stood looking up and down the street. Then drawn by the mingled fragrances of coffee, bacon and biscuits, he headed for breakfast at a café on the nearest corner.

On the way, he saw Dr. Gabriel step outside a mining office and begin sweeping the wooden platform in front of the place. Something deep inside nudged him to avoid her, but he couldn't be that rude. Tipping his hat, he said, "Good morning, Dr. Gabriel."

"Lon Mackey, good morning."

"Is this where you stayed last night?" he asked.

"Yes," she replied. "A man, Digger Hobson, let us stay. I'm just tidying up a bit to thank him for his kindness."

"I'm glad to hear you found a place. Yesterday, I saw you going door to door…" He caught himself before he said more.

"It is always difficult for Indigo and me in a new place." She also paused and gazed into his eyes.

He glanced away. "You still think you can establish yourself here?"

"I do. I hope…" Her voice faded.

He denied the urge to try to talk sense into her. Still, he lingered. This woman had earned his regard. And the feeling of working together to fight the cholera had taken him back to his previous life when he'd had a future. He broke away from her effect on him. "I'll bid you good day then."

Mercy wanted to stop him, speak to him longer. But even as she opened her mouth, she knew she must not. Their paths should not cross again except in this casual way. Why did that trouble her? Just because she had found him so easy to work with meant nothing to her day-to-day life. She went on sweeping, quelling the sudden, surprising urge to cry. Lon had believed in her abilities and trusted her in a way that few other men ever had, and it was hard to simply let that go.

At the sound of footsteps on the office's wooden floor, she turned to greet Indigo. "Thee slept well?"

"Yes. I feel guilty for lying in so long. You know I never sleep late."

"I think thee needed the extra rest." She watched as Lon Mackey walked into the café on the corner. She had no appetite, which was unusual, but the two of them must eat to keep up their strength. "Indigo, would thee go down to the café, buy us breakfast and bring it back here?"

Indigo's stomach growled audibly in response. The girl grinned. "Why don't we just go there and eat?"

Because he's there. "I'm not in the mood for company this morning." That wasn't a lie, unfortunately. Mercy pulled her purse out of her pocket and gave it to Indigo. She gave Mercy a penetrating look, then left, singing quietly to herself.

Mercy walked inside the office and looked out the

smudged front window. She thought of going around town again this afternoon, trying to get to know all the residents, trying to begin to soften their resistance, to change their minds about a woman doctor. But the thought of stepping outside again brought her near to tears.

For the first time she could recall, she had no desire to go out into the sunshine. No desire to go on doing what she must in order to change opinions about her. To carry out her mission. This sudden absence of purpose was alien to her.

The fact was she didn't want to talk to or see anyone save Indigo. Or, truth be told, Lon Mackey. Though she'd been hurt that he hadn't come to her aid, the fact that he'd gone looking for her in the early morning had lifted her heart some. She wrapped her arms around herself and shivered in spite of the lingering warmth from the potbellied stove.

She went over in her mind the brief conversation with Lon about his concern and about his opposition to her way of life. What they had said to each other wasn't as telling as what they hadn't said. She couldn't have imagined the strong connection they'd forged, and she couldn't believe it had ended when the cholera had.

Something was shifting inside her. And she was afraid to venture toward its cause.

A week had passed. Friday was payday and the saloon was standing room only. The poker table was ringed with a few farmers, but mostly miners and lumberjacks watched the game in progress. In the back of Lon's mind, the fact that he hadn't seen Dr. Gabriel on the street since she'd moved into the mining of-

fice niggled at him. Had she fallen sick? Should he go
check on her?

He brushed the thought away like an aggravating
fly. He'd done much this week to rebuild his reserves.
And tonight's game was not for chicken stakes. Nearly a
hundred dollars in gold, silver and bills had been tossed
into the ante. If Lon lost this game, he'd be broke again.

His three competitors included the same small, mustached man whom Lon had gambled with every night
the past week. The other two were a tall, slender young
man and a dark-haired miner. The young half breed
spoke with a French accent. Perhaps he was a mix of
Métis, Indian and French. Either way, Lon pegged him
as a young buck out to have all the fun he could, no
doubt with the first good money he'd ever earned. The
miner looked ill-tempered, old enough to know better
than to cause trouble. But wise enough? Time would
tell.

Lon stared at his cards—just a pair of red queens.
That scoring combination was all he had worth anything
among the five cards dealt him. He hissed inwardly in
disgust. A pair was just above a random hand with nothing of scoring strength.

He gazed around at the other players, trying to gauge
by their expressions and posture how good their hands
were. Could they have gotten even worse hands? Was
that possible?

The small man was tapping the table with his left
hand and looking at Lon in an odd way. Lon decided
he would lay two cards facedown and deal himself another two. He hoped they'd be better than the pitiful
ones he'd dealt himself first.

The miner hit the other man's hand, which was tapping beside him. "Stop that. You tryin' to fiddle with my concentration?"

Lon held his breath. He'd seen fights start with less provocation than this.

The small man hit back the offending hand. "If you been drinking too much, don't take it out on me."

The miner lurched forward.

Fortunately, the onlookers voiced loud disapproval of the fight—it would spoil their fun. The miner scowled but sat back in his chair.

Reminding himself of the pistol in his vest pocket, Lon put two cards facedown and drew two more cards. His pair of queens became a triple, two red and one black. *Better. But not much.*

Then, as the dealer, he went from player to player asking if they wanted to draw again. There was another round of calling and betting. The small man was still watching Lon with an intense gaze. Was there going to be trouble?

The man asked, "You fight in the war?"

Lon shrugged. "Most of us did, didn't we?"

This appeared to aggravate the small man even more. He looked at Lon with narrowed eyes. Lon tried to ignore him. Winning the game was what mattered. Nothing was going to distract him from that.

The final round ended and each player laid down his cards. Lon wished he could have had another chance to make his hand better, but he laid down his three queens. And nearly broke his poker face when he saw that he had won. Victory and relief flowed through him.

The sullen miner's face twisted in anger. "You sure you're not dealing from the bottom of the deck?"

Lon looked at him coolly. "If you don't want me to deal, you deal." He began shuffling the cards with rapid and practiced hands. The men standing around liked to watch someone who could handle cards as well as he could. He didn't hold back, letting the cards cascade from one hand to the other and then deftly working the cards like an accordion. He held his audience in rapt attention.

The young Métis who'd lost his gambling money rose, and another man slid into his place. Lon nodded to him and began dealing cards for another game. One of the saloon girls came over and tried to drape herself around Lon's shoulders. Not wishing to be impolite, he murmured, "Not while I'm working, please, miss." She nodded and moved over to lean on the dark-haired miner.

Lon hoped she would sweeten the man's temper but the miner shrugged her off with a muttered insult. Lon looked at the cards he'd dealt himself and nearly revealed his shock. He held almost a royal flush: jack, queen, king, ace and a four.

The odds of his dealing this hand to himself were incredible. The other players turned cards facedown and he dealt them the number of cards they requested. Lon put the four down and drew another card. He stared at it, disbelieving.

The betting began. Lon resisted the temptation to bet the rest of his money on the game. That would signal to the other players that he had good cards, which in this case was a vast understatement. He bet half the money he had just won. The other players eyed him and each raised. The second round of betting took place. Then Lon concealed his excitement and laid out the royal flush—ten, jack, queen, king, ace.

He reached forward to scoop up the pot. The small

man leaped from his seat, shouting, "You can't have dealt honestly. No one gets a royal flush like that!"

Lon eyed the man. He'd played cards several times with him over the past days, and the man had been consistently even-tempered.

"You're right!" The dark-haired miner reared up from his chair and slammed a fist into Lon's face. Lon flew back into the men crowding around the table. He tried to find his feet, but he went down hard on one knee. He leaped up again, his fists in front of his face.

The gold and silver coins he'd just won were clinking, sliding down the table as the miner tipped it over. "No!" Lon bellowed. "No!"

The miner swung again. Lon dodged, getting in two good jabs. The miner groaned and fell. Then the small mustached man pulled a knife from his boot.

A knife. Lon leaped out of reach again. He fumbled for the Derringer in his vest. The small man jumped over the upended table. He plunged his knife into Lon just above the high pocket of his vest.

As his own warm blood gushed under his hand, Lon felt himself losing consciousness. The crushing pain in his chest made it hard to breathe. He looked at the man nearest him, a stranger. He was alone in this town of strangers.

No, I'm not.

Lon blinked, trying to get rid of the fog that was obscuring his vision. "Get the woman doctor," he gasped. "Get Dr. Gabriel."

Chapter Four

Pounding. Pounding. Mercy woke in the darkness, groggy. More sights and sounds roused her—the sound of a match striking, a candle flame flickering to life, padding footsteps going toward the curtains. "Aunt Mercy, get up," Indigo commanded in the blackness. "Someone's nearly breaking down the front door and shouting for the doctor." The curtain swished as Indigo went through it to answer the door.

Mercy sat up. Feeling around in the darkness, she started getting dressed without thinking, merely reacting to Indigo's command. With her dress on over her nightgown, she sat down to pull on her shoes. She found she was unable to lift her stockinged feet. The listlessness which had gripped her over the past week smothered her in its grasp once more.

She had not left the mining office—in fact, could not leave it. She knew her lassitude had begun to worry Indigo. Her daughter had given her long looks of bewildered concern. Yet Mercy had been unable to reassure Indigo, had been unable to break free from the lethargy, the hopelessness, the defeat she'd experienced deep,

deep inside. And somehow it had been connected with Lon Mackey, but why?

With the candle glowing in front of her face, Indigo came in with three men crowding behind her. "Aunt Mercy, Lon Mackey has been knifed in the saloon."

Cold shock dashed its way through Mercy. As if she'd been tossed into water, she gasped and sucked in air.

"It's serious. We must hurry." Indigo set the candle-stick on the potbellied stove and began pulling a dress on over her nightgown. Then in the shadows, she bent, opened the trunk at the end of the room and pulled out two black leather bags, one with surgical items and one with nursing supplies.

Mercy sat, watching Indigo by the flickering candle-light. Her feet were still rooted to the cold floor.

"Ain't you gonna get up, lady—I mean, lady doctor?" one of the men asked. "The gambler's unconscious and losing blood. He needs a doc."

Indigo turned and snagged both their wool shawls from a nail on the wall. "Aunt Mercy?"

"Yeah," one of the other men said, "the gambler asked for you—by name. Come on."

He asked for me. The image of Lon bleeding snapped the tethers that bound her to the floor. Mercy stirred, forcing off the apathy. She slid her feet into her shoes and dragged herself up. "Let's go."

Outside for the first time in days, she shivered in the October night air, shivered at once more being outside, vulnerable. Thinking of Lon and recalling how he'd done whatever she needed, whatever she'd asked during the cholera outbreak, she hurried over the slick, muddy street toward the saloon. In the midst of the black night, oil lamps shone through the swinging door and the win-dows, beckoning.

The men who'd come to get them hurried forward, shouting out, "The lady doc is coming!"

Mercy and Indigo halted just outside the door. Having difficulty drawing breath, Mercy whispered, "Pray." Indigo nodded and they entered side by side. The bright lights made Mercy blink as her eyes adjusted. Finally, she discerned where the crowd was thickest.

She headed straight toward the center of the gathering, her steps jerky, as if she were walking on frozen feet. "Nurse Indigo," she said over her shoulder, "get the bar ready for me, please." But a glance told her that Indigo was already disinfecting the bar in preparation.

The gawking men parted as Mercy swept forward. One unfamiliar man popped up in front of her. "Hold it. A woman doctor? She might do him more harm than good."

Before Mercy could respond, the dissenting man was yanked back and shoved out of her way, the men around all chorusing, "The gambler asked for her."

Unchecked, Mercy continued, her strength coming back in spurts like the blood surging, pulsing through her arteries. Her walking smoothed out.

She had never doctored with such a large crowd pressing in on every side. She sensed the men here viewed this as a drama, a spectacle. Still, she kept her chin up. If they'd come to see the show, she'd show them all right.

Then she saw Lon. He had been stretched out on a table, a crimson stain soaking the front of his white shirt and embroidered vest. An invisible hand squeezed the breath from her lungs and it rushed out in a long "Oh."

A young woman in a low-cut, shiny red dress was holding a folded towel over the wound. She looked into Mercy's eyes. "This was all we had to stop the bleeding."

Mercy nodded, drawing up her reserves. "Excellent." She put her black bag on the table beside Lon and lifted out the bottle of wood alcohol. She poured it over both her trembling hands, hoping to quiet her nerves as she disinfected. To hide the quivering of her hands, she shook them and then balled them into fists. "Let me see the wound, please."

The young woman lifted the blood-soaked towel and stepped back. She was the only one who did so—everyone else pressed in closer. "Please, friends," Mercy stated in a firm tone, forcing the quavering from her voice, "I must have room to move my arms. I must have light. Please."

The crowd edged back a couple of inches. The girl in the low-cut dress lifted a lamp closer to Lon.

Mercy wished her inner quaking would stop. She sucked in more air laden with cigar smoke, stale beer and sweat. She looked down into Lon's face.

She had tended so many bleeding men in the war, yet her work then had been anonymous. She had never before been called to tend someone whom she knew and whom she had depended on, worked with. Seeing a friend like this must be what was upsetting her. She must focus on the wound, not the man.

In spite of her trembling fingers, Mercy unbuttoned and tugged back his shirt. She examined the wound and was relieved to see that the blood was clotting and sluggish. The wound, though deep, had not penetrated the heart or abdomen. That would have been a death sentence. Her shaking lessened. This was her job, this was what she had been called to do.

As she probed the wound, she felt a small part of the lung that may have collapsed. She had read about pulmonary atelectasis—once she closed the wound, the lung would either reinflate or compensate. But she needed to act quickly.

She turned toward the bar. "Nurse Indigo, is my operating table ready?"

"Almost, Dr. Gabriel." While working in public, both women used these terms of address. The dean of the Female Medical College of Pennsylvania had insisted on using their titles to imbue them with respect.

"Please carry the patient to the bar, and bring my bag, too," Mercy asked of the men. "I will operate there." Mercy turned and the way parted before her. She was accustomed to disbelief and disapproval, but never before had she been forced to endure being put on display. Her face was hot and glowing bright scarlet.

She had heard of circuses that had freak shows, displaying bearded women and other humans with physical abnormalities. Here she was the local freak, the lady doctor. But her concern for Lon's survival outweighed her embarrassment and frustration. He was depending on her.

For a moment, she felt faint. She scolded herself for such weakness and plowed her way to the bar. Now Indigo was helping the bartender position the second of two large oil lamps.

"How bad is it, Doctor?" Indigo asked.

"Can you do anything for him? Or is he a goner?" asked the bartender.

The word *goner* tightened Mercy's throat. "The wound may have collapsed part of the lung. I will need to stitch up the wound."

There was a deep murmuring as everyone made their opinion of this known, discussing it back and forth. Mercy focused on Lon and her task. In the background, the voices blended together in a deep ebb and flow, like waves on a shore.

Indigo laid out the surgical instruments on a clean linen cloth. Mercy looked to the saloon girl, who was hovering nearby. "What is thy name, miss?"

"Sunny, ma'am—I mean, Doc."

"Sunny, will thee help me by unbuttoning the shirt and vest the rest of the way and helping the bartender remove them? I must scrub my hands thoroughly before I begin surgery."

Sunny nodded and began undoing Lon's vest buttons.

Mercy moved farther down the bar, where Indigo had poured boiled water and alcohol into a clean basin. She picked up a bar of soap and began scrubbing her hands and nails with a little brush, hating each moment of delay.

"Hey, Lady Doc," one of the men asked, his voice coming through the constant muttering, "shouldn't you wash up *after* you mess with all the blood and stuff?"

Mercy kept scrubbing as she addressed his question. "A young English doctor, Joseph Lister, has discovered that mortality rates decline in hospitals that practice antiseptic measures before surgical procedures."

"Really? Is that a fact?" the man said. "What's *antiseptic* mean?"

"*Sepsis* is when a wound becomes infected, and it usually leads to the patient's death. *Anti* means against, so antiseptic measures try to prevent sepsis."

"My ma always said cleanliness is next to godliness," another man spoke up.

"Thy mother was a wise woman. In my experience, women with cleaner houses lose fewer children to disease."

Mercy held out her hands, and Indigo poured more

boiled water and then wood alcohol over them. Mercy took a deep breath and turned to her task. "Nurse Indigo, will thee please spray the patient with carbolic acid?"

Using the large atomizer, Indigo sprayed carbolic acid over Lon's broad chest and then directly over the wound, which she had already sponged clean of gore. Mercy proceeded to inspect Lon's wound, feeling for the deepest point. There was silence all around her—thick, intent silence—as everyone watched her every move. She located the point, reached for her needle and silk thread and began to close the wound with tiny stitches.

"Hey! Look!" a man called out. "She's doin' it. Look!"

Mercy felt the press of the crowd. "*Please,* thee must all move back. I must have room to work." *To breathe.*

The men edged back. She drew in air and prayed on silently. She could only hope that Indigo's pressure, plus natural clotting and healing, would help seal the wound and allow the lung to reinflate.

Mercy set and tied her final stitch and blinked away tears she couldn't explain. She was thankful that Lon hadn't stirred during the probing or suturing.

"You done, Lady Doc?" the bartender asked.

"Yes. Now we must hope that Lon Mackey will sleep a bit longer, then wake and begin to heal. Do any of thee know where Lon has been staying?"

"He's bunking in the back room," Sunny said.

Mercy had wondered where Lon roomed. And though his living arrangement fit his gambling, she could not like Lon in this place. She pursed her lips momentarily.

"I suggest that he be carried to his bed, then," Mercy said. "Nurse Indigo and I will take turns staying with him."

A censorious voice came from behind. "Decent women don't hang around bars."

Mercy turned and recognized the speaker as the same man who had tried to prevent her from treating Lon. "I am a doctor. I know my job, and I do it wherever my patient is."

She turned her back on the disapproving man, who had a distinctive shock of gray hair. She wouldn't forget him any time soon. "Please, some of thee carry Lon to his bed very carefully. I don't want sudden jarring to disturb the wound."

Several men lifted Lon from the bar. He moaned. The men halted. Though Lon's eyelids fluttered, he didn't revive. Mercy waved the men on and she followed them. It wasn't uncommon for a person to remain unconscious for a long while after surgery, but Mercy prayed that Lon wouldn't remain asleep for many more hours.

She had just displayed her abilities to many. The outcome of her surgery must be positive, or she might be forced to leave this place in disgrace.

This cold thought brought back the trembling deep inside. She had done for Lon what he needed her to do, and now she needed him to get well. *I need thee to wake up and move, Lon Mackey, our only friend here. Please wake up.*

Lon realized that he was breathing, just barely. Something wasn't right. He felt pain, like his chest was on fire. Like it had been crushed. He recalled loud voices and a table tipping. Something bad had happened. He tried to open his eyes but the lids were heavy, so heavy. Finally, he managed.

He blinked several times to rid himself of the fog

that clung to his senses. Then he saw her. Just a few feet from him, Mercy sat in a chair, her eyes closed. He squinted. What was Mercy doing sitting beside his bed? In the back of the saloon? Was he hallucinating?

He tried to speak and couldn't. What had happened? He couldn't gather his thoughts. They were like popcorn sizzling in a hot pan, hopping and jumping out of reach. His face felt like it was that hot pan. A fever? Had the cholera got him this time?

He looked to Mercy. Maybe she would speak to him and then he would know what had happened, why his chest hurt, why he couldn't speak. But Mercy's eyes remained closed. Her thick, golden-brown lashes fanned out against her pale skin. She'd taken off her bonnet. Her flaxen hair had slipped from the tight bun at the nape of her neck. Her small nose was pointed downward; her pale-pink lips were parted slightly. He couldn't look away. How lovely she was. How untouched.

He drew a deep breath. Pain stabbed his chest. He stopped the flow of air, then let it out slowly, slowly. He lifted his hand, or tried to. "Mercy," he whispered. "Mercy."

Her eyelids fluttered and opened. "Lon." She leaned forward in her chair. "Lon, how is thee feeling?"

He moistened his mouth and tried to speak again.

"Thy mouth is dry, Lon Mackey." She reached over, lifted a cast-iron kettle and filled a cup. "Here. Drink this. It has more to it than water and thee needs strength. If thee can stay awake, I have venison broth ordered for thee."

He drank the lukewarm, bitter coffee with gratitude. He hadn't realized how thirsty he was until he had seen her pouring coffee into the cup. "More."

She refilled the cup and he swallowed it down, lay back, gasping as if he'd just sprinted a mile.

"What happened?" he whispered.

"Thee suffered an injury. Does thee want some venison broth?"

"Yes." He wasn't hungry, but he knew eating was necessary.

Mercy rose. "Sunny!"

He heard footsteps and turned his head. The petite blonde came down the stairs. "Yes, Doctor?"

"Will thee go to the café and ask for broth for my patient? The proprietress said she would keep some on the stove for me."

"Of course, Doctor."

"I thank thee. I don't know why Indigo hasn't returned."

Lon remembered then. This blonde girl had been there when—what had happened? "What kind of injury?" Hearing his own words startled him.

"Thee was stabbed." Mercy's voice was matter-of-fact.

"Stabbed? By whom?"

"I do not know. I did not see it happen. I was called to the saloon to doctor thee."

He rolled her answers around in his mind like marbles, but he could call up no memory. Mercy wouldn't lie, so it must be true. Anger flickered in him. Had the man been apprehended? The fog was blowing into his mind again. *No, no, let me think...*

Lon woke to Mercy's coaxing voice. "Lon, Lon, thy broth has come. It's nice and hot, and smells delicious. Please open thy eyes."

He looked up into her face and was swamped with

the comfort of seeing her. He stiffened himself against the pull toward her. *I'm weak and getting strange thoughts. It's just good to have a friend, and one who's a doctor.* He tried to raise himself. Pain lanced down his left side. He couldn't stop a groan. "Help me sit up."

"Friend," Mercy said in that tone people used with children and invalids, "thee were stabbed, remember? That will pain thee on the left side. Let me raise thy head and I will help thee with the broth."

"I'm a grown man. I don't need help eating," he snapped. The words exhausted him. If he'd had the strength, he would have cursed. *No, not in front of Mercy.*

"Thee is weak from thy wound. Thy blood loss was considerable. Thy strength will return if thee will only let me help." Mercy slid another pillow under his head and shoulders. Then she picked up the bowl and spooned some broth into his mouth.

The broth was salty and hot. It made him feel better as it coursed down his throat. He wanted to tell her again that he could feed himself. Then he realized he was wrong.

"How soon," he asked, swallowing between spoonfuls, "will I be up again?"

"I cannot say. All I know is that thee will need careful nursing. Thee will need to eat as often as thee can and drink plenty of liquids. Thee has a fever, which is completely normal under these circumstances."

He wanted to ask, *Can I still die?* But he didn't. Of course he could still die. They both knew that from the war. His fever was due to infection, and infection could kill him. He fought the rush of moisture to his eyes.

"After thee has drunk this broth, I will begin fomenting thy wound. It will help keep thy fever down—"

"How's Mackey doing?" the bartender interrupted as he entered from the rear of the saloon. He held out his hand. "I'm Tom, remember?"

Mercy began to reply, but Lon cut her off. He could speak for himself. "I'll be up in no time." His bravado cost him.

The hearty red-faced bartender had the nerve to chuckle. "Yeah, well, I hope so. I like having an honest gambler in the place. It's good for business."

"Did the man who stabbed me get arrested?" Lon asked, feeling his thin vitality leak out with each word.

"He took off and we couldn't find him," Tom said. "We telegraphed his description to the territorial sheriff in Boise. That's about all we can do."

Lon made a sound of disgust and then sipped another spoonful of broth, hating that he needed to be fed.

"Friend," Mercy said, looking at the bartender, "I am concerned about Lon Mackey staying here at night. He needs his sleep, and the noise from the saloon will keep him awake."

"I slept all night, didn't I?" Lon demanded, regretting it instantly. Every time he spoke, it sapped energy from him.

Tom folded his arms and leaned against the unpainted, raw wood wall. "I see what you mean, Doc. But there's not many places available."

Lon forced himself to stay silent and just swallow the broth. He couldn't afford to waste more effort on words. He stopped listening to the conversation. Feeling her soft palm on his forehead, he turned into it and let himself enjoy the sensation. The fever had wrapped him in its heat.

He had been wounded before and knew that the pain would pass—if his luck held. He'd made it through nearly four years of war. Thousands of others hadn't. He tried to block out the images of battle and the charge of fear that they brought. *The war's over. It's done. Maybe I'm done.* He didn't like that last idea. *She doesn't think I'm done.*

He managed to open his eyes enough to glance up into Mercy's face. Did she know how pretty she was? He noticed that she had a widow's peak that made her face heart-shaped. Her blue eyes looked down at him with deep concern. And compassion. How could she care so much about strangers? How had the two of them ended up in this place? Hadn't she seen enough of pain, misery and death in the war?

His leaden eyelids drifted down. Maybe the answer lay in the fact that while she had nursed the wounded and dying, she hadn't ordered them into the line of fire and watched them die. Consciousness began to slip from him and he welcomed oblivion, even as he fought to stay awake, stay alive. There was something about this woman that made him want to live. Why hadn't her father kept her at home and married her off to some neighboring farmer, out of harm's way?

Out of my way?

After the bartender went to unshutter the front door for another day's business, Mercy looked at Lon as he slid into sleep. He'd almost finished the broth, and that was heartening. Even his crankiness was a good sign. She stood and stretched her back and neck.

"Hello!" a woman's voice came from outside the front door. "Is the lady doctor here?"

Mercy sent one last glance at Lon and then walked through the saloon. Outside, she saw a large, blowsy woman, one of those who had refused to let her board. Mercy approached her with caution.

"Good day, may I help thee?"

Something beyond the woman caught Mercy's eye: Indigo, across the street, down a few storefronts. She was talking to a man.

"Remember me? I'm Ma Bailey. You still looking for a place to board?" the big woman asked.

Mercy was incredulous. *She wouldn't take us in a week ago. Now she wants us. Why?* "We have been staying in the back of the mining—"

"Know that. But you can't stay there forever. It's not a house. I got room for you in my place. Two dollars a week. That includes food. You got to go to the Chinese for laundry. What do you say?"

"I will consider your offer." *Your belated offer.* The woman looked disgruntled, glancing up and down as if she had more to say.

Gazing at Indigo over the woman's shoulder, Mercy waited for her to come to the point. Indigo was behaving in a most unusual fashion while speaking to the man. It suddenly struck Mercy that Indigo was flirting. Mercy wished the young man would turn around so she could see his face. Indigo and she had never discussed it, but as a woman of color, Indigo faced special risks with white men. But she couldn't see the color of his skin. There were men called half breeds in town. She had yet to see a black man hereabouts.

"Ya see, it's this way," Ma interrupted. "My daughter and her man are coming here before winter. Just got a letter when the supply wagons came in today. And she's expecting." Ma Bailey looked up at her, suddenly beaming. "I was thinking that when her time comes, she could use a good midwife. The first baby's always the hardest. I mean, you don't know if she'll have an easy time or not."

Ah, now this makes sense. Self-interest is *always a good bet when guessing a person's motivation.* "Whether I board in thy home or not, I will be happy to attend to thy daughter's first delivery."

"Yeah, but it's like this." Ma hemmed and hawed with the best of them. "I was thinkin' you might give us a deal on the cost, since you'd be livin' with me."

Mercy gave the woman a thin smile. Stinginess, another reliable incentive for some. Did she want to live with a grasping, unkind, prejudiced woman? No, she did not. "My fees are not exorbitant. I'm sure thy son-in-law will be able to meet them. I thank thee for thy invitation."

The man Indigo was flirting with turned a bit, but his hat cast a shadow over his face. *Be careful, Indigo.*

In spite of Mercy's obvious wish to conclude the conversation, the woman lingered. "You really patched up that gambler?"

"I did indeed," Mercy said.

"Never heard the like. You must really know what you're doing."

"I studied for three years at the Female Medical College of Pennsylvania and passed all the tests."

The woman shook her head. "That beats all. Women doctors. What will they think of next?" She walked away, calling over her shoulder, "Let me know when you make up your mind."

But Mercy was studying the young man's tall, lean profile. And then Indigo glanced toward her and quickly looked away. Mercy hoped the gentleman would turn out to be a fine young man with courting on his mind. She should have been expecting something like this—

Indigo would be sixteen on Christmas Day, just the right age to start thinking of romance.

Yet Indigo was at risk. Mercy hadn't yet seen any men of color in the Idaho Territory, and some white men would be more than willing to take advantage of Indigo's innocence. Even if they were serious about her, mixed marriages were unheard-of and could unleash the nastiest kind of race hate. Mercy had realized that her life's mission didn't include a husband. A doctor was at the beck and call of everyone. How could a woman care for a house, children and a husband with such a demanding schedule? So Mercy hadn't given Indigo's future much thought. However, she didn't want to force her spinsterhood onto her daughter. Her observations today gave her a new concern to consider and to address.

Her thoughts turned to Lon, and she headed back to check on him. She walked into the back room and found Sunny sitting in her chair. Some strong emotion rocked Mercy. She paused for a moment, letting the unusual feeling lap over her like sea waves. She realized that she didn't like finding Sunny alone with Lon.

And then she noticed that Sunny was evidently trying to hide the fact that she was expecting. She looked to be near her last trimester. When the girl was standing, it wasn't so evident. But sitting, yes, it was unmistakable.

Sunny glanced up and then popped out of Mercy's chair. "I was just watching him while you were gone, Doc."

Mercy nodded. She forced herself from the clutches of her unusual reaction, and then pity came swiftly. This young woman, who was just a few years older than Indigo, was going to need help soon. The world was not kind to babies born out of wedlock. More than once,

Mercy's parents had welcomed young girls in this situation into their home. Mercy thought of her sister, Felicity, who was running an orphanage.

Mercy smiled kindly at Sunny. "I thank thee. My nurse will come soon to relieve me."

Mercy watched the young woman leave, wondering how to speak with her about her condition, a condition that she hoped Indigo would never find herself in without a good husband to look after her.

Lon Mackey stirred, and Mercy waited to see if he were about to wake. She felt a rush of tenderness toward the man who had stood by her when she'd first come to town. Despite his unusual choice of profession, the man had the potential to make a woman a very good husband, since he seemed to take a woman at her word and didn't mind if she knew more than he.

Lon's eyes opened and he caught her gazing at him. She didn't have time to look away, so she smiled instead. After a moment, he smiled back at her. Warmth flooded her face as he slowly slid back into sleep.

Chapter Five

Late that night, Mercy woke once again to the sound of pounding on her door. Would that sound ever stop making her heart race? She lit the bedside candle and padded on bare feet to open the door. "Yes?" she asked, shivering in the cool draft that made the candle flicker.

"Please, you come. Please. Wife bad. Baby not come."

This speech was delivered by a young Chinese man. Still waking up, Mercy stared at the man. Was this a dream?

"Please, you come. I pay. Wife bad. Baby not come. People say you doctor, good doctor."

Mercy snapped awake. "One moment." Leaving the door open, she pulled her sadly wrinkled dress on over her nightgown, then slid into her shoes and grabbed her bag. She wished Indigo were here, but she was watching over Lon Mackey, who was still feverish and sometimes delirious in the rear of the saloon.

Mercy stepped outside. Shivering again in the moonlight, she locked the door behind her. "Please lead the way. I'll do what I can for thy wife and baby."

The man bowed twice and then took off running

down the dark alley. Mercy hurried to keep up with him. After a week of idleness, even a late-night call was welcome. If she weren't so tired, she would have rejoiced.

Then the stress of this call punched her with its ugly fist. Childbirth loomed over all physicians as the leading cause of death among young females. She began praying as she hurried through the chill darkness, *Father, be with me tonight. Give me wisdom and skill.*

She was aware that there were Chinese immigrants in town. Ma Bailey had mentioned earlier that Mercy would have to take her laundry to the Chinese. How had these people found their way to the Idaho Territory? And why?

Before long, the two of them arrived at the far end of town, where a group of small wooden houses had been built very close together. The Chinese quarter was, of course, set apart from the rest of the town.

The man opened the door of one of these houses; a lamp was burning low inside. Two Chinese women were in the room, one sitting beside another who was lying in bed, obviously pregnant and in distress. Mercy's nerves tightened another notch. Had she been called in too late? Would she be able to save both mother and child?

There was a flurry of rapid Chinese. Mercy pulled off her wool shawl and tossed it onto a peg on the wall. Then she turned to the man. "Water. I need hot water. *Now.*"

He hesitated only a moment to repeat her request. When she nodded her approval, he hurried outside. She turned to her patient whose face was pale and drawn, and whose hair was damp with perspiration, all signs of a prolonged labor. "I am Dr. Mercy Gabriel." Then she gestured to each of the women and asked, "And thee are?"

The man returned with a bucket of water and hung it over the fire in the hearth as he answered for the women. "I am Chen Park. She Chen An, wife. The other, friend, Lin Li." He bowed again.

Mercy repeated the names and nodded. She began to lay out her birthing instruments on the table with a trembling hand.

The young wife shouted again as an evidently strong labor pain gripped her.

"How long has she been in labor?" Mercy asked.

"Before dawn. I worry."

Nearly twenty-four hours of labor. Her hope for a healthy birth dimmed, but there was still hope for a live birth. Praying, Mercy nodded and washed her hands in the basin he'd just filled with fresh water. *Please, Father, let the child and mother live.*

She motioned for the lamp to be held near and examined her patient. Chen An moaned and whimpered. Mercy didn't blame her. She used her stethoscope to listen for the baby's heartbeat. She thought she heard it, but the mother's crescendo of moaning made it difficult.

"The baby is lodged in the birth canal." Buzzing inside with worry, Mercy went to her instruments and selected a long, narrow forceps.

They looked at her questioningly.

"The baby is stuck, can't get out. I will help baby come out." Mercy demonstrated how she would use the forceps. She didn't like using pidgin English and sign language, but she didn't have time for a long explanation.

Praying still, she sprayed carbolic acid around the birthing site, made a quick, small incision, and proceeded to use the forceps. The woman writhed and moaned, obviously calling for help. When Mercy sensed the next contraction, she gently applied pressure and righted the baby's head in the birth canal.

Chen An called out louder, frantic. Mercy held the child in place. "One more, Chen An," she coaxed. "One more push and this will be over."

The next contraction hit. Mercy held the forceps in place, keeping the baby from turning the wrong way. The baby slid onto the bed. A boy!

She dropped the forceps and cut the cord. Within seconds, she had the baby wrapped in a white linen towel, suctioning out its mouth and nose. In the lamplight, the little face was so pale. Mercy slapped the bottom of the baby's feet. "Come on. Thee must breathe, little one." She slapped the small soles again. *Please. Please.*

Then in the silent, tense room, the baby gasped, choked and wailed. Chen Park whooped and laughed.

Mercy felt gratitude wash over her in great swells of relief. *Alive.* She couldn't help herself. She whirled on the spot like a girl, silently praising God for this new life.

She nestled the baby into the mother's arms. "Thee has a fine son, Mr. Chen Park," she said. "What will thee name him?"

"He will be called Chen Lee," the father pronounced, grinning.

Mercy nodded. "Hello, little Chen Lee. Welcome to this world, precious child."

Lon opened his eyes. Mercy was sitting in the chair beside his cot, smiling. The early morning light made her pale hair gleam with subtle gold. He admired the wide blue eyes that were looking at him with tenderness. The sight took his breath for a moment.

He'd spent the war and the past three years in saloons, far from respectable ladies like Mercy Gabriel. Nonetheless, his whole self experienced the pull toward her, toward the glimmering light, toward home and hearth…and peace.

He closed his eyes. *Get hold of yourself, man.*

"Good morning, friend." Her voice was low and velvety, kind to his ear. "Here's some tea for thee."

Her hands slid under his shoulders and added two more pillows. He turned his face to let her palm cup his cheek. *So stupid of me.* He broke the contact.

"Does thee think thee can hold thy cup today?"

He opened his eyes. "Yes." He accepted the cup, trying to keep it from shaking. The fever still burned inside him and the cup trembled in his hand.

She closed her soft hand over his, steadying it.

He braced himself to resist the feeling of her touch, of connectedness with this good woman. But the fever worked against him. If he tried to hold the cup himself, it would fall and break. Better to just let her hold it. "You can do it," he said ungraciously. He let his arm fall back to his side, free from her touch.

She held the cup to his lips. He sipped and then said, feeling disgruntled, "You look happy."

"I am. I had the privilege of helping a beautiful little baby boy safely into this world. He is little Chen Lee."

From what he had seen of the way the Chinese were treated here in the West, where they had immigrated to build the railroads, he thought that someday this little boy would rue the day he was born in the Idaho Territory. If he survived.

"I'm always happy when I deliver a baby alive and well. It's such a marvel." Mercy's face glowed.

He wanted to say something to bring her back to reality. He quoted harshly, "'For all flesh is as grass, and all the glory of man as the flower of grass. The grass withereth, and the flower thereof falleth away.'"

"Yes," she replied, "Peter wrote that. But Isaiah declared, 'The grass withereth, the flower fadeth: but the word of our God shall stand forever.'"

He cursed himself for bringing up a Bible verse. The idea of God was hard to let go of completely. But after four devastating, bloody years of war, if God was still there, Lon didn't like him very much.

"Where's Indigo?" he grumbled. *Let the subject of man and God drop, Mercy.*

Mercy nodded her head as if acceding to his unspoken request. "She has gone to take a nap. I will watch over thee this morning."

"Don't need someone watching over me."

The Quaker had the nerve to chuckle at him. "Thee will be better sooner if I am here to give thee tea, broth and maybe even oatmeal."

"Sounds delicious," he snapped and then took another sip of hot, sweet tea. It was appetizing and strengthening. He ground his teeth in seething frustration as hot as the fever he couldn't shake.

She chuckled again. "I know thee is the kind of man who doesn't want anyone fussing over him. I will not fuss, but someone must see that thee has liquid and nourishment often. Who else is there to do this, friend?"

He had no answer for her. He had made certain that he developed no friendships here. Now he wished he had befriended someone, anyone. Having this gentle, gracious woman nearby awoke so many memories from the past—his mother, sister and Janette... No, not Janette. His mind wouldn't let his memories of her intrude. He crushed them now without mercy. Janette had nothing in common with this caring doctor, save their gender.

Without Mercy. He must find a way to get better quickly and go back to gambling without this woman who made him long for the life he'd once known.

He tried not to think that this fever might best him yet. Had he survived four years of carnage only to be felled by a knife in a barroom brawl?

Later, Mercy glanced once more over her shoulder as she stepped from the back room of the saloon into the alley. Indigo was sitting beside Lon Mackey, who was sleeping again. Still a little drowsy herself from the interrupted night's sleep, Mercy walked around the front of the saloon and stood looking up and down the street, trying to decide how to find living quarters and an office. Then a thought occurred to her. Maybe what she was looking for wasn't on Main Street. She began to walk the long alleys on both sides of Main Street.

Her thoughts strayed back to Lon Mackey. Was his crankiness just because he felt weak? Men didn't like to feel weak, especially not men like Lon. Or was he angry with her for some reason? The name Janette came to mind. Lon had uttered this name more than once in his delirious moments.

She shied away from thoughts of Lon Mackey's personal life—and the feelings those thoughts raised— and recalled last night's delivery. She looked toward the Chinese quarter. Out in the fresh air, men were working—boiling clothing in large washtubs over fires, hanging sheets on clotheslines. Some were ironing. She had never seen a man do laundry. She had never seen loose cotton clothes like the ones they were wearing.

The sight fascinated her. Why had they come to live here in this place so far from home?

Of course, that was what she had done, too. Was a female doctor any more welcome here than a person of Chinese descent? She couldn't even rent a place to live.

The early autumn twilight was coloring the sky as she turned back and walked to the general store, where she had met Jacob Tarver. "Jacob Tarver," she greeted him, "I see that thee has a storeroom behind thy store."

He looked startled, then said, "Ah, yes."

"Have thee thought of renting it out?" she asked with a bright smile.

"I don't understand." He eyed her as if she'd just dropped from the sky.

Mercy explained to him that she wanted to rent the storeroom for her medical practice. She talked on, overcoming his objection that he needed the storage space with the suggestion that he build a larger warehouse at the edge of town to stock his supplies, thereby increasing his income even more. He could rent her the rear storeroom for her medical practice and then rent out part of his new warehouse to other merchants.

And before she was done, she left him with the comfortable belief that this was what he had been intending to do all along. He promised to have the storeroom cleaned out and ready for her in a day or two.

Mercy would have felt guilty about this friendly persuasion except that it benefited Jacob Tarver as well. As she left the store, she heard a woman call her name. She recognized the pretty dark-haired mother of Missy.

"Miss Gabriel, I mean Dr. Gabriel," the young woman stammered, "I'm Mrs. James Dunfield, Ellen Dunfield. I have been so busy helping my husband and daughter regain their strength after the cholera and taking care of my infant son that I didn't realize that you had been sleeping in the mining office. Please, you must come and stay in our vacant cabin. My husband did so well in panning for gold that he built us a regular house. But the cabin is in good repair and will be a snug home for you this winter."

Joy lifted Mercy. "God bless thee, Ellen Dunfield. Yes, Indigo and I are still looking for a place to stay."

"Well, my Jim and I talked it over, and we don't care what anybody says about mixing races. You and that Indigo saved our family, and we don't give bad for good. And having an able midwife in town is good news for all us wives."

Concentrating on the positive sentiment behind Ellen Dunfield's words, Mercy asked for directions to the cabin and told Ellen that Indigo would bring their things soon and thanked the woman again. Mercy walked back toward the saloon. *Why did I give in to despair? God is in this place, too.*

Three nights later, Mercy supervised while Lon was moved to the new office, where a bed had been set up for him. The storeroom was large enough for an office, a treating room with an examining table and a bed for patients who needed nursing but had no family to provide it.

A stout black stove had been added to the storeroom. Everything was new, clean and neat. Though pleased with her first formal office, Mercy had no time to admire her surroundings. She turned her thoughts to Lon. His fever wouldn't let go. If she couldn't break his fever…

Lon mumbled. He was somewhere between waking and sleeping. Mercy wished this move had not been necessary on such a chilly night, when he was still so vulnerable. But autumn was progressing and there was no holding it back. And this quiet place would be better for him. The loud nights in the back room of the saloon had been a trial.

"Thank thee, friends. Thank thee much," Mercy said to the volunteers.

"Our pleasure, Doc," one of the older men said. Then he hurried out the door as if this kind act were a form of mischief he might be caught doing.

She shook her head and then shivered sharply. November had come today, and the crisp air was penetrating. She added another log to the stove and then sat down in a rocking chair she'd purchased the day before. She wet a cloth with wood alcohol and bathed Lon's face with it. The heat from his skin warmed her hand.

This fever could kill him. The thought opened a deep abyss within her. She prayed aloud, "Father, I know this fever always comes with surgery. How can I break this good man's fever?"

She bathed his neck and wrists with the alcohol. *Lon, keep fighting. Don't give in.*

"Janette," Lon mumbled, "Janette."

That woman's name again. Mercy froze in place, hand on his arm. He mumbled the name a few more times and then spoke with agitation. Mercy only heard, "Wait…heart… Thomas…fickle."

Inside her came an explosion of feelings. Her heart pounded. Her breath became shallow and short. A startling realization she couldn't ignore pierced her. *I care for this man, this gambler.* No, she couldn't let this be true. *No.*

"Mercy," Lon interrupted her. His eyes had opened. His voice shocked her as much as the unexpected feelings that had welled up because he had said the name of another woman. Clamping down on the riot inside her, she braced herself and assured him, "I am here, Lon Mackey. Thee is in my new office."

"Thirsty."

She lifted his head and helped him drink a full glass of water. Tendrils of unwanted feelings made the act torturous. "Can thee drink more?"

"Tea?"

She busied herself at the stove where a cast-iron kettle sat. She made a pot of sweet tea and sat down. Lon drank the cup of tea eagerly. She stopped her unruly fingers from smoothing back his tousled hair.

"You shouldn't have to take care of me like this," he said in a harsh tone. His eyelids slid down. She touched his hot forehead with her wrist. He was awake enough to turn his head from her touch. She tried not to take offense at his rudeness. But it was hard not to, especially now when she sensed that she felt more than friendship for him.

What had caused this overwhelming cloudburst of feeling? Could she be feeling jealousy?

Mercy's innate honesty forced her to look at her reaction without equivocation. Did she have a right to feel jealous over Lon? Of course not.

But she did. Mercy sat back in her rocker and closed her eyes. Where had this come from? Why hadn't she realized the direction her emotions were taking? And how could she stop this imprudence before it went any further?

Over two weeks later, as the local café was just brewing its first morning coffee, Lon knocked on the door of Mercy's office. *Dr. Gabriel's office. Not Mercy's.*

Thinking of her as "the Quaker" might be a better, more aloof way to think of her. He stepped inside.

The Quaker looked up from her desk and smiled. Recovered from his fever, he had taken pains to present himself freshly shaved and sheared, dressed in his brushed and ironed gambler's clothing.

He would pay his bill for this doctor's service and make sure that she didn't think of him as anything except an acquaintance, a former patient. And then he'd go back to his life in the saloon. "You look as if you've been up all night," he said gruffly. He immediately regretted it, since it revealed his concern for her.

"The Dunfield baby had a fever last night. His parents have been so good to let us rent their cabin, I could not but help them. I just stopped here to leave a note that anyone needing the doctor should come to our cabin. Thee is looking well," she added, her blue eyes glowing with warmth.

He turned on the spot, as if showing off the suit to a prospective customer. "So glad you noticed, Miss Gabriel." Why had he called her that, as if she were some young lady he was interested in? "I mean, *Dr.* Gabriel."

She tilted her head to one side, studying him.

Before she could speak, he said, "I've come to pay my bill." Some of the men who'd witnessed his stabbing had picked up his winnings and held them for him. It was nice to know a few decent men still walked the earth. A few.

She turned back to her desk and lifted out a paper, which she handed to him. He was slightly surprised that she had the bill ready. This must have shown on his face.

"I must earn a living, too, Lon Mackey. And I don't think I would make a very good gambler."

He wished she wouldn't look him in the eye, as she

always did. It was unnerving. Young women just didn't look into a man's eyes. They had special ways of… How did a woman like this grow up without the slightest idea of how to entice a man? *Why am I thinking that?*

He pulled out his wallet and counted out her fee. She took the money from him, wrote "Paid in Full" and the date on the bill, and returned it to him, saying nothing. She just looked into his eyes.

Her blue eyes were her most attractive feature. He gazed into them as if discerning afresh the innocence of her soul. Janette had blue eyes, too. This snapped him back to the present. "I'll bid you—"

"Are thee certain thee wants to return to the saloon?" she asked.

Her question ignited his irritation. Of course Dr. Mercy Gabriel would want to "save" him. "I like gambling," he retorted. "It's an easy life. No work. Nobody counting on me. I do what I like."

"An easy life as long as no one shoves a knife into thee again." Her tone was desert-dry.

"I don't expect you to understand me—"

"But I do understand thee," she interrupted him. "Were thee a major or a colonel?"

"A colonel." He gripped his walking stick, angry at his slip. "What has that got to do with anything?"

"I was in the war, too, thee recalls." She gazed up at him. "It isn't hard for me to see that thee…thee possesses the ability and habit of command. Thee took charge in the epidemic here and helped bring it to an end. I'm a doctor. I hold the lives of my patients in my hands. I understand the wish not to be responsible—"

Lon burned, and disliked the reaction. How could this woman understand him better than he did himself? He didn't want anybody's sympathy, much less that of this woman who wouldn't leave him alone—even when she wasn't in front of him. Why couldn't he banish his concern for her? His awareness of her?

"You understand nothing." He turned and left.

Mercy rose and walked to the door Lon Mackey had slammed behind him. She walked out into the alley and glimpsed his back as he turned toward Main Street. The conversation had been brief in the extreme, but much had been revealed. The war had left its mark on their generation. Not just in the countless lives lost, but in all the shattered bodies, shattered dreams and shattered lives. And would the nightmares ever completely stop? Sometimes she still woke with her heart pounding, her ears ringing with cannon fire and a barrage of rifle fire. The sound of drums and the Rebel yell echoed in her mind. *Yet I didn't have to face battle and dread death, as Lon had. All I had to do was stand helplessly by and watch men die...* Mercy swallowed a moan of remembrance. No wonder Lon shied away from any connection to her or anyone else. No wonder.

Lon Mackey deserved a home, a loving wife and healthy children. When would the long, bitter fingers of the war release them all?

Down the alley, she glimpsed Indigo talking to that same man she had previously seen her with. Mercy stepped back into the doorway but was still able to observe them. She heard Indigo laugh. Evidently, love was in the fall air here in the Idaho Territory. Soon, Mercy would have to steel herself to speak to Indigo, to find out about this man who was making Indigo smile even when he wasn't near.

Suddenly, Jacob Tarver came around the corner of

the building. "Miss Gabriel, I'm sorry! I hate that this has happened!"

"What has happened?" she gasped.

"Come on! It's all over the front window. I've never seen anything like it."

Picking up her skirts to run, Mercy followed the agitated man around to his storefront. All over his large front windows someone had used soap to print the words *Kick out the female doctor. Or else.* Scrawled under this was a string of curses.

Mercy stared at the words, stunned.

"I never thought anything like this would happen here," Jacob Tarver said.

Anger flashed through Mercy. "Coward!" she shouted.

Jacob Tarver jumped and stared at her.

"Not thee, Jacob Tarver. I'm not holding thee responsible," Mercy declared. She gestured angrily at the soap message. "Only a coward tries to frighten women!"

She swung around to glare at the crowd of people gathering in the street to gawk at the hot news of the day. "Does any of thee know who wrote this vile message? Does thee?"

Her mind sifted through all the people she'd met who had objected to her profession. She couldn't pinpoint one who stood out from the rest. Would this event lead to worse? Perhaps violence against her or against Indigo?

No one replied. Most looked worried. But a few looked pleased. Was it one of them? How could she find the culprit?

Chapter Six

Yesterday's ugly words had been scrubbed from the general store's front window, but not from Mercy's tender mind and heart. The same melancholy that had plagued her after the cholera epidemic was creeping over her, trying to imprison her again.

Mercy sat at the table in the snug log cabin. By the window's faint, gloomy light, Indigo was washing the breakfast dishes. Lon had recovered, which was good. But the shadow remained over her heart. *What am I to do? Why do I keep hearing Lon say, "You understand nothing"?*

"I know you're disheartened, Aunt Mercy," Indigo said, drying her hands on a dish towel and glancing over at Mercy.

Mercy smiled even as tears stung her eyes.

Indigo had taken a job as a waitress in one of the cafés in town to make extra money. Now she was leaving for work. Soon, Mercy was all alone in the cabin. Lifelong habit made her pick up her Bible. She turned to the Beatitudes, which her father had taught her was the best place to start when faced with a challenge. In the dim, lonely cabin, she read aloud, hearing her father's calm, measured voice in her mind.

Blessed are they which are persecuted for righteousness's sake: for theirs is the kingdom of heaven.

Blessed are ye, when men shall revile you, and persecute you, and shall say all manner of evil against you falsely, for my sake.

Rejoice, and be exceeding glad: for great is your reward in heaven: for so persecuted they the prophets which were before you...

Let your light so shine before men, that they may see your good works, and glorify your Father which is in heaven.

Mercy stroked the well-worn, black leather binding of the Bible. Words could be deeply loving, as her father's had always been to her and her sisters. Or they could be cruel because of the hate and fear behind them.

She thought she had become inured to the general objections to her joining what was deemed a "male" profession. Sometimes she even tried to be amused by the repeated litany of protests. But yesterday's offensive act took opposition against her to a new level of hostility.

Would the words on Jacob Tarver's window keep sick people away from her when they needed doctoring?

"No," she said aloud. Yet she still did not want to go to her office. In fact, she felt as if bands were holding her back. She rose and carried the open Bible to the window. "I follow this unusual path because I was chosen to do this work. When the circumstances get desperate enough, they will come for my help."

This reminder triggered a new flow of confidence. She continued, "They needed me when the cholera was killing people. Lon Mackey needed me when he was stabbed. Chen An needed me to deliver her baby. How do I get them to come to me *before* the need is dire, Father?"

She looked down and her gaze fell on the verse, "Let your light so shine before men, that they may see your good works, and glorify your Father which is in heaven."

She glanced around her. Except for the faint light from the cabin's two windows and the glow of the low fire on the hearth, there was no light here.

Lon Mackey came to mind. But he always came to mind whenever she felt under stress. Could he help her here? Persuade others that since he'd fully recovered that she was a good doctor? That was tempting, but she didn't want to have to beg for help or involve Lon. He'd been through enough battles. She needed to face this one alone—or at least, without human help. God had never forsaken her. And hadn't now, either.

Closing her eyes, she prayed, *Father, let my light shine before men and let them praise Thee.* And to herself, she said, *I can stay here and wait for a special miracle, or I can proceed with one of my plans for this town right now, today. Release me from this holding back.* She resolutely closed her Bible, set it on the table and donned her shawl and bonnet.

If the people of Idaho Bend were not going to come to her, she would go to them. She stepped out into the dreary morning, trying to draw in the cool air. Her anxiety made it difficult to take more than shallow breaths.

With a decisive snap, Mercy shut the door of the cabin behind her. She approached the modest white-frame Dunfield house and tapped on the door. Young, pretty Ellen Dunfield, with her rich brown hair and matching eyes, answered the door. She was holding her one-year-old son with his halo of curly brown hair.

Blonde, four-year-old Missy huddled close to her mother's side. "Dr. Gabriel, what can I do for you today?"

Courage. Mercy suppressed her uncertainty. "I just wanted to ask thee a question. Would thee be interested in learning more about the new ways of keeping thy family in good health?"

The young woman blinked. "What do you mean?"

"Great strides are being made in understanding how the body works and how to keep it healthy." Mercy infused her words with as much confidence as she could muster. Low, gray clouds hung overhead. Her breathing remained shallow. "Would thee, as the mother in thy home, be interested in learning some of these discoveries?"

"I'm terrible busy, ma'am."

Smiling, Mercy held up a hand. "I should have been more specific. What I would like to do is set up an afternoon meeting for townswomen, perhaps in one of the churches. I would have Indigo and a few other young girls babysit the children. Do thee think that thee would attend a meeting like this? Perhaps with tea served?"

Mrs. Dunfield pursed her lips, considering this. "There are new ways to keep children well?"

Gratefully, Mercy felt her lungs loosen. She was able to draw a deep breath. "Yes, there are. In Europe and America, doctors are learning more about the causes of disease and how to prevent it."

The boy interrupted by holding his arms out to Mercy. She reached out and took the child, who patted her cheek with a pudgy hand.

Missy looked up at Mercy. "You like babies, don't you, Dr. Mercy?"

Mercy chuckled. "Yes, I do."

"Why don't you got any?" Missy asked.

Mrs. Dunfield scolded Missy, "Hush! Where are your manners?"

"I don't have a husband," Mercy replied. "To have babies, there must be a father and a mother." She tapped Missy's nose, teasing.

"You are a good woman," Mrs. Dunfield announced, as if someone were there, disparaging Mercy. "I hate what that sneaky coward wrote on Mr. Tarver's window." The young woman glared at the unknown scoundrel. "So if you know ways for me to keep my family healthy, then I should learn them. What church will you be holding the meetings at?"

Mercy pushed on, her usual sturdy confidence nearly restored. "I was wondering if thee would ask thy pastor if I might use thy church building some afternoon next week, perhaps Friday at 2:00 p.m. I need time to let everyone know about the meeting."

"I will ask him," Mrs. Dunfield said. "I'm going to a prayer meeting tonight. I'll do it then."

"Excellent. And if he says I may, I will put an ad in the paper." The little boy babbled and Mercy handed him back. "Now I'm going to talk to a few of the other good mothers here in Idaho Bend and see if they would come."

"Can I go, too?" Missy asked.

Mrs. Dunfield hushed the child again.

"If thy mother doesn't need thee, I would be happy to have thee with me for company." Mercy looked to the mother.

"If she wouldn't be any trouble to you," Mrs. Dunfield said.

"Missy is no trouble at all," Mercy said. "Go get thy shawl, child. And we will set out to make our round of visits. I will have her home by lunchtime," Mercy assured the mother.

Soon she and Missy were walking down the rutted streets of the town, knocking on doors. Predictably, most of the women were hesitant or guarded, a few were hostile and a sparse few were enthusiastic. As they walked down Main Street, Ma Bailey flagged them down. "Why do you have the Dunfield girl with you?"

Mercy stared into the woman's pudgy face. Nosy, nosy, nosy. "Missy is accompanying me. Missy, why doesn't thee tell Mrs. Bailey why we are walking through town?"

"Dr. Mercy is going to teach lessons on how mamas can keep their children from getting sick. Will you come?"

"All children get sick," snapped Ma Bailey, ever the cheery ray of sunshine. "Have you found out who wrote those nasty words about you?" The woman didn't look upset, just eager for information.

Mercy tried to divine whether Ma Bailey knew the answer to her own question. "When does thee expect thy daughter and her husband to arrive?" she asked.

Worry etched itself into the deep lines of Ma Bailey's face. "I don't know, exactly. I'm so hopin' that they'll get here before she delivers. I heard you're good at deliverin' babies. I hear you even delivered a Chinese one." Ma Bailey frowned and shook her head, resuming her normal attitude of general disapproval.

"I'd never had the privilege of delivering a Chinese baby before. And the baby's mother and father were as thrilled with the birth of their son as thy daughter and son-in-law will be with their newborn." Mercy turned to leave this grumpy woman.

"What do you think of that half breed courtin' your girl?" Ma Bailey's voice was sly.

Unable to speak, Mercy made no reply but merely waved her hand and walked away with Missy. She had not gotten a clear look at Indigo's beau, but had thought he looked dark enough to have Indian blood. She hated the demeaning phrase *half breed*.

When they had crossed the street, Missy said, "I don't like that woman. She has mean eyes."

Mercy made no direct reply, but said, "I think we will stop at Jacob Tarver's store and buy a certain little girl a peppermint drop. What does thee think of that idea?"

Missy smiled. "I like peppermint."

"I do, too. And I think thy mother might enjoy a peppermint drop also." But Mercy's mind was preoccupied with Ma Bailey's gnarly question. If Indigo's interest in the young man, who evidently was of mixed birth, was common gossip, then it was time that she and Indigo discussed her future. There was no getting around it any longer.

Lon walked out the saloon door and nearly collided with the Quaker and that little girl who'd survived cholera. He cursed himself for not looking before stepping outside the barroom's swinging door.

"Good day, Lon Mackey," the woman doctor greeted him.

"Hello, mister," the little girl said, waving up at him.

"Good day to you both." Though he wanted to, he couldn't bring himself to walk away. He fell into step with them, cursing his own weakness.

"We're going to the store for candy," the little girl said, skipping. "For peppermint candy."

"Aren't you a lucky little girl?" He felt like an idiot, saying those words.

"Where are you going?" the child asked.

"Missy, it is not polite to question grown-ups," Mercy said gently.

"I'm going to see if the supply wagons brought any recent newspapers," Lon replied.

The three of them arrived at the store. Mercy let Missy go inside to have time to enjoy gazing at the array of penny candy in the glass case. She looked up at Lon. "Have I offended thee, Lon Mackey?"

Her frank question bowled him over. He looked into her blue eyes and wished he hadn't. Her eyes were the windows to her soul, her pure, generous, selfless soul. "I am at fault," he admitted against his will. "I was abrupt to the point of rudeness. And after all your...kindness when I was wounded."

"I pressed thee too much, intruded on thy private sorrow about the war. I apologize to thee. Meddling is a sin, too."

He chuckled suddenly. "You? Meddle? Never."

She laughed, too. "Oh, a direct hit."

"You're not letting that incident...about Tarver's window get to you?" His self-protection alarm was clanging. He needed to get away from this woman who somehow always stripped him of his mask.

"It hurt," she said simply.

Missy came out. "Dr. Mercy, I know which peppermint candy I want."

Welcoming this chance to retreat from the field, Lon tipped his hat and hurried away.

The cloudy day did nothing to still his restlessness. He walked faster. Part of him wanted to grab his valise and set out west for Boise and maybe farther. But he found himself bound to Idaho Bend.

At night, he'd been gambling and winning, but he'd begun to hate the saloon—the drunken behavior, the raucous laughter, everything he used to enjoy. Then another upsetting thought hit him.

Who had scrawled those awful words on the store window?

Lon wanted to put his fist into someone's face. Now his stride lagged—he found he couldn't go on. He was still weak from his stab wound and the subsequent fever. He closed his eyes a moment, then turned back to the saloon where he needed to rest until evening. Forced to walk slower, Lon glowered at the sleepy Main Street and lonely sky. Maybe it was time to move on. Yet he couldn't force Mercy Gabriel's face from his mind. He knew she was the anchor that tethered him here. And that must end. Soon.

Evening had come. Mercy watched Indigo setting a new red-and-white-checked oilcloth on the table. It was pretty and gave the humble cabin a festive appearance. This, along with a morning spent in Missy's lively company and the setting in motion of Mercy's plans for better public heath, should have revived her spirits. But it was her meeting with Lon that had truly lifted her up. She had been surprised by his honest apology and heartfelt thanks, and she'd spent the rest of the day fighting the urge to smile constantly. She was trying very hard not to think about what it all meant.

"I've been meaning to tell you," Indigo said with her back to Mercy, "that I've invited someone to eat with us this evening."

Mercy inhaled. Was Indigo finally ready to share

with her the man she'd become interested in? Would he be suitable or dangerous to Indigo's reputation? Mercy plunged ahead. "Is he the young man I've seen thee talking to?"

Indigo turned and grinned. "You miss nothing, Aunt Mercy."

Neither does Ma Bailey. Any kind of gossip could make Indigo the target of… Mercy didn't want to put it into words. But a certain kind of man would take advantage of any woman deemed less than respectable. And it could tinge the standing of Mercy's fledgling medical practice. Mercy closed her eyes, resisting the temptation to worry.

Indigo began singing to herself, "There'll be peace in the valley for me someday, I pray no more sorrow and sadness or trouble will be, there'll be peace in the valley for me, there the flowers will be blooming, the grass will be green…"

Listening to Indigo's low, sweet voice, Mercy turned her thoughts back to the present. *No use borrowing trouble.* "I certainly haven't missed seeing how this young man has succeeded in bringing out thy smiles and laughter," Mercy said, feeling guilty over her reservations. *Lord, let me be wrong.*

"He does make me laugh," Indigo replied as she began to set the table for three.

"Then he must be a good man."

"At first I tried to avoid him," Indigo said. "I mean, I am a woman of color and he's part white. But he says his mother won't care."

"He has a mother living?" Mercy asked.

"Yes, farther north, near Canada. He came down to see if he could make some money mining or logging."

"And what is this young man's name?" Mercy

watched Indigo trying to hide how much joy merely speaking of her beau gave her.

"He is Pierre Gauthier."

The names sounded good together. "I will, of course, make him welcome. What are thee preparing this evening?" Mercy glanced at the covered cast-iron pot hanging over the fire, gently humming with steam.

"Pierre went hunting and brought the meat over earlier. So I put it to roast with some wild onions and a few potatoes. I'm baking a pie, too." Indigo pointed to the covered Dutch oven on a trivet sitting in the back of the fire. "I picked some late berries this afternoon. One of the miners eating at the café told me where to look for them. Wasn't that nice?"

Mercy nodded her agreement. "Sounds like a lovely meal." *I hope Pierre Gauthier is worthy of it.*

A jaunty knock sounded on the door.

"That's him." Indigo's face lit up like a lightning bug. She hurried to the door and opened it.

"Bonjour, ma jeune fille."

The man spoke French?

He walked inside, carrying a basket of fall leaves and pinecones. "I thought you might dress up your cabin with these."

Mercy couldn't help herself—she was impressed. "What a lovely gift."

He strode to her and executed a bow. "I am Pierre Gauthier, Dr. Gabriel."

She gave him her hand. "Welcome to our home, Pierre Gauthier."

"Merci, Docteur."

Another knock on the door sounded. Mercy glanced at Indigo who shrugged and went to the door.

"Hello, Indigo. I've come to speak to Dr. Gabriel."

Lon? Mercy was caught completely off guard.

Indigo looked back at her. "Please come in, Mr. Mackey."

Lon entered, doffing his hat. Then he paused, obviously surprised to see Pierre. His face changed in a moment from the honest one he had worn when they had spoken together earlier to the gambler's cool veneer.

Lon nodded toward Pierre. "I'm so sorry to intrude. I didn't know you had company."

"Lon—" Mercy began, but couldn't finish her sentence. How did she say, *Don't act like this?*

"You must come in, sir," Indigo said, managing to take his hat from his hand. "We were just about to sit down to supper and we have more than enough for four."

Lon looked ready to decline. And Mercy felt her former good spirits vanishing.

"*Mon ami,* stay," Pierre said expansively. "You will even up the numbers." He grinned. "Two ladies and two gentlemen."

Mercy lifted her tight lips into a smile. Having another man at the table might give her a better perspective of this young man. If only Lon wouldn't carry on his "I am just a carefree gambler" role. "Yes, Lon Mackey, please stay."

"As you wish, Doctor," he said archly.

Soon the men sat on the bench on one side of the table. "Mademoiselle Indigo, something smells delicious," Pierre said.

Indigo beamed and turned toward the fire.

"Thee are French, Pierre Gauthier?" Mercy asked, trying to relieve the tense atmosphere in the small cabin.

"Please, call me Pierre. And I am Métis."

Mercy didn't want to seem rude, but the words popped out. "What is that?"

"It's the name given to Indians who intermarried with the French fur traders much earlier, before the U.S. was even a nation," Lon said smoothly.

"*Oui,* I am French and Ojibwa and Dakota Sioux also. Most Métis live in Canada, but my family settled on this side of the border."

"Ah." That explained the mix of French in his English and the blend of races in his face and build.

Lon looked pained with the polite conversation. Or was it something else?

"Indigo says thee has a mother," she said, forging on.

Pierre nodded. "Mackey, do you not gamble tonight?"

Lon cleared his throat. "I will be in the saloon tonight if you should wish to try your luck with the cards." His mouth quirked into a faint smirk.

In spite of Lon's provocation, Mercy kept her face impassive. *Lon, I won't let thee lure me into any discussion of thy gambling.* She hated that their new accord was slipping through her fingers.

"I was stopping to let Dr. Gabriel," Lon said, watching her, "know that I intend to leave town in the next few days. Since our paths rarely cross except in passing, I didn't want her to find out secondhand."

Mercy's insides turned over. "Thee plan on leaving?"

Indigo stopped on her way to the table. "Leaving? Why?"

Lon shrugged. "Gamblers never stay in one place for long. Miss Indigo, that certainly does smell delicious."

Indigo set the meal on the table and began serving. Lon lifted an eyebrow, his expression almost a challenge to Mercy.

Mercy tried to keep up the conversation while trying to decide why Lon had come and if he was sincere in planning to leave.

An hour after the meal, Pierre excused himself. "I must go home and sleep. I begin work at dawn." He bid Mercy a formal goodnight and then lifted Indigo's hand, kissed it, and left, murmuring, *"Bon nuit, ma chère,"* before he left.

Lon had not followed the young Métis out. He rose. "I thank you, ladies, for an excellent meal. But I must go earn my living at the saloon. I will need sufficient funds to leave town."

"Is thee really leaving town?" Mercy asked, unable to stop herself.

"Indeed. I hope to leave by week's end." He bowed, donned his hat and departed.

Indigo closed the door and then leaned back against it. She straightened, looking directly into Mercy's eyes. "What do you think of Pierre, Aunt Mercy?"

Mercy tried to sort through all her impressions, but Lon's unexpected announcement had distracted her. "I like him," she said at last. "I don't know how anyone could not like him."

"But you don't think that's good enough." Indigo's face looked downcast.

"I didn't say that." Mercy had no room to talk. She knew by now that Lon commanded her attention more than he should. She also tried to think of a way to ask the question that had not been asked.

"You're wondering if he's friends with the Lord?"

Mercy walked to Indigo and put an arm around her. Lon did not appear to be friends with the Lord. War could do that to any man. But when her daughter didn't answer the question, Mercy's smile slipped away. *Oh, dear.*

"I don't know the answer to that, Aunt Mercy."

Mercy gazed at Indigo's lovely face. So young, so pretty, so wanting to be loved. "We will pray about it."

"But I am going to have to ask him, right?" Indigo looked as if she were hoping Mercy would say no.

Mercy nodded. "Thee *must* know the answer."

Sudden tears sprang into Indigo's eyes. "I don't want to lose him."

Lon Mackey slipped into Mercy's mind, and her mind repeated Indigo's words, *I don't want to lose him.*

How can I lose what I never had? Yet Lon Mackey was the only man who had ever lingered in her mind like this. This left her feeling empty. If Lon left town, would every day fill her with this sense of loneliness and loss?

It had taken a bit longer than Mercy had hoped to get the meeting arranged at the church where she and Indigo had treated the last few cholera patients. Nonetheless, today, humming with anticipation and nervousness, Mercy walked to the front of the church. She looked out over the small gathering of around thirty women all dressed in their Sunday best. Would they listen with understanding to what she had to say? Or would they reject what she longed to teach them?

"Good afternoon, ladies. I'm so glad that thee has come to hear about some of the discoveries doctors here and abroad have been making about the human body and how to keep it healthy."

Ma Bailey sat front and center, glaring at Mercy.

Mercy resisted the temptation to lift her chin. However, if Ma Bailey thought she could take this hopeful beginning and turn it to dust, she was mistaken.

"The recent cholera epidemic is an example of a disease that can be stopped with public sanitation."

"What's public sanitation?" Ma Bailey snapped.

"Public sanitation is the name of the emerging movement to keep people healthy through clean water and food." Mercy forged on, preempting Ma Bailey, who was trying to be heard. "As early as the 1830s, New York State passed laws to keep their water sources free of contamination from animal carcasses."

As Ma Bailey opened her mouth again, Mercy hurried on. "Here, the first family to succumb to the cholera was the family that had made and brought the berry juice to the church meeting. Subsequently, dead rats were found in their well."

A communal gasp went through the women. "No one told us that," Ellen Dunfield declared, an angry edge to her voice.

Mercy nodded. "Thee may ask Lon Mackey and the bartender, Tom Banks. They discovered the rats themselves."

This revelation was followed by a buzz of upset voices. Mercy hoped she had as good a poker face as any gambler because inside, she was rejoicing. The truth was a powerful force.

Mercy was about to go on when the door at the back of the church opened slowly. In the shaft of sunlight, Mercy couldn't see who had come late. Her eyes adjusted, and she saw Chen Park and his wife standing just inside the church. *Father in heaven, I never expected them to come. Help them be welcomed, not shunned.* "Chen Park and Chen An," she greeted them as she went up the aisle.

Both of them bowed low several times. The husband spoke, "We hear you tell women how to keep babies well."

"Yes, I'm speaking on how to keep babies healthy.

Please take a seat." She motioned toward the nearest pew, which was far behind the nearest woman. Mercy hated the separation, but realized that this was neither the time nor the place for a lesson on the evils of discrimination.

The Chinese couple made their way into the pew and sat down. Mercy walked back to the front, ignoring the low rush of disapproving voices discussing the arrival of the Chens. She heard Ma Bailey hiss, "Heathens in a church."

Before Mercy could reply, another woman said, "Mrs. Bailey, there will be every tribe and nation in heaven."

To stem this theological debate, Mercy began speaking again. "Now many of thee have known women who have lost children due to milk fever."

At these words, an anxious silence fell on the assembled parents. Milk fever killed many infants each year in the warm months. "Thee should know," Mercy continued, "that a scientist named Louis Pasteur has shown that boiling milk destroys bacteria. And bacteria are what carry disease."

"Bacteria?" Ellen echoed.

"Yes, as early as the 1600s a Dutchman, Antonie van Leeuwenhoek, developed lenses that could see living bacteria, which is too small for the human eye to see—"

"If it's too small for us to see, how did that ol' Dutchman see it then? Answer me that," Ma Bailey crowed.

Mercy held her temper, which wanted to break away from her like a racehorse. Did this woman never have a helpful thought?

"Thee has seen spectacles, hasn't thee? Antonie van Leeuwenhoek ground glass lenses finer and finer, and as he did, he saw more. Pasteur used the microscope that Leeuwenhoek developed with finely ground lenses to view bacteria and their effects."

Ma Bailey scowled.

"These bacteria are what make us sick?" another woman asked with a shyly raised hand as if she were in school.

"That is what scientists think. They are studying how bacteria do this, but we all know that contact with a sick person or even their clothing and bedding can spread a disease."

"That's right," Ellen agreed.

"Well, what do these scientists have to do with what we're doin' in the Idaho Territory?" Ma Bailey demanded.

"Very simply, some scientists have had good results after boiling questionable water and milk. So if—"

The pastor of the church ran inside, startling Mercy and the ladies. He halted at the pull rope and began tolling the bell. "Mine cave-in!" he shouted.

The women leaped to their feet, some with a shriek. Mercy's audience fled down the center aisle and outside. The pastor continued to yank on the bell rope. The steeple bell joined what sounded like the fire bell, bellowing on Main Street, calling for help.

The frantic tolling blasted through Mercy like gunpowder. She had read once in a newspaper that a woman had confessed to being "drenched with terror." Now Mercy knew exactly how that felt. The familiar twin jolt of energy and alarm rushed through her, the same jolt that had come whenever a cannon had roared.

She rushed from the church and over to her office to gather up supplies she might need for victims of a cave-in. Instead of wounds caused by grapeshot and lead bullets, she would no doubt be faced with the aftermath of bodies crushed or struck by falling rock and wood supports.

Like a bee straight to its hive, a sudden thought whizzed through her. Pierre Gauthier was a miner. *Father, protect this fine young man. Indigo's heart would be broken if anything happened to him.*

Chapter Seven

Lon stood, looking over the still-swinging doors of the saloon. He watched the town race like a pack of rats up the street toward the mountainside. He fought the urge to grab his hat and join the exodus. He gripped the top of the doors and stopped them from rattling. Or tried. Not only did he hear the pounding footsteps pelting down the wooden sidewalk in front, but the sound also communicated through the wood vibrating in his hands.

He released the doors and turned away. As he did, he saw Mercy. He cursed himself for his weakness in continuing to think of her as "Mercy." He saw that she was hurrying along with the others, her black bag in her hand, racing to the rescue. Lon turned away, resisting the urge to follow her.

He recalled that recent evening when he'd ended up going to her cabin. Why had he felt the need to tell her he intended to leave? Had he somehow hoped she'd try to talk him out of going? While she hadn't, her startled-wide eyes at his announcement had haunted him ever since. *But I'm right. This town is bad news.*

Would the Quaker never learn to watch out for herself first? Had she already forgotten that after saving countless lives from cholera, this town had handed her less than five bucks for her tireless efforts? Had she already forgotten that no one in this town would rent her a room because she had adopted a Negro orphan in the war? His gut burned with the injustice. *Well, perhaps St. Mercy can forget, but I won't.*

Mercy arrived at the mine as angry gray clouds scudded fast and free overhead. In the milling crowd, she tried to decide whom to approach. Who was in charge? Who would *take* charge?

Mercy began looking around and then realized she was seeking Lon. For all she knew, Lon was already gone. That thought gave her the familiar empty, lonely feeling.

Even standing on her tiptoes, she couldn't see a leader of the rescue effort. If only she were taller, or she'd been a tomboy, like her sister, Felicity. If Felicity were here, she'd climb a tree to get a bird's-eye view of the crowd.

Then Mercy glimpsed a tall man with red hair. It was Digger Hobson, the mining company manager. She began threading her way through the crowd, which was becoming larger and larger by the minute. As she ventured toward the man, the throng surrounding him became tighter and tighter. She was soon forced to beg men to give way to her. They did, of course. Even though she was an odd woman, she was still a woman and must be treated with deference.

"Digger Hobson," she said, arriving at his side, panting. "How serious is it? Are men trapped?"

Amid all the other voices clamoring for information or giving advice, he glanced down at her. "I'm glad you're here."

His simple, direct words were both welcome and unwelcome. If he were glad to see her, it must be gravely serious. Heart throbbing, she drew in a calming breath. "Has the rescue effort begun?" she asked.

During this exchange, the men around him had quieted, listening. Raising both hands, Digger spoke in a strong, ringing voice, "We're trying to figure out what exactly has happened. There are some men inside assessing the situation."

"Have there been cave-ins here before? Does thee have experience in recovering miners alive?" she asked. At her questions, more and more people fell silent around them.

"I've been in mining most of my life, so, yes, I have experience." Digger gave her a grim look. "We've had a few minor cave-ins, but this sounded bigger to my ears."

His words hung in the air over them all. "I will stay as long as I am needed," she said.

He reached for her hand and gripped it momentarily. "If you weren't here, we'd have to transport any injured a day's journey to Boise. So thank you."

Mercy's insides clenched, thinking of injured men lying on buckboards, being rattled over bumpy trails and getting reinjured on that rough trip. Some would die from the journey itself.

From the mine entrance, a younger man came forward, shoving his way to Digger Hobson. "The rescue party is ready, Monsieur Digger. We have filled already our oil lanterns. The equipment, it is ready, and we have the new beams to hold up the unstable walls. You must only give the word."

Mercy was relieved to recognize the young man as Pierre Gauthier. She learned much about him in that moment. He was at the forefront of the rescue effort, which meant Digger Hobson trusted him. And Pierre Gauthier was concerned—very concerned—for others. Indigo had chosen well.

Digger nodded to Pierre, then raised his hands and his voice again, saying, "The crew has cleared away the loose debris. Now they're going to work their way into the mine. They have to move slow so they don't set off another cave-in. Everyone should fall back so we can maneuver—"

"Please!" Ellen Dunfield called out from where she stood with the other miners' wives. "Please, we need to know who's in the mine." The women around Ellen added their voices in agreement.

Digger Hobson frowned. "If you don't see them here, they're probably in the cave-in." Many of the women gasped in unison. "Now everyone fall back and open paths for my men to work."

"I'll stay with the women until I'm needed," Mercy declared, mustering all her strength and will. She headed straight for Ellen. She took Ellen's small, cold hand in hers and led her away from the workers. And as if she were the leader, most of the women followed her. She led them higher on the nearby slope so that they would be able to see yet not be in the way.

"We must not give in to fear," Mercy declared. "'God is our refuge and strength, a very present help in trouble,'" she quoted. Spontaneously, all the women joined hands and bowed their heads.

"Please pray for us, Dr. Mercy," Ellen said, her brave voice quavering.

The anxiety mounting all around Mercy pulled at her, weighing her down. Still, in this request, she discerned the silent pleading for reassurance and hope. She took a deep breath and prayed aloud, "Father, we need Thy mercy and provision. Loved ones may be in the mine. We ask that Thy presence enfold them, that help will be able to reach them in time. Help us pray as we ought to." Then she began the Lord's Prayer and the women all joined in.

When Mercy looked up, tears still streamed down the women's faces. But they had all drawn together. They had put this awful occurrence into God's hands. They would face this together.

Then the waiting began. Strong winds from the southwest buffeted them, making Mercy tie her bonnet ribbons tighter. The racing clouds darkened. They became a moving gray-flannel roof over each head. And, below, the gloom of fear hovered over each heart. How long would it take the rescuers to reach the trapped men, the husbands and fathers who loved and protected them?

Lon stood alone in the dim, shuttered saloon. After hours of no customers, even the bartender had been unable to resist the call of the mine cave-in. Alone, hands in his pockets, Lon walked to his bunk in the back room. He sat on it and stared at the blank wall. It was time to start packing—Idaho Bend was not working out for him. First had come the cholera, then being stabbed nearly to death and now a cave-in. It was time to move on to a luckier place. He pulled his valise toward him. His belongings were sparse. His hand touched his father's gold pocket watch and his mother's locket. He held one in each hand. Who could have predicted that they would die while he was away, facing bullets, sabers and grapeshot? *Mother would have liked Mercy.* He crushed this errant thought and thrust the two mementos back into the pouch where they belonged. Maybe going all the way to the Pacific would be a good change for him. Mercy Gabriel was claiming too much of his mind.

Near evening, Indigo led the children she had been watching during the church meeting to the mine site. They walked hand in hand up the last few feet toward the women around Mercy. The children ran to their mothers, who folded them into their arms. A sudden harsh gust of wind grabbed their skirt hems, twirling them. Some mothers lost their bonnets to the wind and their children chased and caught them.

Mercy overheard children asking about fathers and uncles and older brothers, and mothers soothing them. The wind snatched at their voices, carrying them far. But Mercy's heart ached for these little ones. They could barely understand anything, except that something bad had happened in the mine and that something more dreadful might come.

"I kept them away from here as long as I could," Indigo murmured into Mercy's ear, "but they need supper."

Mercy took Indigo's hand in hers. "Pierre is helping with the rescue effort."

"You saw him?" Indigo's eyes revealed the strain of unspoken worry.

Mercy nodded and squeezed Indigo's hand. She knew the longer it took to reach the trapped miners, the less hope there would be for survivors. The rescuers were also in danger of subsequent cave-ins. Closing her eyes, she grappled with this hard fact. She opened her eyes, refusing to give in to the despair that clutched at her spirit like icy fingers.

She faced the women. "If thee must go home to care for and feed thy children, go. Indigo and I will stay, and she will bring word to thee if any progress is made." *Or if thy loved one is pulled from the mine—living or dead.* She didn't need to say this out loud. Why should she? It was what they all were thinking, fearing.

Blinking rapidly, Ellen Dunfield swallowed down obvious tears. "Thank you, Dr. Mercy. The children must be taken home for some care and comfort. It's best for them."

Mercy appreciated this young woman's quick response and the assurance it brought to the rest of the waiting women. Ellen lifted her son into her arms and took Missy's hand in hers. Together they started down the rise toward town. Soon only women without children remained on the hillside.

Mercy noticed that several older men were starting a fire at the mine entrance. Even protected as it was from the wild wind, the blaze sent sparks flying high on the relentless gusts.

Ma Bailey came into sight around the bend, walking between the shafts of a two-wheeled cart, dragging it behind her. From the cart, the wind carried the scents of biscuits, bacon and something sweet. Ma stopped by Digger. "I made biscuits and fried bacon, Mr. Hobson, for the men working to open the mine. And I'd already baked cinnamon rolls for tomorrow's breakfast."

Mercy waited to hear what the tightfisted woman would be charging for this needed and welcome food.

"It's free," Ma barked as if arguing with someone unseen, "to the workers."

Mercy stood, astounded. The wind took advantage of her distraction and untied her bonnet ribbons. She caught the bonnet just before it sailed away.

"I just hope no one comes out dead," Ma said, looking mournful.

Mercy wished Ma Bailey hadn't added this, but she couldn't find fault with this cantankerous woman today.

Indigo spoke up, "I have food I can bring, too. I baked bread last night. I'll go home and get it." Several other women hurried along with Indigo, calling that they would be back soon with more food and drink for the vigil.

The older men continued to tend the fire at the mine entrance. A few held spades, ready to put out any sparks that might escape and ignite the grass. The orange flames were welcome against the graying sky and the chill from the damp ground.

Suddenly, Mercy missed Lon Mackey. Had the whole town come out to work together—even ill-natured, stingy Ma Bailey—while he had stayed behind? Could it be that he was truly gone already? *Lon Mackey, if thee is still here, thee must come. Thee will never forgive thyself if men die and thee did nothing. Thee may deny that, but I know thee better.*

The long evening stretched into a long night, and the rushing wind brought the scent of rain. Mercy wrapped her shawl more tightly around herself. Men kept working, digging through the blocked mine shaft. The sound of their picks and shovels could be heard even above the surging wind. The men took turns coming out periodically to warm their hands by the fire, drink strong coffee and swallow any food handed to them.

The mothers had returned with their children. They had tucked them, wrapped in blankets and quilts, into mining wagons to sleep together, to comfort one another. It was touching to see little children patting each other and talking softly.

In light of the coming storm, large canvas sheets had

been set up and lashed over the wagons, making snug
tents. Mercy and the mothers clutched shawls around
themselves and paced around the fire, shivering and
praying.

Distant thunder sounded against the stiff wind, stirring the night. She found herself glancing at the mining shack where the rescuers would take anyone they
carried out. And then her gaze would return to the fire
at the mine entrance. There lantern lights flickered as
men went in and out.

The impetuous, worrisome storm rushed toward
them—closer, closer. Over the western mountains,
lightning flickered ominously. Which would come
first—survivors from the mine or the big storm bearing down on them? Finally worn out, she leaned back
against one of the wagons filled with sleeping children.

"Mercy."

She jerked upright. Lon was standing beside her.
He had come. Golden joy surged within her spirit. She
threw her arms around him, so solid, stalwart—so welcome.

Bright lightning splintered overhead.

Sudden thunder hammered like a blacksmith working iron.

By the crackling lightning, she glimpsed two men
carrying a miner from the cavelike entrance. She ran
toward them, Lon's hand in hers. Lon jogged beside
her, trying to make himself heard. Mercy couldn't understand what Lon was shouting in her ear, but there
was no time to stop. The brunt of the violent storm had
reached them.

Lightning flashed quick and steady like the tapping
of a telegraph key. Cold rain poured down on them,

snatching Mercy's breath. Thunder pounded, battered them. Jagged lightning streaked, struck and ignited.

The cold rain had soaked Lon in a moment.

Struck by lightning, a nearby tall pine exploded, flinging branches, pine needles and flaming sparks over them. Mercy ducked as Lon threw his arm around her shoulders to protect her.

When they reached the men with the stretcher, one of them shouted into Lon's ear, but Lon couldn't hear the words over the thunder. Then another two men came out carrying a man by the shoulders and feet. Mercy waved the men toward the mining shack. Lon continued into the mine. Maybe he hadn't delayed too long, maybe he had come at the right time to help support the injured as they staggered out.

Thunder continued, blasting overhead like an artillery barrage. The sound battered him physically, shook him until his teeth rattled. Then an explosion like a cannon shell threw him to the mud.

Panic. He yelled, his voice vanishing into the maelstrom. Rocks cascaded down the slopes around them. Some bounced high, barreling into the valley where he lay facedown. He covered his head with his arms. Squeezed his eyes shut. And prayed.

At last the earth ceased vibrating. He opened his eyes and sucked in air. He was alive. He hadn't been snatched up in the whirlwind. Pushing up with both hands, he got to his feet. He staggered and caught himself.

The storm was already past them, moving east. Yet the flashing lightning still illuminated the surroundings. And thunder boomed so close, too close. When he looked to the mine, he gasped, shock rippling through him. An avalanche of rocks had fallen, blocking the entrance. *Dear God, help.*

He glanced around for Mercy. Was she out of harm's way? He saw an oil lamp shining dimly through the mine shack window, illuminating her silhouette. She was safe.

Soon he was surrounded by the few men left and several women. He couldn't tell if it was rain or tears streaming down their faces. They all looked to him, beseeching him to tell them what to do.

The urge to turn tail and run hit him like a blast of buckshot. But one glance at their faces and he was powerless to desert them. "Form lines!" he shouted against the receding yet still roaring thunder. "Like bucket brigades! Start moving out rock! If it's too big to lift, roll it!"

He ran forward and they followed. He hefted a large rock and then started it down the line. Two more lines formed. The horror of what had just happened twisted inside him like the tightening of a screw. The rescuers had been swallowed up by the avalanche, along with Digger, the mine manager.

Even as the work began, he despaired. There weren't enough rescuers. Too many had been swallowed by the mine. How many would they find still alive?

The rocks cut his soft gambler palms, gouged his knuckles. If only there were more hands. Then he saw movement by the light of the retreating storm. Suddenly, another line formed beside his. Who was it?

Then he saw—the Chinese had come to help. The men formed another line and began moving rock away from the blocked entrance. He didn't know why they'd come to help. But he was humbly grateful. Choked up, he couldn't utter even a word of welcome.

The rock brigades worked steady and determined for hours. The storm finally moved beyond their valley, no doubt still spreading destruction eastward. Lon's arms and back ached. The black night wrapped around them. Drenched, Lon shivered in the cold. He gasped for air.

Occasionally a man would grunt; a woman would moan. Someone was praying aloud—the Twenty-third Psalm. The phrase "the valley of the shadow of death" repeated in his mind. *Lord, bring the sunrise. Let some live.*

Mercy had never passed a more terrifying night. First the cave-in, then the storm, terrifying in its destruction. Rampaging thunder. Lightning exploding and flaming about. Then rocks pouring down, shattering, crashing, smothering.

In the mining shack, she stood, looking out the one small window into the murky gray of predawn and an early mist. Her arms were folded as if holding back a well of shock and distress. Was Lon still out there working? She didn't know and couldn't leave her patients to find out.

A moan sounded behind her. She turned to one of her two patients lying on the earthen floor and took his pulse. She hadn't been able to do much for either of them. She had managed to clean the area around their gashes and stop the bleeding. But if they had sustained internal injuries, there was nothing she could do.

A knock sounded on the door. Indigo rose from the floor and opened it. The pastor of the church where Mercy had been speaking just hours before peered in.

"We haven't spoken directly, but I'm Pastor Stephen Willis. My wife and I have prepared the church for the injured."

"Thank You, Jesus," Indigo murmured. Mercy repeated the words silently.

"The wagon is all ready to take the injured there," he said.

Mercy looked at her two patients, who took up almost all the floor space. Only these two had been brought out of the mine before the storm and avalanche. How many remained trapped? How many remained alive? Tears clogged her throat.

Indigo must have sensed this. She responded for Mercy, "We just have these two so far, Pastor. I'll help you carry them to the wagon."

Mercy wished she could give in to the tears that crouched just behind her eyes. However, she knew intuitively that any show of emotion on her part would weaken her reputation as a physician. Male doctors showed little emotion—she must do the same or be dismissed as just an emotional female.

She sighed and put her bonnet on again. She prayed for the men still trapped in the mine as she went out into the chill, damp fog that misted her face. She glanced at the lines of people ferrying rock away from the mine entrance. Ma Bailey had somehow got a fire started in spite of the heavy soaking they'd received. She was giving mugs of steaming coffee to tired workers.

Then the fog lifted; Mercy halted. She looked more closely toward one line passing rock away from the avalanche. The Chinese men were working along with the Americans. Praise for God flowed through her. How touching that these unwanted strangers in this land were willing to help in this time of disaster. And she hadn't imagined Lon arriving, or the feel of his arm protecting her. A few times last night she'd doubted her memory.

Lon was still there, directing the rescue. He had come late, but he had come.

Mercy hurried to Lon. He broke away from the brigade and took her hands in his. "Mercy, where are you taking the injured?"

She felt the roughness of his hands. "Pastor Willis has opened his church as a hospital." She wished she had time to treat his lacerated hands.

"The progress is slow." He wiped his grimy, damp forehead with his sleeve. Once again, Lon's flashy gambler clothing clashed with the man and his actions in a crisis. *Thee may try to make thyself and everyone else believe thee wants to live as a gambler, Lon Mackey. Thee will never make me believe it.*

"How are thee faring?" she asked, leaning close to catch his low voice.

He squeezed her hands in reply. Someone called to him. "Take care," he said as he rushed off.

"And thee!" she called after him, missing his touch immediately. A spark of warmth flared within—hope.

Lon glanced over his shoulder, watching Mercy and Indigo mounting a buckboard. A man with a clerical collar was helping them up. He wished he could call her back. Her presence always lent strength. But another woman already sat in the wagon bed, obviously to help Mercy. Two pairs of feet protruded from the end of the wagon bed. They must be taking the two victims of the cave-in to town. Were they being taken for treatment or burial?

Death. Death was their real enemy, their constant adversary, always ready to suck out their breath and put them in the ground.

A shout sounded. Lon turned.

"We're through!" one of the miners yelled.

Lon hurried to the hole they had finally cleared through the rock barrier. "Let's be careful. We need to widen this opening and get a rescuer who will fit through it."

One of the Chinese waved and bowed. "I can go through." Lon blinked away deep emotion that was trying to surface. These immigrants were barely deemed human by many of the miners they were offering to save. Their willingness to help was humbling.

"Thanks," Lon said, returning the bow.

The Chinese man said, "I Chen Park. Woman doctor bring my baby."

Lon nodded. "Dr. Mercy Gabriel is a good doctor." *A good woman. Too good for this bunch.*

"Yes," Chen Park said. "Dr. Mercy. Good."

Lon noticed that everyone else had fallen silent, watching this exchange.

"Thank God Dr. Gabriel came to town when she did," said Ellen Dunfield. "If she hadn't, many of us would already be in the grave." She glanced over her shoulder toward the wagons where the children were still sleeping. Then she sank to the ground, exhausted from hours of nonstop labor.

"Is this hole big enough?" the miner closest to the opening asked.

"Big enough for me." Chen Park hurried forward and accepted a lantern. "I go in."

The other miners called out encouragement, "Good man! God bless!"

The man ducked low and entered the hole.

Lon could only hope that this brave man would be able to reach someone alive—and stay alive himself.

Chapter Eight

The watery morning sun had finally burned away the fog. Lon passed another rock down the line. His back felt broken; his arm muscles trembled. He was so exhausted he could have sunk to the ground and fallen instantly into a deep sleep. But each labored breath reminded him that men trapped inside might have little chance to go on breathing if the rescuers didn't work faster—if they didn't reach them in time. The old feelings that had plagued him before each battle—the cramping in his stomach, the tautness in his neck—flared to life. He would have no ease until all were accounted for—living and dead.

The Chinese men were taking turns going into the hole, carrying or rolling out large rocks to make room for the injured to pass through. But the progress only inched forward. Lon fought his impatience.

Then Chen Park returned, grinning. "I see men. Touch men."

"It must be the rescue party," Lon said, gasping, his breathing shallow and his pulse suddenly racing. "They rushed in and were caught by the avalanche."

"Three—" he held up three fingers "—under rocks."

He shook his head. "Not breathe. Four still breathe but sleep." The news horrified but invigorated the men and women still moving rock. Close, so close. Lon and the rest who were still able to work began frantically widening the hole.

Lon passed rock after rock, straining with their weight. His whole body ached and he often found his eyes shutting. But he was used to pushing himself beyond the limits of his strength. The women who had worked all night staggered away to care for their waking children.

Panting and wheezing, some of the older men fell where they stood in line. Younger men carried them near the fire and covered them with blankets. Everyone's willingness to work until they dropped stoked a flame in Lon's heart. *We'll save some. God help us.*

Chen Park came out backward, gasping, obviously laboring hard. He was pulling a man. Lon hurried forward to help along with the other workers. He could see Digger Hobson's red hair. Hands grabbed Digger and helped carry him out. An incredible rush of energy charged Lon. He saw it reflected in the grinning faces around him. They had broken through. Finally.

"Chen Park," Lon said, "well done. Thanks."

The man bowed low. "Hole big enough for bigger men to go in." He wiped sweat from his forehead. "Hole bigger inside."

Then Lon noticed Digger's right foot. His boot looked crushed. Chen Park nodded. "Foot under rock. Bad."

Lon squeezed Chen's shoulder. "You did your best. You need to rest. You men have been carrying the brunt since early morning. Rest."

Chen nodded and motioned toward his fellows. "We go home. Eat. Come back."

"Thanks," Lon said again, his voice low and gravelly. He didn't want them to stop, yet they were only flesh and blood.

The Chinese men walked away, stretching their backs and rotating their tired shoulders. The women and children waved and called out their thanks.

Pastor Willis, who had been waiting for survivors, drove the wagon close to the mine. Lon turned his attention to another survivor who had just been brought out. It was that young Métis he'd played poker with and later met at Mercy's, the one who was sweet on Indigo. He was still unconscious.

Men helped Pastor Willis load both injured miners into the wagon, and he drove away. Then more men were carried out, but they were dead. The rescuers covered them with wool blankets as women knelt beside them and mourned.

Let down after the brief elation, Lon turned away. The cries of the women shredded his heart. *At least during the war, I didn't have to hear the widows mourning.* But he'd had to write letters to them, telling them of their husbands' last days and how they had died. He rubbed his chest over his heart, trying to banish the physical pain these memories always caused him. Here and now, however, he had not given the order sending these men into the mine. This had not happened under his command.

He stood very still, drawing up, hauling up all his reserves of strength. They had one more barrier to break through to reach the men who'd been trapped in the original cave-in. Once again, every eye had turned toward him, asking for direction, encouragement. Why was everyone here depending on him? He had no answer. But then he was depending on Dr. Mercy to save as many survivors as she could. Yet he knew that even she couldn't save everyone, either.

At the church hospital, Mercy looked with dismay at Digger Hobson. He had just regained consciousness and was writhing with what must be unbearable pain.

A long, rectangular table had been brought from the saloon and set up where the pulpit usually stood. Mercy directed the men to carry Digger and lay him on it. She must perform surgery on him as soon as possible. His foot was crushed and might soon become gangrenous, which could kill this good man.

Mercy looked around and saw that they had carried in another patient. As soon as she heard Indigo's outcry, she knew it must be Pierre. She hurried to Indigo and lifted Pierre's wrist. "His pulse is slow but steady," she said. But she didn't like the look of his bruised and bloodied head. Mercy ran her hands over him, checking for other injuries. His right arm was broken.

She looked to Indigo, feeling the sting of her daughter's pain as her own. "He is not in immediate danger. We must treat Digger Hobson first."

Her lips trembling, Indigo looked into Mercy's eyes and said quietly, bravely, "I'll prepare for surgery."

Mercy squeezed Indigo's shoulder and then went to prepare herself for this ordeal. Dread opened inside her, sucking away her composure. She hated what she must do. She had assisted in so many amputations during the war that she'd already known how to perform one before she started medical school. But that didn't lessen her loathing of them.

Soon, she stood wearing a clean, white apron. She

looked down at her gleaming surgical instruments, which Indigo had laid out for her on spotless cotton. Mercy took up the scalpel. Indigo was administering ether from a sponge and Digger had just become unconscious. The familiar rush of energy and clarity sharpened her mind and bolstered her will to do this thing.

About halfway through the operation, someone came into the church and demanded, "What's going on here?" Heavy footsteps hurried up behind Mercy. The same voice challenged her, "Good grief, woman, what are you thinking? You can't do an amputation!"

Mercy didn't, couldn't pause in her surgery. "I'm very sorry, but I must ask thee to step away. I am at a very delicate part of the operation and cannot allow any distractions." From the corner of her eye, she glimpsed an older man.

"You stop that right now. I'll take over. I'm a qualified physician. No nurse is up to this kind of surgery."

"I, too, am a qualified physician," Mercy said, keeping her main focus on the operation.

He grabbed her arm.

Wild outrage shot through Mercy. Digger's life hung in the balance. "Get this man off me!" she called out. "He's keeping me from my work! Digger could die!"

A number of women hurried over. "Let go of Dr. Mercy. She's right in the middle—"

Hot words boiled out of the man, and he did not release Mercy's arm.

So Mercy did something she had never done before. She kicked the man's shin as hard as she could and swung her hip at him, knocking him off balance. Releasing his grip, he fell, shouting a curse.

Hot anger bubbling, Mercy continued suturing. She heard the door open and Ellen's voice.

Pastor Willis hurried over and helped the man up, but guided him away from Mercy. "Who are you, sir?"

"I am Dr. Gideon Drinkwater. I practice medicine in Boise. The sheriff got a telegraph about the mine cave-in and I came to treat the injured. What do you mean by letting a woman perform surgery?"

"Dr. Gabriel is a qualified physician—"

"She's lying," the man objected. "There is no such thing as a qualified female doctor. No medical college admits them."

"I've seen her diploma from the Female College of Medicine in Pennsylvania. She helped end our recent cholera epidemic. And by the way," Pastor Willis added in a stern tone, "we telegraphed Boise for help with the cholera, but no doctor came that time."

Mercy had forgotten that. She wondered what excuse this doctor would use for not coming to help then.

"There is no cure for cholera," the doctor grumbled. "I thought my efforts would be wasted here."

"Well, thanks be to God, our Dr. Gabriel didn't take that attitude," Pastor Willis said. "We only lost some seventy souls when we might have lost nearly half our population."

"That is neither here nor there," Dr. Drinkwater said, sounding cross. "You can't let a woman practice medicine here. I won't stand for it."

Mercy tried to ignore her irritation, tried to block out the man's blustering words. Her hands needed to remain steady.

"Why do you have to stand for anything?" Ellen's clear voice rang out. "Dr. Mercy is taking care of things. You're not needed here."

Not needed? Mercy realized that she must intervene. She steadied herself, dampening her buzzing exasperation with the man. "Thank thee for thy support, Ellen, but this is only the first wave of survivors. We don't know how many patients will be needing medical help. Dr. Drinkwater, why doesn't thee observe me and see if I am equal to the task?"

"I will do nothing of the sort," he snapped. "I will not lower myself to work alongside a female who is posing as a physician. Either this woman goes, or I go."

"Well, go then," Ellen said. "We know what Dr. Mercy can do. We don't know how good a doctor you are."

Dr. Drinkwater sputtered and marched out.

Troubled, Mercy concentrated on doing the rest of the operation without being distracted. She sent a prayer for wisdom heavenward and went on with her intricate work.

Having two doctors would certainly increase the injured miners' chances for survival. If she stood down and let this doctor have his way, they'd be down to one doctor again. Both of them were needed. Would prejudice against her cost lives?

When Mercy had finished the surgery and washed up, she walked outside. Weariness had invaded her very flesh. Her back ached; her feet were wooden from standing so long while operating. And now she must contend with the same old hostility. How could she convince this doctor that they needed to work together?

After the storm, the air was cool and clear, the wind gentle. Nearby, under an oak tree whose leaves were turning bronze, the doctor and the pastor were sitting on chairs, talking. Now she saw that the doctor must be in his later middle years with a pronounced paunch, the Boise doctor had salt-and-pepper hair and an ill-natured expression. Mercy prayed silently as she approached the two. "Now I am free to talk."

Both men stood until she sank down on a third chair. Then Dr. Drinkwater snapped, "Did the poor man survive your butchery then?"

Mercy looked him in the eye. "I assisted in thousands of amputations while nursing during the war."

"I'll probably have to fix what you have botched."

Mercy merely stared at the man. Indeed, she was too tired to argue. Crows cawed in the distance. The sound mimicked the doctor's tone and voice. Ellen joined the threesome.

Finally, taking a deep breath, Mercy looked once again into the doctor's hostile gaze. "Gideon Drinkwater, I am a free woman and a qualified physician."

Drinkwater cut in, speaking to Pastor Willis. "I won't practice medicine here if—"

"Neither of us knows how many injured there may be," Mercy interrupted. "If thee goes, I will continue trying to save as many lives as I can. But I believe that there will be more injured than *one* doctor can successfully treat alone. Will thee let men die because thee disapproves of me?"

"Let's have no more time-wasting discussion," Ellen said, attempting to soothe tempers. "We need two doctors and we now have two hospitals. The church at the other end of town is ready for you, Dr. Drinkwater. You won't even need to see Dr. Gabriel."

"Excellent!" Pastor Willis beamed at her. "Just the solution we need. Thank you, Mrs. Dunfield. I'll walk the doctor to the church." The pastor turned to the obviously aggravated man. "Let's be going then. We don't have time to waste."

Gideon Drinkwater rose and gave Mercy a scathing look. "This is not over, madam." He turned and marched away.

"Good riddance," Ellen whispered when the men were out of hearing distance.

Mercy just sank back farther in her chair. She believed Gideon Drinkwater's threat. He would do what he could to make matters even harder for her than they were. But she wouldn't think about that now. "Ellen, how are things at the mine?"

"They're working their way through the rock that sealed off the original cave-in. They're making good... progress." Ellen's voice broke on the final word.

Mercy gripped the woman's hand. "I am praying that thy good husband will be restored to thee."

Ellen nodded, holding back her tears.

After dark, Lon shuffled as quietly as possible into the dimly lit church hospital where he'd been told Mercy was treating patients. The smell of carbolic acid hung in the air. The work at the mine was done. All around him, people had rejoiced that every miner, living or dead, had been found and brought out. For him, there was no joy and no going back to the saloon tonight to celebrate. The cave-in, the storm and the avalanche had sucked him dry. He should have just gone back to his cot in the saloon and picked up the thread of his normal life there, continuing with his plan to leave Idaho Bend behind.

But, try as he might, he had been unable to stop himself from seeking out Mercy. Before he could speak her name, she was there in front of him. Her flaxen hair glimmered in the low candle and lamplight.

"Thee needs some nourishment and rest." Just as she had the first day they met, when she'd served him coffee, Mercy tended him now. She took him firmly by the arm and led him to the front of the church hospital where the pulpit had been pushed to one side. Tall shadows danced on the walls. She opened the back door and said in a low voice, "Lon Mackey is here. Will thee bring him a bowl of stew and coffee, please?"

He wished she didn't always do that, try to take care of him. "I hear you have competition," Lon said gruffly.

Mercy led him to a chair and pushed him gently into it. "A very opinionated man, unfortunately." She sounded only mildly interested. "I just finished treating my last patient. Soon I will be checking on all here again. Since you have come, it must mean…" She fell silent and touched his arm.

Her words caused him physical pain. He rubbed the back of his neck and forced his lungs to inflate. "About two hours ago, we broke through the final barrier and all the injured…and deceased have been removed from the mine." The memory of the crushed and broken bodies that had been tenderly carried out knotted around his lungs. Tears hovered just below the surface.

I shouldn't have come here—come to her. But he had been unable to stop himself. The desire to be in this woman's consoling presence had been undeniable, uncontainable. He bent his head over his folded hands. She took his hand and held it. He didn't pull away. Couldn't.

Then Mercy cleared her throat. "Thee took the remaining injured to the other church then?"

"The last two living, one of them was Dunfield."

"I'm so glad James Dunfield came out alive," she said, sounding more worried than relieved.

Maybe they should have brought Dunfield here to her, instead of the Boise doctor, but they had been told there was no more room. He couldn't stop the old feelings of loss and failure that the past hours had reignited. He'd done his best but, as always, it wasn't enough. Why hadn't he just stayed at the saloon? Why couldn't he have just been another rescue worker? Why did people turn to him? A bleak silence stretched between them.

The back door opened and he dropped her hand. He recognized the pastor's petite wife and thanked her for the large bowl of stew and mug of coffee she'd brought him. "After this," the woman said in a stern, motherly tone, "you should get some sleep. You look played out."

"I am. Thank you, ma'am."

"They tell me you're a gambler. And that after the avalanche, your quick action saved lives. I think your talents would be better used in a different line of work." With that admonition, she turned and went back outside to the detached kitchen.

Mercy had the nerve to chuckle softly. "She has a point."

Their levity fired his anger. "I told you I like living a free life—"

"Lon Mackey, thee may fool others, though in light of the past day, I doubt it. Thee didn't demand the lead in the rescuing effort, but thee was there. And everyone turned to thee without thee saying a word. Leadership is a quality that some are born with. Thee was born for command."

He couldn't curse in her presence though he sorely wanted to. "I don't want to lead. I just want to be left alone."

Mercy merely shook her head at him. "Eat thy food and then it will be time to rest."

He began spooning up the venison stew. It tasted better than he'd expected and he resented that. He didn't deserve good stew and comfort. Men had died.

At least the Quaker let him eat in silence. He hoped she would fall asleep where she sat and then he could just slip away. *Why did I come here? She can't do anything for me, for the way I feel.*

"Why aren't you resting?" he asked, unable to hold back the words, letting his ill grace be heard.

Mercy looked up. "I am going to. Indigo fell sound asleep when she sat down over there." Mercy gestured to the shadows near the far wall. "When she wakes, I'll lie down and sleep."

"And if someone's wound reopens, you'll just tell him you need your rest so they should stop bleeding, right?" he growled, scraping up the last of the stew.

She said nothing, making him feel like a scoundrel. Still, he couldn't bring himself to apologize. He'd spoken the truth about this woman. Mercy Gabriel couldn't help herself. She was impelled to help sometimes thankless people. For some reason, that made him angry. He set the empty bowl on the floor and began sipping the strong, hot coffee.

"Lon Mackey, thee has carried a heavy load and not just yesterday and today," she said at last. "I don't blame thee for seeking some ease, some pleasure. When I think of the war, I wonder how I survived it. How any of us survived it."

She passed a hand over her forehead as if she had a headache. "I often wonder if the men who framed our Constitution to continue the practice of slavery would have changed their minds if they had known what it would cost their grandchildren in human suffering."

"I'm not in the mood for a philosophical discussion," he said, hating the disdain in his harsh voice. He drained the last of his coffee and set the cup by the bowl on the floor.

"It is not thy fault that all the miners were not saved, Lon." Mercy's rich, low voice flowed over him. But it didn't soothe him; it raised his hackles.

"Thee did thy best, and some lived who would have died if thee hadn't stepped in to lead."

"I don't care!" He said the words with a force that surprised even him. He jumped to his feet, suddenly enraged.

"Thee does care. That's why thee is so angry."

He had to stop her words, make her stop prying up the scab that covered unhealed wounds.

"Lon, thee is a good—"

He pulled her to him and kissed her. This halted her words, but it also unleashed something within him. She was so very soft, so womanly in his arms. The sensation was intoxicating. How long had it been since he'd held a woman close and kissed her?

Mercy's gasp of surprise died on Lon Mackey's lips. No man had ever touched her like this. No man had ever kissed her. Sensations she'd never experienced rushed through her, overpowering, uplifting, breathtaking.

Lon pulled her tighter, and she reveled in the contact with his firm chest. The strong arms wrapped around her gave her a sense of sanctuary she'd never known. So this was what the poets wrote of…

Suddenly, Lon thrust her from him and rushed down the center aisle and out the front double doors. Mercy stood, blinking in stunned silence, and then she sank into her chair. The quiet of the church hospital was disturbed by a loud moan. Mercy rose and went to Pierre, who was writhing in his sleep.

She touched her wrist to his forehead. Just a slight

fever. She sank to her knees on the hard floor beside him and prayed that he would regain consciousness.

As she prayed, Lon's kiss kept intruding on her thoughts. She remembered everything—the strength of his arms, the stubble on his chin rubbing her face, his lips moving on hers. She tried to block it out, but couldn't.

Why did he kiss me? She had done nothing but try to encourage him to accept who he was. Was that so hard for him to do? Then her conscience pinched her. She was not always up to carrying on her work, either.

After the cholera epidemic, hadn't she spent a gloomy time in the back room of the mining office, trying to hide from who she was? And after the horrible words had been soaped onto Jacob Tarver's window, hadn't she been tempted to withdraw again? *Forgive me, Lord. I'm not invincible, either.*

"Both Lon and I have been called to step out from the crowd," she murmured aloud in the darkened church, "called to carry more responsibility than most." She sighed and rubbed the back of her neck. She slid down to lie on the floor, too exhausted to move.

"It's hard, Father," she whispered, gazing up at the dark ceiling. "How can I help Lon heal and be the man—the leader—you created him to be?"

Mercy woke, the floor hard beneath her. All was quiet. She felt a few moments of disorientation. Where was she? Then she recognized the sound of Indigo's footsteps as she moved through the aisles, checking on her patients.

The memory of Lon's kiss assaulted her senses, bringing her fully awake. She couldn't deny the kiss's effect on her. But had he simply done it to stop her words? She had made him angry with the truth, she was certain of that. But though she knew little of kissing, Lon had not appeared untouched by the kiss, either. Intuitively, she realized he would not have kissed her only to silence her. He never did anything from casual motives.

What if Lon kissed her again? What if he never kissed her again? The second question caused her the more powerful reaction. She realized she wanted Lon to kiss her again. But kissing Lon Mackey didn't mesh with her calling. Hers was a lonely path. Now she truly experienced a loneliness she had never anticipated. She had put her hand to the scalpel and now couldn't turn back. No man, not even Lon, would want a wife who was a doctor. Who could argue with that truth?

Two days later, holding her gray wool shawl tight around her, Mercy stood on the church steps. She watched another funeral procession make its solemn way to the town cemetery. These processions took place every morning and afternoon. The mortician and the town pastors were busy all day and each evening, preparing the dead and comforting the mourning. Mercy's heart went out to the widows and orphans who walked behind the wagon bearing their loved ones. As the flag-draped bier passed, she bowed her head in respect.

When she looked up, she saw two men approaching. Gideon Drinkwater, fire in his eyes, and behind him, Lon. She drew herself up and called upon God for strength and wisdom for the coming battle. "Good day, Gideon Drinkwater." She smiled.

"I have never approved of Quakers," he snapped. "Letting women think they are the equal of men is a dangerous idea. Now, I've done all I can for the patients sent to me first. I'm going to check on your patients and do what I can for them—"

"I am afraid that I cannot allow thee to do that." She had prepared for this. Usually Quakers did not believe in arguing with others, preferring to turn the other cheek. However, Mercy had decided that to permit this man to treat her patients would be to admit she was not a qualified physician and his equal. More importantly, since she had been told by the relatives of patients that this doctor did not practice sanitary medicine, he could actually do harm to her patients.

"Thee knows that no doctor presumes to encroach on the patients of another."

The man made a scornful sound and tried to push past her.

Lon hurried forward. "Stop that."

Gideon thrust her aside. Mercy lost her footing and fell. She gasped. Lon shouted in disapproval as people rushed forward. Lon jerked the doctor around and put up his fists as if challenging him to a fight. Women helped Mercy to her feet.

"Don't you try anything," Lon threatened.

"Dr. Drinkwater," Mercy said, still breathless from his assault on her, "no man has ever offered me physical violence merely because of my work."

"I'll do more than that!" he raged, shaking free of Lon.

Mercy put out a restraining hand, silently asking Lon for no violence. "I will see that you are run out of the Idaho Territory!" Drinkwater shouted. "Madam, either you stick to midwifing from now on or the next time I come to Idaho Bend, I will see you barred from doing even that. Territorial law does not permit women to hold professions such as physician."

"I believe that thee is making that up." Mercy rubbed her shoulder where it had bumped the door behind her. "In no state is it illegal for women to practice medicine."

But Gideon Drinkwater was already stalking away. "I am going to seek payment for my services and then I will be riding back to Boise. You've not heard the last from me!"

"Good riddance!" one of the men yelled after him.

"Are you all right?" Lon asked her, drawing near.

"I'm… I'm merely shaken." She tried to smile. "Thank thee for helping me."

"I'm sorry you were subjected to such abuse. I was on my way to visit Digger."

"Good. He needs cheering."

Lon nodded his gratitude and headed away. Just before he disappeared inside, he glanced back. His gaze told her much. *Lon, what am I going to do with thee?*

As she turned to walk away, a familiar voice stopped her.

"I just don't like that Boise doctor," Ma Bailey said. "He thinks we're dirt under his feet. If we've decided to let you doctor here, what business is it of his?"

Surprised again by this unexpectedly complex woman, Mercy turned to her. Just the two of them remained.

"And don't worry," Ma said, glancing around, "I won't blab your secret all around."

"What?" Mercy asked.

Flushed with obvious triumph and glee, Ma grinned with cat-in-the-cream-pot satisfaction. "About the gambler kissing you last night." She chuckled. "It's good to see nature taking its course. You and him make a good pair. And he'll give you something more than doctoring to think about." Ma winked, then walked off, chuckling to herself.

Mercy stared after her, appalled. The most notable gossip in town would keep Lon's kiss a *secret?* Mercy wasn't a gambler, but she thought the odds of Ma Bailey keeping that secret were over a hundred to one.

Chapter Nine

Mercy tottered back inside the church, still reeling from Ma Bailey's parting shot. She tried to think of a way to stop the news of Lon kissing her from becoming public knowledge. No idea came to her. It was only a matter of time before the juicy details of her first kiss would pass from gossip to gossip. And it didn't help that at the mere mention of the kiss her lips had tingled and her face flushed with uncomfortable warmth.

Lon sat on a chair beside the pew where Digger lay, speaking in low tones. Should she warn Lon?

The church was nearly empty. All the men who had family had been taken home for nursing care. Later today, Mercy would make her rounds in the community, checking for infection and informing the families about the best ways to help the mine accident victims return to health. Mercy turned her mind to the present challenge—away from Lon.

Indigo was sitting beside Pierre, who had regained consciousness yesterday. But he had said nothing, merely eating and drinking while looking at everyone with the most peculiar expression. Mercy had an idea as to why Pierre wasn't speaking, but she hoped she was wrong. Still, she had to test her theory, no matter how painful it might be for Indigo. The truth always became harder to face the longer one delayed in tackling it. Her sympathy for Indigo weighed on her heart. To avoid Lon, she paused to speak to Pierre and Indigo. Unable to stop herself, she tracked Lon's every word and gesture. Finally, Lon departed.

Unwilling still to confront Pierre's condition, Mercy moved to Digger and touched his heated forehead. "Thy fever is expected," she assured him.

He touched her arm. "I don't know if I can stand this."

She knew he was referring to the loss of his lower leg. She sat down in the chair beside the pew he was lying on. "It is hard." She took his hot, dry hand.

He stared at her, tears leaking from his eyes. "I came through the whole war, and now this."

She wiped his tears with her handkerchief. "Thee is a good man, Digger Hobson. Thee will recover. Thee will still be a good man and a capable mining manager."

"What woman will want me?" he whispered.

Mercy took a small, dark bottle from her nursing apron pocket and poured a dose of medicine into the large spoon lying nearby on a square of white cotton. "A woman who loves thee."

He shook his head, suddenly chuckling. "I know it was a stupid thing to say. I haven't even been thinking of looking for a wife."

Mercy smiled and held the spoon to his lips while he swallowed the medicine. The memory of Lon's kiss fluttered through her. "From what I've observed of life so far, not many men need to go far to find a bride. 'And a man who findeth a wife findeth a good thing,'" she quoted.

Digger inhaled long and deep. "How will I walk?"

"I have already ordered a prosthesis for you. Jacob Tarver made out the order form. Thee can pay him when thy fever has left thee."

"So they'll call me Peg Leg Digger." His attempt at humor failed as his voice broke on the words *peg leg*.

She kept her tone matter-of-fact. This brave man needed calm understanding, not pity. "The new artificial leg will not show in public. Thee will have a slight limp. And remember, thee has much to be thankful for. Thee might have died."

His face flushed from fever and emotion, Digger nodded. "I'll sleep a little now. I'm so tired."

She nodded. "The fever does that. Thy body is fighting for thee. And rest with regular food and drink is the best way thee can help thy body win this war."

He closed his eyes. "You're the doctor."

Mercy sat, clinging to his words—his precious, truly heartwarming words. The route to this moment had been like scaling a cliff, handhold by handhold, while men and women had taunted her. Now she felt as if she'd swallowed the sun. *Yes, I am the doctor here. Thank Thee, Father.*

Silently rejoicing, she rose and checked on several of her other remaining patients. Most were feverish. She had no weapons for fever except for the liquid infusion from the bark of the willow in the dark bottle in her pocket. And no one knew why this worked. The longing for better medicine, better science, twisted through her.

She rose and walked to Pierre—no longer able to put off the inevitable. Indigo was sitting beside him. Mercy looked down at the tanned face that was still handsome in spite of injury. Near the hairline of damp chocolate-brown curls, his head wound had been cleaned. And his arm was in a splint and a sling.

Pierre looked up at her with that odd expression.

"Pierre, can thee hear me?" Mercy asked, wishing she could postpone or deny her hunch.

He nodded, looking uncharacteristically sober.

"Does thee know who I am?" Mercy asked.

Indigo started at these words, her gaze switching back and forth between Pierre and Mercy.

He stared at Mercy for several moments, his face twisted. "No. Why do you talk funny?"

Eyes wide with shock, Indigo looked to Mercy. "What's wrong, Aunt Mercy?"

Her stomach roiling over the unappetizing truth, Mercy went on talking to the injured man. "Thee is Pierre Gauthier. Thee is a miner who was caught in an avalanche. I think thee is suffering what is called amnesia. It can happen after a blow to the head. This young woman is Indigo, my adopted daughter and someone who has been special to you over the past weeks."

Pierre looked at Indigo and then to Mercy. "Who are you?"

"I am Dr. Mercy Gabriel. Thee must not worry. Thy memory will return soon. Just eat and drink as much as thee can and thee will recover thy strength and memory."

"You're sure?" he asked, sounding relieved.

"Yes, indeed thee shall." Mercy hoped what she was saying was true. She had seen a couple of victims of amnesia in the war and they had all recovered in time. But there was no guarantee. Unwilling to face Indigo's crestfallen expression, she walked outside, suddenly needing air.

Back at her office, Mercy was cleaning her medical instruments after making rounds of a few patients with less dramatic ailments—a man with a case of gout in his foot, a little boy with a broken arm, a three-year-old with an earache. Hearing a timid knock, Mercy turned to see Sunny at her door. "Come in!"

Dressed in the same faded blue dress Mercy had seen her in when she was nursing Lon, Sunny walked in and closed the door behind her.

"How may I help thee, Sunny?"

The girl looked at the floor. "I don't need to tell you what's bothering me, do I?"

"Is thee referring to the fact that thee is carrying a child?" Mercy finished putting the examining instruments into a basin of wood alcohol. She turned and walked to her desk. "Why doesn't thee take a seat and we will talk?"

Sunny did so. Mercy waited, letting the quiet build between them.

"I don't want to raise a kid in a saloon." Sunny continued to speak to the floor.

"Is that where thee was raised?"

"Yes." The blunt word was said with a wealth of ill feeling.

"I see." One of the worst things about how women were treated in this world was the fact that there were no good options for someone like Sunny. She had been born into a situation there was little hope of leaving. Society was very unforgiving of women who weren't deemed "decent," even though the same stigma didn't attach itself to the men who used these women. "Does thee have any family?"

"No, my ma died a year ago. A few of her friends came here and I came along." Sunny was slowly shredding a white hankie in her lap.

"Sunny, I will be happy to deliver thy baby when

thy time comes. Does thee want to give up thy child for adoption?"

This question finally brought tears. Mercy took one of Sunny's hands in hers.

Sunny was finally able to speak again. "I don't think anybody would want my baby. And it hurts me to think of giving it away. It hurts to think of it being raised like I was. So lonely. No decent mothers would let me play with their children..." Sunny couldn't speak, her weeping was too strong.

Mercy's heart was breaking for this young woman and for her child. "I have a sister who runs an orphanage near St. Louis. If there is no one else to take thy child, I will write her." Mercy squeezed Sunny's hand. "But, Sunny, I would prefer to help thee leave the saloon and find a better life where thee can keep thy child."

Sunny rose, looking suddenly anxious to go. "I'm a saloon girl. I seen how it was with my ma. But thank you anyway, Doc." Sunny gave her a fleeting smile and then hurried out the door.

Mercy bowed her head and prayed for Sunny, her child and for this world that wouldn't welcome this new life. *God, how can I help her?*

The answer came quickly. Not only did she have Felicity, she also had her loving parents. Mercy pulled out paper and her pen, and began writing.

For the first time since the mine rescue, Lon walked from the back room into the saloon where the lively evening was in full swing. The mining disaster had interrupted his routine. And he still felt strange, as if someone had taken him apart and then put him back together again wrong. It was like donning a shirt that didn't fit.

But tonight he'd get back to his normal routine. And stay that way. No more interruptions to his easy gambling life.

"Hey!" the nearest man hailed him. "How're you doing? My arms are still aching from moving all that rock."

Lon recognized him as one of the older men who'd helped with the rescue. The mention of the mine disaster made Lon feel as if he was walking barefoot on hot sand. But he managed a smile for the old guy who'd worked himself to exhaustion. "Fine. You're looking in good fettle."

"Come on," the man said, "I'll buy you a drink."

"Later, friend. I need to make a few dollars first." Lon headed toward his chair at his usual table. Three more men hailed him with thanks and praise, so he was forced to shake several hands. Each kind word and smile pained him as if he were biting down on a cactus. Couldn't everyone just let it rest?

Finally, he got to his table and did what he always did while waiting for men to sit down for poker—he made a show of shuffling cards. He let the snap of the cards lull him, mesmerize him. The place wasn't crowded, but conversations hummed at the bar. Laughter punctuated words periodically.

Usually, the friendly sounds of the saloon lightened Lon's mood, made him relax. Now each greeting or comment directed toward him tightened his nerves.

Two men left the bar and walked toward him. *Good.* He smiled. Everything would go back to normal now. He'd spent the past night and day lying on his bunk in the back, staring at the ceiling, wondering why he hadn't left yet. And ignoring the answer.

Sunny had finally come and talked to him, asking

if he needed the doctor. That had galvanized him. He'd realized that he had to start gambling again or everyone would think he'd gone strange. And no, he did not want to see Mercy Gabriel.

The two men sat down across from Lon. One was a logger. The other was Slattery with his shock of gray hair.

"We need one more, gentlemen," Lon said, sending the cards back and forth between his hands.

"How about me?" The voice came from behind Lon and the shocked expressions on the faces across from him made Lon swivel around fast.

"Hello," said the pastor, who had ferried injured miners to the churches. He slid into the remaining chair at the poker table.

The cards flew out of Lon's hands and scattered over the tabletop.

The pastor chuckled. "Sorry if I surprised you."

Lon was aware that the saloon was quieting. No doubt not only because of the appearance of this unusual customer, but also because everyone wanted to hear what the tall, thin, blond pastor had come to say to the gambler. Disgruntled, Lon nodded to the pastor and began picking up his cards. "We need a fourth."

The pastor laughed, looking genuinely amused by Lon's suggestion. "I'm Stephen Willis, and I won't take much of your time. My wife suggested that I invite you to the community dinner this coming Sunday."

Of all the things Lon had imagined this man saying, that was not one of them. His scalp tightened with surprise. "What's your angle?"

Willis shook his head. "No angle. Just want to thank you for all you did during our recent—"

"Don't want any thanks." The same anger that had pushed Lon to kiss Mercy into silence flamed inside him.

The pastor nodded, still smiling. "We're going to have a special service of thanksgiving on Sunday."

"What's there to be thankful for?" Lon snapped. "We lost good men."

Willis's face grew solemn. "That is quite true. But all the dead have been buried and properly mourned. And there are many who survived because of the good people of Idaho Bend." The man raised his voice. "The whole town is invited. The churches are going to come together for the service. This service is for the living. To begin the healing of our broken hearts."

The man's final words fired up Lon, boosted him upward. He stood up, knocking over his chair. He dragged in drafts of air, his face flaming. Words jammed and stuck in his throat. The anger washed through him in hot waves.

Willis rose, squeezed Lon's shoulder and then walked out of the saloon.

There was silence in the large room and every eye turned to Lon. The heat drained from him. He reached down, picked up his chair and sat down. "We need one more player." His voice betrayed him by cracking again. Another logger came over, gave Lon a cautious look and sat down.

Lon nodded in greeting and picked up the remaining cards scattered on the table. Then he shuffled and dealt the first hand. The conversations at the bar began again, now buzzing. Lon tried to ignore the sound, knowing all the talk was probably about the preacher singling him out and about his curious and intense reaction to the man's invitation. What had gotten into him? Why had this simple invitation wound him up so fast and so hot?

And why was it that the only person he wanted to talk to about it was Mercy? But after his kissing her like that, how could he just go and talk to her? Maybe the kiss had set up a barrier between them. That would be for the best. Dr. Mercy Gabriel had proven to be dangerous to his peace of mind.

In the evening of the tenth day after the avalanche, Mercy watched the pastor and another man carry Digger Hobson to the wagon. Pierre walked beside them, and they helped him to sit beside Digger. She and Ellen had agreed that Digger and Pierre would be moved to the Dunfield house where Jim had already returned for care. Mercy still visited the other recovering patients daily and would until they were well enough to care for themselves. She tried to keep her mind on the present, but she could not stop thinking of how Lon Mackey had once again vanished from her life. Could it be because of the astoundingly perplexing kiss? Was he full of regret? Or was it something about her?

Mercy and Indigo walked beside the wagon as it bumped its way toward the far end of town.

"You're sure that Pierre will get his memory back?" Indigo asked, looking down.

Mercy sighed, trying to hide her own worries about this. If Pierre didn't, how would this affect her dear daughter? "I've seen other cases and those men did regain their memories. And if he fell in love with thee once, can't he do so a second time?"

"It's hard to look into his eyes and know he doesn't remember what he said to me," Indigo confessed, her voice faltering.

Mercy took her daughter's arm and pulled her closer. As they walked, Mercy put herself in Indigo's place. Or tried to. Her unruly mind insisted on bringing up Lon's kiss. She fought to keep her fingers from tracing the path of his lips on hers. Did she want her fingertips to feel the kiss again or erase it?

She sighed, feeling lonely even here with friends and her daughter. How could the absence of one person make a sunny day chilly and dismal? *I do know how you feel, Indigo. Lon Mackey appears not to want to remember me. And I miss him so. I've never missed anyone as much. I know I shouldn't, but I do.*

The wagon pulled up in front of the cabin. The men helped Pierre down from the wagon and Indigo walked with him into the house. The men followed, carrying Digger on a stretcher. Mercy entered and took off her bonnet.

Ellen turned a worried face toward her. "I didn't want that other doctor to treat my Jim," Ellen said, wringing her hands. "I don't think he'd be doing so poorly if you'd doctored him."

Mercy went to Ellen and put an arm around her. She heartily agreed with every word, but it wouldn't help Ellen's state of mind for her to say so. "Dr. Drinkwater is definitely not a…conciliatory man, but he is a qualified doctor."

"But he didn't wash his hands or instruments when he treated Jim. And it was plain to everyone that the men you treated got better faster. A few of the other wives noticed that after that quack left, you knew what to do to help their men get better faster."

Mercy nearly smiled at the way her brief, simple teachings on sanitary methods had begun to sink in and take hold. She pulled Ellen into a one-armed hug. "I couldn't have treated all the patients. There were too many."

Ellen chuckled ruefully. "Yes, and you're not the kind to speak against anyone. But I saw you kick that man in the shins and knock him off his feet."

Flushing warm around her collar, Mercy shook her head. "I—"

"You don't need to explain that to me. I felt like kicking him myself."

Mercy couldn't stop herself from laughing. Dr. Drinkwater didn't know how lucky he'd been, evidently. "I'm going to examine your husband's wound and see if it needs another fomenting."

Ellen stopped her with a touch on her sleeve. "I've heard talk about you and the gambler."

Mercy gasped.

"People always have to have something to gab about. I just…forewarned is forearmed, my mom used to say."

Mercy managed to nod. *I must put everything but my patients out of my mind. And gossip never lasts.* But Lon Mackey persistently refused to budge from her thoughts.

In the saloon, Lon sat in his accustomed chair, shuffling the cards, listening to the chatter and hubbub. He used to enjoy all the voices and laughter and bright lights. Now it just irritated him.

"I'll take another card," one of the players said.

As Lon dealt to him, a sudden hush fell over the saloon. Lon looked up to see the pastor again. Lon felt like growling. He reined in his instant antagonism and looked at the man coolly. "I don't have a place for you in this game, preacher. You'll have to wait."

The man laughed. "I came this time not only to invite you to the thanksgiving service and potluck but to remind everyone who worked in the rescue that you're welcome. We just want to make sure that those who helped are given recognition."

I don't want any recognition. I want to be left alone. Lon held tight to his flaring temper. "I'll keep that in mind. Now if you don't mind, I need to win this hand."

"I'll bid you good evening, then." With a wave, the pastor strolled out the swinging doors.

"That preacher's got guts," Slattery said. "I wonder what his church board will say about him walking into a saloon."

"If we're lucky, they'll fire him," Lon snapped. "Ante up."

The other three players stared at him, looking shocked.

Lon ignored this and went on dealing. He lost this game and the next. As he dealt the third hand, another hush came over the saloon. Lon recognized the sound of Mercy Gabriel's purposeful footsteps.

"Lon Mackey," Mercy said, "may I speak with thee? I have a message."

He wanted to slam his fist straight through the tabletop. He even felt the blow as if he'd actually done it. Yet he rose politely. "Dr. Gabriel, at the present I'm working—"

The other three players all rose and tipped their hats at Mercy. "That's all right, Mackey," one said. "We'll just lay our hands facedown, and when you've finished talking to the lady doctor, we can continue the game."

Mercy smiled.

And Lon was left with no recourse but to speak to her. "Dr. Gabriel, let's go outside." He motioned toward the door. She preceded him, nodding and greeting men who rose to say hello.

Outside in the chilly autumn night, he faced her.

"I'm sorry to bother thee when thee is working, but

Digger Hobson is fretful with fever and he has sent me to bring thee to him. I don't think he will be able to rest till he has spoken with thee tonight. And he needs his sleep." She gazed up at him.

The light from the saloon glistened in her blue eyes. His gaze drifted down to her pale pink lips and he couldn't help but think of how they'd felt when he'd kissed her. *Stop.* He inhaled. "Let's go."

She turned and he walked beside her. Neither spoke until the Dunfields' house was in sight. "Digger is making the best of the situation. And I think with careful nursing he will recover his health. Please try to speak to him as thee would—"

"I know. I'll speak to him as if you hadn't cut off his leg," Lon interrupted. No sooner had the words escaped him than shame consumed him.

Mercy said nothing further, but led him into the Dunfields' house.

He trailed in behind her. In the small parlor, Digger, Dunfield and the miner Indigo fancied lay on rope beds side by side, all flushed with fever and looking weak and miserable, much worse than the last time he'd seen them. He wanted to turn and hightail it back to the saloon. But he forced himself to see *them,* not flashes of past scenes from army hospital tents in battle after battle.

He cleared his throat. "Digger, you wanted to see me."

The redhead grinned feebly. "Come here."

Lon shot a nasty glance at Mercy. Had she brought him here to sit beside the man and watch him die?

"I'll get you a chair," Ellen Dunfield offered.

"Digger is doing well," Mercy said, as if she'd noticed Lon's reaction. "I think his fever will break in the next few days. I must thank Ellen for helping me nurse him, along with her husband."

So Mercy thought Digger was going to be all right. Lon felt the tightness in his gut loosen. He sank into the chair. The three women drifted away, giving the men some privacy.

"Gambler, I need you to take over for me at the mine," Digger said, his voice reed-thin.

"What do you need me for?" Lon asked, feeling resentful at being brought here to be asked to do something he couldn't do. "I'm not a miner."

"You're a man who can get things done. I'm getting better, so I'm able to think what should be done at the mine. But I'm not able to do it and see that it's done right."

Lon geared up for a good argument. "I might be able to tell your crew what you want done, but I wouldn't know if it was done right."

"Not a problem. I got a guy working for me who's about a hundred years old." Digger chuckled, sounding like a creaky gate. "He can tell you if they've done it right, but he hasn't got the energy to give orders. You met him when you were running the rescue brigade."

Lon wanted to continue arguing, but didn't want to upset Digger. Keeping calm was important for someone who was running a fever—even he knew that. "I still don't know why you want *me* to run the mine while you're laid low. There must be someone else—"

"The miners will do their best for you because they know you care about them," Digger interrupted. "They won't talk back to you or try to get away with anything. You've already won their respect."

"That's right," Jim Dunfield spoke up. "We all know

that more of us—if not all of us—would have died without you moving things along like you did."

Lon pressed his lips together to hold back an angry response. Why did everyone act as if he'd done something great? "I just did what anybody would have done."

"There were a lot of people in this town who ducked out when the going got tough," Digger said. "You stayed and did what had to be done. So no more arguing. I need to know in the morning."

Digger's final sentence ended the conversation. Lon rose and shook the three men's hands, then turned toward the door. Now if only Mercy would let him leave without having to add her bit.

He nodded at the women who had gathered around the table pushed against the wall. They waved at him and wished him goodnight. He walked out the door into the faint moonlight and found he was not looking forward to going back to the gaming table.

He also found he was more than a little disappointed that Mercy hadn't followed him out as he'd expected her to.

"Hey," someone with a rough voice said. Lon felt a nudge in his ribs. "Hey, gambler."

Lon opened one eye, ready to commit murder. "What?" he snapped.

"I'm Athol Dyson. I come to take you to breakfast so I can explain what's got to be done at the mine today."

Still with only one eye open, Lon stared at the gray-whiskered old-timer who was bending over him. He recognized him as one of the older men who'd worked at the mine cave-in and who'd tried to buy him a drink not long ago.

"Come on," Athol chided, the wrinkles on his face

moving with each word. "Digger told me to come and fetch you. We got to get to the mine before the miners arrive."

Waves of disbelief rippled through Lon. "I told Digger I'd think about it and get back to him."

"Well, to me and Digger that's a yes. If you didn't want to do it, you'd have just come out and said so. Wouldn't you?"

Lon asked himself, was this true? Then a thought occurred to him. If he went to breakfast and to the mine, Mercy would be relieved. He'd seen her concern for Digger, her patient, last night. And Digger deserved any help Lon could give him. Another advantage—he wouldn't have to spend tonight trying to act the charming gambler. He sat up. "Give me a minute to shave and comb my hair."

"You young fellers—" Athol shook his head, his long beard waving back and forth "—always got to look good for the ladies."

Lon rose, shaved, dressed and rejoined the old-timer at the back door. "Did you mention breakfast?"

Athol chuckled. "That's a good sign. I like a man with an appetite."

The two of them ambled down the alley and onto Main Street to the café. When Athol entered, he was greeted warmly. Indigo was waiting tables this morning. Athol and Lon sat at a small table and accepted mugs of steaming coffee from her.

Lon tried to ignore the fact that news of his capitulation in this matter would soon be known to Mercy. Why did that bother him? He was glad to do something to help Digger. It bothered him because Mercy was clearly trying to get him away from the saloon, and because the lady doctor was way too knowing. He was a pane of glass to her and he didn't like it. He didn't want her to think he'd changed his mind.

Lon forced himself to listen to what Athol was telling him about the day's mining agenda. *This is just temporary. I'll do this for Digger and after this break, I'll be more than ready to go back to the gambling table.*

On Sunday morning, Lon found himself standing at the back door of the church, idly listening to the large group service. The two pastors in town had combined their congregations and invited the whole town. The pews were filled with women and children, and men leaned against the walls and spilled out onto the steps.

People were subdued and that hit Lon as the right spirit. Lon had planned not to attend, but in the end, so many miners had urged him to come that he'd given in. He'd just stand at the back and slip out before the service was over.

In spite of his best intentions, he found himself looking around for Mercy, but he didn't see her anywhere. Maybe someone had needed her doctoring. Then he heard rustling behind him and quiet murmuring. He turned and blinked, not trusting his eyes. Didn't the woman ever know when to quit?

Mercy was walking down the main aisle, leading the Chinese men and their families toward Pastor Willis. The murmuring increased to an agitated buzz. Lon gritted his teeth. Why did Mercy want to embarrass the Chinese by bringing them here where they wouldn't be welcome? Why couldn't she see that this would discredit her with the people here? His nerves jangled. And against his will, he prepared to do battle for the woman who never left things as they were.

"I'm so glad you were able to persuade our Chinese

friends to come today," Pastor Willis said, stepping away from his pulpit. "As you all know," he addressed the gathering at large, "we owe a debt of gratitude to these strangers in our midst. I asked Dr. Gabriel to invite them so that we as a community could thank them for coming to the aid of our miners."

There was utter silence as the congregations digested this. Then Mrs. Dunfield, with her chin high, rose and began to applaud. Her little girl popped up and began clapping, too. One by one, other women rose and then the whole gathering—except for a few sour-faced dissenters—rose. A few men whistled. The sound enveloped Lon and his throat thickened with emotion.

Finally, Pastor Willis raised his hands for quiet. He approached Chen, who had gone into the hole first. "I believe that you were the man who bravely went into the mine after the avalanche."

A sudden memory nudged Lon. Before he considered what he was saying, he blurted out, "Why don't you ask him why they came to help?" All faces turned toward him. He felt the hot flush of embarrassment on his face.

"I Chen Park. We hear loud noise. Rocks falling. We come see rocks over mine. Bad. I say, woman doctor help wife bring baby. We help miners."

Now every face turned to Mercy. She gazed back with her usual honest-eyed serenity. What would her response would be? She stepped forward. "I am grateful, Chen Park," she said, nodding toward the man, "that thee came to help the miners. It reminds us that we are all human and all need each other. I was happy to help deliver thy first son, and I hope he will grow strong and wise."

"Yes," Pastor Willis agreed, "and please stay for the meal."

Voicing his thanks, Chen Park bowed several times toward Willis, Mercy and then toward the congregation. Then the Chinese began to walk back down the aisle. But as they passed, Ellen Dunfield came to the aisle and held out her hand. "Thank you," she said and then continued, sounding a little uncertain, "Chen Park, I'm Mrs. Dunfield."

Chen Park took her hand. "Good day, Mrs. Dunfield." Though the man had trouble with her name, both of them smiled. Then at each row down the aisle, hands were shaken as they made their way to the open doors.

Inside Lon, disbelief vied with sincere gratitude. He'd seen the Chinese who worked on the railroads and at mining sites hated and degraded by the white settlers, treated worse than animals. How was this event happening? When Chen Park passed him, Lon thrust out his hand. "Thanks again, Chen Park."

When the Chinese families had assembled at the rear and on the steps, Lon looked at Mercy. Awe expanded within him. What a woman. She was a miracle worker. And he was a witness to this one. The admission made him feel how far he himself had missed the mark.

The pastors ended the service with prayers and the gathered congregations answered the benediction with a loud "Amen!" The women hurried outside to where tables had been set up. Soon the tables groaned with pans of roasted venison and elk, bowls of cooked greens, huge bowls of mashed potatoes with puddles of melted butter and, at the end, a crowd of pies, cakes and cookies. Lon hung back by an ancient oak.

He wanted to leave, but found he couldn't make himself turn away. The mixed aromas of the food and the rumble of happy conversation ebbed and flowed over the churchyard and drew him irresistibly, though he'd halted at the edge.

He'd felt a part of this community during the cholera outbreak and the mine cave-in. But would they welcome the gambler? A deeper, more disturbing thought stirred within him. Did a man who had ordered men to battle and to death deserve a part in this celebration? He half turned to leave.

"Isn't thee hungry?" Mercy asked, coming abreast of him.

Lon startled against the oak. "Where did you go off to? I thought I saw you come out with everyone else." He spoke in a provocative tone and didn't apologize for it. This woman had a way about her that a man had to watch. She wouldn't wrap him around her finger as she had in the past.

Holding a cast-iron skillet with both hands, she smiled at him. "I went in the back entrance to get this pan for Mrs. Willis."

The mention of the church's back entrance instantly dragged his mind again to the kiss he'd stolen from her there on that night not so long ago. His collar became tight.

"Thee must come and sample the dishes or thee will insult the ladies."

He wanted to say no and walk away, but that would call attention to the situation, causing gossip about the lady doctor and him. So he forced a smile. "After you, Dr. Gabriel."

She led him toward the laden tables. He resented every step and the effort the charade cost him. When they were almost to the table, Mercy turned and gave him one of those smiles that he didn't want to admit made him weak in the knees.

He nodded and headed for Digger Hobson, who was sitting on a chair, wrapped in a blanket. As Lon walked away, he made a vow to himself. *I'll be leaving town as soon as Digger is on his feet.*

Chapter Ten

Several days after the thanksgiving service, Mercy sat in her cabin. It had been a long time since she'd had a quiet morning to herself. How long would it last before she'd be called out to a sick child or some other emergency? She sipped the now cool cup of coffee Ellen had brought her with a breakfast tray. Mercy's mind rolled over and over in circles of confusion.

Pierre still didn't recall anything of his life before the mine accident. How was that going to play out? Lon Mackey had kissed her and was now avoiding her. Why did Lon's drawing away hurt her so?

In spite of these worries, Mercy had been able to sleep in her own bed last night, uninterrupted for the whole night—fatigue had simply overcome worry. Since Indigo didn't have to work at the café this morning, she had kept watch over the three patients last night, allowing Mercy the night off. Indigo had returned a short time ago.

Indigo had told Mercy that every morning, Lon Mackey ate breakfast at the café and then left directly for the mine. Would Lon leave his gambling days behind? She scolded herself for thinking about a man who was fighting himself so hard, there clearly wasn't room for anyone else in his life. She would do herself no favors harboring any illusions about Lon Mackey.

Not that she had room in her life for him, either, she reminded herself. She rose and walked to the window, gazing out at the majestic mountains surrounding the valley. The trees blazed with autumn colors—bronze, red, yellow and orange—and stood out against the evergreen trees on the slopes to the towering Rocky Mountains. It was a breathtaking vista and she often wondered how she had been allowed to settle here amidst this grandeur.

She stopped the rim of her cup at her lips. Curiosity halted her.

A man she didn't recognize was limping with a crutch under his arm straight for the Dunfields' house. His expression was intent.

Mercy turned and placed the cup on the tray where the remains of her breakfast had cooled. She scooped her hair into a tail, twisted it up and secured it at the nape of her neck with several bent hairpins. She donned her bonnet, picked up the tray and opened the door quietly so she wouldn't disturb Indigo.

Who was this man and what did he want? And why did she expect bad news?

Mercy tapped on the door and entered as Ellen called, "Come in!"

Dressed in a mix of buckskin and plaid flannel, the stranger was standing by the cot where Pierre sat. The man swung around on his crutch to face her, his expression cautious. "You're the woman *docteur, n'est-ce pas?*"

Refusing to give in to her concern, Mercy handed

the tray to Ellen and offered her hand to the man. "I am Dr. Gabriel. And thee is…?"

He squinted at her and then replied, "I am Jacques Lévesque, *Docteur.* This is my *bon ami,* Pierre Gauthier. When I returned to town, I heard he couldn't remember, and now I see for myself. He doesn't recognize me—we who have known each other since we were children."

Mercy looked to Pierre, who appeared puzzled. He should have started to regain his memory by now. Weeks had passed since his injury.

The door opened and a disheveled Indigo entered. "I woke and you were gone, Aunt Mercy." At the sight of the stranger, she halted.

"You are Indigo?" Jacques asked. "Before the mine accident, Pierre and I worked together. He pointed you out to me. I am a friend of Pierre and of his family who lives north of here."

Mercy stood very still, her clasped hands tight.

Indigo moved forward and greeted Jacques. He shook her hand, but kept looking at Pierre. "How can I help my friend, *Docteur?*"

Mercy was torn between concern for Indigo, her daughter, and concern for Pierre, her patient. She decided she must voice an idea she'd been considering, but had thought impossible. "You say you know Pierre's family? Do you know where they are?"

"*Oui, oui,* I had heard that *mon ami* had been injured and had trouble with his memory, but I thought he would be well enough now. I am planning on leaving for home this morning and hoped that Pierre would come with me and finish healing there." Jacques looked pained. "A few supply wagons are headed north. We can hitch a ride with the wagoners."

Mercy took a deep breath. "I think, Mr. Lévesque, that thee should take Pierre home with thee."

This forced a sound of wordless denial from Indigo.

Mercy moved to her daughter, her heart wrung with pity. "Indigo, seeing his family may jog Pierre's memory. He should be starting to recall things by now."

Indigo visibly struggled with tears and then nodded. "If it's for his best."

"It is." Mercy put an arm around Indigo's shoulders, trying to lend her daughter strength. "Jacques, Pierre can walk well enough and his fever broke yesterday. Take him home to his mother and we will pray that she will help restore his memory."

Pierre rose from the bed and donned the hat and jacket that Ellen handed him. He thanked Ellen for her kindness and then paused beside Indigo. "I... You..." His expression tugged at Mercy's heart as she ached for Indigo. "Take care, Indigo." He touched her cheek and then the two men departed.

Indigo remained silent until the door closed behind the two. Then, weeping, she bent her head to Mercy's shoulder. "I love him so."

Mercy stroked Indigo's back and murmured comforting sounds. Regret lodged in her throat, making further speech impossible. This falling in love was chancy at best. It came without warning and left one without recourse.

For a moment, she lost track of whether she was thinking of Indigo, or of herself.

A week later, Mercy stood at the front of the church. The ladies who had come to her first lesson on sanitary practices had returned—and brought friends for today's lesson.

While she waited to begin her talk, she recalled the nights and days she'd spent in this building, treating the injured from the mine cave-in and avalanche. Digger was resting at the mining office while Lon ran the day-to-day operations of the mine with Athol.

Since Pierre's departure, Indigo walked around in a daze of misery for which there was no cure. Would Pierre return and know Indigo again as he had before? Mercy ached for her child, but dwelling on what one couldn't change helped no one. She tried to keep Indigo as busy as possible.

Standing straighter, Mercy began the topic for the day. "Ladies," she announced, the quiet murmuring fading, "today I want to let thee know of something thee might not have heard of but which has been done for nearly seventy years now in Europe. It is called a vaccination, and it will protect thee and thy children from smallpox."

"What's a vaccination?" Ma Bailey asked, from the front row, back to her old pugnacious self.

Mercy couldn't help but grin. "Very simply, a vaccination is dosing thyself with a very mild form of a disease so that if or when thy body comes in contact with a virulent form of the same disease, thy body can fight it off."

"Is that possible?" Ellen asked, sounding hesitant.

"No, it isn't!" a voice boomed as the doors at the back of the church burst open.

Mercy looked up, nearly groaning aloud with dismay. Dr. Drinkwater was bustling up the aisle toward her with a stern-looking man in his wake. She forced a smile. "Dr. Drinkwater, I see thee has come for another visit."

He gave her a scathing glare and then rudely positioned himself right in front of her, facing her audience. He said, "You women shouldn't be listening to this quack female. She's filling your heads full of nonsense—"

"Why're you so rude?" Ma Bailey demanded, leaping to her feet. "You walk in here and treat Dr. Mercy like a…like a slave or something. You're no gentleman."

Mercy stood straighter, stunned as much by Ma Bailey's defense of her as by the man's extreme nerve and bad manners.

The other women surged to their feet, and a clamor billowed through the church. The Boise doctor shouted to make himself heard and was ignored. The other man, who wore a large brass star on his chest, stayed to the side, silent but with an uneasy expression.

Cringing at the noisy argument, Mercy stepped around to Dr. Drinkwater's side and raised her hands. "Ladies, please."

The women, most red-faced and glaring, sat back down and pointedly gave their attention to Mercy. Mercy turned to Dr. Drinkwater, who looked as if he were about to have an apoplectic fit.

"Doctor, perhaps it would be best if I proceed, and then we can discuss the merits of vaccinating against smallpox later."

"We'd like to hear how to protect our children from smallpox," Mrs. Willis said.

"No!" Dr. Drinkwater objected.

The women jumped to their feet again, scolding the doctor.

Mercy closed her eyes, praying for inspiration. She opened them. She would give this man one more chance to prove he wasn't as foolish as his behavior branded him. "Dr. Drinkwater—" she began. The women fell silent again. "—why doesn't thee have a seat and listen to what I have to say, and if thee wants to give thy—"

"I will do no such thing," he snapped. "I told you I'd come back and stop you. I've brought the territorial sheriff with me—"

The rest of his words were drowned out by the general outcry. Fuming, Mercy pressed her lips together. This man was one of those unreasonable people her mother had always warned her about. "You can't persuade an unreasonable person with reason," she'd said. "Go to the real issue and stick to it." Mercy raised a hand.

Instant silence.

She smiled, knowing that this would goad Dr. Drinkwater to reveal more of his foolhardiness. "Doctor, I am a qualified physician and will continue to practice medicine. Thee does not intimidate me."

He leaned toward her, his face contorted with anger. "Does the sheriff intimidate you?"

Mercy looked to the other man, who had kept his distance and now appeared unhappy. Mercy decided to follow her mother's advice and be done with this irritating man. "Did thee bring the sheriff to arrest me?"

The sheriff chewed the ends of his mustache.

Silence. Every eye was on the sheriff. Mercy decided to push one step further. She walked directly in front of the sheriff with her hands outstretched, wrists together, as if ready for manacles. Was this sheriff as determined as the doctor to make himself a public spectacle of folly?

"If I am doing something against the laws of the Idaho Territory," Mercy stated calmly, "arrest me."

The story of Mercy's near arrest blazed through town within an hour. Lon was seething when he finally tracked down the obnoxious doctor and the territorial sheriff with the big brass star on his chest. The two of them were sitting at a table in the café, eating supper. "You!" Lon declared, advancing on them. "Foolish doctor! I should have blacked your eye the day you pushed Dr. Gabriel down. For two cents, I'd do it now."

The sheriff looked up, his fork poised in midair.

Len switched his attention to him. "What do you mean coming to town and threatening to arrest our doctor?" Lon stood, glaring down at the man.

The sheriff merely gawked at Lon, but the doctor was fired up. "We didn't arrest that blamed woman, though she should be put away where she can't be a danger to others with her quackery!"

"You be quiet, you old goat," piped up Ma Bailey, who'd been chatting with the café owner at the counter.

The doctor reared up from his chair. "Don't badger me, woman. The females in this town obviously don't know their place."

Lon gave the man a disapproving look. Regardless of Ma Bailey's foolish tongue, Lon didn't want the confrontation to descend into a public free-for-all. And while he was at it, he had another complaint to air. "You're the sheriff, right? What have you done to track down the man who stabbed me months ago?"

The sheriff put down his fork and rose. "You the gambler who got stabbed here?"

"No one else that I know of here has been stabbed," Lon said in a mocking tone. "Have you arrested the man responsible?"

"Well, it's a big territory—"

"If it's so big, what're you doing here?" Ma Bailey interjected, looking as if she were enjoying herself. "Is our woman doctor that big a problem?"

For once, Lon was forced to agree with the quarrel-some woman.

The sheriff frowned and looked at Lon, ignoring Ma. "I came to town to talk to you. I've got my deputies looking for him. And when we find him, we'll arrest him and you can identify him and testify against him."

Lon didn't believe for a minute that the sheriff had come to town to see him. He settled his hands on his hips, still glaring at the man. "I think you two had better go back to Boise. I would think that by now you'd have realized that we've adjusted to having a lady doctor in town. And we don't like interference from outsiders."

"For a gambler," the doctor said in a sneering tone, "you act like you're a pillar of the community—"

"Oh, he's not a gambler anymore," Ma Bailey crowed, rosy with excitement and in her element. "He's managing the mine and kissing the lady doctor. He'll be a respectable husband before you know it!"

A moment of shocked and total silence held them all in place. Then chatter erupted, cascading over and around Lon.

Furious now, Lon stalked out the café door and headed straight for Mercy's cabin. He rapped on the door and walked in before Mercy could even say "Come in."

She looked up from her chair, startled. "Goodness, what is the matter?"

Lon struggled to contain his outrage. *I shouldn't have come here. This is the last place I should be.* "Nothing's wrong. I heard that the territorial sheriff tried to arrest you."

She rose. "I told him to arrest me if I was breaking the law by practicing medicine. Of course I'm not, so the sheriff and the doctor left the church. And I went on with my talk about smallpox vaccinations. Lon, are thee all right?"

He wanted to say, "No, I'm not." Instead, he clapped his aggravation tightly under control. "Why would you tell Ma Bailey we kissed?"

"I didn't, of course. Does thee think I've taken leave of my senses?"

Now he burned with chagrin. Of course Mercy wouldn't have revealed the kiss to anyone, least of all the town's busybody. Why couldn't he think straight when it came to Mercy Gabriel?

His irritation still molten, still flowing, he said, "Fine. Good. Great." He turned toward the door and then said over his shoulder, "Tell Digger I won't be working at the mine tomorrow. I've got to leave Idaho Bend. It's time I finally got out of this town."

With that, he marched out the door.

"Hey!" A hand shook Lon's. "What're you doin' here? You forget to get up for our breakfast meetin'? Digger's drinkin' coffee at the café, waitin' for you."

It was Athol. Lon rolled onto his back and stared up at the ceiling. He'd been bunking at the mining office, but last night he'd returned to the saloon. After working all day at the mine and gambling all night, he'd staggered here and collapsed, falling into an almost drugged sleep.

"I heard about you tellin' that sheriff and the Boise doctor off. Still hasn't got a lead on who stabbed you, huh? And that doctor has a nerve stickin' his nose into our town's business. Who does he think he is, tellin' us who we can have doctorin' us?" Athol asked. "My ma always said, 'Keep your nose out of other people's business and it won't get snipped off.'"

Paying scant attention to Athol's rant, Lon thought over last night. He had hated every moment of last night's gambling. Why?

Mercy intruded into his thoughts unwelcomed. He might as well face the truth. He didn't want to spend another night gambling. What he really needed to do was leave the town. But he didn't want to leave Digger and the miners high and dry. At least that was what he told himself.

"Well, ya sick? Or you comin'?" Athol demanded.

"Isn't Digger well enough to go back to work?" Lon hedged.

"Needs his new leg the lady doctor ordered from Tarver."

"Okay, then," Lon capitulated. He rose, shortened his morning routine and was soon walking beside Athol and smoothing back his hair as he donned his hat.

Athol squinted up at him. "Heard you kissed the Quaker."

Lon waited for a rush of irritation at this, but instead found himself amused to be discussing such things with Athol. "You did?"

"Yeah, and you know she's the kind of woman who gets under a man's skin."

This keen observation startled Lon. "What do you mean?"

Shading his eyes, Athol looked to the clear sky directly above. "I'm not too good with words. But here's the thing. Most women're interested in doo-dads and furbelows and such. But the lady doctor's a woman who cares about what a woman ought to care about—bein' kind and doin' good. That's what my ma said I should look for in a wife."

"Is that why you're a bachelor, too?" Lon asked, grinning.

"Ain't a bachelor, I'm a widower."

Lon instantly felt bad for making a joke. But Athol smiled in reverie. "I been married twice. First wife was Merrillee and the second was Violet. Both of 'em cared about bein' good to others." Athol slanted a look up at Lon. "And good to me. If I were younger, gambler, I'd set my cap for the Quaker."

"I'll take that under advisement, Athol," Lon said lightly, as if the man's words hadn't been like an acid wash to the heart.

"You'd be smart to do so," he replied.

Deep in the November twilight, Lon approached the snug little cabin on the edge of town. He'd spent a long day at the mine, and it had been a good one except for his regret over the harsh words he had tossed at Mercy the day before.

Snowflakes floated down around him. Winter was coming and this morning on the way to the mine he had bought himself a wool coat. The change in the weather mimicked the change in his life. He had come to town a cheerful gambler, living by his wits. Now, nothing much was fun.

He walked more slowly, trying not to reach her door before he could come up with what he wanted to say to Mercy, how to apologize to her for his hasty, rude words.

The door opened and Mercy stood in the doorway. For a moment, he was transfixed. The candlelight behind her formed a halo around her slender, petite figure. He often forgot how dainty she was in body. Her spirit towered over most other people he'd ever met.

"Good evening, Lon Mackey. Come in from the cold."

Her softly spoken words captured him. He hurried forward and slipped inside past her. She shut the door behind him. The cabin was lit with two candles and warmed by the fire. He was thankful to see that Indigo was not present. "Where's Indigo?" *That wasn't what I wanted to say.*

"She is visiting a friend in town, a girl near her age. I'm very pleased that the girl's parents have welcomed Indigo into their home." She held out her hand for his coat and hung it on a peg by the door.

He added his hat and stood awkwardly in the center of the small, sparsely furnished, one-room cabin. Her neatly made bed sat against the far wall, the table and chairs were by the window, and two rockers flanked the hearth. He felt like an intruder.

"Come sit with me by the fire," she invited, claiming one of the chairs and waving him toward the other. "I thought thee were planning to leave Idaho Bend as soon as possible."

Was she taunting him? He walked, feeling like a windup toy, and sat down. The chair creaked under him in a friendly way, yet he was unable to relax. "I am leaving," he said with emphasis, "but I came to apologize—"

"For what?" She looked at him, her gaze open and honest, as always.

"I wasn't very polite the last time I arrived at your door." There, he'd admitted it. But he didn't feel any release of tension. He couldn't meet her gaze.

"Thee doesn't need to apologize for being concerned about me."

"That's not what I was referring to."

"Oh?" She tilted her face.

He ground his teeth, then said, "I know you didn't tell Ma Bailey about…" He couldn't bring himself to say the word *kiss*. He fell silent, nettled by her gracious words.

"So Ma Bailey broadcast…" Now she faltered. "What happened that night in the back of the church."

Now her careful wording goaded him into speaking the truth. "You mean when I kissed you."

She didn't reply right away. He waited as she rocked, the chair creaking in a steady rhythm that was making his neck tighten.

"Yes, when thee kissed me." She looked down at her hands folded in her lap.

He had come here with the best of intentions. And here in this soothing setting, with this soft-spoken and gentle woman, every word punctured his peace like sharp teeth. Where was this anger coming from?

"Thee is angry. I'm sorry, but I knew that Ma Bailey would not be able to keep a secret."

"So you knew she'd seen us?" He nearly stood up.

"Yes, she mentioned it to me the day Dr. Drinkwater left. I don't know how she managed to see us. She must have been dozing in one of the back pews and must have heard us…and woke. But as I said before, Lon, I did not discuss what happened with anyone."

"Now everyone knows." His words came out more harshly than he'd intended.

"I have not replied to any plain or veiled questions about it. It will blow over."

Her casual tone and the way she neutralized the kiss—which had shaken him to his core—infuriated him. He leaped to his feet, lifted her from her chair and kissed her again. For a second he felt resistance. Then she melted against him. He tightened his embrace and kissed her as if the world were about to end and this was his last chance to show her how much he cared.

The thought froze him in place.

Chapter Eleven

Mercy felt Lon's sudden stiffening and sensed what might come next. To prevent it, she wrapped her arms around him and hung on tight. As she had anticipated, he tried to pull away. She tightened her hold on him more, refusing to release him.

"Thee did that the last time, Lon. Thee kissed me and then left. This is all very confusing. What's happening?" She gazed at Lon's face. He looked as if he were in pain. Her throat tightened. "What's wrong, Lon?"

He looked upward, avoiding her eyes. "I shouldn't be kissing you. I know that."

"That is not the issue, Lon Mackey. I am not married and thee is not…or are thee married? Is that it?"

"No, I'm not married." He laughed in an unpleasant way. "She had the good sense to marry my best friend."

Realization dawned on Mercy and her heart nearly broke for Lon. "Is that why thee runs off every time thee kisses me—"

"This is only the second time I've kissed thee, I mean you. Don't make a big fuss about it. You said yourself that Ma Bailey's gossipmongering will blow over." His voice was climbing, sounding more and more annoyed.

"I am not making a fuss," she defended herself. "I just want to understand. Thee is an honest man. Face the truth. Thee has kissed me twice, and more than just a gentle brushing of my lips." The physical memory of how he'd kissed her thrummed through her.

"Thee has kissed me with…with ardor. I know a friend's kiss is different than…thy kisses." She took his stubborn chin in one hand and tugged it down so he was looking at her. "Now who is this woman who married thy best friend?"

"I don't want to talk about her."

"I probably don't want to hear about her, but tell me anyway."

He looked startled by her admission, and something changed in his face. "I went to war. My friend paid three hundred dollars bounty for someone else to serve in his place. So she married him. That's all there is to it."

Mercy brought her other hand up and captured his resisting chin within both hands, forcing him to look at her. "What a dreadful woman. Thee is well rid of her, Lon."

"In the end, she did me a favor. She was a woman with no loyalty. You, on the other hand…" Lon suddenly bent to kiss her again.

She stepped from his embrace, though it cost her. She wanted to stay within the circle of his arms. "Lon Mackey, I must be truthful and admit that I enjoy thy kisses, but now we must talk. Kissing means something more than friendship is forming between us."

He couldn't help himself. He grinned. How like Mercy to come out and just tell him she liked his kisses. And how like her to insist on being told why he'd kissed her. He leaned his head back and exhaled. He felt her take his hand and then nudge him back into the chair he'd left.

"We will talk now, Lon Mackey. Thy troubled spirit has long been on my mind." She moved her chair closer to his, but still faced the fire.

A log collapsed in the flames, sending up bright orange sparks. He rose and took the poker, pushing the logs around and adding one from the nearby stack. "Who's been cutting your wood?"

She chuckled. "Lon Mackey, I am not going to be distracted by such a foolish question. Now it is time for truth telling. A faithless woman abandoned thee for a friend. That is hurtful, but I cannot believe that is the reason thee denies who and what thee are."

He nearly snapped, "Who am I then? And what?" He caught himself. If he asked this woman those rhetorical questions, it was predictable that she would give him her opinions. And she had stated the truth. Janette's betrayal had not given him this deep hurt, this deep ache.

"Thee has no answer for me then?"

He sat back down. Her simple words were aggravating him, and he was aggravated at himself for being annoyed. "Why don't you tell me?"

She began rocking. "I already have told thee and on more than one occasion. This time thee must tell me what I do not know about you."

"I don't want to talk about me," he said, hating the belligerence in his voice.

"Has thee told anyone about what troubles thee? Why thee decided to become a gambler? Is there someone better than I who is willing to listen and understand?"

He pictured her with her stethoscope to his chest, listening to his heart. "Want to diagnose my illness?" he quipped.

She turned and looked at him full in the face. Firelight flickered shadows over her pale features. How had she become so beautiful to him? "I want to understand thee. I want thee to understand thyself so thee stops kissing me and leaving. And I want thee to stop going back to the saloon to gamble when thee knows thee doesn't want to."

He began marshaling his arguments to avoid disclosure. Then he stopped. His feelings had suddenly ignited. Scorching fury surveyed within him. "I'm so angry," he blurted out.

She nodded. "I know. What fires thy wrath?"

The erupting anger became a volcano like ancient Pompeii. It uncapped inside him, scalding and bubbling. He felt her cool hand rest on his forearm. He tried to pull away.

She held tight. "Please, Lon Mackey, here in this room, just the two of us, thee can tell me. Purge the anger. I can stand the storm."

An image flashed in his mind. Mercy and he at the mine, the storm pounding above. Drenched, they were running hand in hand. Another image seared across that one. In the midst of battle, he was urging his men forward. Grapeshot and bullets were whizzing through the air. His men were falling around him. He heard them screaming, calling for God. Fear and terror forced him out of his chair.

"Don't leave me, Lon." Her voice was urgent, yet gentle and completely disarming.

He moaned God's name and then sank back into the chair and began sobbing. He tried to stop the wrenching cries that boiled up from deep inside him. He couldn't. He buried his face in his hands. Mercy knelt in front of him and wrapped herself around him, laying her head on his arm, a sweet presence. Tears poured down his face. Time passed, but he could not stop until finally he was empty, purged.

Finally, he opened his eyes and looked down. Mercy's white-blond hair had come loose and flowed onto his lap. It reminded him of a painting he'd seen once of angels with hair like spun white-gold. *Mercy, what are you doing to me?* "I'm sorry," he said, his voice still thick from weeping.

She raised her head and looked up into his face, a tender smile curving her pale pink lips. "Thee has nothing to apologize for. Thee has been carrying that heavy, sorrowful burden much too long."

"Crying doesn't do any good." He wiped his wet face with his hands.

"Oh, that's right. Boys don't cry." She tilted her head. "But, in truth, they do, and men should sometimes, too. God gave us the ability to weep because sometimes we must weep. Jesus wept at the grave of a friend. Is thee better, stronger than he?" She rose then.

He wanted to pull her back, keep her close. His arms reached for her, and then he remembered that she didn't belong to him. He let them fall back to the chair arms.

She leaned forward and kissed his cheek, a soft, fleeting benediction he wished he could save. Then she sat in her chair and lifted some white yarn from the oak basket on the floor next to her. "Tell me."

"Tell you? What?"

She gave him a narrowed look as if scolding him. "About the war. What thee hated most. Who thee misses most. What keeps coming up in thy mind that has the power to make thee try to be a different man?"

"That's a lot of talking." He snorted. His limbs felt weak as if he'd just been ridden hard and put away wet. He couldn't have stood up if he wanted to. "It's too much."

"I agree," Mercy said. "It was a long, devastating war and the losses to all were overwhelming. Thee knows that I was there, too. Sometimes I wonder how I did what I did."

His head felt heavy. Bending, he leaned his cheek on his upturned hand, hiding his face from her gaze. "I'm spent."

"Weeping takes more energy than one would imagine."

He leaned his head back against the chair and began rocking. The woman near him began knitting, and the rhythm of the needles joined the creaking of the two rockers. It had been a very long time since he felt this much at peace. The weeping had cleansed him somehow. Washed away the sins of the past. *I'm becoming poetical,* he jeered at himself.

Mercy knitted, clicking her wooden needles, and Lon rocked, matching her rhythm with the creaking of the chair. It was a companionable quiet, peaceful. She didn't push him to reveal more, but he knew she would not let this go. "You're right," he admitted at last. "I don't want to gamble anymore. I used to, but that's changed."

"Thee needed a break from responsibility. I see that." She paused, studying her knitting. "But I think that the cholera epidemic and then the mining accident forced thee to face who thee really is."

"And who am I, really?" The fact that she insisted she knew him better than he did remained irksome.

"Thee is Lon Mackey, a good man, a born leader. Thee has a path, too. The war wasn't meant to be thy path—"

"I thought it was when I went to West Point," he interrupted. Uncapped by her fearless words, emotions he couldn't identify easily were sliding, swirling through him. "I wanted to be an officer in the U.S. Army. And we see how wise that was."

I've lost all my youthful zeal and idealism, Mercy. I can't get it back no matter what I do.

He gave a dry laugh. "Colonels are not as needed as before. What would you suggest I choose as a career now?" He couldn't keep the mocking note from his tone, even though it was directed at himself, not her.

"Thee must find that thyself. I have faith, however, that God will show thee the work, the path He has for thee if thee asks Him." Her hands, pale in the dim light, worked the needles and white yarn.

Lon still couldn't wrap his mind around this woman's God. The faith he'd been raised with had failed him in the war. He'd called out to God during the cave-in, but that was not faith, merely desperation. "It's as simple as that?" he asked with an edge to his tone.

"People like to make God complicated. But once thee accepts that He is God, Ruler of all who live, life becomes easier. He has a plan for each life."

"God didn't hear my prayers in the war. Why would He now?" he grumbled. The old question still hooked him with a barb.

"We live in a fallen world. People like to think that God wants them to go to war in His name, but God doesn't want war any more than you do, Lon Mackey. Thee prayed and thy prayers did not appear to be answered because the war went on and on. But God cannot make humans do something they do not want to do. The Confederacy would not surrender until it could no longer go on."

"So evil exists because people won't surrender to good?" he asked sardonically.

"Yes, thee has stated it very well." She was counting her stitches on one needle, moving them two by two. "If we all put our efforts into doing the good for others that God wants for us, this world would be a better place."

How could he argue with her about that? He didn't have the strength to form more words. But his mind took him back to the war. The few times he'd tried to protect his men in battle, his caution had only caused more loss of life. *I don't have your faith, Mercy. I don't see any path for me.*

"Lon, how long will thee deny they true self and God? Thee does not want to play the gambler any more than thee truly wants to leave this town."

He went to counter her words, but couldn't make the effort.

The door opened and Indigo walked in, letting in a rush of chill wind. "I'm home, Aunt Mercy— Oh!"

Lon rose from the rocker, feeling at least eighty years old. Mercy had exhausted him. "Good evening, Indigo."

"Good evening, sir. I didn't know you were visiting."

"We were just talking," he said, feeling vulnerable, yet certain Mercy wouldn't betray knowledge of his loss of control. How had this happened? He hadn't wept like this even during the war over his fallen comrades in arms.

"If you two want to speak in private, I'll go see Mrs. Dunfield," Indigo offered, staying by the door.

"No, no." He went to the pegs and donned his hat and coat. "I'll see you ladies around town then."

"Please think about what we have discussed. I will be praying that thee finds thy path." Mercy had turned to him, casting her face in shadow. Still, her bright hair gleamed in the low light.

He conquered the urge to return and kiss her good-night. "Indeed I will. Good night." He opened the door and stepped out into the cold night. The darkness around him reflected his dim outlook. What was he going to work at now? And when could he kiss Mercy again? That last was a perilous question. She demanded a lot with her kisses. Would he ever live up to her expectations? Or would he merely disappoint her? Could he live with himself if he did?

In the café's clatter of dishes and silverware and surrounding chatter, Digger, Athol and Lon sat around a table the next morning.

"Lon, I still need you for about a week or two," Digger said. "I can walk now with this prosthetic leg but I don't have the stamina I need to work sunup to sundown. I'll go to the mine in the morning to look matters over, go back to the mining office and come back just before the end of the day."

Lon nodded. He had been expecting this. But the question of what he would do now loomed, mocking him.

"Are you… I don't think…well…" Digger stammered.

"I'm not going back to gambling, if that's what you're trying to ask." Lon felt his mouth twist down on one side. "But I don't know what I can do to make a living. The only thing I know besides gambling is the army." He tossed up both hands and then folded his arms over his chest.

Both men surprised him by looking as if they'd expected his words. "You're an educated man, aren't ya?" Athol asked.

Lon nodded, watching the two closely. They couldn't really be serious.

"Well, then, you ever think of reading the law?" Digger asked. "Or maybe getting some territorial job?"

"Digger's right," Athol agreed. "You could do somethin' like that easy."

Lon lifted his coffee cup to his lips, playing for time. He lacked the will to take any of these suggestions, couldn't take them seriously. He still felt flattened from last night. When would what the French called *joie de vivre* return? Or would it ever return? "I'm grateful for your confidence in me."

Athol squinted at him and Digger looked as if he were weighing Lon's words.

"Well, you'll have to find your own way," Digger said at last. "But if you need a good word, feel free to give my name."

That struck a chord deep inside Lon. "Thanks," he managed to say. They ended their breakfast meeting and headed off toward the mine for the day.

Hours later, Lon walked back into town alone. His conversation with Mercy the night before and his talk this morning with Digger had finally stirred him to action. He couldn't let them persuade him to venture forth into paths that would bring failure to him and disappointment to them. His mind cleared. He wouldn't delay. As soon as Digger no longer needed him, he would pack up and leave the next day. He walked through the swinging doors of the saloon and was hailed by the bartender.

"Hi, Tom," Lon greeted him and leaned against the bar.

"I hear your job at the mine is almost over," Tom said.

Lon was amazed again how fast news spread through

Idaho Bend. Someone must have been listening to his conversation at the café in the morning. "Digger's getting back to work."

"You'll be back again, then?" Tom looked at him sideways as he swabbed the bar with a wet cloth.

Lon grinned. Tom's tone told him the bartender didn't expect him back. "Digger thinks I should change my line of work."

"Well, you know, what we need in town here is a bank." Tom paused and looked at him.

Lon burst out laughing. "You think I've got enough money to start up a bank?"

"No, but you're the kind of man who can go to Boise and maybe Portland and Seattle and get investors interested. It's obvious you're an educated man."

Lon shook his head, restraining the urge to reply sharply. "You have more confidence in me than I have in myself."

"That's for sure," said Sunny, whose shiny red dress could no longer hide her delicate condition. She walked up beside Lon. "Are you really going to marry Dr. Mercy?"

Lon did a quick burn at the town's infernal nosiness. "Dr. Gabriel is a fine lady. Any man would be proud to have her favor. But there's been no talk of marriage."

"Well," Tom said, "she's not the kind of woman you can kiss without it meaning something."

"Thank you for explaining that to me," Lon said, heading into the back room to collect his few possessions. Moments later, he walked out of the saloon with a wave. He couldn't get away soon enough. This town was way too interested in him and the doctor.

His thoughts were interrupted by the sound of firecrackers going off nearby. Along with everyone else on the street, he turned and saw that it was coming from the alley behind Tarver's store. Mercy's office! He began to run, and others who obviously jumped to the same conclusion joined him.

He arrived in front of her office and gaped at the simple one-word message soaped onto the window: LEAVE. A burned string lay before the door, the remnants of the firecrackers. Lon looked around, hoping Mercy was nowhere nearby. "Quick! Let's get this wiped off—"

Carrying her black bag, Mercy appeared in the alley and looked puzzled by the crowd of people clustered around her office door. Everyone parted, letting her pass. She halted at the door and stood very still.

Lon watched her light complexion turn pink and then pale again. He clenched his fists, wanting to batter the culprit to a bloody mass. "I'll get it off," he muttered.

She glanced at him, her face drawn and sad. "If thee please, I would be grateful." Then she unlocked her door and went inside.

Tarver bustled up with a buckle of water and a couple of rags. "I'll help you wash it off. I wish I knew who was doing this. I'd like to box his ears."

After rolling up his sleeves, Lon accepted the wet rag and began washing the window. His intention to steer clear of the Quaker frustrated yet again. *I intend to find out who's doing this, and when I do, I'll run the rat right out of town. Then I'll go, too.*

Mercy sat in her office for a long time after the unpleasant word had been wiped away. She was fighting the urge to go home to her cabin and hide. Why did such opposition hit her much harder here? She had faced the same anger when she'd entered the nursing profession and worked with Clara Barton. She closed her eyes and pinched the bridge of her nose.

Indigo walked in. "I don't want to cook this evening. Let's go to the café for supper."

Mercy gazed at her daughter. Inside Mercy, unruly emotions clamored, insisting she go home to the cabin, shut the door and not face anyone for days. She forced herself to rise from her office chair. "I think that's a wonderful idea."

Mercy turned down the wick in her oil lamp and blew out the flame. Then she donned her bonnet and wool cape. Outside, she slipped her arm through Indigo's for the short walk to the cheery café.

As soon as they entered, Mercy saw Lon sitting with Digger. This did not help Mercy's mood. Still daunted or distressed somehow by the one-word message on her window, she tried not to glance his way, as if she were embarrassed that he'd had to help her in that way.

Gossip about them was sweeping its way through town as it was. She would do nothing to add any fuel to it. The coffee in her cup rippled from the slight trembling in her hand. She pulled herself together and smiled at Indigo as they sat down.

When the bell on the café door rang, Mercy looked up. Her spirits sank lower than she thought they could. *No, Lord, not him, not now. Help.* Blinking away tears, she murmured to Indigo, "Dr. Drinkwater has just walked in."

"Oh, no," Indigo whispered.

Mercy didn't like the self-satisfied look on the doctor's less-than-attractive face. The sheriff wasn't with him. Instead, a lean man of medium height wearing a small brass star followed him inside. The two of them made their way to Mercy's table. The other diners stopped speaking and the café grew quiet—only the sounds of the cook in the kitchen behind the dining room were audible. Mercy's stomach clenched, but she kept her polite smile in place.

When Dr. Drinkwater reached her table, he stepped aside. The other man stopped beside Indigo, pulled a paper out of his pocket and began reading, "Indigo Gabriel, I, Martin Blank, do arrest you for breaking the law of the Idaho Territory—"

The rest of his words were drowned out by the exclamations from the other diners. Mercy's mind had halted on the word *arrest*. She closed her eyes and prayed for strength and wisdom. Then, in the midst of the hubbub, Mercy rose, her heart beating fast.

This quieted the café. She forced herself to stay outwardly calm. "Who are thee? Is thee trying to arrest my daughter? On what charge?"

"I'm Territorial Deputy Martin Blank," the man with the star replied. "The 1857 constitution prohibits new in-migration of Negroes, as well as making illegal their ownership of real estate and entering into contracts. They were also denied the right to sue in court. It's all in Article 1, Section 35. Therefore, this warrant for the arrest of Indigo Gabriel was ordered by the Circuit Territorial Judge Chance Solomon." The deputy looked up from the paper.

"May I read that, please?" Mercy held out her hand.

"See what I mean?" Dr. Drinkwater mocked her. "This woman thinks she's the equal of a man."

Though she was tempted to lash out at him, Mercy stared hard into the doctor's face and kept her hand out. She willed herself to hold on, give no quarter. Finally, the deputy handed her the paper. She read it and went colder inside. The warrant said exactly what he'd stated. "Idaho Territory has an exclusion law?"

"Yes." Dr. Drinkwater looked elated. "And if I have anything to say about it, we'll add an amendment excluding quack women doctors."

"Well, if they had a law against quack male doctors, they'd run you out of the territory!" Ma Bailey announced. "You're just jealous because Dr. Mercy's a better doctor than you." Many diners agreed to this loudly.

Dr. Drinkwater's face became mottled with red and white blotches, and for a moment, he couldn't speak.

Mercy handed the paper back to the deputy. "I believe that this exclusionary law is against the Constitution of the United States. The Thirteenth Amendment freed the slaves, and the Fourteenth Amendment enfranchised male Negroes. How is it possible to exclude American citizens from any territory?"

"That's not for me to say, ma'am," the deputy replied, rolling the paper scroll-like. "It's just my duty to arrest this woman and take her back to Boise for trial."

At this, the men in the café rose as one. Lon quickly covered the short distance to Mercy's table. "We're not letting you take Indigo out of this town," Lon said.

"Yes," Digger, at Lon's elbow, agreed. "If you have to arrest her, fine. But she's staying here. The circuit judge will see to her case when he comes here next week."

Indigo edged around the table away from the deputy. Heartened by the men's support, Mercy wrapped her arms around her daughter and glared at the two interlopers. Her heart was sending her blood out in strong waves and her face felt flushed. "Dr. Drinkwater, thee is a coward. Thee cannot drive me from the territory, so thee moves against my daughter."

"I told you, woman, I'd see you run out of the territory," he blustered. "And you broke the law bringing this black girl into white territory."

"And I said we're not letting you take this young woman from our town. You can arrest her and put her in Dr. Gabriel's custody." Lon spoke with stern authority in his voice. "Do I make myself clear?"

The men in the room all drew out guns. Shock flashed through Mercy like chilled blood. "Please, I don't want any violence."

"There isn't going to be any," Lon said, with steel in his voice. "We've all witnessed the serving of the arrest warrant. And we'll all make sure this young woman is here when the circuit judge arrives. But Miss Indigo stays in Idaho Bend. We're not letting you take her anywhere. She's an innocent woman and we won't allow it."

"That's right," Digger agreed. And the rest of the men in the café made their agreement loud and clear.

Dr. Drinkwater looked ready to explode. The deputy gazed around, a shocked look on his face. Finally, he cleared his throat. "Okay, but remember, you'll all be held responsible for this girl being here when the judge arrives." He turned and marched out.

Dr. Drinkwater sputtered words that weren't intelligible, yet Mercy got his meaning, and anger heated her neck and face. "No, this isn't over, Dr. Drinkwater. I won't be bullied like this."

"Yeah," Ma Bailey chimed in, "we aren't impressed with you, Doc. Go back to Boise."

Gideon Drinkwater turned and marched out, slamming the door behind him and nearly dislodging the jingling bell.

Applause broke out, but Mercy sank into her chair.

Indigo sat back down, too, looking stunned and wounded.

"Don't let this upset you, ma'am," Digger said. "No judge from Boise is going to tell us what to do."

Mercy tried to smile in response, but her attempt was less than successful. Many in town had accepted her as their doctor. These were the ones she had been able to treat and help. But the one-word message on her window proved that there were some who still wanted her to quit. What should she do about this charge against Indigo? What would be the outcome? Would she be forced to leave Idaho and start all over again somewhere else? Would she be forced to part from Lon, who had just come to the defense of her daughter in a way that had renewed her faith in his goodness?

After they'd eaten the little they could with their spoiled appetites, Mercy and Indigo walked home through the chilling November wind. At home in Pennsylvania, the autumn would still be warmer and golden, but here the wind blew briskly. However, the scene at the café was chilling Mercy more than any wind. Neither of them was speaking. They finally reached their own door and hurried inside.

For the first few moments, Indigo was busy stirring and feeding the glowing fire on the hearth and Mercy hung up their bonnets. Then they sat down, warming their feet by the fire.

"Aunt Mercy, sometimes I just get so tired of it all."

Mercy knew what Indigo was talking about. *I get tired, too, Lord.*

"Why does it always have to be about what color I am? Why can't people just see me?"

Mercy merely reached for Indigo's hand and held it.

"I know you didn't like Pierre, but he saw *me,* not a black girl."

"You're wrong. I liked Pierre. I just hoped he wouldn't break your heart," Mercy said, aching for her child.

"How could he do that?"

Mercy sighed and sank back against her chair. The warmth from the fire was beginning to thaw her physical cold, but had no power to melt the ice within her. "I guess I'm just especially watchful about you. You're my only child. I want to keep you safe."

Indigo gazed into the fire. "What are we going to do? If the law says I can't be in the Idaho Territory, how can I stay? And if I leave, how will Pierre find me? If he ever remembers me?" Indigo began to weep.

Mercy got up and hugged her daughter. "If we have to go, we will leave word for Pierre as best we can. We have each other, daughter, and I will not give in so easily. I'll telegraph Boise and hire a lawyer. You won't go into court without legal counsel. This law is wrong and we must fight it."

"Why do we always have to fight things like this?" Indigo's tone was plaintive. "Other people don't."

"Other people don't see things the way we do." Mercy straightened, but rested a hand on her daughter's shoulder. "We believe men and women are equal in God's sight and that God loves all tribes and nations equally. Since we refuse to agree to the popular way of thinking, we will always face opposition, here or elsewhere."

Indigo was wiping away her tears with her white handkerchief. "I don't like it."

I don't, either. "Indigo, this world is not our home. We're just passing through." Mercy spoke the words of a spiritual she'd heard slaves sing in the South during the war.

But it's hard, Lord, never fitting in. She thought of leaving Idaho, leaving her friends, leaving Lon Mackey. *He's still fighting You, Lord. Please look after him.*

As Mercy comforted her daughter, she steeled herself for the fight ahead. And for the possibility that she might lose Lon Mackey, just when she was starting to find him.

Chapter Twelve

Another busy day at the mine past, Lon stalked around Tarver's storefront to the rear alley, his anger over Mercy's unjust treatment still simmering. Light from the lamp shone out into the alley. Mercy was indeed in her office. Was she alone? He'd stayed away from her for the past twenty-four hours because he wanted to calm down before he spoke to her. But peace had not come near his reach. He had to talk some sense into her. Then maybe he'd calm down.

The incident with the firecrackers and the soaped message on her office window, plus the scene in the café the night before, played over and over in his mind. He had said and done little of benefit to Mercy and Indigo in either uncomfortable situation.

He must speak to her, reason with her. He must convince her that he had the solution to her problems. Anger had ridden him with its spurs for years now. If he persuaded Mercy, would his lightning-quick temper calm and recede? Would he once again be able to think and act with measured prudence?

Lon approached the door and turned the knob. He stepped inside and felt the warmth from the Franklin stove in the corner of the small office. He had rarely seen Mercy like this in a private moment. She had taken off her bonnet and her soft hair fell around her shoulders. She sat at her desk, writing in her ledger. She looked up. "Lon, is something wrong?"

The fact that her first thought was one not about her own troubles but one concerned for him blasted his self-control to shreds. He reached for her, lifted her from her chair and kissed her. For a moment, she clung to him, but then she tugged free. "Thee is kissing me again, Lon. Why?"

Her hair gleamed, catching the golden lamplight. With one hand, he lifted a handful, letting it fall through his fingers—silken, enticing, irresistible.

"Lon," she scolded, "this is my office. Someone might see us." She stepped back and tried to gather her hair into its usual knot at the nape of her neck, blushing and looking delightfully flustered. How could he not want this woman in his life?

"I've decided that we should marry." He blurted out the unexpected and audacious words in the most blunt, unromantic manner possible. He cursed his clumsiness. *What am I saying?*

She gaped at him, her lips parted in shock.

That sparked his irritation anew. "Don't look so surprised. Do you think I go about kissing women indiscriminately? You are the one woman in this world I trust, the one woman in this world I must care about."

She stumbled down in her chair, facing him. "Lon, thee does not sound very confident of thy feelings for me. Thee 'must' care about me? That does not convince me. What has caused thee to propose marriage to me?"

"Why do you always have to talk everything to death?" He began pacing. Voicing the proposal fired his determination. He would never be free until he and Mercy left this town behind them. "I want to marry you. I know that you'll be faithful and honest."

"I do not talk things to death." She continued fiddling with her hair.

His fingers twitched, urging him to reach again for her hair, to let it flow over his palm. He grimaced at himself. *I must concentrate and convince her.*

"I only speak when there is something I must communicate or learn," Mercy said. "If thee cannot tell me plainly why thee wants to marry me, I cannot marry thee."

He turned his back to her and continued pacing in the space near the door. The small office felt like a box. "I want to go to California." These words shocked him. But his mind was suddenly very clear. "I want to marry you and then the three of us will go to California."

"Why?"

Her incredulous tone jabbed him. He turned to glare at her. Why didn't she understand what was going on here? "Because you aren't wanted here, that's why. That Boise doctor is not going to stop bothering you till you leave the territory. So let's go. There will be sick people in California who need you, too." How could she argue with that?

She looked directly into his eyes—as she always did. He read the concern for him there and looked away. *This isn't about me, Mercy.*

"Lon, I believe I am wanted here. I have been accepted as a doctor by most of the people in town. Why should I let one foolish word soaped on my window and one nasty, ill-natured man make me turn tail and run?" Her voice strengthened with each word. "I am not a coward. And neither are thee."

He ignored her last sentence. "Of course you're not a coward. But we could be happy in California—"

She gave up trying to control her hair, her hands dropping to her lap. "I suppose," she said, looking up at him and speaking in a wry tone, "thee will spend thy nights gambling and I will practice medicine?"

"Of course not." Her words and sarcasm tightened his forehead. He rubbed it, trying to ward off a headache. "I'll find gainful employment. I'm educated. I could read law there."

"Why can thee not do that here in the Idaho Territory?"

Her cool question drew the headache nearer. "I've had it with this place." He struck his open palm with his other hand. "I was stabbed here. Now this doctor is harassing you. Let's go. Start fresh in California."

She shook her head stubbornly. "I will not run."

He wanted to lift her out of her chair and shake her. "It isn't worth the fight. *Now* some of these townspeople accept you. But wait and see—if a male doctor comes to town, they'll drop you like a hot rock. You can't count on them. The people here will let you down."

"I don't think so," she said slowly.

"You don't know that for sure. And there's worse coming. Have you considered Indigo? Do you want to put her through the indignity of a trial? To make her go through that public humiliation?"

"I hope it won't come to that." She wouldn't meet his eyes.

"What's going to stop it from coming to that— I've just proposed marriage to you. Isn't that of more importance to you than Dr. Drinkwater?"

Mercy gazed at him, mouth open and wordless.

"Do you love me or not?" Lon asked.

"Thee has not spoken of love—"

"I will," he cut her off, enjoying the sensation of at last leaving her without much to say, "if that will persuade you to leave with me. Do you love me?"

Mercy fussed with papers on her desk.

The door opened and Ma Bailey walked in. "Oh!" she exclaimed, looking back and forth between the two of them with palpable curiosity and glee. She must have seen him heading here and followed him.

"What can I do for thee, Ma Bailey?" Mercy asked in a colorless voice, blushing.

"I hope I'm not interrupting anything…private," Ma said, thick innuendo layering her words.

"No, we were discussing this business with Indigo," Mercy responded with aplomb and a lift of her chin.

"That Boise doctor sure has his nerve," the older woman agreed, her face darkening. "Anyway, I just wanted to let you know my daughter and her man arrived in town today."

Lon gritted his teeth to keep from sending the woman away with a few choice, pithy words he'd long wanted to unleash upon her.

"Well, that is good news." Mercy smiled. "I'm sure thee is glad to have her safely here with thee."

"I am." Ma glanced at both of them. Her eyes spoke volumes of nosiness.

Lon paced again, sure that this private tête-à-tête would be broadcast through the community within hours. The headache began throbbing right under one eyebrow.

"I'll leave you two alone then." The older woman left with a wave and a self-satisfied grin.

Lon halted in front of Mercy and leaned toward her. "If for nothing else, come with me and get away from that snooping, meddlesome woman."

Mercy grinned but then grew somber. "No matter

where we would go—" she reached up and touched his hair, smoothing it back from his face, soothing the pounding of his headache "—there would be a Ma Bailey there, too."

He shoved his hands into his pockets and hovered over Mercy, willing her to agree with him. "I want to leave this town. And I want you and Indigo to go with me."

She gazed up at him with maddening calm. "I must not leave till I know that is what God wants me to do. Until then I will stay and fight."

Lon gritted his teeth. When was this woman going to realize that their lives were *their* lives and they must live them their own way? He tried to put this into persuasive words.

He couldn't. He made a sound of disgust and walked out into the brisk evening. Why couldn't she see that she was setting herself and Indigo up for indignity and scorn? Could he bear to stand by and watch?

Mercy woke to a knock on her door. "Who is it?" she called.

"It's me, Sunny. My time's come."

Mercy quickly opened the door. "Come in. How long has thee been having contractions?"

Groaning, Sunny entered and halted, clutching the back of a chair. "For most of the night. I finally decided—" Sunny paused, wincing "—I didn't want to have the baby in my room over the saloon so... I decided to come here."

Mercy reached for her robe on the end of the bed. Indigo sat up and rubbed her eyes. "Indigo, Sunny will need the bed. Will thee prepare it for her?"

Indigo yawned and nodded, rising.

Mercy helped Sunny sit on the chair. Then she turned

to hang the full iron kettle on the hook over the fire. She added some more wood to the fire and stirred the coals. Soon Indigo had the bed ready. And then Mercy started walking Sunny. The contractions came closer and closer and stronger and stronger.

Dawn was just breaking at its fullest when Mercy helped Sunny's little girl into the world. The exhausted woman wept and laughed, touching her little one gently.

Watching Sunny hold her newborn daughter brought tears to Mercy's eyes. Every baby was a gift from God. Would she ever hold a newborn of her own? It was a startling idea—one she'd never had before. Lon, of course, or kissing Lon was what had put this in her mind. How would this all turn out in the end? She knew she didn't have the power to change Lon's mind and heart. Only God could heal the pain of the past. Then Mercy noticed tears streaming in Indigo's eyes. Because Pierre had not returned.

Mercy drew in breath, pushing all these concerns aside. She'd received a letter from Felicity saying that she would send someone by train to get the child. But Mercy hadn't heard from her parents, who lived so much farther east.

She decided she would telegraph them today. She couldn't leave Sunny to bring her child—though unwillingly—into the life Sunny had been born into. Sunny obviously didn't want that. And Mercy was absolutely certain God didn't want that, either.

Later the next day, Mercy stood at the front of the church for her latest venture in teaching public health practices. On the table beside her were the items needed for smallpox vaccinations. The scent of freshly sprayed carbolic acid hung over them. Seven mothers had lined up to receive the vaccinations. Mercy tried to keep her mind on this—not on Sunny, who was recovering in her cabin, not on the troublesome Boise doctor, and absolutely not on Lon Mackey.

Mercy smiled, hoping to reassure the women; each looked back at her very anxiously. "Now, Indigo is going to allow thee to see her smallpox mark so thee will know what to expect after the vaccination. Please go one by one behind the screen—" Mercy pointed to the screen set up behind her "—and Indigo will show thee."

The women took turns. As Mercy watched this procession, Lon Mackey's words ribboned through her mind. His visit to her office had tangled her emotions into a terrible knot. She knew she could do little to alter her feelings for Lon. What a predicament she was in.

Lon had changed so much over the past few months that she had let herself hope that he would at last put the past behind him and find peace with God again. And, yes, that they might have a life together. She admitted this to herself now. Lon was angry, and she knew that it had to do with what he'd gone through in the war. He was angry at himself, and at God.

The four bloody years had been dreadful enough to live through. Why would someone as intelligent as Lon hold on to the horror and grief and regret? Of course, perhaps Lon didn't see it that way. Perhaps he didn't believe he had the right or the power to release the past. How could he expect her to leave with him when his life and his faith were so unresolved?

Finally, all seven mothers had seen the vaccination mark on Indigo's upper left arm. Most of them looked determined. A few looked frightened. Mercy took a deep breath and focused on the task at hand. "Now, if thee is not certain that thee wants to do this, thee doesn't have to."

"This really will protect us from smallpox?" Ellen asked, gazing at the needles and the small brown bottle of vaccine.

"Yes, it will," Mercy said firmly. "But remember that thee may experience redness and swelling at the site of the vaccination. Thee may run a slight fever for a few days. Thee might actually get some of the symptoms of the disease, such as a mild rash. When I was a child, my parents had all of their daughters vaccinated in Philadelphia. Each of us had a combination of those side effects, except for my sister, Felicity, who had none. But we were fine after a few days."

Her mind kept calling up the image of Lon pacing in her office. Had she made the right decision, not accepting Lon's proposal? The answer came quickly: she couldn't say yes to Lon until he had broken free of the past. Until he'd allowed God to make him whole again, and had acknowledged God once more. If she consented to become one with him before that had taken place, it could stunt his healing and leave him wounded longer still. She felt this unpalatable truth like a stiff rod up her spine.

Mercy cleared her throat. "These vaccinations have been given for the past seventy-some years. And I know that they do work. I myself was exposed to smallpox several times during the war and did not fall ill."

"That's good enough for me." Ellen unbuttoned her starched white cuff and rolled up her left sleeve. "I'm ready."

Mercy smiled and began the process of pricking Ellen's arms and introducing the vaccine solution. Maybe Mercy should seek Lon out later and help him see that she was right, that they had to stay and fight—

The double doors of the church flapped open. Ma Bailey hurried inside, shutting the doors against the stiff November wind. "Sorry I'm late!" she exclaimed, sounding breathless and hurrying down the aisle. "I want to see this." She halted and stared at Mercy and Ellen. "I don't see how sticking a needle over and over into Ellen Dunfield's arm is going to keep her from getting smallpox."

Mercy didn't turn. "I have explained it—"

"Did you know that the gambler just left town on a supply wagon heading for Boise?" Ma gazed at Mercy with avid interest.

Mercy's breath caught in her throat. Despair and shock washed over her in debilitating waves. Nonetheless, her training stood up to the challenge; her hands didn't falter in their work. She went on pricking Ellen's skin and infusing the vaccine.

It was good that her hands knew their work because her mind had whirled away from her, her stomach churning with acid. Lon Mackey had gone to Boise. And without a word of farewell to her. What had she done? And would she ever see him again?

When Lon climbed down from the supply wagon's bench near dark, he was chilled to the marrow and stiff. He needed to buy a warmer hat and some gloves. Still aching from the hard bench, he limped slightly, heading toward the brightly lit saloon. His spirits limped along, too. He'd left Mercy behind. He'd finally decided that the only way to make her see sense was to leave. But how long would it take for her to come to her senses and follow him here? He didn't like to think of her facing Indigo's trial alone, but that might force her to leave Idaho Bend.

Putting this from his mind, he kept walking. He'd

warm up in the nearest saloon and see if they had a gambler already. He needed to get started making money again. He walked into a large saloon, saw the stove against the back wall and walked straight to it. He stood with his back to it, letting the fire warm him as he viewed the gathering of men.

He observed that a professional gambler was already plying his trade. When Lon was completely thawed, he tipped his hat to the gambler and headed outside to find the next saloon. Boise was twice as big as Idaho Bend and had more than twice the saloons.

At the third saloon he visited, he sat down in his favorite spot in the middle of the room, but near the back wall with his face toward the door. He took off his heavy wool coat and began to shuffle the cards. He suppressed the feeling that he didn't really want to be here doing this.

When Mercy came to her senses and was forced to leave Idaho, he'd keep his promise and find a more genteel way to make a living. Through the yellow cigar smoke, two well-dressed men and a man who obviously worked with his hands sat down at his table. Lon grinned. He broke the seal on a new deck of cards, shuffled them and asked the first man who'd sat down to cut the deck. Then he dealt the first hand, the cards slipping, whispering expertly through his palms.

Yet something strange was happening. Lon had the oddest sensation, as if he were outside his body watching himself, as if he were acting a part in a play. It was as if he'd split himself in two and only one part was aware of this. He shook off the odd impression. Leaving Mercy behind so she would wake up and realize that he was right must be causing havoc with his mind.

He'd left her a letter, which he'd read and reread so many times he'd memorized it.

Dear Mercy,

When you come to your senses, I will be in Boise waiting for you. I think it's wrong to put Indigo up on public display in a court of law and allow her to be humiliated before the common herd. Come to Boise. We'll marry and the three of us will move to California. I'll give up gambling and pursue some sort of work. And you can start your practice again.

Now he forced himself to think only of the cards and the faces of the players sitting across from him.

In the middle of the third game of the night, Lon heard the swinging doors open and looked up. Lightning flashed, sizzling through him. He almost leaped to his feet. His heart thudded in his chest. But he retained enough sense to make no outward sign that the man now standing in the doorway was the very man who had stabbed him. Lon held this all inside as the game proceeded. How should he handle this? Why wasn't the sheriff around when he was needed?

At the end of another hand, Lon saw his quarry turn to leave. That decided him. He leaped to his feet. "Stop that man!" he shouted. "He's a wanted man!" His shouts stirred up confusion. The men in the saloon looked around, exclaiming, questioning.

Lon shoved his way through the crowd in time to see the small mustachioed man hurrying out the doors. Lon burst through after him, drawing his pistol from his vest pocket. "Halt! Or I'll shoot!"

Chapter Thirteen

Still grieving Lon's desertion, Mercy froze in her tracks on Main Street. Four men had ridden into town—one was the unwelcome doctor and the other three were strangers, but they all wore black suits and tall stovepipe hats, the sign of professional men. The judge perhaps? Another deputy? A lawyer? She could practically feel her stomach sliding down toward her toes.

Digger had said the territorial circuit court judge wasn't due until next week. *I might be jumping to conclusions.* Mercy's beleaguered mind slipped away from Main Street. *Lon, I want you here. Why did you leave me?* The raw ache over Lon's leaving Idaho Bend throbbed throughout her whole being, physical and emotional. Her spirit whispered, *Isn't God sufficient for thee?*

"You think that's the judge?"

Mercy jerked and turned to Ma Bailey who had appeared at her elbow.

"I don't know." The four men tied up their horses and stopped at the door of the new hotel that had opened last week. The doctor was now pointing her out to the other three and sneering.

As Mercy grappled with what this might mean, she didn't relish the prospect of a conversation with this intrusive woman. Yet she smiled politely, if not sincerely. "Is thee enjoying having thy daughter and son-in-law with thee?"

"Yes," Ma said in a sad voice, twisting the apron she wore over her faded brown dress and shawl. "But my son-in-law says he won't have no woman doctor tend his wife when her time comes. I told him you're a good doc, but he forbid it."

Irritation crackled through Mercy. For a moment the urge to snap at the woman nearly overwhelmed her better sense. Then she looked into the older woman's deep brown eyes, now filling with tears.

As always, Ma had said exactly what she meant to say without much consideration of another's feelings. Sometimes that was good and sometimes that was bad. But a person always knew where she stood with Ma.

Now Mercy read in Ma's tear-filled eyes worry for her daughter's safety. This son-in-law's verdict against Mercy was an untimely and unnecessary reminder of how the world at large judged her. It nearly triggered her own tears. She inhaled sharply. "I'm sorry to hear that."

"Maybe he'll change his mind," Ma offered, the lines in her face trembling as she fought against weeping.

Her words echoed in Mercy's mind and shifted her thoughts to Lon. The thought didn't ease the pain of Lon's desertion, but it did put it into perspective. Lon was a man and he'd made a mistake. But if he wanted to turn back, he could change his mind.

"Maybe." Mercy put an arm around Ma's shoulders, offering sympathy. "Maybe he will."

Ma lifted the hem of her apron and wiped her eyes,

whispering, "I don't want anything to happen to my girl."

Mercy stood there, comforting this rough woman who had a good heart buried deep inside her crusty exterior and nosy ways. Resting her head heavily on Mercy's shoulder, Ma wept without making a sound.

Mercy thought of her own daughter. Should she follow Lon's advice? Was she wrong to hold Indigo up to public scrutiny, and perhaps ridicule and humiliation? *Should I have gone with him?*

Usually when Mercy asked one of these deep questions, an unmistakable leading—usually a strong feeling—came to her, revealing a clear answer or direction. How often had she heard her mother or father say, when faced with a difficult decision, "Way will open"? That meant that if God wanted them to take action, He would prepare the way, show them the way.

Here and now, Mercy only felt dry and empty—bereft. She wanted to go home and pick up her knitting and never leave her snug cabin again. She gazed up into the slate-gray sky.

No, I can't give in to that gloom again. Lon is still running from himself. I can't. I won't run from this challenge. No more hiding.

"I'm sorry he thinks that way," Ma murmured, pulling away.

Mercy forced a grin. "I am, too, but I will not despair. Thy son-in-law is new in town. We will hope that as he gets to know people he will accept me as a doctor."

"You're always nice to me."

Ma said the words like a little girl. They stung Mercy's conscience like darts. How often when she was near Ma had she spoken kindly but inwardly let annoyance consume her?

"Thee has a good heart, Ma Bailey. Thee showed that when the miners needed help. Thee didn't hesitate to do what thee could for others that night."

Ma tried to smile, then turned away and hurried toward her house.

It was then that Mercy noticed one of the men who had arrived with Dr. Drinkwater walking across the street toward her. Was he the Boise lawyer she had telegraphed?

Lon, I wish thee had not left me. But I must stay here and fight for Indigo, fight for myself. Ma Bailey's daughter might need my help and I must stay here for her and the others. Lon, thee must break the bondage of the past completely or there is no future for thee or for us. Father, please, I need Thy "way" to open.

Night folded around Lon as he slipped through the moonlit forest higher on the mountain slope. He was still pursuing the man who stabbed him. And to make things even more difficult, he was favoring one ankle. Someone in the crowd outside the saloon had tripped him and he'd fallen, twisting his ankle. He hadn't wasted time finding out if it had been on purpose or not.

The cold December wind shook the dried oak leaves nearby. Though slowed by his injury, Lon had managed to follow the man out of town and far up this slope at a distance. Or had he lost him? Darkness had come much too soon for his liking.

From behind, a blow caught him in the kidneys. Pain. He doubled up, falling to his knees. Another blow struck his right ear. Head ringing, Lon rolled onto his back. He jumped up. The man caught him with an uppercut to the jaw. Lon began throwing punches. The near blackness made it difficult to find his target.

A fist punched him in the jaw again. For a moment, stars of light flashed before his eyes. Then he came fully back to consciousness. He heard the man running off, stirring the branches of the fir trees and the underbrush.

With the back of his hand, Lon wiped the blood from his split lip and continued his pursuit. He threaded his way between trees. The man must have stopped. Lon paused, straining to hear movement. An owl hooted. Something—a bat?—swooped overhead.

Again, Lon was struck from behind. This time the man missed his kidneys. Lon rode the punch. He turned, and with a fist to the jaw, downed the man. Then, bending over him, Lon planted a powerful punch to the side of his attacker's head.

The man lay, gasping in the faint moonlight. Lon pulled the pistol out from his vest. The man cursed him. "Well, go ahead and shoot, Yankee colonel!"

Lon stood stock-still. He couldn't make out the man's face. "What did you call me?"

"I called you what you are, you Yankee colonel. I seen you." The man sounded as if he were fighting tears. "I know you. Your regiment killed practically every man in my company that day at Antietam."

Bloody Antietam. The worst slaughter of all. But Lon couldn't put what the man was saying together. "What has Antietam got to do with your stabbing me in Idaho Bend? You and I played cards together for several nights."

"I didn't know who you was at first," the man said, panting. "You just looked familiar somehow. And then that night I recognized you. Something you said triggered my memory and I seen you again, your sword in the air, leading your men down on us."

"We were at war," Lon said, shaking his head as if he weren't hearing right.

"That don't make it right!" The man cursed him.

Lon stared down at the shadowy shape on the ground. "Are you crazy? The war's over." His words rebounded against him as if an unseen fist had landed a blow to his own head. *The war's over.*

"The war will never be over—not in my mind!" the man retorted. His tone was sick, hateful, venomous.

"Four years of war wasn't enough for you?" Lon asked, feeling disoriented and dazed himself. "You didn't get enough of killing and dying in four years?"

"No. Not while Yankees like you live."

The quick, hot reply shocked Lon. "Why would you want to go on fighting the war?"

"Stop talking. Just shoot me or let me go. I got nothin' more to say to you."

Lon was at a loss. He couldn't release the man he was sure would try to kill him again—and perhaps others. But it was a long way back to town, and Lon had nothing with which to tie the man's hands. Then it came to him.

"Get up," he ordered the man. "You're a prisoner of war. Put your hands on your head and keep them there." Lon waited to see what the man would do.

His prisoner obeyed his orders, just as if they were both in opposing armies and Lon had captured him. Clearly, the war had not ended for this man. It was a startling, stomach-churning realization.

"Go on then," Lon ordered. "We're heading back to the sheriff. You'll be charged there."

The man began walking and Lon followed at a safe distance, his pistol poised to fire. He couldn't trust this man, not if he were still trapped in the war.

A cloud covered the sliver of a moon, hiding his prisoner from him. Would he try to get away? No, the man kept moving forward, his elbows out at that awkward angle. Maybe the man was relieved to have been caught. If he was in custody, he wouldn't be compelled to try to get revenge. What a weight he must carry—trying to right all the wrongs of the war. That was worse than death. He pitied the poor wretch.

Still, Lon recalled the excruciating pain he suffered after being stabbed, and the long feverish days and nights. He couldn't let this man go free to do that to some other former soldier.

Lon kept trying to grapple with what it all meant, how it had all happened. The man's words kept echoing in Lon's head. *The war will never be over—not in my mind.*

Deeper into the cold-night hours and with his pistol in hand, Lon steered the man into the dimly lit sheriff's office. The sheriff looked up from his chair, where he had obviously been dozing. "What's this?"

Lon told the man to halt. "This is the man who stabbed me in Idaho Bend."

The sheriff looked at Lon and then at the man. "You're sure?"

"Yes, I'm sure. Can you arrest him, or do I have to do that, too?" Lon growled, cold and irritated.

Frowning, the sheriff grabbed manacles from a peg on the wall, and with a couple of sharp metallic snaps, secured the man's hands. He motioned for Lon to follow him as he led the man to the cell in the rear of the office. When the prisoner was in the cell, the sheriff slammed the door.

The man glared at the sheriff and Lon. "You a Yankee, too?"

The sheriff gave him an irritated look. "The war's over. If you think you're still fighting it, you're loony."

Lon followed the sheriff out to the office area again. He shook his head, wincing from the pain caused by the blows he'd taken tonight, and then collapsed into the chair by the desk.

"You're sure this is the man who stabbed you?" the lawman asked again.

"Yes, we played cards several times before he decided to stab me." Lon had thought that catching the man would have given him more satisfaction. Instead, he was gripped by an odd feeling. Something had happened to him during the exchange with this Johnny Reb, the label Yankees had for Confederate soldiers. This Reb who had decided to continue the war single-handedly.

Lon said, "I need a place to stay tonight. Which hotel in town is best?"

The sheriff replied with a few short words and Lon rose.

"Is that it?" the sheriff asked.

"What do you mean?" Lon turned, already heading out the door.

"Well, you sounded all fired up about this man when I talked to you in Idaho Bend. Why aren't you...?" The sheriff gave him a sideways glance. "You don't seem mad or excited or anything."

Lon paused, completely still. He probed his emotions and found no anger, just peace and a deep desire to eat his fill and then fall asleep. "Why should I be? I caught him, and now you've arrested him." Lon shrugged and headed out the door to find his late supper and a bed.

Outside in the bracing night air, he shivered and began walking fast. As if touching a recently healed wound, he probed his heart and mind once more. He found no pain. Instead, there was something he'd longed for but which had eluded him until now. He felt a deep peace inside. And suddenly he wanted nothing more than to get back to Idaho Bend and share that peace with Mercy.

Mercy walked into the saloon, which had been turned into a courtroom. She recalled the night she had operated on Lon's stab wound, and the nights spent in the back room nursing him. The agitating memories rushed through her like a flight of raucous crows.

He's gone. He left me. Mercy kept her back straight and her chin level. She would show neither fear nor pain. Was she doing right by fighting? Or was this court case a sign for her to leave Idaho Bend? *My trust is in Thee, Father.*

Indigo walked beside her with her head down.

Mercy didn't blame her. It was hard to look into faces that held condemnation or censure. The Civil War had outlawed slavery, but what of the bondage of prejudice? How did one fight that invisible war?

The Boise defense lawyer who had come to town yesterday motioned for Indigo to come with him and for Mercy to sit with the other people who'd come to watch the trial. She made an effort to smile at the bystanders she knew and sat down on the edge of a hard chair.

The judge in his black robe, the prosecuting attorney and Dr. Drinkwater entered the room. The people rose and stood until the judge sat down behind a rough-hewn table and motioned for them to be seated.

Mercy followed the exchanges between the two lawyers and the judge. Dr. Drinkwater sat on the opposite side of the room, glaring at her. She smiled at him and refused to show how upset and anxious she was.

For one brief, traitorous moment, Mercy let herself think of leaving Idaho Bend with Indigo and meeting Lon in Boise. *But that isn't what I want. This town is home. That's why I couldn't just leave here. This is where I am meant to be. I feel that, know that now.* This gave her a measure of confidence, but fear lurked, ready to take her captive.

The selection of the jury began. Men were lined up and questioned by the two lawyers and the judge. When she spotted a few of the locals who had openly disapproved of her profession, Mercy's spirits weren't improved. She folded her hands in her lap and continued to pray that God's will would be done here.

In the quiet Boise café, Lon was eating a leisurely late breakfast. He'd slept better than he had in months and had awakened with the appetite of a lumberjack. Now he chewed, savoring the golden toast soaked with melted butter and coated thickly with red huckleberry jam. Delicious.

He breathed in the intoxicating fragrance of bacon, fresh coffee, melted butter and cinnamon. This blessed morning every sight, sound and taste around him was fresh, brilliant, vital—as if he'd spent the past few years looking at life through smudged spectacles. Today he saw clearly that this was a great morning to be alive.

A man with wild white hair sticking out from under his hat came in and stood glancing around. Then he made a beeline toward Lon. "Hey! You that gambler that caught the man who stabbed him?"

Lon paused, his forkful of egg and sausage halfway

to his mouth. He went ahead and took the bite but he nodded in answer to the man's question.

"I'm Jeffries. Own the newspaper here in Boise. Tell me what happened." As the man spoke like he was sending a telegram, he sat down. He drew out a pad of paper and a roughly sharpened pencil and licked the lead.

Lon chewed and swallowed, still comfortably at his ease. "The man stabbed me in Idaho Bend. I saw him here and caught him last night."

"What's his name?"

"Don't know." *Don't care.* "Ask the sheriff."

"Why'd he stab you? Were you cheating?"

"A skilled gambler doesn't have to cheat to win." Lon considered whether he should reveal the man's reason for stabbing him and then decided not to. The Reb had been unbalanced by the war and Lon had suffered something similar until last night.

And did this newspaper man expect Lon to confess to cheating? Though Lon had read this man's paper in the past, in light of this he might have to reconsider what he thought of it. Something niggled at the back of Lon's mind, something he'd read in this man's paper. Or was it in some other newspaper?

Jeffries stared at him, pencil hovering. "I hear you're sweet on the woman posing as a doctor over there."

The intrusion and the word *posing* shattered Lon's peace. "Are you a gossipmonger? And let me tell you, Dr. Mercy Gabriel saved my life and has saved many others this year." Lon glared. "She nursed with Clara Barton during the war and no doubt saved hundreds of lives there also. I've seen her certificate and I've seen her operate. And my only comment is that anyone who would prefer Dr. Drinkwater over Dr. Gabriel is an idiot." Lon felt like punching the man in the nose, just to make sure he'd gotten Lon's point.

Jeffries made a humming sound. "You don't say?"

"I do say." Lon took a long, reviving swallow of the good coffee.

"Drinkwater's been bad-mouthing her all over town." The man's gaze darted from his notes to Lon's face and back again.

"That means he's not only a bad doctor, but also no gentleman."

Jeffries nodded, tapping the pencil on the pad. "I think you're probably right. Now, what about this trial that's going on against the black girl—what's her name?"

Lon froze. He'd awakened this morning feeling so good after last night's capture that worry even about Indigo had drifted from his thoughts. He'd been a fool. "Has the trial started? I thought the judge wasn't expected in Idaho Bend till next week."

"No, he left here yesterday—"

Lon downed the rest of his coffee and handed the waitress what he owed with a generous tip and a smile. Then he headed straight for the door.

"Hey!" the newspaperman called, following him. "Hey, I'm not done interviewing you!"

Lon ignored the man and hurried down the street toward the livery. He'd have to hire a horse. *I must have been out of my mind to leave Mercy to face that trial alone.*

Chapter Fourteen

Mercy was so proud of Indigo. Throughout the hours spent choosing the jury, her daughter had sat beside the lawyer, straight and composed. And then as the case began, she had faced those who testified about the exclusionary law that said she couldn't live here.

"Your honor," Mercy's tall, reedy lawyer said, "the intent of the exclusionary law is attached historically to the slave state versus free state conflict, which is no longer a reality. The Civil War settled that controversy once and for all. Our Negroes are no longer slaves but free citizens. And as such, free citizens cannot be stopped from entering any U.S. territory."

"Counsel," said the judge, who looked as if his face had been carved from rock, "I understand your case, but this is a circuit court, not the Supreme Court. It is not in my jurisdiction to declare a law unconstitutional."

"A little over a year ago, on January 10, 1867," the defense lawyer continued, "the U.S. Congress passed the Territorial Suffrage Act, which allowed African-Americans in the Western territories to vote. The act immediately enfranchised black male voters in those territories. Doesn't it follow that the U.S. Congress wouldn't have passed this if territories could indeed exclude black citizens?"

"That still doesn't address the coming of new immigrants to Idaho," the judge countered.

The prosecuting attorney—young and very well dressed—gloated with a smile. "Your honor, since the defense counsel has no way to discount the law, I ask that the jury bring in the only logical verdict. Indigo Gabriel is guilty of entering the Idaho Territory unlawfully."

The judge looked to the defense attorney. "Defense counsel, do you have any other witnesses or arguments you wish to present at this time?"

"No, your honor. The defense rests."

Mercy felt each of these solemn, hopeless words like a knife thrust.

The judge turned to the twelve men sitting together along one side of the saloon. "You men have heard the evidence. Now go into the back room, elect a foreman and then talk this all over. When you have your decision, come back out and have your foreman announce it."

The judge banged his gavel and adjourned court. The jury filed out, and the onlookers who were standing against the walls or sitting on chairs began talking in low tones to each other.

Indigo turned around to Mercy. As she looked over Mercy's shoulder, her brave smile transformed to an expression of shock.

Mercy whirled around and saw Lon Mackey walking into the saloon.

She rose. "Lon Mackey."

"Mercy Gabriel." Then she was within the circle of

his arms and he was kissing her. She heard the gasps of surprise around them, but she found she didn't care.

"I'm sorry I left. Is this Indigo's lawyer? Is there anything I can do?"

In reply, Mercy remained pressed against him and rested her cheek against his coat. The lawyer turned and shook the hand Lon offered him. "You're a bit late. The jury just went out to deliberate."

Lon's face fell.

Mercy looked up at Lon. "I'm so glad thee came." She couldn't say more, turning her face into Lon's shoulder, hiding her distress.

"I'm sorry I'm late. But—"

Then Mercy looked back up at him, really seeing his condition. "Lon, why does thee have a split lip and a black eye?" The shock of his unexpected arrival had, for a few moments, evidently overwhelmed her normal perception. "Is thee hurt?"

"It's a long story." Lon kept Mercy close.

"We have time," Mercy said and drew him down to sit beside her.

Lon squeezed her hand and whispered, "I'll tell you later."

Mercy accepted Lon's words, overwhelmed again by his sudden return. She reveled in Lon's presence and his firm but gentle grip on her hand.

"This is really a matter that the Supreme Court should take up," the lawyer said to Mercy. "There are black settlers in Oregon State and the Washington and Idaho Territories, in spite of the exclusionary laws. The black pioneers just keep to themselves and are for the most part left alone."

"Well, we explained to you why this has all come about," Indigo said, sounding angry. "I certainly have not done anything to call attention to myself. It's all about hateful prejudice, not the law." She rose. "I'm going to walk outside a bit. I can't sit here." Indigo hurried toward the door and the lawyer put on his hat and left for the café.

Mercy suddenly realized that she had kissed Lon in front of the whole town and was actually holding hands with him. Suddenly embarrassed, she tried to withdraw her hand from his.

He wouldn't let go. "Please, Mercy, forgive me for leaving. I don't know what I was thinking…" He halted. "Yes, I do. I was thinking that—"

He was interrupted by the jury filing back into the courtroom. Their quick return appeared to surprise everyone. There was some commotion as the temporary bailiff, Tom the bartender, went out and summoned Indigo and her lawyer back into the saloon.

Once everyone was in place, the judge returned. Everyone rose; he gaveled court back into session. He then looked to the jury. "Have you come to a verdict?"

Foreman Slattery, with his distinctive gray shock of hair, rose. "Yes, your honor. We find the defendant not guilty."

For a few moments, Mercy distrusted her ears. Did he say "not guilty," or was it just that she wanted him to say those words?

"Would you repeat that?" the judge requested, looking and sounding incredulous.

"Your honor, we find the defendant not guilty," Slattery repeated, looking straight at Dr. Drinkwater. "And we also think that doctors from Boise ought to mind their own business and not mess in ours." The jury murmured their agreement.

Dr. Drinkwater leaped to his feet. "This can't be

legal!" The doctor's words shattered the polite reserve of the bystanders. They all began talking, arguing. Their outburst swallowed up the rest of Dr. Drinkwater's rant. Both the doctor and the general public were silenced when the judge began pounding his gavel. "Order in the court! Order, or I'll empty the room!"

An agitated silence settled over the barroom court. The judge looked to Slattery. "How did you come to this…unexpected verdict?"

"Well, your honor," Slattery said, looking toward Indigo and Mercy, "we decided that you out-of-town people made a mistake. Indigo isn't black. Anyone can see that."

Another jury member popped up. "She's just been out in the sun a lot." He looked at Mercy. "Dr. Gabriel, you need to make sure your girl wears a bonnet and gloves outside from now on. We don't want anyone else getting the wrong idea." He sat down, looking puckishly satisfied.

The rest of the jury nodded their agreement. A few men behind Mercy actually chuckled and a man called out, "That'll teach Boise people to stick their noses into our business!"

The judge pounded his gavel, glaring at the loudmouth who called out those words. He turned his gaze to Indigo. "Will the defendant please rise?"

Indigo did, facing him, her head high.

Mercy was so proud of the way her beautiful daughter stood, tall and unflinching.

"Miss Indigo Gabriel, you have been found to be not guilty of this charge by a jury of your peers." The judge looked resigned but disgruntled. "Jury, you're dismissed with the thanks of the Idaho Territory." He hit the tabletop with his gavel once more, rose and withdrew into the back room.

The outcome had come so swiftly and with such an unexpected twist that an intense, watchful mood quieted the room. Slattery made his way through the crowd to Mercy. "I want to apologize, ma'am, for the ugly words I wrote on Tarver's store window. When I seen how you took care of the miners, I changed my mind."

Mercy rose and offered the man her hand. "What is thy full name?"

"Irwin Slattery, ma'am."

"Irwin Slattery, thank thee for thy honesty. But I still don't understand how the jury came to this conclusion. Thee all know that my daughter is—"

Slattery cut her off with a conspiratorial grin. "Your girl showed her stuff, taking care of people, too. And besides, we're not letting that quack doctor from Boise push us around. We'll decide who gets to live in Idaho Bend *and* who practices medicine here."

Instantly, a hubbub of voices filled the room as everyone started discussing what Slattery had just revealed.

Slattery turned to leave and then turned back. "I didn't set off the firecrackers and write that word. I think that was kids. Firecrackers is usually boys. Trust me."

Mercy smiled. Her mind whirled with all that had just happened. She turned and saw Lon's incredulous expression, which she guessed must mirror her own. Before she could say another word, he pulled her into his arms again.

Dr. Drinkwater pushed through the crowd of wellwishers who surrounded Mercy and Indigo. Lon wanted to punch the man and send him sprawling. People let the doctor through, but the looks they were sending his way weren't welcoming. "I am going to take this to the territorial governor—"

"I think it's time you went back to Boise—for your own health. Leave right away so you can get back there before dark. The woods around here are dangerous at night," Lon said.

Silence descended. Prickly. And foreboding.

The Boise doctor stopped speaking and looked around. He found himself surrounded by Digger Hobson and the largest men from Digger's mine. Each one was staring at him intently, unkindly. For once, the man was speechless.

Indigo's defense attorney slid through the men and took the doctor by the elbow. "Why don't you head to Boise with me now? The prosecutor and judge have to stay and finish a few more land cases, but we can leave."

Dr. Drinkwater nodded, his jaw still working as though chewing words he feared to voice. People parted, letting the two men leave the saloon.

The minute they went through the doors, Tom called out, "Well, I'd buy everybody a drink, but court's still in session for the rest of the day!"

Many men laughed and started a jovial argument about Tom's spurious offer. Under cover of this, Lon led Mercy and Indigo from the saloon. Outside, the air was downright cold.

Mercy clung to his arm. "Lon, why did thee come back?"

Lon gazed into her honest, blue eyes and wondered how he could tell her all he wanted her to hear.

"Aunt Mercy, I think you should take Mr. Mackey

to our cabin for a cup of tea. I'm invited to my friend's house to celebrate."

Lon grinned with gratitude. *Sharp girl.* "Thanks, Miss Indigo. A cup of tea would be most welcome."

Lon offered Mercy his arm and proudly led her down Main Street. They stopped often to accept congratulations from friends and others whom they knew only on sight. Lon felt as if he had passed from night to day. The fight last night had torn down the high walls he'd built around himself. He could even breathe more easily. And the woman beside him drew him more than ever.

Finally, they arrived at her cabin. He opened the door for her and she led him inside. As if it were his usual chore, he went to the hearth and busied himself stoking the low fire. Mercy filled an iron kettle and hung it over the fire on the hook. Being in her home and doing these mundane tasks beside her touched Lon. It was like coming home at last.

"Come and sit down, Lon, and tell me why thee has a black eye, a split lip and probably other hurts."

Doing as she suggested, he grinned at her in the low light from the two small windows. "Mercy, I found the man who stabbed me in a saloon in Boise. I chased him down and..." He shook his head, still unable to believe how much had changed within him over the intervening hours.

She put a hand over his on the table. The simple act rocked him to his core. *Mercy, sweet Mercy mine.*

He drew her hand to his mouth and kissed it. "I think I've been changing all along—ever since you arrived in town. But last night I discovered that the man stabbed me not over the card game but because he recognized me as the commander of the Union regiment that decimated his Confederate unit."

He kissed her hand again and was pleased that she didn't try to draw it from his grasp. "He's still fighting the war. And in doing so he's losing his present life. That's what you've been telling me all along. Telling me to let go of the war. To be free of it. Free of the deaths I was powerless to prevent." The final phrase cost him. He had to stop and let the pain flow through him once more and then let it drain away. "I still feel the pain, but I'm no longer angry at God, or myself."

Mercy then did something he would never have expected her to do. She leaned forward and kissed him as if it were the most natural thing for her to do.

"Mercy," he murmured, "I love you." Though he knew he was speaking the truth, his own words spoken aloud surprised him. To make sure she knew he meant it, he repeated, "I love you."

"And I love thee, Lon Mackey. When shall we marry?"

Her frank words shocked a bark of laughter from him.

She turned bright pink. "I shouldn't have said that. *Thee* is supposed to propose to me." She turned even pinker.

He rose and drew her up with him. "Mercy Gabriel, if you recall, I did propose to you, just not for the right reason. I'll marry you as soon as you wish. Today, if you want." He tugged her hand and reveled in folding her into his embrace.

"Not quite today, Lon," she whispered. "But soon. Yes, soon."

For several wonderful moments he held her to him. He loved this woman and she loved him. And he had a future—they had a future together. He kissed her and let the feel of her against him ease the old pain, the old resistance. "Mercy," he murmured.

Someone pounded on the door. "My girl's in labor!" Ma Bailey said from outside the cabin. "You got to come."

Lon couldn't believe it. Did this woman always have to pop up when he least wanted to see her?

Mercy went to the door, brought the older woman inside and helped her sit down. "Thee shouldn't be running like this. When did the labor begin?"

"A few hours ago when you were busy in court."

"Well, first labors usually take longest. I'm sure we'll be in time if we walk." Mercy stopped, frowning, and then said, "Ma, I thought thy son-in-law didn't want a woman doctor attending his wife."

Still panting, Ma grinned. "He's talked to some of the men in town and they all said that you should do it. And today he got a look at that Boise doc, didn't like him and changed his mind. Will you come?"

"I will." Mercy turned to Lon. "I'm afraid, dear one, that I must leave before I have made thee tea."

"That's all right. I'd better get used to this. Marriage to a doctor certainly won't be boring." He grinned the widest and happiest grin he'd ever known.

Ma Bailey whooped with pleasure. "I knew it! I knew you two would make a good match!"

The long hours of labor ended just at dawn. Lon sat at Ma Bailey's kitchen table across from the young father, Aaron Whipple. Lon had kept the gangly young man company through the long hours, making conversation and drinking coffee. At the sound of a baby's cry, Whipple rose from the table, looking stunned and somewhat stupefied. He wobbled a little on his feet.

Lon stood also and gripped the man by his upper arm to steady him.

Then Ma Bailey walked out, beaming. "Come in and meet your son."

Whipple staggered into the room down the hall. Lon held back, but Ma motioned for him to come, too. Lon stayed outside the room but looked in at the new father and mother and the infant in the mother's arms. The sight warmed him to his heart.

His Mercy came to him. He put an arm around her shoulder and pulled her close. His wife-to-be was responsible for this happy outcome—he was certain of that.

"Thanks," the new father said, looking to Mercy. "Thanks, Doc."

"We call her Dr. Mercy around here," Ma Bailey said, looking happier than she ever had before.

Lon knew what the older woman was feeling. He was happier than he could ever remember being. And as long as Mercy was in his life, that happiness would continue. *God, I have been avoiding You for a long time, but no more. Thank You for Your mercy and for my Mercy, too.*

Epilogue

The town east of Idaho Bend was decorated for Christmas. Every store window displayed festive clothing, food or gifts. Lon had driven Mercy, Indigo and Sunny, with her baby girl, Dawn, to meet the train. They stood in the depot, watching for it. The sharp December wind blew against them.

Holding on to his hat, Lon tried to ease the tension that was twisting up his spine. He was about to meet his in-laws for the first time. And since they had left home before he'd married Mercy a few weeks ago, they didn't yet know about Mercy being his wife. They'd had no way to telegraph the news to her parents already in transit.

"My parents will love thee," Mercy said, straightening his collar.

He grinned. He was still a clear pane of glass to his wife. He hoped she was right.

The only touch of sadness was the fact that Pierre Gauthier had not returned to Idaho Bend. Lon knew that first loves often went astray. For her part, Indigo was still keeping faith that Pierre would return, focusing on waitressing, working on filling her hope chest and helping Mercy.

They heard the train whistle and puffing steam engine. Soon the passengers, mostly people who would be heading farther west, filled the platform and depot.

Mercy shepherded her party toward an older couple dressed in sober black—a tall man with white hair and a petite woman who reminded Lon of Mercy.

"Mother, Father!" Mercy called out. The three took turns embracing and then Mercy turned to Lon and Sunny. "Father and Mother, this is Sunny and her little girl, Dawn."

Adam and Constance Gabriel greeted Sunny warmly, and the young woman curtsied and smiled shyly.

"And this is my husband, Lon Mackey." Mercy blushed at her own words.

There was a moment of wordless surprise. Lon wished he could speak, but his tongue had turned to wood. He wanted to tell them how much he loved their daughter, how her love and God's had healed him. But words failed him.

"Well, welcome to the family, Lon Mackey," Adam said, shaking Lon's hand with a much younger man's vigor. Adam studied Lon, as if delving into him deeply.

"Yes, welcome, Lon Mackey," Constance said, holding up her hands. "Mercy, I don't know what to say. I thought thee had decided never to marry." Mercy's mother smiled at her with a knowing sparkle in her eyes.

"I couldn't marry a man who didn't want me to continue my profession, of course," Mercy said, still rosy pink. "But Lon does and he loves me."

"I am one hundred percent behind Mercy continuing to practice medicine," Lon declared.

"And I am happy to announce that Lon is reading

law. I hope he will run for territorial office in the next election." Mercy glowed with joy.

"Excellent!" Adam said, punctuating all the good news. "Mercy, thy mother and I are very tired. Could we go to a hotel?"

The group headed to one of the nearby hotels where Lon and Mercy had already secured rooms for Mercy's parents.

After letting Adam and Constance have a few moments to freshen up, they went to a nearby café. Lon still fought twinges of nerves. So far, Mercy's parents had been welcoming. But an unexpected son-in-law could make a poor impression—he hadn't formally asked Mercy's father for her hand in marriage. Lon didn't know how to rectify this faux pas.

When the waitress delivered their meals, Mercy's father bowed his head and said a brief prayer. The quiet prayer soothed Lon's nerves. He began to sense the natural peace that his in-laws brought with them.

"So thee is the man who has won my eldest daughter's heart," Adam said with a grin.

"Yes, I am the lucky man." Lon suddenly choked up. Truer words had never passed his lips.

"Where is thee from, Lon?" Constance asked.

"Maryland. But I have no family there except for a couple of older aunts and a few cousins. I wrote to them of my marriage, of course."

"I am sorry that thy parents aren't here to share our joy," Constance said, beaming. "We are so happy for thee. I see thy love for our Mercy in thy face."

Creating a small commotion and grabbing everyone's attention, little Dawn cooed and wriggled as if reaching for Constance.

The woman put down her fork and held out her arms

for the baby. Sunny hesitated and then complied. Constance talked to the baby with soft, cheery words.

Sunny wiped tears from her eyes. "I'm just so grateful."

Constance laid a comforting hand on Sunny's sleeve. "We are the ones who are grateful. When we offered to come and take thee and thy little one home with us, we didn't know that we would end up meeting our new son-in-law. What a wonderful surprise, such a wonderful blessing. God had it all planned for us."

Lon again felt the deep tug of intense emotion, of the brilliant truth that radiated from his mother-in-law's simple words. He reached for Mercy and clasped her hand in his. *I couldn't have said it better myself, God. Thank You.*

* * * * *

Dear Readers,

I hope that you have enjoyed reading the stories of these three special sisters, Verity, Felicity and Mercy Gabriel. I've enjoyed doing the historical research for each story and have grown to love these characters.

Very few people have the audacity to go against popular opinion. It takes a special kind of faith and strength. But Mercy needed a support system, too—Indigo, Mercy's new friend, Ellen Dunfield, and, of course, her help-meet, Lon. As Solomon said in Ecclesiastes 4:11–12a: "…if two lie down together, they will keep warm. But how can one keep warm alone? Though one may be overpowered, two can defend themselves." Two are better than one.

As for Indigo and the other African-American characters in The Gabriel Sisters series, it's hard to believe that it took nearly a hundred years to finally put to rest laws that discriminated against African-Americans in the United States. Though some prejudice lingers in the dark corners of America, our laws no longer uphold it.

Nevertheless, if Verity, Felicity and Mercy walked the streets of the U.S. today, they would still find plenty to keep them busy. I hope that these three sisters will make you sensitive to those who need God's love. I hope they will inspire you to let His light shine in this present darkness.

Please drop by www.craftieladiesofromance.blogspot. com for more about stories by me and other Love Inspired authors.

Lyn Cote

WE HOPE YOU
ENJOYED THIS

LOVE
INSPIRED®
BOOK.

If you were **inspired** by this

uplifting, **heartwarming** romance,

be sure to look for all six Love

Inspired® books every month.

Love Inspired®

SPECIAL EXCERPT FROM

Love Inspired®

*When a young Amish woman has amnesia during
the holidays, will a handsome Amish farmer help
her regain her memories?*

Read on for a sneak preview of
Amish Christmas Memories *by Vannetta Chapman,
available December 2018 from Love Inspired.*

"What's your name?"

The woman's eyes widened and her hand shook so that she could barely hold the mug of tea without spilling it. She set it carefully on the coffee table. "I don't—I don't know my name."

"How can you not know your own name?" Caleb asked. "Do you know where you live?"

"Nein."

"What were you doing out there?"

"Out where?"

"Where was your coat and your *kapp*?"

"Caleb, now's not the time to interrogate the poor girl." His *mamm* stood and moved beside her on the couch. She picked up the small book of poetry. "You were carrying this, when Caleb found you. Do you remember it?"

"I don't. This was mine?"

"Found it in the snow," Caleb said. "Right beside where you collapsed."

"So it must be mine."

Caleb noticed that the woman's hands trembled as she opened the cover and stared down at the first page. With one finger, she traced the handwriting there.

"Rachel. I think my name is Rachel."

Rachel let her fingers brush over the word again and again. Rachel. Yes, that was her name. She was sure of it. She remembered writing it in the front of the book—she'd used a pen that her *mamm* had given her. She could almost picture herself, somewhere else. She could almost see her mother.

"My *mamm* gave me the pen and the book…for my birthday, I think. I wrote my name—wrote it right here."

"Your *mamm*. So you remember her?"

"Praise be to *Gotte*," Caleb's *dat* said, a smile spreading across his face.

"Is there someone we can call? If you remember the name of your bishop…" Caleb had sat down in the rocker his mother had vacated and was staring at her intensely.

They all were.

She closed her eyes, hoping to feel the memory again. She tried to see the room or the house or the people, but the memory had receded as quickly as it had come, leaving her with a pulsing headache.

She struggled to keep the feelings of panic at bay. Her heart was hammering, and her hands were shaking, and she could barely make sense of the questions they were pelting at her.

Who were these people?

Where was she?

Who was she?

She needed to remember what had happened.

She needed to go home.

Don't miss
Amish Christmas Memories *by Vannetta Chapman,*
available December 2018 wherever
Love Inspired® *books and ebooks are sold.*

www.LoveInspired.com

Love Inspired®

Save $1.00
on the purchase of any
Love Inspired® or Love Inspired®
Suspense book.

Available wherever books are sold, including most bookstores, supermarkets, drugstores and discount stores.

Save $1.00
on the purchase of any Love Inspired® or Love Inspired® Suspense book.

Coupon valid until April 30, 2019. Redeemable at participating retail outlets in the U.S. and Canada only. Limit one coupon per customer.

52616033

5 65373 00076 2   (8100)0 12391

Inspirational Romance to Warm Your Heart and Soul

Join our social communities to connect with other readers who share your love!

Sign up for the Love Inspired newsletter at **www.LoveInspired.com** to be the first to find out about upcoming titles, special promotions and exclusive content.

CONNECT WITH US AT:

Facebook.com/groups/HarlequinConnection

 Facebook.com/LoveInspiredBooks

 Twitter.com/LoveInspiredBks

LISOCIAL2018